CODA

Book 1

XN5

CODA

Book 1

XN5

G. M. Ellerbeck

[www.gmellerbeck.com]

[Publisher: www.gmellerbeck.com]

Ellerbeck, G. M.
CODA Book 1 XN5
First edition

ISBN   978-0-9566047-0-5

Book Design by G.M.Ellerbeck

To my wife

Mary

Acknowledgements

A very special thanks to my wife Mary and my children for putting up with me while writing this book. To the ladies of the Aisling writers group; without your help this story would never be told. To Nicola Jennings for your invaluable advice and editing. To Pierre Maré for the early days.

Prologue

Perhaps an hour, he thought. That's all he had, to prepare for his final crossing to the altered state. He would finally join the ones he loved and contribute his life energy to the fabric of creation. He was not afraid of death. It was the challenge of life that held the most pitfalls for him. His wet body, strapped into the battle station seat, seemed to be floating in outer space. He looked down at his bare feet resting on the rudder pedals and the fantastic vista of stars beyond. None of the constellations were familiar to him and directly ahead was a massive black cloud that he was powerless to avoid.

He checked the Universal compass reading and realised where he was...the first Universe. Galaxy sized black clouds, with temperatures of minus 250 degrees Celsius and below, plagued its outer reaches...one of which was about to engulf the remains of his now crippled ship. He was doomed with no escape. Even with his capacity to endure extreme temperatures, this was beyond his formidable strength. The Universe he was in was almost entirely depopulated except for its home world, Moeba, the first world, the one that had started it all. It was not the Universe he would have chosen, but the unstable vortex that had brought him here had been his only escape from certain death.

It had jettisoned his war ship directly into the collision path of an enormous asteroid, which had torn off the aft end and ripped the main engines out like a tooth violently extracted. He sealed off the bridge and activated the explosive bolts. As they exploded, his smaller ship separated from the remains of the wrecked war ship and floated free.

He tried to start the engines but nothing worked. The smell of melted circuitry and burnt metal sowed a sense of foreboding.

The bridge was uniquely designed around a large glass ball water tank. The entire structure was a plasma touch screen he would operate from the inside, while he was submerged. To engage in battle, he would eject through the battle hatch, directly into the external cockpit seat, which was not under water. Once in the seat, a total surround screen was activated from the base. The view was generated

1

by the ship's vision sensors. The seat was designed as a battle station, with controls on the armrests that would steer the ship and rotate the screen in the direction of flight or fire. Its controls were compatible when connected to the superstructure of a bigger war ship with its more powerful engines and armaments.

With most of the ships solar skin ripped off and the power packs damaged, there was maybe two hours of power left to run the emergency lights. The oxygen would last maybe five hours, after that...there was only the oxygen left in the water. Ultimately, none of it mattered, as the inexorable momentum of his wrecked ship took him directly into the gaping black maw of death. With no power to run the survival systems, his body would freeze in the cloud...suspended in darkness for hundreds if not thousands of years before it exited on the other side.

He removed the target specs; fatigue and tension etched deeply into the contours of his face. His glowing red-brown eyes held a profound sorrow for his comrades who had died this day. Among them was his closest friend who had been there with him from the beginning and had saved his life on countless occasions. He felt consoled by the knowledge that he would join them soon.

He hit the button on the left armrest console and the screen retracted into the base of the seat, to reveal the observation deck. It was sometimes used as a war room, but mostly, he would just sit in the old red leather wing-backed chair and contemplate the view in the wide half surround observation port. The darkness was illuminated only by the glow of the emergency runners and a distant star now partially obscured by the black cloud. Everything loose was floating in the air permeated with fine drops of water, which meant the gravitation drive was also lost.

He sighed and punched the harness release buckle on his chest and floated free of the cockpit seat. He made his way to his space boots, moved over to the observation port, put them on his bare feet, activated the magnets and put his feet on the metal floor. He took hold of his coat and put it on. For what seemed like an eternity, he stared out of the observation port at the fast approaching cloud. So this was how he would die, he thought, alone in space, in a hostile universe, in a dismembered ship. Was there any reason to live...now that they had all perished? After such long lives, it had all come down to this. It was not a bad way to die; after all...he was used to the cold.

He picked up his father's flute. A unique instrument his father had made of ditholium, a very strong alloy used in aqua mining. He had modified it after his father's death. It now not only made beautiful sounds, but also made terrifying ones that could jar the bone of the staunchest enemy. Occasionally he had used it as a weapon...but now he would play.

He thought of his father and the haunting mysterious notes of the tune he'd always played, before and after meditation. Those notes started to flow with the memory of his father's gentle encouraging voice and his gift of music. He remembered his mother's loving face, her soft hair, and her passion for mathematics. The tone of the notes darkened, as he recalled his enemies and their treachery. War notes ripped into the melody, as he paid tribute to those worthy adversaries on the battlefield. The mood changed with a frightening cacophonous crescendo, as he recollected the monsters of the deep. The tune lifted and thundered with joy and fascination at the wonders of space and the adventures of his life. The loss of his comrades and friends brought a more pensive and sorrowful tone, like a soothing salve after the lash.

The melody ended abruptly, the air in his lungs choked off as he remembered...her... The vision of her death was still vivid in his mind. The pain of it was overwhelming. A soft, agonising wail escaped his throat, that once free, grew into a frustrated and angry roar that ended in a pitiful sob. He could still feel her sensual touch; smell her musk and feel the glow of her intimate love and understanding. He could still see the grace with which she moved and feel the power of her soul. With suffocating heartache...he missed her.

The observation port had become dark and ice was forming around the edges. In an almost trance-like ritual, he slowly removed his clothes except for his black leather loincloth. Once undressed, he drifted across to the top of the tank, opened the hatch, and submerged himself into the water. It was a soft embracing cocoon, illuminated only by the shafts of light from the emergency runners.

As he started to meditate, in his mind's eye, he saw the vast expanse of his father's aquatic origin. He felt the peace of its beautiful under-sea mountains and valleys. As his thoughts drifted in, he let them pass until his mind was still. To the sound of a bubbling brook in his ears, he slowed his bodily functions down, until his heart rate dropped to one beat every two minutes. As the ships power ran out, he felt the water slowly freeze. He watched it solidify around him and take hold of his body. As the emergency lights faded, a bright white light grew in his mind. As he moved into the light, he felt free at last, a release from the physical burden of pain and suffering and left his body in the blackness, preserved for eternity, in the confines of its glass custodian...

Present
Planet Moeba, Mt. Ross,
Ajari Province.

Looking through the immense oval window, at Var, the moon of Moeba, Captain John Masters' attention was drawn by a small patch of clear crystal glass. Like a stain on a pure white sheet, he thought. It remained unaffected by the constant battering of sand storms that pitted the rest of the glass and turned it almost opaque. It obscured a breathtaking view of stony planes and rocky outcrops, illuminated by the enormous opalescent moon. Its warm incandescence filtered into the room and filled it with the deep amber of early evening twilight through a thin dust-laden atmosphere.

He took a sip of his drink. The liquor rasped down his throat like a jagged rock and ignited that familiar fire in his corpulent belly. Its weight seemed to counterbalance his deceptively powerful shoulders that supported the heavy round head on its stump-like neck. He looked comfortably tailored in his lightweight dress uniform. His balding, neatly cut red hair with the greying temples, blended well with the now unbuttoned collarless jacket. It was waist length and the colour of rust with blood maroon brocade on the lapels and cuffs. The matching maroon silk shirt collar with the gold Captains' tri-circle insignia was unbuttoned. His broad back was turned towards his guests when Ehzhu Moriwe, his guest of honour, had put the question to him.

'So, Captain…do you believe there is such a place?'

Ehzhu was an influential Sabalian trader, who had graced his table before, with very profitable results. The heavy perfume he wore on his toxic fat body, failed to compete with the pungent odour of stale sweat on his shiny blue skin. He had seven wives, two of whom always travelled with him; his head wife Uli and his latest Feen.

Captain Masters turned to face the oval room. It was a double height room, carved into the gold coloured marble of Mt. Ross. Its cold polished surfaces would not be softened, despite the warm exterior glow. The walls and floor were made luminescent with subtle embedded lighting. Rows of lit alcoves in the walls proudly displayed artefacts, hunting trophies of aliens and animals he had killed and collected from exotic worlds. Like macabre spectators, each had its own story to tell.

He surveyed his six guests with pale blue eyes. His face was fleshy and his complexion ruddy with a boxer's nose and thin lips. It was a face that belied his intelligence. He was a difficult man who had come up the ranks the hard way, but who had grown into a comfort zone and had become bored and restless with the confines of Mt. Ross. On his left were Ehzhu Moriwe and his two wives. On his right were Lieutenant Shay Duncan and Dr. Monica Lynn. Directly in front of him was Mentor Etha Dax. They were seated on oversized sofas and armchairs covered in luxurious bottle green silk and arranged around a golden onyx table. It was a low table that served up drinks, snacks, sociable drugs, music, and 3D holographic entertainment, controlled by small touch pads along its outer edge.

The Captain took a handful of nuts, popped one in his mouth, chewed on it noisily, and answered with disdain. 'The 100th Universe is a myth. There are only ninety nine Universes with twelve realms of life.' He chewed a bit more, relishing the taste and texture of the nuts. 'To think that there might be a thirteenth realm in a Universe that doesn't exist is absurd. Throughout the eons we have extensively explored the Multiverse and there has never been even a hint that this Universe exists. Unless it's somewhere out there beyond the Multiverse; in the Megaverse perhaps. We know all the passages, known and secret, even where most of the unstable vortexes occur. So...believe me, the 100th universe is a figment of your imagination.'

His response was not directed at Ehzhu, but rather at Mentor Etha Dax, but his eyes were on Feen. If she had not been dressed in that skin-tight cat suit, he thought, one could have sworn she was sitting there naked. It was emerald green and offset her challenging green eyes and striking red hair. Her choker, bracelets, and loose fitting thigh-high boots were of raw sienna suede with gold loops attached. At sixteen, her golden brown skin glowed with youth. She looked up at him and her smile was like a warm caress. A stirring in his loins made him tear his gaze away. He looked straight into Ehzhu's cunning black eyes that held a subtle amusement at the lust he saw there.

Captain Masters flushed and to cover his embarrassment, vented his frustration on the Mentor who sat calmly in the oversized armchair. 'You mentors have always perpetuated this fantasy of a watery green utopia with its stable climate that "could sustain the human race as we once knew it.'" Captain Masters' annoyance became manifest as he continued. 'Well, no one alive has ever known this planet or ever will. In search of this non-existent mirage, our ancestors left us for dead on a planet they had destroyed. All based on a fictitious novel, created in the fevered mind of an ancient old pathfinder who went mad from all the time spent alone in his tiny little spacecraft!'

He looked around the room and took note of the expressions on their faces. 'Now...you brandish this book as the definitive text on a planet that doesn't exist, with a nonsensical navigational code that no one can understand or interpret, on how to get there.' Captain Masters sat down in his huge wing backed chair that dominated the room. He finished his drink in one gulp and tapped out another from the table's service hatch. He could barely contain his intolerance for these so-called psychics. 'You have taken this story-book, embellished it with all kinds of psychic rubbish, and turned it into some sort of religious philosophy. This is now used as the prime justification for the aimless wanderings of the Pathfinders' guild.' He pointed his chin at Monica. 'Anyone with even an inkling of psychic ability, you draw into this brainwashing web and they then spread this fantasy tale like an insidious cancer.'

Monica looked at him with indignant fire in her cautious blue eyes. 'On the contrary Captain! The Pathfinders are a noble group of sages that have brought light and understanding throughout the multiverse. They have done excellent work at mapping out the Megaverse and improving our understanding of different alien species and cultures. Speaking as a scientist, Captain, their contribution is of infinite value,' she ended with a sarcastic tone.

The Captain's lecherous eyes roved her taut body, dressed in her knee length plain black dress with its square front and bare arms. His gaze rested on her small but shapely breasts. 'The only true value is that which can be seen, touched, and turned into hard currency.'

Before Monica could respond, Mentor Etha Dax interrupted with his deeply timbered voice. 'As you know Captain, the price of currency is dependent on your intent. You can never escape appropriate consequence, no matter how well you cover your intent. It is only intent that will generate true proportional value.' His bald head seemed to glow with an inner light and his ageless black eyes taunted him with their tantalizingly humorous secret. At sixty-two, his six foot five athletic body still held a slumbering power that hinted at his warrior prowess. 'And keep in mind Captain, that the very star charts you use on your travels, were explored, and mapped by the Pathfinders of old on those so called "aimless wanderings."'

The Captain was a hard man, but not an uncivilised one. He conceded with an evil grin and lifted his glass. He has a point, the Captain thought, as he finished off his drink; however, this is not the end of it.

●

Mentor Etha Dax hated these private trade dinners, but in this instance he was forced to attend. The detestable Ehzhu Moriwe was particularly instrumental in securing Sabalian trade with Moeba. In order to secure this treaty, as head of the Pathfinders, he had been requested by the guild of Trade and Industry, to maintain a supply of Mannas to Ehzhu for his personal consumption. The secret of Mannas production was held only by a select few of the Pathfinders. It was considered to be an elixir of life, youth, vitality and sexual enhancement. What no one except the select few knew was that it was a corrupted version of the real thing. What was in fact distributed was an addictive drug that strongly enhanced the physical sensations with a euphoric hallucinogenic effect. The real thing was called Manna. It reversed the ageing process and had an intense spiritual effect on a person. His thoughts were interrupted by Uli, Ehzhu's first wife.

'And what say you of the Pathfinders, Lieutenant?

Undressing Lieutenant Shay Duncan with her lascivious grey eyes, she looked at his crotch and said in a throaty voice, 'Surely a young man of your obvious attributes has an opinion on such philosophical matters.' She leaned forward; her heavy sagging breasts shown off by the very low cut cleavage of her blood red dress.

She was past middle age, six foot tall with long limbs and heavy thighs. Her light blue skin contrasted sharply with the big ruby pendant on its long gold chain that drew the eye like a magnet. With her left hand she took her tall drink from the table; her bony fingers with their long red nails like talons, clutching their prize. From her drink she plucked out the small orange fruit with its long glass skewer and sensuously sucked it into her mouth. Her matching ruby earrings offset her close-cropped silver hair and long elegant neck.

Shay cleared his throat self consciously and crossed his legs. 'Well...yes,' he said and cleared his throat again. 'As a navigator, I can only admire the work done by those illustrious men and women.'

To Etha Dax, it seemed like it had suddenly become too hot for Shay in his dress uniform jacket with its ornate navy brocade on the lapels and cuffs. His face was red with embarrassment. His navy silk collar with its double ring Lieutenants' insignia looked like it had become tight and uncomfortable under the dragon's breath of Uli's sexual heat. She sat back and opened her legs just enough for him to view her inner thigh before she crossed them in the same flowing movement. Shay looked before he could stop himself, falling neatly into her trap. She had a subtle, triumphant smile on her full-bottom-lipped mouth.

To recover from his shock and self-loathing he leaned over to tap out another drink from the table. Before he could think of something else to say, he clumsily hit the wrong button and the 3D holographic system came on with "Nebula" blaring out their high-energy club music. With explosive volume, the percussive beat echoed off the hard walls with bludgeoning ferocity. It seemed to go on for an eternity as he desperately attempted to find the "off" button. When he finally did, the shocking silence left the party deaf and numbed.

Etha Dax could not contain his mirth at the expressions on their faces. His deep rolling laughter burst from his belly and washed over the room like a cold shower. Feen erupted with her hysterical giggle that was coupled with Uli's derisive cackle. Captain John Masters joined in with a loud hoot accompanied by Ehzhu's blubberous chuckle. The moment was so spontaneous that even the sympathetic Monica could not suppress her shy smile.

While everyone enjoyed the moment, the Lieutenant masked his glowing discomfort with a sporting grin. He was a handsome man, six foot tall with classic good looks. As the room settled down, Ehzhu looked at Etha Dax and asked in his high pitched silky voice. 'Tell me Mentor; how is it that the Pathfinders exist at all. What was the catalyst that created this unusual band of travellers?'

'The answer lies in the nature of the human species.' Etha answered in his enigmatic fashion. The Captain wearily lifted his eyebrows, sighed, and took another sip of his drink as his eyes strayed back to Feen.

Etha Dax ignored him and barrelled on. 'Our planet had at one time been a green planet with vast seas. It had a thick atmosphere that stabilised the temperature and created an almost global tropical climate. If the resources of the planet had been managed correctly it would have sustained an infinite population. However...the nature of humanity is such that as the population numbers grew, their consumption of these resources finally surpassed the supply.' He paused, looked around the room and noted the hedonistic interplay between the Captain and Feen, who loved to tease.

'Greed and total disregard for the environment had caused monumental so called "natural disasters" that left our planet's atmosphere clogged with all sorts of gasses and carbon particles. To make matters worse, the solar wind activity of our sun increased massively; higher than ever recorded in our history. Our weather patterns changed, generating killer winds that created these huge sand storms. They killed off all our crops and livestock and drove the surviving population underground. Then our magnetic field faltered and our atmosphere began to dissipate under the solar winds of our sun. With the decrease in atmospheric pressure our seas literally evaporated out into space. The only water we were left with was the underground aquifers. Now we inhabit the living rock of the mountains and have protective crystal glass canopies built over our cities in sheltered valleys that offer at least a semblance of normal life.'

'Like bats in our little caves,' the Captain interrupted and took another handful of nuts, 'all jostling for a bit of space.' He took a sip of his drink, put more nuts in his mouth and chewed, clicking his tongue as he savoured the oils and textures.

'The Pathfinders, Mentor?' Ehzhu prompted, breaking the awkward silence that followed.

'Oh yes...The Pathfinders...they began as astronauts sent out into the Universe to find a new world for humanity to start over. At first we dispatched probes that returned data from all corners of the Universe. We found two planets that had potential. We sent manned missions to them, but they proved to be uninhabitable. We are still trying to seed these planets. The accidental discovery of the vortex opened up the Multiverse to us. We followed the same formula by first dispatching probes and then small manned missions. We lost many of these ships through various disasters. Then, when things got really bad here, private interests sent out large survival type ships with starter populations and all the necessities to start new worlds. No-one really knew where they were going; our navigational charts of the Multiverse were sketchy at best. At that point the Pathfinders were formed to explore and chart the Multiverse properly. So, it was decided to send out those brave men and women on what were essentially one-way missions.'

'How do you find people, who would willingly go on a one-way mission like that,' Ehzhu interrupted. 'Surely it would be tantamount to a long and painful death sentence?'

'Only unique individuals with strong psychic abilities could cope with the long years of solitary travel. Our very best technology was sent with them to prolong their lives and communicate their findings.'

Ehzhu looked at the Mentor with keen interest at the mention of this technology. He sat forward, his weight straining at the red and black designs of his silk shirt. 'Are there any still alive?'

The Mentor noticed Ehzhu's reaction. 'Yes there are. The last one to be sent out was as recent as fifteen years ago. It's an ongoing movement that still brings in new and interesting results.'

'So, what of the search for this mythological planet, did they ever find it?' Ehzhu asked.

'No...not yet. Most of those early survival ships just disappeared. We have no idea what happened to them. We eventually found some of them that had been...compromised. When our planet seemed doomed, it was decided to build the generation ships and use the information sent to us by the Pathfinders to evacuate the planet in search of a more suitable world. These generation ships were monopolised by the elite and their avarice was such that only those who could afford the fare were able to leave the planet. The rest of us were left for dead. We have a partial navigational code, but as the Captain says, it makes no sense and has not yet been deciphered. In the mean time we continue to map out the Multiverse in the hope that we may find the answer.'

The steady hum of the air conditioners was interrupted by the sound of the Captain punching out a popper on the touch pad, breaking off the top and sniffing the intoxicating gas up his nose. As his heart contracted, it pistoned a hot gush of blood through his body that exploded in his brain and relaxed the nerve ends. In an almost euphoric tone he blurted, 'Yes...well...that's ancient history now isn't it? We have since...evolved into much more civilised and rational beings now, haven't we?' His face was puffed up and flushed and the surface veins could be seen pulsating under the skin. He let out a strained grunt, took a deep breath and laughed with abandon, took another breath and with a satisfied look on his face ended with a long fading, 'Aaaah...'

'We have become more sophisticated yes, however, civilised is debatable.' Etha despised the common use of recreational drugs, which was the accepted norm in Mt. Ross.

Ehzhu pushed Feen's popper clutching hand away from his fat heavy jowled face with its full greedy lips and cascading double chin. He leaned forward with his hard eyes boring into the Mentor. 'It is my understanding that you still possess this long life technology. Is this true?'

'Yes we do.' Etha Dax had a guarded expression on his face.

'How then, does one acquire such technology?'

'It can never be acquired, but its product may be part of a negotiation,' he knew that Ehzhu was now in play.

'This negotiation you speak of, what would that be?' Ehzhu had a slight frown on his brow.

'A fair trade treaty between our planets.'

'Now, now Mentor,' Ehzhu responded with dismay. 'Surely you know that I am not empowered to negotiate such a treaty on behalf of the Sabalian realm.'

'Yes we know that, but we also know that you have sufficient access to those who can. Your influence on the trading fraternity of your realm is legendary.'

Ehzhu was silent for a moment as he thought; this man is not the bumbling priest he is made out to be. To underestimate such a man was folly indeed. There was a price to pay when he used his influence; however, the reward of a longer life was very tempting. Besides, he had just been complimented, so rare these days.

'Do you speak on behalf of the guild of Trade and Industry, Mentor?' Ehzhu's eyes gleamed at the prospect of newfound wealth.

'I do.' The Mentor answered simply. He already knew what the outcome would be, but had to play it out convincingly. Ehzhu put his fat fingertips together and brought them up to his lips. He thought for a moment and said matter of factly, 'You realise of course that the cost in Interversal Gion would be exacting on both Moeba and myself. Vast sums of this currency would be needed for inducement and besides, what incentive would there be for me?'

'Assuming you agree to facilitate such a venture, I'm sure we can negotiate a favourable incentive,' he passed him a small vial of white powder, 'A small token of our good faith.'

'Mannas!' Ehzhu exclaimed with an involuntary gasp and beamed, 'Ah Mentor...you certainly have a way of sweetening the palate.'

'Yes...well...perhaps you might meet with the trade minister and me for lunch tomorrow?'

'Very well Mentor...tomorrow it is. You know where to find me,' Ehzhu leaned back in his comfortable sofa and sniffed the popper Feen cracked open for him. He let out a satisfied sigh and took a drink from Uli. They knew what was in the offing for them at the success of such a venture.

As the Mentor was about to take his leave the holographic com-link came on. A miniature 3D image of the telephonist hovered above the table and asked for Captain John Masters. He was slouched in his chair with a slightly dazed expression on his face. At the mention of his name, he surfaced from his drug soaked fog and responded angrily. 'I gave clear instructions that I was not to be disturbed tonight!'

'I do apologise Captain, however this is a code red. Shall I patch you through?' Her voice was calm and professional. The Captain stared at her for a moment, not quite comprehending; it had been so long since he'd had a code red, that he almost forgot how to respond. Slowly his eyes focused and he sat up straight. 'Very well... patch me through then.'

Her image faded and changed to that of Admiral Walter Green. He was a distinguished tired old man biding his time until retirement. 'Good evening Captain.' Before the Captain could respond he said abruptly, 'You and your crew have been chosen for a unique mission in the Onusa quadrant. You are ordered to proceed to our moon station on Var where you will be briefed and equipped for your deep space mission. Now...I understand that Dr. Monica Lynn is one of your guests tonight, so may I speak with her as well?'

'Over here Admiral, how may I help you?'

The image of Admiral Green turned towards her. 'Ah yes...Dr. Lynn. So sorry to meet you under these circumstances, but we were hoping you might consider going along on this mission, all expenses paid of course.'

'Could you tell me Admiral,' Monica interrupted. 'Where are we to be based and why am I being considered for this mission?'

'You will initially be based at the research station on Upi, the moon of planet Onusa. We have detected a disabled Alien ship on the edge of the Othaxal cloud. Your research into alien physiology and culture has made you our natural choice as the leading scientist in this field. I realise that this creates more questions than answers, however, once on Var, you will be fully briefed at the research facility by Professor Erick Astor through com link, who I believe you are already acquainted with.'

'Oh yes, I have worked with the Professor in the past and I'd be happy to work with him again.' She was excited at the prospect of new challenges and working with the esteemed Professor once more. 'When does the shuttle depart?'

'At 22h00, Vidal flats shuttle station, terminal three. Please meet Captain Masters and his crew at 17h00 in the departure lounge for your pre-flight brief. Good evening and enjoy the rest of your party.' And the Admiral's image faded out…

●

Her lungs were on fire and her heart was racing painfully as she tried to swim up towards the light, desperate to escape the cold dark abyss beneath her. Blackness engulfed her mind, like suffocating ink it sucked at her soul and held her helpless, dangling like bait for what lurked in the deep. Monica woke up in a cold sweat, gasping for breath as she sat up. With a shaking hand she lifted the glass from her limestone bedside cabinet and gulped the water down. She looked around the bedroom. Still breathing hard, she tried to shake off the fear this recurring dream always left her with.

She had lived with the fear of water since she was a young child of six. She remembered the first time she saw a large body of water. Her father had taken her to see one of the many underground lakes. They walked onto a natural shelf of rock that protruded out twenty feet from the cliff over the water. It had a banister along its edge and was often used by visitors as an observation point over the lake. Her excitement was such that she took her father's hand and pulled him with her; elbowing her way through the small crowd that had gathered at the furthest edge of the shelf. The massive expanse of water stretched out into the distance and disappeared into its mists. There were thousands of natural limestone pillars that seemed to grow out of the water to reach up hundreds of feet and support the heavy oppressive stone roof with its ancient stalactites that betrayed the planets earlier rainfall climate. From man-made holes cut into the roof, beautiful shafts of light cascaded onto the water. Hundreds of small electrical fishing craft were on the water with their nets out. At the small harbour, dock men were loading fish from the boats into refrigerated electric road trains that would take the fish to the markets.

She was excitedly gesticulating at the docks when, with a loud crack, the rock upon which they were standing broke off at the base and tumbled into the lake taking all the onlookers with it. As it started to tumble, her father had pushed her out and away from the rock, but could not dive out far enough to save himself from being crushed beneath the rock's weight. Amid the sound of terrified screams she hit the cold water and sank like a stone. The black water beneath her reached up and tried to swallow her in its gaping mouth. It shocked her into panic. She looked up and clawed at the disappearing light, desperate for air. Slowly, she started to lose consciousness as her breath ran out.

As if in a dream, she felt the fishing net close around her. One of the fishermen had cast his net over the place where she had fallen. When he felt the tug on his net he knew he had her. He pulled the cord that closed the bottom of the net and hauled it out with the frantic help of his small crew. Once on board the fisherman breathed air into her lungs and pumped her chest until she coughed up water and took a deep breath of her own. The memory of that event and the death of her father had left her with an emotional trauma that had plagued her all her life.

She slipped her legs out from under the burgundy silk sheets and sat on the edge of the bed. She rested her feet on the warm limestone floor, streaked with veins of white and gold marble like tiny rivers of white-hot magma. Monica stood up and walked across the small round room. As she walked the recessed lights in the walls and ceiling slowly intensified, highlighting the fantastic patterns of the glowing marble. When she got close to the wall, with a soft hydraulic hiss, the stone bathroom door automatically pushed out towards her and slid to the right.

As she walked into the circular bathroom the lights dimmed up. In the centre of the room was the round floor to ceiling, glass enclosed steam shower. On the right was a glass basin sunk into its limestone cabinet with a large elliptical mirror on the wall above it. On the left was the toilet framed by two narrow cabinets. A curved bench along the far wall connected the two sides of the room.

She took off her navy blue nightdress and put it on the bench. As she walked into the shower, fine jets of warm water sprayed out from channels within the glass shower wall. She thought of her mother. She had suddenly become rich through compensation paid out by the Agricultural Guild for the accidental death of her husband. With her mother's newfound wealth came high morals and standards, critically imposed on Monica with fanatical intensity. Eventually Monica had become a tense, self-conscious introvert. At fifteen she had won a scholarship at the Institute of Anthropology and Alien studies and left home for good. She did not hate her mother; only, she could not live with her. Every time she visited her, she always had some criticism to throw at Monica that ended the visit with dramatic argument. Monica had called her yesterday evening to let her know that she was off on this mission which of course ended the same way as usual.

'Who knows what is to become of you Monica!' she had ranted. 'You're always off on a mission to who-knows-where, to some remote corner of the universe to study who-knows-what, when you should be at home with a good husband raising a family! It's such a waste after all the hard work I've put into you!'

Monica knew that there was nothing she could do to help her mother understand her thirst for knowledge, her need for freedom and the joy she felt when exploring new worlds and studying new species. When all her faculties were focused on alien physiology, the last thing on her mind was a man and raising a family. Shay Duncan suited her needs well enough for now. They were both travelling people and accepted the noncommittal nature of their relationship. She knew Shay wanted more, but it was not a viable option under the circumstances and besides, she was not sure she loved him enough anyway.

As she walked out of the shower the water stopped flowing. She took a towel out of the cabinet and dried herself off, took another towel and dried her long straight black hair. She pulled back a glass sliding door under the bench and put the wet towels and her nightdress into the steam washer. She walked over to the basin and pressed a button on the touch pad beneath the mirror. The backlights behind the mirror slowly dimmed up and a low recessed cabinet containing her toiletries rose up from the stone counter top.

While brushing her teeth, she thought about the mission she was about to embark on. She looked forward to spending several weeks if not months with Shay. The unpleasant part would be sharing the time with Captain John Masters. He normally captained freighters that were sometimes used to ferry passengers on special assignments. He was militarily trained, but with Moeba's neutral status there had been very little call for such activity. Some officers had gone off to far-flung universes to work as mercenaries or to join other militaries, but only a few had returned. Captain Masters was not one of these. His rank was achieved through the merchant fleet, helped along by the fact that he lined the pockets of key people who could promote his interests.

When she finished she rinsed her mouth and toothbrush and put it back in its place. She put on some deodorant and left the bathroom. On entering the bedroom, the bathroom lights dimmed out and the toiletries cabinet sunk back into the counter top. Still naked, Monica padded unabashed across the room towards the opposite wall. She was comfortable with her body and in her own space she enjoyed the unrestricted freedom of no clothing. Her five foot eight body was long limbed and lithe with the finely toned muscle structure of an athlete and the grace and posture of a dancer.

As she neared the wall, another stone door swung out, giving access to her dressing room. The left and right walls were lined with the usual assortment of hanging spaces. However, what gave the room its character was the alien origin of its furniture. Standing on the floor on the far side of the room, was a very narrow full-length oval mirror. It had a narrow silver frame that rested on an ivory base that was beautifully carved and finished. It resembled fine wisps of smoke emanating from the floor, so finely carved; it was almost transparent and completely surrounded the mirror. The backlight picked out these transparent areas and emphasised the illusion.

Dominating the room was the central dressing table. It was carved from the two tusks of the Giant Oselha, a gigantic arctic beast that once lived on the now extinct planet Eko. A unique and fantastic piece with silver trim and small silver handles. All the edges and surfaces were softened with the smoke motif flowing and boiling in subtle relief. It had the curved shape of a horseshoe open at one end. An elegantly formed silver stool stood in the centre, its padded seat upholstered with the exquisitely soft white fur of the Giant Oselha's underbelly.

Monica stepped up to the hanging closet to her left, took out a royal blue silk robe and put it on. She strode over to the stool and sat down. She looked at her reflection in the dressing table mirror with its silver frame. It was suspended in its fine carving that held hundreds of tiny day glow bulbs scattered like glitter on a carpet of snow. She sighed and while brushing her hair, thought of that mysterious tribe of inter planetary hunters she had lived with for three years. She had been studying their culture and gene pool when their leader had fallen ill. Her knowledge and equipment had helped to save his life. They had given her this dressing table as a gift of gratitude.

She thought about the flight she was about to go on and how much she hated the take off and re-entry. Although she had done light years of travel, it was always these two aspects that she feared the most. It always seemed a small miracle that the craft survived and everyone arrived safely. Even more dangerous was passage through a natural vortex. It was highly unstable and could tear a ship to pieces. Fortunately they would use the teleports. They were stable man-made portals that could transport space ships, crew and cargo to predictable destinations light years away almost instantly. Every realm had their teleports and charged exorbitant fees for their use.

Monica finished brushing her hair and tied it back. She stood up, walked over to the right-hand hanging closet and took down her flight suit. From the drawers she dug out her underclothes and got dressed. Her flight suit was an all black coverall type outfit with multiple pockets that hugged the body and was normally worn under the space suit. It had a pressure membrane on the inside that equalised under heavy G forces. She put on her flight boots and took another look at herself in the mirror.

She always felt transformed when she was dressed for flight. She felt empowered, ready to take on the universe, with conflicting emotions of dread and excitement; she felt flushed and energised. Oh yes, she was ready all right. It had been almost two years since last she was on a mission. The idea of getting off this dust bowl again was almost euphoric. Her bags had been collected last night, so all she took with her was her small carry on holdall with a few personal effects. She took a last look around her, walked out of the dressing room and through the double stone doorway that led into the main open plan living space. She stepped out the front door and pressed the button on the remote key that locked the apartment. As the lights went out, the only sound was the hum of the air conditioner as it slowly wound down to its silent hiatus until her return.

●

At the back of Shay Duncan's mind there was a place where all his painful memories were supposed to remain…secure behind sturdy locker doors in neat rows in that dim, dank and airless space. From one of these lockers burst a gale of agony so intense, it pinned him to the sidewalk. He felt powerless as it tore through the barriers he had taken so long to build. The raw intensity of emotion was such that it felt as if his spirit had left his body and was standing next to him; watching himself fall to pieces. With an exhaustive effort he finally shut out the emotional storm and cauterised its effect.

His numbed body slowly tingled back to life. The sight of the young girl speeding by in the auto-tram had unlocked the emotional assault. He had noticed her as he looked up from the tram call console and there she was, seated on the near side window seat. She was the spitting image of his daughter when she was five. She had the same smile with those expressive eyes and the dark hair. It was not her of course, it couldn't be; she and her mother had passed away in the tragic quake of Mt. Toyin. He had been away on a merchant ship that carried harvested ice from the ice caps of Taras when he had heard the news.

With a sigh, Shay calmed himself and looked up at the crystal glass dome that covered the city. Its embedded Polaroid layers filtered out the intense ultra violet rays of Moeba's sun and made it possible to still inhabit this planet. Shay could see a weak dust cloud driven by the wind. He was still in awe at the power of that wind and the destruction of the dust storms it generated. It was almost the end of the nine-month dust storm season…almost, but not yet. He had seen a spaceship caught in one of those unpredictable storms. It had ripped off one of its fuel cells and had blown it so far off course it eventually crashed in the arctic region where the entire crew perished in the minus seventy two degree Celsius climate. It was still however a good day to fly.

He looked at the traffic loop on Chestnut Avenue, but found no available auto-trams. You'd think that on a road that is five miles long they'd have more auto-trams, he thought. Fortunately he had ample time for his rendezvous with Monica at Millie's breakfast club, so he decided to take a walk. With the roadway on his right and the apartments on his left, he took the wide footpath, which was bordered by tall chestnut trees. They created a leafy canopy that always struck Shay with a sense of tranquillity. Its cool shaded protection helped assuage his nerves and recover his fractured emotions.

He passed the workmen taking a break from harvesting the fruit of these versatile trees. Shay didn't know them, but greeted them anyway. He remembered his teenage years, working beside peasants like these in the olive groves to make enough money to pay his way into the right schools to qualify for space academy. The pathway was crowded and he felt he was floating down a pedestrian river that would end up in a sea of humanity somewhere.

The population of Moeba had changed somewhat since the Multiverse had opened up. Shay noticed several Sabalian traders with their deep blue skins and expensive clothes. A small group of Adovacian fighters, sinister and secretive, were standing in the shadows watching the passers-by and a mentor in deep discussion with a very tall Nekobian priest. Nekob was one of the strangest places Shay had ever visited. All its population were very tall and thin; humans stretched up like an elastic band. It had to do with the atmospheric pressure there. Visitors to their planet had to remain in de-pressurised buildings or eventually suffer pressure sickness. His crew could not stay long and even then it was only in their de-pressurised terminal building.

Shay took one of the pedestrian footbridges that crossed the street every two hundred and fifty yards. When he had crossed the bridge, he turned left onto an identical footpath with its double row of chestnut trees and continued walking in the same direction as before. With the road now on his left, more pedestrians crushed in on him, augmenting his already heightened sense of claustrophobia. On his right was a wheat field; one hundred yards deep and the entire five-mile length of the road. As he approached the next footbridge he noticed the walkway was partially blocked by another harvesting team, so he turned right on the path that crossed the field. The contrast was almost liberating in its emptiness. The path had very few pedestrians and no trees with wheat-fields stretching out for miles on either side. The wheat was still green and waved slightly in the gentle breeze generated by the fans of multiple giant air-conditioners that regulated the air quality of this man-made habitat.

Shay turned left again onto the terrace promenade that ran parallel to the road and bordered the field. There was a row of chestnut trees on his right with recreational benches in their shade. They faced out over the open expanse of the valley beyond. The view seemed particularly clear this morning so he decided to stop for a few minutes and take it in. He dodged some runners and angled across the path towards one of the benches that had an unoccupied space next to an old man. He was feeding the doves that often came begging for a snack. Shay greeted him and sat down. Putting his light bag of personals at his feet, he crossed his legs, sat back and marvelled at the cityscape in front of him.

Across the valley the same terraces were cut into the mountainside and followed its meandering contours. The three bottom levels were reserved for underground industry; hydroponics agriculture, silk farming, clothing, textiles, medicine, and recreational drugs. All other manufacture like electronics, vehicles, heavy machinery, and warehousing was also on this lower level. The upper layers were reserved for housing. The higher up the more it cost. Many of the upper terraced apartments had private walled gardens and crystal glass windows that looked out over the wasteland. Each plateau was similar in that they all had a road that ran along its length bordered by different fruit or nut trees with an irrigated wheat, maize, bean, potato or hemp field along the edge.

The valley floor was carpeted with more hemp and wheat fields. Groves of mulberry trees flanked a narrow winding river that ran through the centre. It was crossed by footbridges and roads that formed a maze through the fields and mulberry groves. The leaves were harvested for silkworms and the hemp was harvested for the textile industry. There were many insects crawling and flying that had found refuge with the human population. Several different species of bird added variety to the wildlife; chief among them was the falcon. Field mice and rats were plentiful and were preyed on by hawks, falcons, owls and snakes.

There were two huge stadiums on the valley floor used for sport, music, theatre, and political rallies. About three miles to the north the valley forked, split by an enormous outcrop of rock. Tapered on both ends; it was eight miles long and three miles high. Like a subterranean axe blade it cleft Mt Ross in two and dominated the city. Its steep sides were smoothly encased with glass walls that covered the entire length of the outcrop. It enhanced its sharp powerful presence, which housed the planetary administration in its honeycombed centre. Air traffic was heavy as usual with light cargo and passenger craft that created a constant hum from their magnetic pulse engines, the smell of which left a sharp metallic taste at the back of his mouth.

The old man looked at Shay. 'We don't often see you flyboys taking in the scenery here, you're always too busy going somewhere aren't you?' Without waiting for a reply he tossed some more seed at the doves.

'I suppose that's true enough,' Shay responded. 'How about you, do you come out here much?'

'Most mornings...I'll come and sit here with the birds. Sometimes they are better company than people, you know. Look at that one there; with the dark ring on its neck...it's almost as if he's trying to tell me something, as if he understands what I'm saying.' The old man cast him some seed which was instantly pecked away. 'I was a flyboy like you, you know,' he continued. 'Merchant fleet like yourself. Traded eight universes and cost me forty-five years until I was "replaced" by a younger engineer. Back on Moeba, the whole family were gone, I had no friends, no wife, no kids, so now I sit with the doves every morning, take naps in the afternoon and read or use the entertainment centre at night until I finally fall asleep.'

Shay felt a deep sympathy for this man and not a little fear for himself. Here was the living manifestation of what might be his future. 'Why not write your memoirs perhaps or even a novel based on your experiences?'

'My memory has faded and my imagination is not that good,' he said and sowed more seed for the doves.

'Oh... I'm sure an interesting man like yourself will find a good woman to keep you company through those long nights hey?' Shay said with a wink.

With an incredulous look on his face, the old man hacked a cackle of mirth, 'Yes...perhaps... maybe hey!'

'Good luck!' Shay took his bag and stood up.

He took a drink from the water fountain next to the bench and continued his walk down the boulevard. This day had not started well he thought. The sooner he got out of this place the better. Millie's

Breakfast Club was only a mile further down the road, so he stretched his pace and hurried along.

●

Millie's was packed as usual. It was popular not only for its great food, but also for its location. It was on the outer edge of the all-glass shopping centre that spanned between two terraces. With entrances at the upper and lower terrace it had five levels of shops, eating houses and markets. Millie's was on the top level and enjoyed the best view.

To Shay's surprise, Monica had arrived early and had found a good table at the window. He caught her eye and she waved at him as he elbowed his way past the hot drinks bar. He always felt a light-headed thrill whenever he saw her and loved her deep blue eyes that were like warm oceans in which he could lose himself.

When he got to the table he wanted to kiss her hello, but was never sure if it was okay to do so, however Monica offered, so he kissed her and sat down opposite her. 'How are you this morning?' he asked.

'Fine thanks Shay,' she said, admiring his fresh good looks augmented by his dashing navy blue flight suit. 'I had that dream again,' a fleeting moment of despair flashed behind her eyes.

He reached across the table and touched her hand in sympathy, knowing that nothing he could say would make it any better.

'Every time I have that dream, it feels like it happened yesterday...intense.' She looked out of the window at the auto-tram traffic on the lower terrace road, ferrying passengers to the great elevators that would take them up or down the mountain. 'I have never been able to get over my fear of water you know,' she looked at Shay. 'Since that day I have avoided anything to do with going on water. It frightens me...I hope this mission has nothing to do with water.'

'Oh, I don't think so,' Shay said reassuringly. 'The captain seems elated, so there's money to be made...for him at least. It's most likely some sort of alien discovery. Besides, you don't have to do anything you are not comfortable with.'

'I know, I know, it's just...I have this feeling that it has something to do with water. Every time I feel this way, something happens.'

'Are you sure its not just pre-flight nerves playing tricks on you, I know how you feel about take-off and re-entry?'

'Now Shay, I know the difference between nerves and intuition,' she responded with mild annoyance.

'Very well then,' he picked up the menu. 'Let's eat.'

●

After breakfast they made their way down to the valley floor and took the mainline train out to Vidal flats. The train had no wheels and ran silently on magnetic tracks. Its carriages had polaroid glass domes and offered unobstructed views. Mt. Ross was one of several cities created in a long mountain range; all connected by underground tunnels and overland glass domed railroads. These railroads were lined with fruit trees of apple, cherry, apricot, peach or plum.

Other more long distance railroads were lined with olive, orange or lemon trees. Every five miles there was a worker's compound for agriculture, road and rail workers. Along some sections of the line the air was replete with blossom petals, picked up by the slipstream as the train sped by.

As they reached the edge of the flats, the train took the tracks that branched off from the main line and headed straight across three hundred miles of stony plain. There was no agriculture along this line, only the four rail tracks that carried people and freight to and from the space station in its glass tunnel. From horizon to horizon the stony countryside was flat and scorched black by the intense heat of Moeba's giant sun. It was a desolate inhospitable place that promised only a slow agonising death to anyone who was trapped out there in its vast hunger. Like a javelin the straight line impaled the extinct volcano that housed Vidal flats space station in its hollow centre.

An ensign met Monica and Shay on the station platform and fast tracked them through security and immigration. On exiting the station they boarded an open EV (electric vehicle) that drove them the three miles to the western elevator which took them up to the seventeenth level. They stepped out of the elevator and walked down the corridor. It had a glass wall that looked out over the crater.

Monica was always in awe at the scale of this complex. It was not only a launch pad with five terminals, but also a maintenance and spacecraft production facility. It had sixty-four levels, twenty-five of which were under the launch pad. It was built on an elevator system that could lower craft to the bottom levels and bring other craft up to the surface for launch. The lunar shuttle was on the surface being made ready for take-off. It was an undistinguished craft; big, bulky with its hull burnt black from repeated entries into Moeba's atmosphere.

The ensign showed them into the conference centre at the end of the corridor where the crew were already assembled. Captain Masters was in animated discussion with Admiral Green who looked distressed and seemed to be trying to move away from the Captain. Shay and Monica's entrance offered him the excuse he needed so he turned his back on the Captain and walked up to the podium.

'Can I have your attention please,' the Admiral said.

The Captain, who was left in mid sentence, strode purposefully to his seat and sat down. The crew had not heard the Admiral and continued with their conversation. The Admiral tapped on the microphone and said in a more commanding voice. 'Attention crew!' The crew settled down and the Admiral continued, 'As you all know by now this is a code red mission.' He gave that a few seconds to sink in and noted the expressions on their faces.

'What we know so far is that five days ago an Alien ship or part of it was discovered on the edge of the Othaxal cloud. Our radio telescope on Upi cannot give us any information other than a rude outer image of the ship. It would seem that it has travelled through the cloud and presents us with a possible time capsule. However, this might be a war ship and we don't know what we are dealing with.'

There was a murmur among the crew who had not often if ever been in a military or first contact situation before.

'You have been assigned to make contact with it and find out if there are any survivors. If so what are their intentions and if not to tow the ship back to the research station on Upi for further analyses. Your weapons will be issued to you on Var where your ship is now being prepped and supplied. You are scheduled for teleportation three days from now, so that should give you ample time to rest and make final preparations.'

The Admiral wished them well and left the room. The ensign took over with their flight log details and assignment sheets. There was a heightened sense of excitement and expectation among the crew that rubbed off on Monica. She felt elated and slightly light headed at the prospect of the new…

Othaxal Cloud, Onusa Quadrant, the Nullax Rover

'It's a war ship!' the Captain said. 'Or what's left of it.' The creeping fatigue of constant space flight over the past six months lifted in that instance of first sight. The atmosphere on the bridge was tense with anticipation. Everyone was focused on the screen.

'It has Adovacian letters on it, but looks nothing like an Adovacian war ship,' the Captain continued. 'Too small. It also looks like it was fast and elegant, more like a fighter than a war ship. What do you make of it, Lieutenant?'

Shay looked up at the screen. 'Most likely a mercenary ship, Sir.'

'Are there any survivors on board?'

'Our scanners have picked up hydrogen, oxygen, methane, carbon and...water. Lots of it Captain!' Shay was incredulous at the quantity of it. 'Fifty two percent of the ships internal volume is filled with water now turned to ice. All systems are off line and there are no signs of life.' He looked up at the screen. 'It seems we have a dead ship that has come through the Othaxal cloud.'

'Ah ha,' the Captain nodded in agreement. 'Cloud status?'

'We have a fifteen hour window to tow the wreckage out of there before the cloud closes in on it again.'

'Then we have no time to lose. We are close enough, fire the grapples, Lieutenant!'

Shay hit the release and the magnetic grapples shot out with their fine metal alloy cables. They spread out like ever lengthening tentacles reaching out for its prey. They created small dust clouds as they hit the hull and took hold.

'Take us out, Lieutenant, nice and slow.'

Shay released some pressure on the forward thrusters and the Nullax Rover slowly started moving backwards. Once they were out of harm's way he released the grapples and let the wreckage float past them. He manoeuvred the Nullax Rover along the side of the wreckage and lined up with its docking station. Once docked, he set a course that took them a safe distance away from the cloud.

'That's far enough,' the Captain said. 'Put us in a slow holding pattern. I think its time to take a look at what we have. Call the doctor and three of the crew to go with us.' He stood up from his seat and headed for the docking hatch.

Shay put them into a holding pattern on autopilot. He then called Monica and the three crewmen on the comlink. He handed the bridge over to Chief engineer David Wall and went to the docking hatch.

At the hatch the boarding party were changing into their space suits when Shay said to Monica. 'There's a lot of ice on board. Fifty two percent of the ship's volume is filled with it.' He noticed a darkness come over her, but her expression remained determined. He knew there was no going back for her. 'I don't know how much of it has melted, but watch yourself.'

'Thanks for the warning Shay, but I can take care of myself. Now, help me with these clips please.'

Shay smiled and Monica wrinkled her nose at him as they went through the ritual of tying down the clips on each other's backpacks. They helped each other with their helmets, checked their weapons and joined the rest of the crew. The Captain opened the door that led out onto the docking platform. There was no gravity in this area, so they activated their magnetic boots and walked up to the alien craft.

The door was frozen shut and could not be opened, so the Captain ordered one of the crew to use his heat laser on the door mechanism. When it had cooled down the crewman pulled the two levers that unbolted the door. There was a release of pressurised vapour as the door pushed inwards and slid to the left.

What greeted them was a large floating fish unlike any they had ever seen before. Its oversized head with its dead eyes and long glistening teeth had an electrifying effect on the boarding party. In shock they had all pointed their weapons at it. As if it had finally been set free, the frozen fish slowly floated out and past them. They all stared at it in disbelief. Monica broke the spell by taking hold of the fish's tail and put it in a large bag for further analysis.

'Come on you lot!' the Captain said. 'Look sharp now,' and walked in. No matter what was said about him, he had no fear. They all followed him into what seemed like an ice cave. Their flashlights picked up more dead fish and icicles floating everywhere. As they walked, the air that had been still for eight hundred years was disturbed and seemed to come to life. Icicles bounced off them and frozen fish started to swirl with the air current.

'Have you ever seen anything like this?' Monica asked no one in particular.

'No.' said Shay.

'The fish are an unfamiliar species too. Look at the colours on that one, even dead it looks almost luminous.'

They walked into the central chamber and took in their surroundings. Ice had formed on all the surfaces. The edges were softened and rounded. For a spacecraft it was highly unusual to find hand crafted wood panelled walls and wood banisters along the metal gangways. The central gangway that led from the bridge at the front, to the glass elevator towards the rear of the ship spanned the large open space over the surface of the ice, which filled the bottom half of the ship. Beyond that was a storeroom that was almost entirely filled with empty laser generator packs and plasma torpedo cases. This ship had clearly not been on a mission of peace.

The Captain led the way across the central gangway towards the bridge door. It was a double door also made of wood panels. Its handles were made of a dark hand-beaten alloy, the same as the mesh floor. The Captain twisted the handles and pushed the doors open.

Shay and Monica stepped into the room behind the Captain and stood awestruck for a moment. Dominating the circular room was a huge glass ball water tank, now frozen ice. The walls were completely lined with wood panelled cabinets. In front of the tank was a cockpit seat devoid of any instruments. Further ahead were two large red leather wingback chairs that faced the floor to ceiling observation port window. It was a wide window that gave a hundred and eighty degree view. On the floor was a hand woven carpet that formed a ring around the tank and cockpit seat. The designs on it were complex and aquatic with the main colours being blues, greens, burgundy reds and gold. Floating in the room were articles of clothing and a three-foot long black metal flute.

'Fan out!' the Captain ordered as the crew moved forward, training their flashlights in all directions. Monica was about to move forward when one of the flashlight beams trailed across the tank from the opposite end of the room. She reacted with a sharp intake of breath when she saw the dark silhouette in the centre of the tank.

'Look!' She pointed at it.

They all heard and trained their flashlights at the tank. No one could see anything out of the ordinary as they were all behind their flashlights. Monica slowly pushed Shay's flashlight down to reveal the silhouette against the back light. The Captain came over and stood next to Shay. They stared in fascination.

'Well now...I assume that would be our pilot,' the Captain said. 'Lieutenant, find an auxiliary power input and hook some power up to this craft. Get Chief Wall to recycle the air with heated oxygen so that we can take off our helmets and start work.' He walked over to the crew to give further instructions and Shay got on the comlink to Chief Wall.

Monica had started work on the articles of clothing in the lab on board the Nullax Rover. The black full length coat, trousers and boots were all made of a patchwork of leather. She found the coat the most intriguing. It was made of different types of leather, as if when one part got damaged or worn, it would be repaired with whatever good leather was at hand. The back panel and shoulders were made of a single skin of a large aquatic reptile with an interesting scale pattern that was deceptively soft and malleable. The inner lining was of a very soft chamois that had an ingenious system of black wooden buttons that made it easy to remove and replace. The coat was double breasted with a high collar that would close across the face and form a hood over the head for extreme weather. The patchwork was not done randomly, but with more deliberate sinuous design. It was like nothing she had ever come across before. The textured reptilian leather patches were shaped to accentuate the negative spaces which created a visual effect that seemed to resonate with power and sensitivity.

Why keep repairing the same old coat when surely a new one would have been easier? She decided to start dating it with carbon dating and a few other more accurate methods. What she found was even more mystifying as the youngest piece was approximately eight hundred years old and the oldest was three and a half thousand years old. Even more fascinating was the size of the man who wore this coat. He would have had to be over nine foot tall. The trousers and boots confirmed this. The trousers were also unusual in that all the leather was eight hundred years old. They were more like leggings with no crotch or seat. It would most likely be worn with a loincloth, she thought. She had read about this before; some of the ancient communities on Moeba had worn this type of clothing. That's where the similarities ended. Attached to rings at the beltline was a leather web that spread from a point at the navel across the front to the hips. The same design was repeated behind and came together at the small of the back.

Two straps that extended over the shoulders were attached to rings at the navel and the small of the back that braced the trousers. Attached to the webs, were long strips of leather that hung down the front and back to about half way down the thigh. Attached to the ring at the navel was a beautiful pure white scallop shell. The straps and the top edge of the webs were adorned with small white shells sown into the leather. There was no other decoration apart from the sinuous patchwork design of the leather itself.

Monica's thoughts were interrupted by the coms-monitor. On screen was a grainy, flickering image of Professor Erick Astor calling from Upi; the third moon of Onusa. 'Monica, are you there?' he asked breathlessly as he stared blindly into the camera. She walked over to the monitor and activated it. 'Ah...there you are. How are you, my dear?'

'Fine, thank you Professor.' She was shocked to see the condition he was in. He was very pale and his hair was dishevelled. He had an oxygen tube attached under his nose that was pulled too tight across his face. Overhead neon lights accentuated his haggardness. 'You don't look too well, Professor. What's the news on your heart, when will it arrive?'

'Yes, well...things have taken a turn for the worst I'm afraid. The heart muscle has finally failed, so it's the heart machine that's keeping me alive.' Taking a deep breath he continued. 'That's to say, until they can successfully grow another new one for me at the genetics lab on Moeba.'

'I thought they already had one for you.'

'Oh they did, yes, but it failed in transit. Something to do with a power failure coming through the teleports. Those vortexes are just never as stable as you would like them to be. Now...I received your message this morning, so tell me what you have.'

Monica went through the list of articles and uploaded the visuals for him. They went through her findings and agreed on the dates according to her methods used to establish them. On further analysis they also agreed that eight hundred years would most likely have been the time it took for the craft to drift through the Othaxal cloud.

'Looking at the fish species, especially the big one with the long teeth, it reminds me of something I came upon in my research of the Urohan realm. It is reminiscent of the mythological "shoal hound". It was supposed to be a doglike fish that could be trained to round up great shoals of fish. If they existed at all is debatable, but to find one in such pristine condition and floating in space, defies logic.' His excitement was such that his aura seemed to expand. It felt as if he was standing in the room beside her.

'Can you tell me more of that realm, Professor?'

'Yes...Uroha is the dominant planet of that tiny realm, but is possibly the most mysterious planet in all the Multiverse. It is permanently covered with clouds and has constant storms. The entire surface is covered with water apart from two very small islands. Too small to support any number of population. It is said that it was once populated by humans, but that the sea levels rose to finally engulf them. So, what you have today is a planet in constant turmoil that is beset with violent storms and which is too dangerous even to explore.' He picked up a glass of water and took a sip, wheezing for breath and continued. 'Now...what can you tell me of the boots?'

'The soles are of very durable synthetic type silicon laced with magnetic strips activated by a power pack in the heel. The uppers are made of two layers of handmade leather. The inner layer is of a sturdy but soft chamois. Between these layers is an insulation of tightly packed strips of chamois. They come up to just above ankle height and are laced together by leather thongs.'

She looked up at the coms-monitor. 'The quality of the craftsmanship on all the leather work is very high. It also dates at eight hundred years. I suspect it must have been done by the same person. The stitch work is the same style throughout, but the mystery is that some of it seems to have corresponding timelines to the leather. It's almost as if the craftsman had lived and repaired these clothes for three and a half thousand years.'

'Fascinating. How soon will we be able to get a look at our pilot?'

'Shay and Chief Wall are working on that as we speak, but I'm told it could take another three days. Until then I have plenty to keep me busy.'

'Speaking of Shay...how are the two of you getting on?'

Monica blushed involuntarily at such a direct question. 'Fine thank you,' she distractedly tucked a strand of hair behind her ear. In many respects Professor Astor was like a father to her and her mentor, but she could not confide any further details of her relationship with Shay.

'Ah well...everything seems fine then,' he had a knowing smile. 'Keep me posted and if I can be of assistance call me any time, okay?'

'Okay then,' Monica smiled back at him. 'You take care now.' She stood watching the monitor as he waved goodbye and hit the exit button. As the screen went blank, Monica was left with a haunted smile and a hollow feeling in her stomach.

Shay ran his hand along the counter top that separated the upper panels from the lower ones. It was fine craftsmanship made with hand tools. He remembered his father who had chosen to be a carpenter in his youth and had died a pauper. Before he died, he'd passed on to Shay his love of creating in wood and a good grounding in mathematics. At the age of twelve Shay watched his father die of cancer. After that he watched his mother drink herself to death. He then worked the olive groves with the peasants and lived in the compounds next to the railroads. With the help of the station master he continued his education through a distance learning college and finally had graduated with honours. With the money he made working on the olive groves he paid his way through space academy and the rest is history.

He had not worked in wood since his father died, the memories were too painful. Over time he found a way to ignore wooden furniture or for that matter anything made of wood. Especially if it was well made, he would hear his father's commentary on how the joints fit together and how the wood was treated. How to use the crosscut and the rip saw. How to plain, sand and polish it until the wood came to life. Once again he was confronted by his emotional ache at the sight of his father's emaciated body on his death bed.

The spell was broken when his fingers found a small indentation that seemed a bit odd. He looked and found that it was deliberately made. The edges were rounded onto a recessed button that when pressed released a small lever on one of the upper panels. He pulled on the lever and the panel opened outward to reveal a cabinet that was filled with the pipe work, power cables and relays of the technical workings of the ship. He looked along the counter and found these buttons at regular intervals. Shay hit the coms button and spoke into the mike on his collar.

'Chief...this is Shay. I have something of interest here I think you should take a look at.'

'I'll be right over Lieutenant!'

The Chief was as wide as he was tall. A solid block of a man who knew everything about the technical workings of spacecraft. His belt rattled with measuring instruments and tools. He took out a small flashlight and looked in behind the panels.

'How did you open this panel?' Shay pointed out the recessed buttons on the countertop which they then pressed and opened up all the upper panels on the starboard side. Shay then ran his hand along the underside of the edge of the countertop and found more recessed buttons that opened the lower panels. The Chief took two flood lights and pointed them at the now open wall.

He whistled softly. 'This is a deceptively serious piece of machinery. All along the bottom there...' he pointed, making sure Shay could see, 'those are all plasma torpedo bays. There are also four laser generators there. All that stuff up there...' he pointed again. 'Those are assault lasers and force field actuators that could stop practically anything you could throw at this craft. If the portside is the same then I'm convinced that this is part of a bigger ship that would have contained bigger and faster long range engines and perhaps more crew. Now... I wonder if there is perhaps a panel or a point where I can connect a power source to.' He bent over towards the machinery and started to inspect it with his flashlight, losing all interest in Shay.

Shay walked to the rear of the bridge to investigate the two consoles. One on each side of the double doors. They were more reminiscent of old roll-top writing desks that should be in someone's study or library, rather than in a spacecraft. The desk top in line with the counter top was higher than normal. The leather padded chairs in front of them were higher and oversized, as if it had been custom made for a very tall person. The roll-top extended all the way to the edge of the desk and was made of four inch strips of wood, tied together by leather straps attached with hand made metal studs. He was about to go to work on the locking mechanism when with a hum the gravity drive was activated and the lights went on.

'Ha ha!' Chief Wall let out a satisfied laugh as he connected up the power cable.

There was an instant sound of icicles showering down in the central chamber amid the thuds of frozen fish as they hit the floor. Shay felt the gravity pull on his limbs and found it almost impossible to move his feet. He deactivated his magnetic boots and turned to face the room. What surprised him was the subtlety and warmth of the lighting. It gave the room the comfortable ambiance of a sitting room, rather than the bridge of a war ship. All the wood was a hardwood with a deep red colour running with a sinuous grain. To work this wood would have taken great skill, Shay thought. He turned back to the desk, picked the simple lock with a small tool and pushed the roll top back. He was astonished to find how dry the interior was. In the centre of the desktop was a recessed glass plasma touch pad. Directly ahead of it was a glass plasma monitor. The shelves and wooden pockets to the sides of it were filled with rolls of what looked like thin sheets of leather. There were several fishbone quills and now dry ink pots. The rest was filled with leather bound books of paper and clay tablets. Shay opened the two panels under the desk and found many layers of glass panels that pressure released outwards. Imbedded in the glass was an array of electronics that made up the computer.

When he opened the panels above the desk he was astounded to find the ancient library extended up to the ceiling, over the door and down to an identical console on the opposite side. The only difference with this console was that it had no shelves under the roll-top. The monitor was much bigger covering the entire back panel and the recessed plasma keypad was also bigger. Shay was amazed to find it still worked. He recognised some of the symbols on the keypad and realised that he was looking at the navigation console. On the monitor was a star chart that he did not recognise.

His thoughts were interrupted by another whistle from Chief Wall. Shay turned and found him standing on the portside in front of the panelled wall. Two panels were open and he was removing what looked like two curved swords with a hook cut into their points. The three foot blades were slender with a single very sharp edge. There were complex patterns on the surface of the metal that were a result of internal structural elements in the steel. The eighteen inch ivory handles screwed into each other and resulted in a long single weapon with a hooked blade on each end. The Chief found a small button on the handles that, when pressed, released a small inner blade that covered the gap made by the hook; effectively making it possible to release the blade from its victim.

'Now here's a lethal piece of gear,' the Chief mused with fascination. 'This could rip a man to pieces in no time.'

Shay walked up to him. 'Yeah...looks deadly. What else do we have?'

'These two leather tubes. They are shaped a bit like they could fit on the forearms. There seem to be metal rods in them. Some sort of armour, I'd say.'

'And what would that be?' Shay asked pointing to four tubes on the upper sides of each arm guard that were open at their forward ends. The Chief looked in the open ends and saw four arrowheads. He tried to shake them out, but they would not budge, so he took a closer look at the surrounding leather. At the back of each tube was a small button. He pointed it at one of the panels and pressed the button. The load spring released and the arrow shot out with surprising force and embedded itself into the hard wood. Attached to the shaft of the arrow was a long thin line that connected to the arm guard.

'The line seems to be made of some sort of soft sinew. Obviously to hold onto whatever it was shot at.'

'Fish perhaps?' Shay suggested. 'Apart from battle, that double sword seems to have had a similar function with that hook on the end. Bag it and I'll get it up to Dr. Lynn. What's that over there?'

The Chief opened up a leather roll that contained a belt of eight throwing knives and two eighteen inch fighting knives with ivory handles and made of the same metal as the swords. There were also two, two foot long needle like blades with double edges and slender black stone handles. He opened an upright case with Adovacian printing on it and gave out one of his silent whistles again.

'Now these are state of the art pieces of hardware. That's an Adovacian laser pulse rifle and hand gun. They are a little out of date, but still massive fire power. The cabinet next to it here holds an Adovacian battle suit with invisible masking technology and can be used under all weather, terrain and space conditions. There is no doubt in my mind that what we have here is a warrior of note and a big one too.' He took down the helmet. 'This helmet is much bigger than a normal man's and I have not seen a face plate like that before. Definitely custom made.'

Shay helped the Chief bag everything and was about to take it all up to Monica when he was summoned to the Captain's quarters. He put the artefacts onto a trolley and decided to drop them off at the lab on the way.

●

'**B**last it all to the snake pits of Azul!' the Captain banged his fist on the desk. His face was flushed with frustration. 'Those damned technocrats on Upi are going to be all over this craft for months if not years. My salvage rights did not come cheap and now it seems that it will be years before I can realise a profit.'

'Perhaps not, Captain. It is still possible that the alien being is one we are familiar with and of course the technology might be familiar. We have no idea what we have yet.'

'I know you mean well Shay, but the truth of the matter is that the novelty of a practically handmade space craft, actually in space, will on those grounds alone tie it up in a museum somewhere for the foreseeable future.' The Captain poured two drinks and passed one on to Shay.

'Do your salvage rights not give you at least part ownership of the craft?' Shay took a sip of the strong liquor.

'That bastard, Admiral Green, stitched me up on that score. He made damned sure that my rights were only valid if there was no scientific or archaeological interest. However,' he turned to look out the window that offered a view of the craft. 'We have a job to do. I want a full report on all of it as soon as the ice has melted. Maybe we can still find a way.'

'Very well, Captain.' Shay finished his drink and walked towards the door.

'Oh...Lieutenant,' the Captain said absentmindedly as he stared out the window. 'Keep an eye on Monica will you, I don't want too much information to get out.'

'Yes Captain.' Shay left the room, his back stiff with annoyance at the Captain's assumption that Monica could not be trusted…

●

The ice had melted in the tank, but like a cocoon it had remained solid and opaque around the body. The opening at the top of the tank was only just big enough to winch it out. Chief Wall climbed up the ladder and stood on the gangway that led up to the opening and watched one of the crew chopping bits of ice off the cocoon so that it did not break the glass as it was hauled out. 'Be careful there!' he bellowed. 'You don't want to damage the contents now!' In his fifties, he was a man's man, tough, popular and commanded respect from everyone. As the cocoon came free he reached over and pulled it towards himself and then along the gangway. He stopped it just past the ladder and directed the crew to lower it onto the lab trolley.

'Easy...easy!' He indicated with his right hand until it touched the trolley. 'Stop!'

The crew then lowered the cocoon until it lay on the trolley. They unhooked the winch and waited for the Chief to climb down the ladder. When he got down, two of the crew helped him to wheel the trolley out to the lab on board the Nullax Rover.

Monica looked up from the microscope as Chief Wall and the crew wheeled the alien in. 'Now missy...where would you like us to put this cold hearted feller?' he gushed. Whenever the opportunity presented itself he loved to flirt with her in his own paternal way. He knew he had no hope, but was always encouraged by the fact that she sometimes blushed and seemed a bit flustered by his comments. It was all in the spirit of fun and at times generated a good laugh. She liked the Chief who always seemed to change colour from calm and in control to bright red and falling apart whenever he was in her presence. She feared that he might internally combust and marvelled at how he managed to keep himself from melting just long enough to still flatter her. She smiled warmly. 'Over here David, the cold room is the best place for him. The temperature is better controlled and the ice will melt evenly.' The Chief glowed at the mention of his first name and pushed the trolley through the door into the cold room.

'How are things on board his ship, anything new?'

'Oh yes, it's all very mysterious. The technology used is familiar on the one hand and totally unknown on the other. Some of it has only existed in theory so far, so to find it in reality is fascinating. What I find even more fascinating is the hand made stuff. Almost the entire internal structure is hand made. We haven't got to the lower levels yet as most of it is still frozen. What did you make of that weaponry we found?'

'It's as you say...enigmatic.' She adjusted the flood lights onto the cocoon. 'The ivory is aquatic and the stone handles are black obsidian. The throwing knives are perfectly balanced as are the fighting knives. I have to admit that the designs of these instruments are unique and lethal. The steel was hand forged with iron, glass and charcoal which gives it that unique pattern and offers flexibility and a very hard, sharp edge. The laser weapons are your department, so I'll leave that up to you.'

'Right then.' The Chief left the room.

Monica walked up to the cocoon and touched it. At first it was cold, very cold, considerably more than she thought it should be. As the bite chewed its way up her arms she felt a profound sorrow pierce her heart. Her soul quaked and shrank from it as tears burst from her tear ducts. She fell back and landed heavily on a trolley laden with instruments that crashed to the floor. The Chief heard the commotion and rushed back into the room. He was shocked by what he saw. She was curled up on her side in a foetal position staring at her shaking hands. Her ashen face was distorted, tears streaming down her cheeks.

'Monica! Are you all right? What happened?' he rushed to her side.

Monica saw his mouth moving, but couldn't hear anything except the wailing scream of agony inside her head. She knew it wasn't her screaming; that something or someone had taken hold of her mind. She saw the Chief come to her side, turn his head and shout something at one of the crew, then turned back to her with his mouth moving. Suddenly the sound stopped with a whimper and she could hear him again.

'...nica! Can you hear me? Speak to me! Are you all right?' He took her cold hands and started to rub some heat into them. 'You're ice cold. The medic is on his way, just stay with me now.'

Monica struggled to get her emotions under control. What just happened she did not know, but had the idea that it had to do with some sort of energy transfer from the ice. The ache in her heart slowly started to abate and the sorrow she felt began to lift. The tears finally stopped and she gained control of her breathing. The Chief helped her sit up and she took the proffered handkerchief from him.

'Now...have you hurt yourself? Do you feel pain anywhere?'

'No,' she wiped her eyes and blew her nose.

'What happened?'

'I slipped and fell.' She said, not able to find the words to explain it.

'Seems like more than a mere slip to me. Now, what really happened?'

'I touched the ice...a strange sensation...intense sorrow and an awful scream...' she shook her head. 'I can still feel it.'

'All right now, you need a bit of rest and you'll feel right as the sun on a dusty morning. Now...do you feel okay to stand up?' He helped Monica up and walked her over to a nearby chair and helped her to sit down.

●

Shay could not believe how far the alien craft had come. It just didn't seem possible. He had done some research on the Rover's computers for any known star charts that matched up with the one he was looking at on the navigation console. The one that had some similarities had been buried deep in the Rover's archives. Obviously, it was one that never got used and probably never would have, had it not been for the discovery of this ship. The chart was of a star constellation in one of the galaxies of the Bidan realm's fifth universe that was way out on the outer rim of the multiverse. A bit more digging found that none of Bidan's universes had a teleport that could bring a ship here. The only possible explanation could be a natural vortex. He had read of travellers who had used natural vortices, but only a small handful had survived. Could it be that the pilot had made it through one of those, he thought?

Shay's Adovacian was good enough to read the alphabetic and math symbols on the keyboard, so he hit the flight plan button and the computer instantly responded. It showed a course that took it and several other craft from the home planet Adovac across fifteen universes. Using three different teleports, the journey ended at the Nev galaxy. They then made way for the Jexxar star constellation. Shay assumed they had gone there to do battle as the Adovacian realm was almost exclusively warlike and recruited mercenaries from all over the multiverse. But why so far away from their home planet, he thought. What could have been so important to travel all that distance to do battle? Who did they do battle with, he wondered. He tapped the log button and the most recent live log exploded onto the screen.

The inexorable pull of the vortex sucked the ship into its maw with increasing velocity. The 360 degree cameras gave the impression of not being in a ship at all, but bodily speeding through space. As it crossed the event horizon the vibration became so intense that all light and objects lost definition and colour to become white noise. Then...black silence crept in from the edges until there was only a pinprick of white in the centre. It stayed that way for almost a full minute and then started to grow. As it grew the white light started to change colour and with it came a high pitched whine that deepened the bigger the light became. As it filled the screen, objects and light became more defined until the vista of space became clear as the craft exited the other side.

Suddenly everything went mad as something crashed into the side of the craft. It was thrown into a violent spin. The cameras caught glimpses of a giant meteor and bits of space craft as it spun away into the path of the black cloud. Slowly the craft was brought under control, but now faced the cloud. Shay relaxed his fingers that were gouging into the leather armrests of the chair in front of the console. He felt as if he had been in the craft himself and marvelled at the skill of the pilot. As he brought his breath under control, he heard the sound of the explosive bolts as the pilot ejected the wrecked engine bay. So, the Chief was right, this was part of a bigger craft, he thought.

The tiny comlink in his left ear crackled to life and a small voice interrupted his thoughts.

'Shay...its Monica. Are you free at the moment?'

Shay was shocked at how vulnerable she sounded. This was not the Monica he was accustomed to. He tapped the coms button and spoke into the mike. 'Are you alright Monica? Where are you now?' His sense of alarm threatened to overwhelm him so he stood up and started walking out of the alien craft.

'I'm in my cabin.'

'I'll be right over.'

What could have precipitated this, he thought. It was very unusual for her to be in such a fragile state. When he got to her cabin he found her standing with her back to the door and looking out of the small porthole that offered a view of the starscape. Shay walked over to her and put his hands on her shoulders.

'Monica.' he said tenderly.

She turned towards him and rested her forehead on his chest. Her shoulders started to shake as her body was raked by a new spasm of grief. Her forearms were lifted across her chest with her hands still clutching the handkerchief the Chief had given her. Shay could feel her trying to fight the tears and almost deliberately keep her arms between them in an effort to defy her urge for solace. As if by letting Shay any closer the dam would burst and she would betray her vulnerabilities.

Shay was in awe at the intensity of her emotion. He had always known her to be passionate and strong, but never vulnerable and overwhelmed like this. Gently he pulled her closer and whispered, 'Come to me...let it out...let it out.'

Slowly, she began to shake as the emotion waxed within her. He felt her arms go around his waist and hold him with clutching despair. He held her like that for the longest time. It was as if something or someone had taken hold of her and finally had the chance to cry for the first time. It came from the depths of her soul, a sorrow he knew she did not normally possess. Gradually the paroxysms of grief subsided and her body started to relax. She looked up at Shay who was struck by the hollow angst in her eyes. His heart swelled with love and sympathy for her and he kissed her tenderly on her parted lips. They were moist and her tears were salty.

There was a subtle shift of expression in her eyes and she kissed him back, tenderly at first and then with more urgency. He felt her body crush into him as she reached up with her right hand. He felt her pull him closer as her tongue entered his mouth, probing and reaching for him. It felt as if he had unlocked the door to a passion deep inside her he had not expected and had only ever hoped for. He felt her heat surround him, consume him and fill his senses. All he could taste, smell and feel was her. Beyond the whirlwind of blood rushing in his ears he could hear her soft moans as she took his left hand and put it on her breast. The stirring of his loins was rapid and almost painful with each hot pulse of blood that throbbed his manhood into a hardness that strained against the fabric of his flight suit.

Monica felt his response and broke the kiss. With an intense urgency she took hold of the zip at the collar of his flight suit and pulled it down to his waist. Shay took over and slipped out of the coverall type outfit while Monica took off her t-shirt, trousers and panties. Shay took off his t-shirt and was about to remove his boots so that he could get out of the coverall leggings when Monica kissed him again. With her back to the wall she drew him towards her and pushed down his shorts. Shay felt her fingers release his penis from its material confines and explore the well formed muscle. He sensed her urgency and supported her thighs as she mounted him.

The first penetration, at first, gentle and tender, grew into slow deep thrusts. Shay could feel the tension grow in her back and thighs as she gyrated with his rhythm. As the heat grew within her he could feel himself get even harder. He felt her thighs start to quiver and her breath come faster as the heat became exquisitely unbearable. He felt as if he would burst at any moment, not only in his loins, but with love and passion that was concentrated into a white hot pin point. He felt her start to spasm as her intense orgasm finally relieved her aching heart. Her heat suffused his lower belly and melted away his final control. His release was strong and copious while his heart raced, fuelling a tempest of joy and emotion that left him spent.

It was like a shape-shifting black blob floating in from the edge of her mind. She was in a room, but couldn't discern the size of it. She could only see a door with more darkness beyond. The room was dark, airless and felt oppressive and claustrophobic. She found it hard to breathe as if there was a massive weight on her chest. The blackness seemed to expand and recede, obscuring her vision one moment then opening up to let the dark vision in. Suddenly the blob expanded completely absorbing the room. A small white light started to glow in the centre. She felt fascinated and warmed by its brightness. Slowly the frightening visage of a colourless face took shape beyond the light. It was ugly and full of menace with eyes that pounded nails of fear into her breast. Suddenly its massive jaws snapped open and rushed at her.

Monica awoke with a start with Shay's arm across her chest. Her mouth was dry and her breathing came hard and fast. They had fallen asleep on the cramped single bunk of her cabin. Her heart was racing and she felt anxious and edgy after the emotional excesses of the past eighteen hours. She pulled back the privacy curtain and got up, careful not to disturb him. She took a steam shower in the tiny bathroom cabinet at the end of her bed. It consisted of a toilet and basin. The steam emanated from small channels in the walls. She felt the heat and steam start to un-knot her muscles and wash the blackness away. Since she had touched the ice she had been in an almost uncontrollable emotional state, she thought. Now it seemed like she was dreaming dreams of things she had never experienced. She had to work this out.

When she was done she stepped out of the bathroom cabinet and took out a fresh set of clothing from the lockers in the opposite wall. She got dressed and left the cabin with Shay still asleep on the bunk. It was a short walk down the curved corridor to the officer's mess. At the small galley she hydrated and heated a breakfast pack and took a sealed fruit juice from the refrigerator. She walked over to the table and sat down. As she started to eat she looked at the conference screens at the opposite end of the table.

They had several views of the alien craft's exterior hull and interior views from cameras Chief Wall had installed. She noticed that most of the ships solar skin had been ripped off and that the metal under it was stained black and brown as if it had been exposed to harsh elements for an extended period of time which had rusted it. It seemed a miracle that such a craft could actually be in space at all. It was however elegantly shaped. Like a headless bird with a bulbous body. It looked battered and worn as if it had been repaired many times. It seemed more like a personal war craft than any realm sponsored one. She looked up at another screen and saw two of the crew cataloguing the library and scrolls on the bridge. She wondered at the mysteries they might contain, however, that answer would be for another day. Captain Masters walked in, saw her and greeted.

'Hello Monica,' he said and poured himself a hot brew at the galley. 'I understand you had some sort of ...traumatic episode with the alien body yesterday.' He walked over to the table and sat down. With his elbows on the table he looked intently at her. 'So, how are you feeling now?'

'Better now thank you.' she responded cautiously. She always felt uneasy in his mercurial presence.

'Ah…very good,' he sat back with an unconvincing smile on his face. 'Perhaps you might fill me in then. What sort of assumptions and conclusions have you come to so far?'

'It's too early to tell at the moment. I have not yet seen the body, only then can I give you a report of any value.'

'Oh I understand that, however, I'm curious…I heard there were some anomalies with the age of his effects. Do you think this would reflect the actual age of the being or would he just have found these things along the way?'

'It's hard to tell. The only constant is the thread used to sew his clothing together which would offer an eight hundred year time frame. As for his weaponry and other effects, they are highly unusual and can only be approximated through some dating techniques and historical referencing.'

'I see…' He looked at her for a few moments with a contemplative look in his eye. Monica could see a shift of expression as he continued. 'Monica, I know we didn't exactly get off on the right foot and I'd like to apologise for my remarks back on Moeba. I was way too intoxicated to be rational and well…my judgement was impaired, you know how it is.'

Monica's shock and surprise was complete. Nothing had prepared her for this. An apology from this man had to come with an ulterior motive. All her alarm bells were ringing. In a sense she felt twice insulted that he would insult her in public, but apologise in private, however, she was curious to see what he was up to.

'Oh…accepted Captain.' Monica smiled, but stopped short of shaking his hand. 'Now, if you'll excuse me I have work to do,' and left the room.

●

The ice cocoon had melted down to about half its original size, but not enough to reveal the body yet. Monica adjusted the overhead scanner and sat down at the monitor. She typed in a series of entries and the scanner started to move over the cocoon. 'Now…lets see what we have here.' she said to herself.

The scan started at the feet and slowly worked its way up. She noticed something odd almost immediately. Normally ice would permeate throughout the body, but in this case there was a narrow gap between it and the ice. She looked at the readings on the monitor and found that the gap was filled with a liquid of fatty acids and glycerine. As the scan reached his brain she noticed a small speck of heat at the frontal lobe area. She thought the scan was a bit off or maybe she had messed up one of the entries, so she decided to do the scan again. All was normal as one would expect from a dead body, but when it reached the brain there were now several points of heat. She decided to do a full body real time activity scan. She entered the formulas and a different overhead scanner was activated.

A full body image came up on the monitor. For the first minute nothing happened, and then suddenly there was a very low, but distinct pulse of the heart and the brain lit up in several areas. At first she just stared at the monitor in shocked disbelief as the light faded out. It happened again almost two minutes later. Now she knew!

'Merciful heavens,' she whispered in awe. 'He's alive!'

Her first instinct was to break him out of there and bring him back, but then she decided to follow a more cautious path. She got on the coms network and contacted Professor Erick Astor. His face appeared on the monitor, pale and drawn. The oxygen tube under his nose looked like it was pulled too tight across his face again. He was sitting up in his wheel chair with the oxygen tank attached to the side.

'Monica!' he wheezed. 'It's so good to hear from you again. What news?'

'Our alien is alive, Erick!'

'What's that you say?'

'He's alive, Erick, our alien lives! I'm hooking you up to a live feed of the real time scan as we speak.'

Professor Astor stared intently into the top right hand corner of his monitor as the picture came on. 'Well he's definitely humanoid, but I don't understand, he looks dead to me.'

'Yes, I thought so too, but he has a heart beat every two minutes.'

'That's highly unlikely Monica, as you know...' he stopped in mid sentence as he looked at the monitor. 'My word!' he exclaimed in astonishment as he noticed the heart beat. 'I have never seen anything like it. A humanoid aquatic being that can hibernate for hundreds of years, that's astounding!'

'Something as unprecedented as this I thought would be better dealt with if I consulted with you on how to revive him from his hibernation without killing him. As you can see, his body is excessively emaciated and we are still not sure what we are dealing with here.'

'I would be most honoured to be a part of this, thank you Monica. Now...I would suggest letting the ice melt naturally. Take samples of the fluid around his body and the ice itself...' They discussed their strategy for the next few hours while Monica turned up the heating and kept the scanner active.

Eventually Professor Astor tired and needed to rest. Monica kept the live data feed to him active and continued to work. She took down a core drill and drilled several cores from the ice. She also took samples of the liquid that surrounded the alien. She put them through several different testing procedures and discovered that there was more to this liquid than fatty acids and glycerine. It was also full of all manner of nutrients including several types of microscopic plankton that was frozen in the ice. Like a bolt of electricity it struck her with the realisation that the best way to revive him would be to keep him submersed in the tank water that he was taken out of. To try and do it any other way would kill him. Chief engineer David Wall was the man she would need to consult.

●

Monica had set up a temporary lab around the ball tank on board the alien craft. She had two portable scanners set up to monitor the alien's physiology as the ice around him slowly melted into the surrounding water inside the tank. All the water in the craft had now melted. Chief Wall had worked his magic and got all the pumps working that circulated, filtered and oxygenated the water. All the dead fish had been removed and put in cold storage for further study. She was distracted by the details the Chief was giving her as she set up the last of her monitoring equipment.

'I tell you Monica, this is an amazing machine. It has the oldest engines I have ever seen on a space craft and what do you suppose they run on?' Monica's response was mute, so he continued. 'Water, can you believe it? The active element used is hydrogen and the by-product, water, is then recycled back into the system. It runs through a filtration system and then through an oxygenation system, which is part of a waterfall under the central gangway there.' He pointed at the central gangway that ran over the water in the central chamber.

'There is even a zero point energy system using water as it's source to fire up the laser canons and charge up the plasma torpedoes. Initial energy is derived from the solar skin on the hull. The only reason why this craft failed is because it had lost most of the solar skin, energy cells, and auxiliary power which had been damaged by the meteor impact. It did not have enough energy to fire up the engine. Fascinating stuff.' His face glowed with a smile permanently in place. His expansive euphoria was such that Monica thought if she did not give him something else to think about, the button on his collar might pop off.

'How do you suppose he controlled this craft? I don't see any controls.'

'Ah well...that's the genius of the whole thing. You see this tank here,' he pointed at the ball tank, 'well now, it's not just a water tank, the whole thing is a plasma touch screen from the inside and all controls are activated on it. The seat in front is the cockpit battle station. It has a total surround screen that comes out at the base of the chair. All the visuals are generated from thousands of tiny cameras on the hull. Fascinating stuff.' he repeated. Before he could say anything else his comlink buzzed in his ear and the captain called him to the bridge.

'Must be off my dear, see you later.'

Monica smiled and waved him on. She enjoyed his attention and company and always felt complimented by it, but now she needed to focus on the task ahead. She walked up to the tank and noticed that the ice had melted further. It was almost transparent allowing her to see the shadow of the alien body a little clearer. Shay walked in and she unconsciously crossed her arms across her chest thinking that this was the last thing she needed right now. Shay smiled and stood next to her.

'How are you feeling?' he asked looking directly at her.

She was surprised at how warm she felt inside at his sincere enquiry after her well being. Despite herself, she blushed and smiled warmly.

'I'm much better now, thank you.'

He put his right arm around her shoulders and pulled her closer. They both stared at the alien for a few moments before Monica asked.

'I wonder where he came from, how he got here. It's astonishing that he is still alive you know.'

'I was nearly knocked off my feet when I heard. The Captain left the bridge and has been in his cabin ever since. He is most likely trying to come to terms with the financial loss of his salvage rights. I'd stay out of his way for a while. Now...' he broke the contact between himself and Monica and stepped a bit closer to the tank. 'Our alien here is a first rate pilot. According to the latest log on his navigation console he had done a military campaign in the Bidan realm's fifth universe at the Nev galaxies Jexxar star constellation. He got here through a natural vortex.'

'But that's impossible is it not?'

'So the theory states. But then, that's what theories are, only theories. There's a visual record of him getting through. It has always been assumed that no one has survived such an event, but it would seem that no one has been able to fly through such an event and prove it. His ship sustained this damage when it was hit by a giant meteor as it exited the vortex.'

'Shay...' Monica said staring intently at the alien. 'Do you see that?'

'What?'

'There.' she pointed. 'Is that a crack forming there?'

'Yes it is!'

Once begun, the crack spread rapidly. It cut across the midsection and started to shatter on both sides. It shattered further down until it reached the ankles. It seemed to remain suspended like that for a few moments until slowly a few pieces drifted away.

As if on cue, the rest of the shattered bits floated free, partially releasing its captive of the past eight hundred years. The ice remained solid from the chest, across the face, over the head and down the back to the feet. It seemed reluctant to let the rest of him go. From the scans Monica knew that it was the ankle length hair that the ice was holding on to.

'Good heavens!' Shay exclaimed. 'I have never seen anyone that emaciated before and live. The man is just skin and bone, there's almost no muscle left on him. His skin is all wrinkled up and loose on him, it's as if...he would have had to be a much bigger man to have filled that skin. And look at the colour of it; it's so white it's almost colourless.'

Monica had moved closer and was scrutinising his ribs. 'Look over there,' she pointed. 'Those slits between the ribs...they look like gills don't they?'

'They certainly do.'

'Do you notice a slight movement in them?'

Shay nodded.

'That must be the way he was getting oxygen into his blood stream.' Monica continued. 'I would not be surprised if that was also the way he absorbed nutrients. It would have been impossible to live for so long without some form of nutrition. By the look of his body, there is no fat or muscle left to feed on. I am of the impression that he would not have lasted much longer.' She left the tank and walked over to the table where the scan monitors were.

'There's a lot more activity with his body. The heart rate also seems to have picked up from once every hundred and eighteen seconds to once every hundred and fifteen seconds.' She looked up from the monitors. 'I think he's starting to wake up!'

She felt flushed and excited.

●

Captain John Masters paced up and down his quarters. They were more spacious than the other cabins with a sitting room, separate bedroom and shower cabinet. His desk was also in the sitting room. Now that the alien was alive there was no way he could exercise his salvage rights. He walked over to his desk and sat down. There had to be a way to make his money back, he thought.

He went through the alien ships inventory again to see if there was any opportunity there. After some time pouring over the list of books he decided that he needed to call in a few favours. He went onto his private coms network and called Ehzhu Moriwe who was still languishing in the Captain's home on Moeba. He sent a text message through to a small coms device Ehzhu carried on his person. He was in the throes of entertaining a small group of influential Sabalians to dinner when he got the call. He discreetly left the table and entered the study where he could speak in private.

He sat his great body down on the sumptuous silk covered bottle green chesterfield chair at the oversized obsidian desk. Dark brown, black and red flow lines embedded in its natural glass were offset by the blood red carpet. The padded walls and ceiling of the small round room were covered with the same bottle green silk with fibre optic light buttons recessed deep into the padding. There were two green silk chesterfield couches, one with its back against the front of the desk, the other facing it. They were separated by a low automated obsidian table matching the desk. Behind the facing couch was an obsidian half moon cabinet with two brass tree lamps that had many tiny amber tear drop bulbs. Two identical lamps were on the desk.

Ehzhu pushed a recessed square in the centre of the desk and a flat screen monitor slowly flipped up. He touched the coms button on the key pad and the image of Captain Masters came on screen. 'Captain...your mission has been profitable I trust?'

The Captain looked at the shiny blue faced visage of Ehzhu and wondered if he was taking the right course with him. 'As well as can be expected.' he answered somewhat defensively. 'How are the trade negotiations going? I hope Etha Dax has not been too much of a bore now.'

'Oh...on the contrary, he has been very facilitating. Tell me captain; to what do I owe the honour of this call from five light years away?'

'Well, we found the alien craft, but with a damned alien on board who is still alive, captured in a natural state of suspended animation.'

'I don't comprehend; a natural state of suspended animation?' Ehzhu was astonished.

'You heard me. The alien is an aquatic as well as a surface being that has been frozen in a tank of water for the past eight hundred years or so. It turns out that he has a large library on board, so I'm uploading a catalogue of it to you to see if they would be of any interest to you.'

'Ah yes, I do love a good book.' Ehzhu said as he looked up into the top right corner of the screen. As the catalogue downloaded he maximised the screen and read through the contents. Suddenly his eyebrows lifted and his expression changed from concentrated perusal to intense interest. He sat forward and squinted at the screen. 'This one here, "A Treatise of Manna", is it truly on board?' The Captain knew he had a live one.

'Oh yes and it's in good dry condition too. It looks very old though and seems to be written in an old Moeban dialect of which I can only understand a word here and there.'

'If it is the book I'm thinking of, it is exceedingly old. It has been lost for thousands of years.' His face seemed to be shinier than before, almost aglow with excitement. The Captain wondered at how a book could bring about such a reaction in a man who concluded universal trade deals without breaking a sweat. What came next almost knocked the Captain off his seat.

'Captain...I will meet you at the settlement on Upi in three weeks to conclude this transaction. Accompanying me will be my two wives and their entourage. You are invited to take residence on board my ship for the duration of our visit there. I'm sure the accommodations would be more comfortable than those at the research station.'

The Captain felt a stirring in his loins at the thought of seeing Feen again. He laughed. 'I look forward to it. Until then Ehzhu!

'Until then!' Ehzhu responded glowingly.

●

'What is that there, at his feet,' Professor Erick Astor asked, as if he was in the same room as Monica. 'Those seem like some sort of hooks attached to his hair.'

'Oh yes, they're hooks alright,' Monica answered. 'But not attached to his hair. They are in fact hardened hair, like horns. His hair is like nothing I've come across before. If you look at the scan of his head you will notice a network of muscles on the scull that seem to be attached to the roots of his hair. The hair itself has a fine network of long slender muscle and nerve. They form ankle length rope-like appendages ending in these hooks and spikes. This means of course that the hair can be used as an independent limb.'

The ice had melted further, but stubbornly remained frozen around the head and shoulders. His body had been reduced to skin and bone. Over the past eight hundred years, his body had fed on its own fat and when that was gone, it fed on its muscle. All that kept it alive after that was what little nutrients could be absorbed through the gills from the ice itself.

'Fascinating!' The Professor exclaimed. 'It looks like there are several hooks on each rope. I would venture a guess that they would have been used as a weapon or survival tool like hunting perhaps?'

'My thoughts exactly.' Monica concurred. 'Now if you look at the dark area around the navel that comes together and forms a thin line that goes up the centre of the belly. It then spreads out again from the solar plexus across the centre of the chest. What do you make of that?'

'That's very unusual.' The Professor said, panting with the exertion of breathing and speaking at the same time. He looked to his right side and adjusted the oxygen levels on the tank and then continued. 'Being an aquatic being, it reminds me of the lateral line on a fish, which as you know, lets it feel its environment. It seems very odd that such a being could find itself in space, let alone piloting a ship.'

They were interrupted by Shay who had been studying the journals at the library console. He walked over to Monica with one of the journals and said, 'I think we might have a name for our alien.' He opened the journal and pointed at a word that had very little meaning to Monica. 'You see these symbols here? Every entry logged ends with the same word. My assumption would be a name and that name reads as "Coda."'

'Just Coda? No second name or title?'

'Just Coda.' Shay confirmed.

They all stared at the alien with their own thoughts. By knowing his name, he had suddenly become more human to them, somehow a little less alien, less of a water being, but more of a being. Something that could read and write and had consciousness was far more of a someone and not just an alien in a fish tank. Monica said his name in a pensive tone and as if on cue, the ice that covered his face cracked and slowly drifted away.

A chill crept up her spine and lifted the hair at the back of her neck. It felt as if Coda had waited for this moment to reveal himself. She was struck by the serene expression on his face. At one with himself, almost as if he was in a state of deep meditation. How was it possible for him to still look so young, she thought? He looked more like someone who was in his fifties. Certainly not someone who had been encased in ice for the past eight hundred years. His face was drawn from starvation and his eyes were sunken into his skull, but still, he didn't look like a very old man. As if there was some sort of reversible time mechanism in him. For an alien aquatic being, his features were also remarkably human. On closer inspection she found his nostrils were broad and flat, like two flaps of muscle that would close off the nasal passages under water. Above each eyebrow there were five small distinct holes. Perhaps some sort of sensory passages she thought. If it was what she thought it was, then this man was superbly equipped for the aquatic world and would be a formidable hunter.

'What do you make of those Erick?' She broke the spell and pointed them out.

'Well...they look like ampullae. The kind you find in predatory fish to sense electric impulses. Underwater he would have been able to sense impulses over vast distances, a marvellous adaptation! I notice he has some tattoos there on his thighs and upper arms. Once he is free of the ice we should give them proper study.' Professor Astor was leaning forward and peering intently into the monitor. The overhead light cast macabre shadows on his face, accentuating the oxygen tube pulled tight under his nose and cheekbones. His pale face had a sheen of perspiration from his excitement and effort to breathe. 'In all my years of alien anthropology, this has been a most interesting find. I see on the scan that he has lungs as well, so that would mean he would be equally capable of living outside his aquatic environment.' He sat back in the wheelchair, panting. He dug some pills out of his top pocket and put them under his tongue. 'Monica, I have to get some rest, please excuse me. I'll be in touch soon enough.'

'Thanks for your time and advice Erick, get some rest now,' she said with great tenderness. If he did not get his new heart soon, it was doubtful that he would last very much longer. 'I'll be in touch with another update.' She saw him touch a button on the remote and the monitor went blank. She moved out from behind the table and walked over to Shay who was standing at the tank looking at Coda. 'He's a big one isn't he?' Shay said.

'Yes...over nine foot, but the water makes him look even bigger.'

'It looks like he has seen some extreme action too. His body has a myriad of scars particularly across his chest and arms. He has penetration scars on his abdomen and several slash marks on his thighs. There's a bad one on his left knee there,' Shay pointed. 'I wonder how long that would have taken to heal.'

'The scan showed an impact wound that shattered the shin bone just below the knee and healed quite badly. I'm fairly sure it would have left him with a limp. He has had other fractures along the way, most it would seem, when he was very young.' She looked up at Coda. 'He's lived a hard life this man called Coda.'

It was then that Coda's eyes opened slowly and looked straight at them. They stepped back as the shock of it slapped into them. To Monica it felt as if someone had taken hold of the skin at the back of her head and pulled it tight across her face. Her chest seemed to constrict with sudden impact that left her heart aquiver. Coda's pupils were totally dilated with only a thin line of red brown iris around it. Covering the eye was a membrane that protected the eye, worked as an infra red lens and gave him acute underwater vision.

What astounded Monica was the wisdom behind those eyes; it was like looking into the well of ages. She felt warmth behind her eyes, as if she had made another connection with him, except, it was not sorrow and pain this time, but exhaustion. As if the last drop of energy had been drained from her, she stumbled slightly and leaned against Shay for support. He put his arm around her shoulders and held her there, rooted to the spot. Slowly, Coda closed his eyes again and was gone from them, as if someone had switched the light off.

Monica awoke in the same position she had fallen asleep. She had slept like a dead person with no dreams and no movement. She sighed, opened her eyes and lay there, savouring the quiet for the moment. She turned onto her back and stretched her legs out. Her left arm was numb from lack of circulation where she had slept on it. The previous days events came rushing back as the vision of Coda's eyes filled her mind. She felt an urgency to get back to him. She felt as if she might miss some vital moment, something significant.

After she showered and got dressed she headed directly for her makeshift lab at Coda's tank. When she got there the first thing she noticed was that the ice around his head and shoulders had melted. The tendrils of his hair were floating freely, but what struck her were the tattoos that covered his entire back, buttocks, thighs and calves. The bold designs looked as if the skin had been carved out in the shapes of entwined plant fronds as they unwound in early growth. The negative spaces between were tattooed with intricate chevrons, lines, circles and spikes. There were areas of three dimensional shading that formed shapes like the boiling gases of a star. On closer inspection she noticed that the larger negative tattooed areas covered what looked like damaged skin. It was the design itself that was compelling. From the centre of his spine radiating outwards was a spiral galaxy with an elongated central mass of stars. The black matter of space was tattooed in the swirling shapes of clouds interspersed by the lighter shades of the spiral arms. It was all held together by the clear skin, intertwined plant fronds that seemed to grow from his chest, abdomen, and front of his legs. They formed a beautifully intricate network in black and grey that followed the contours of his body and seemed to hold his soul in place.

For a long time Monica looked at them, following the lines that drew the eye along its myriad shapes and spaces. She wondered how long such an enormous tattoo would have taken and how much pain he would have had to endure. Suddenly his hair, that was floating freely, began to move and wrap itself around his back and torso. It seemed as if he knew he was under scrutiny and thus covered himself in an almost self conscious way. She walked around to the front of him, but found his eyes still closed as if he was in a deep sleep.

On his left wrist she noticed the only piece of jewellery he wore. It was a bracelet of black metal. It looked similar to that used for the flute. It had an unusual, but elegant design. It had no reference to the tattoos. She wondered what the significance of it was. Everything about Coda seemed to have some sort of significance to him. She hoped she would find out some day.

She walked over to the monitor and noted his heart rate had risen significantly to a normal sixty beats per minute. The heat sensors showed that the temperature of his brain and chest area had risen to normal and remained steady. His outer extremities were taking longer. The thrill of working with an alien who was coming alive after being frozen for such a long time was almost overwhelming. How was it possible, she thought? Why was there no cell damage, or was there and they just didn't know? When he was finally conscious, how would he communicate? What was his life story? How would he react and interact with us, she wondered...

Upi, Onusa Quadrant

The planet Onusa loomed large, dwarfing Upi, the only one of its three moons that was stable enough to build a research station on. Captain Masters expertly guided the Nullax Rover onto the landing pad with the alien craft in tow. Once landed, the pad descended into the underground hanger that was re-oxygenated once the roof sealed shut. A general cheer sounded among the crew as the pad came to a stand still, relieved to be back on terra firma after such a long journey.

A flurry of activity burst onto the landing pad as ground crew went about their business of securing the two craft and beginning their general maintenance checks. The crew disembarked and headed for the debriefing room. The Captain, Monica, Shay and chief engineer David Wall were met by Dr. Dennis Craven on board the alien craft. He was the minister of Science, Culture and Technology on Moeba; a cold ruthless politician who reserved his smile only for the camera. At forty five he was young by political standards, but his short cropped white hair testified to the stress of his ambition and rise to power. He wore a black silk embroidered suit with a high collar. His royal blue gathered silk shirt had a stiff mandarin collar. It was pinned in front by the oval cut diamond set in its wing-swept triangular shaped silver setting that was the emblem of the Moeban Progressive Party (MPP).

Chief Wall and the Captain had taken him on a tour of the craft and explained to him what they knew so far. They came to a stop at the glass ball tank and stared for a moment. Dr Craven's cold grey eyes scanned Coda with detached interest. He looked at Monica, acknowledging her presence for the first time. 'Do you think he will live?'

Monica was unaccustomed to the withering effect his gaze had on her. She took an involuntary half step back and crossed her arms in front of her. She cleared her throat. 'We might revive him yes, but what damage he has sustained over the years we don't know. As you can see, his body has...'

'Yes, I can see,' he interrupted dismissively; losing interest as he was satisfied that Coda would most likely be a vegetable. 'Captain, let's have a word shall we.' As they left the craft, Professor Erick Astor trundled through the double doorway of the alien craft's bridge, in his electric wheelchair. As he crossed the threshold he stopped in amazement and marvelled at the scene. The first thing that struck him was the ambiance created by the lighting. It picked up the subtle colouring of the fantastic aquatic designs of the circular carpet. Dominating the room was the glass ball tank with Coda, the alien.

He hit the forward control on the right hand arm rest and was propelled around the tank towards where Monica, Shay and the Chief were standing. Monica's face lit up when she saw him. His grey hair was dishevelled and the oxygen tube under his nose still cut a gash across his pale fleshy face. His intense brown eyes smiled at her from under his bushy grey eyebrows. Her tension fell away as she unfurled her arms and walked towards him.

'Erick! It's so good to see you.' She took his bony blue veined hands in hers and gave them an affectionate squeeze. She noticed the paper thin skin and the weak response. She was taken aback at how much he had aged since she last worked with him.

'How are you my dear, it's been such a long time.' he smiled up at her.

'I have been just fine thank you. Let me introduce you...this is Chief engineer David Wall and this is our navigator Lieutenant Shay Duncan.' The Professor noticed the exchange between Monica and Shay and was pleased that there was more to it than mere professional courtesy. David Wall he liked instantly as the man's expansive nature seemed to affect everyone in the room. His firm handshake and red face was backed by a strong voice. 'Ah yes, Professor, it's good to finally meet you. I trust you're feeling well today?'

'Well enough thank you.' His smile was hampered by the tight oxygen tube, but there was no mistaking the warmth in his eyes as Shay greeted him with equal benevolence.

He looked up at Coda. 'He looks far bigger in real life doesn't he?' Monica nodded. 'How is his recovery coming along?'

'Not as well as I would hope for.' Monica looked grave. 'At first, his recovery was rapid and steady, but it now seems to have levelled off. I fear a further decline is inevitable unless we attempt an intravenous feed. He's hydrated enough, but needs more powerful nutrition to survive. According to his blood scan, we have made up a drip recipe that can be safely administered.'

'Where will you find a vein? To do it underwater will be impossible.'

'If we can lift his head and shoulders above the water line, I'll insert the tube into the subclavian vein of the neck.'

'Excellent!' The Professor knew he had the right person for the job. He had fought a mountainous struggle with Dennis Craven over his recommendation to have Monica do this job. He suspected that Dr. Craven wanted someone he had leverage over, someone he could control, however, Monica's credentials won the day with the help of a few favours he called in. 'When do you plan to do this?'

'We have everything in place so we are going to do the procedure now.' She nodded to the Chief who walked off towards the stairs that led up to the gangway. There was a small cordoned off area where he changed into his wetsuit. He scaled the steps and walked onto the gangway. The hoist was placed over the opening of the tank with the harness attached to the pulley by a chain that would hoist Coda up. The Chief sat on the edge of the gangway and put on the goggles and mouthpiece that was attached to the oxygen hose. He released the catch that held the ladder above the water and it slowly lowered into the water on its hydraulic hinge. The Chief turned around, stepped onto the ladder and lowered himself into the water.

As the Chief entered the water he had the feeling that he should not make any sudden or threatening movements, as if he was with some sort of trapped and dangerous animal. Being this close to Coda made him realise just how big and menacing this alien could appear underwater. He felt an electric chill grip his chest as Coda's hair spread out behind him and several tentacles of hair reached out towards him. With ominous intent, one of the incredibly sharp barbed points pinned him under the jaw at the apex of his throat. Several other tentacles gently explored the contours of his body and wrapped around his limbs. Coda's eyes opened for a moment and seemed to bore through him, transfixing him, reading him and penetrating his mind.

Slowly as if understanding the Chief's intent, the tentacles fell away and Coda closed his eyes once more. The Chief was shaken to the core with the realisation of just how close death had passed him by. Mentally he brushed aside its cold residue and got on with the job. He looked out the side of the tank to where Shay was standing with the controls and indicated to him to lower the harness. Shay hit the button and the Chief took hold of the harness as it descended into the water.

He strapped the harness under Coda's arms and across his chest, careful to keep clear of his gills. Once the harness was secure he indicated to Shay to lift Coda out.

Monica was lying on her belly on a makeshift platform at the edge of the tank opening. With her arms over the side she indicated to Shay to stop when Coda's head and shoulders were above water. To minimise the stress, he was lifted so as to keep his gills submerged. The weight of his hair pulled his head back and with his face close to Monica he opened his eyes again and looked at her. She saw the protective membrane pull back from his eye balls and his pupils return to normal size. She felt his weakness and comprehension of what she was about to do. His steady gaze was reassuring with warm penetration.

'I have to do this or you will die of starvation,' she said, knowing somehow that he understood her.

He closed his eyes again and slowly turned his head away from her, exposing the side of his neck. With her latex gloved hands she drew her surgical mask over her nose and mouth and worked fast. She dried off his skin and swabbed it with an antiseptic solution. She carefully inserted the catheter needle into the subclavian vein. She then withdrew the internal needle and attached the drip tube to the flexible catheter that remained fixed in the vein. She then sealed off the catheter site with a sterile aquatic dressing and taped the tube in place at the back of his ear. She got to her feet and started the feed pump that was mounted on the drip stand. Before she released the feeding solution, she made some fine adjustments to the timing of the pump and checked to see that there was no air in the tube. When the procedure was complete, she indicated to Shay to re-submerge Coda. The Chief checked to see that the harness was comfortable and left it on to keep Coda upright until the feeding period was over. He made sure the dressing was secured and then got out of the tank. He took off the goggles and mouthpiece and sat there on the edge of the gangway for a moment to settle his nerves. Monica too was in a pensive mood as she adjusted the tube length and checked the readings on the feed pump. They were all affected by it, even Professor Astor sat in quiet contemplation of what had just passed. Shay climbed up the stairs onto the gangway where the Chief sat.

'Are you ok?' He put his hand on the Chief's shoulder.

'Yeah, I'm good.' he responded looking at his still shaking hands.

Shay descended the makeshift stairs that led down to the platform Monica was standing on. 'How did it go?'

She looked at him, took a deep breath and sighed. She then stared at him with a perplexed look, but said nothing, as if she was not there. Her mind and her thoughts taken far away to a place he would never know. After some time she blinked, took another breath and sighed again. She shook her head slightly, as if to clear it and said with a soft voice. 'Yes the procedure went well; I just hope it will work.' She put her hands in her pale blue lab coat pockets, walked past Shay and up the stairs.

'His skin was warm you know,' she said over her shoulder to Shay. 'I never expected that. It was almost as if he gave me his permission to go ahead as well. The one moment you would think he was in an almost comatose state and the next he's communicating on some subliminal level. There is far more to Coda than we can possibly imagine.' Using Coda's name in this way struck Shay with the significance of Monica's connection with him. It was becoming personal for her.

'Where did it come from?' Dr. Craven asked as he took a sip of his drink. He was seated on the raw silk couch in the VIP lounge. Its ochre and golden yellows offset the cold grey moonscape of Upi seen through the glass wall. The Captain sat opposite him on an identical couch. He leaned over to the low automated table between them and selected a drink from the array of buttons along its edge. A small panel in the surface of the table slid back and an ice chilled drink ascended. He lifted the glass and swirled the strong golden liquor before he swallowed it down in one gulp.

'Aah…the comforts of home,' he sighed. He looked at Dennis Craven and thought that he had to be very careful how he handled this man. He had had dealings with him before and knew that his power far exceeded the station he held in politics. He was backed by Adovacian muscle and a network of connections that spanned several realms and many Universes. The Captain knew that there was profit to be made if he played it out carefully. 'He had done battle at the Jexxar constellation in the Bidan realm. There is a visual log of the battle that had obviously not gone his way. It would seem that the intended target was a ship called the AXA GAFF.' He noticed Dr. Craven's subtle change of expression at the mention of the AXA GAFF. 'It had taken a serious beating, but its fighters managed to destroy the entire attacking fleet except this craft. It escaped through a natural vortex that deposited him here in the Moeban universe.'

'But going through a natural vortex would be impossible would it not?'

'That's the theory yes.'

'Remarkable.' Dr. Craven stood up and walked over to the glass wall and peered absent-mindedly at the moonscape. 'When did you say this happened?'

'It apparently happened eight hundred years ago.'

Dr. Craven took a large swig of his drink and was quiet for some time before he responded. 'I want that log on my desk within the hour. Now, I understand there is zero point technology on board.'

'Yes.' The captain said looking at his back. He leaned forward and selected another drink from the row of buttons on the edge of the table. There was more to the AXA GAFF than the good Dr. was letting on, he thought. And what of this zero point technology, he thought, energy of that nature was worth a fortune in the right hands.

'Outstanding.' Dr. Craven said. 'I'll have my team of experts there shortly to study this technology. They have top level security clearance and I expect your full co-operation.' There was no answer from the Captain. Dr. Craven turned and looked at him. The Captain avoided his eyes and took another sip of his drink. Dr. Craven realised that the deal had to be sweetened. 'I understand your salvage rights are at stake are they not?' He noted the captain's interest. 'Now let's say you stood to gain say 120% profit after expenses, I'll make you a deal. I'm willing to buy you out at thirty percent.'

'Up the offer to seventy percent, paid out in Interversal Gion and you will have my full co-operation.' The Captain knew it was an audacious thing to barter with him as if they were at a local market.

'Very well then, it will be twenty five percent or I'll confiscate the ship and all its contents, do I make myself clear Captain?'

The Captain stood up and squared his shoulders. 'Perfectly, Doctor.'

'You may go, Captain.'

The Captain left the VIP lounge and walked down the corridor. His face broke out in a wide grin, satisfied with how well things were going so far. He had lost his salvage rights because the alien was alive, but today fortune's glow was upon him. Now, to head off to Ehzhu's ship and Feen for a more relaxed celebration, he thought.

●

'I tell you Shay, that alien looked right through me and believe me he would have run me through with that point.' The Chief knocked back his drink and indicated to the barman for another. 'I could feel him probing my mind, scrutinising my every thought and intent.' He took his refilled glass and showed its contents a little more respect. 'I don't think it's such a good thing leaving Monica with a beast like that. Who knows what might happen.' The cold neon lighting under the glass counter cast pasty shadows up his face and stripped it of its usual ruddy glow. 'I don't even know if the four sentries we put in place will be enough protection.'

'I'm sure she'll be okay.' Shay said. 'Let's look on the bright side. She's a capable woman and while Coda is being fed and confined to the tank, I don't think he can do very much harm.' He took a sip of his drink and continued. 'Monica doesn't feel that there is any reason to be worried. She thinks there is some sort of connection with him that tells her there is nothing to be concerned about.'

'Yeah, until he is in some way threatened and total chaos breaks loose. I'm telling you man, this alien is dangerous beyond anything we have yet come across.' He finished his drink and ordered another. Shay had not seen his friend in such a state before. His usual expansive jovialness had disappeared and was replaced by this brooding depression.

'I think what we should do is use our time off and go somewhere. Why not hire a shuttle and fly over to the Ado crater. The Ado observatory has good spa facilities, is less crowded and the views of Onusa are outstanding. The trail drives in their all terrain vehicles are great. So, what do you say?'

The Chief looked up at Shay. 'You know, I think you're right. That's just what I think we should do, leave the Nullax Rover and its alien to sort them selves out. A bit of rest and relaxation is in order.' His face cracked into a smile and some of his glow came back as he lifted his glass. 'To the spa I say!' and knocked his drink back.

'To the spa then!' Shay said and swallowed the rest of his drink.

Captain John Masters' sense of anticipation grew as his shuttle neared Ehzhu's ship. It was a fantastic ship with enormous power that could cover light year distances in very short time. Everything about it reeked expensive. He was cleared to dock, so he landed the shuttle carefully in the landing bay. He was dressed in his dress uniform with his face shaved and doused with a little too much aftershave. His red hair was slicked back and his teeth were clean. He was ready. He picked up the small metal case that contained the book and left the shuttle.

He was met by one of Ehzhu's assistants. Her almost blue-black skin was stretched taught over her tall muscular body that was dressed in a sober grey tailored cat suit. Its stretch fabric softened the hard edges of her body, but did nothing to hide its power. Her short cropped black hair was offset by beautifully expressive black eyes and a pure white toothed friendly smile. The captain was struck by how feminine she was despite her butch appearance.

'Welcome aboard Captain, my name is Elmee and I've been assigned to assist you. Do you have any other luggage?'

'Yes, it's on board the shuttle.'

'I will send someone for it. This way Captain.' She smiled, turned and walked ahead of him to the docking bay door. As he looked at her thighs and buttocks, the Captain's already keyed up sense of sexual anticipation seemed to wind up another notch. Those were the most muscular buttocks he had ever seen on a woman, he thought, as they moved under the fabric of her cat suit. He almost bumped into her as they stopped at the bay door to wait for it to slide open. He had been without a woman for too long, he thought, this was doing him no good. With a grunt, he cleared his throat in an effort to focus his mind.

As the door slid open Elmee stepped through and the captain walked in beside her. He had to keep his eye on the prize and not Elmee's fantastic buttocks, he thought. Ehzhu was a formidable businessman and therefore he had to stay sharp. Elmee led him into a round room that had an air of intimacy with a small port window that looked out on Upi. The low level lighting glinted off wall panels that looked like beaten copper.

'Please take a seat captain. May I pour you a drink?' Elmee turned towards the wall and opened one of the panels to the drinks cabinet.

'Yes please, Dara, straight up if you have.' He stepped down the three steps and took a seat on the circular sunken couch, the colour of blood. He looked up and from his viewpoint her buttocks and thighs were even more fantastic. Mesmerised by this vision he almost did not notice Ehzhu's great body shuffle through the doorway. Ehzhu had a knowing smile and greeted him with his high pitched silky voice.

'Hello John, it's good to see you again.' Ehzhu made his way down the steps and moved towards him. The Captain stood up and took Ehzhu's proffered hand. It always amazed him at the strength of Ehzhu's grip, as if all his ample weight was concentrated in that big hand. They sat opposite each other and took the drinks offered by Elmee. She left the room and the door slid shut.

'So tell me, how was the Othaxal cloud?' Ehzhu opened; he noticed the metal case at the Captain's side.

'Oh well, you know, cold and dark. The alien ship was interesting at first, but then the alien woke up, so now everyone seems to have an interest.' He took a sip of his drink and rested his hand on the case.

Ehzhu noticed the movement, but pressed on. 'Does our alien have a name?'

'I understand his name is Coda.'

There was a dark shift in Ehzhu's eyes at the mention of Coda's name. 'There are legends of a warrior by that name...' Ehzhu had a thoughtful expression on his face.

'What is it about this Coda that I'm supposed to know?' The Captain leaned forward.

Ehzhu took his time before he answered. 'A terrifying warrior of that name has appeared and disappeared throughout the multiverse for the past three and a half thousand years. If this is the same being then I would urge great caution.'

'Hah!' the Captain scoffed. 'If this is the same warrior, he is a weak and mild invalid being fed like a baby in his water tank.'

Ehzhu sat forward, a focused look on his face. 'A water tank did you say?' The captain nodded. With that Ehzhu suddenly stood up, ascended the steps and paced the room from side to side.

'What is it Ehzhu?' the Captain asked puzzled.

'What does his ship look like?'

'Well... bit like a headless bird with a bulbous body. We could not make out the name of it as the solar skin was ripped off. We only identified three letters A-H-U, but she sure looks fast.'

'Ha ha ha!' Ehzhu laughed. 'John, you have stumbled upon one of the greatest warriors of all time and his ship is the legendary "Awa Na Tahu". It was reputed to be one of the fastest fighters ever built. What a find! I'd love to have a look at it some time. Now let's take a look at that book.'

As Ehzhu made his way back to the couch, some of the pieces of the puzzle started to fall in place for the Captain. He now began to understand Dennis Craven's interest in the technology and he wondered how much Ehzhu was not letting on. He was sure he would find out soon enough...

●

The banquet had turned out to be a delicious feast. Ehzhu seemed to have pulled out all the stops for this one, the Captain thought. There were several Sabalian dignitaries on board who were in discussion with Dr. Dennis Craven. There were women from all corners of the Multiverse, dressed to please. Everyone was served by a member of the crew who doubled as waiters, dressed in deep red waist length jackets with black trousers.

The Captains' mood was expansive as he had secured a fantastic deal with Ehzhu and to cap it off, a night with Feen was on the cards. It seemed as if she had dressed solely for his enjoyment. She wore a turquoise ankle length latex dress. It reached up over her abdomen and breasts to the choker collar around her neck. The back was very low cut across her buttocks exposing the top of their cleavage and leaving her entire back and shoulders bare. Her soft creamy brown skin augmented their fine muscle structure and narrow waist. She wore long fingerless latex gloves that ended above her elbows. Their black and turquoise vine pattern matched her flat soled boots. Her red hair was pulled back by a black Alice band with her wild curls cascading over her shoulders. Her flirtatious green eyes were tinged with turquoise as she flashed them at the Captain.

'Would you like another drink Captain?'

'Please, call me John,' he repeated. He was already intoxicated and the pills Feen had put in his drink had made him feel more sensual than ever. He pushed his empty glass towards her. 'Let's go somewhere more private shall we.'

Feen looked over to Uli who gave her an imperceptible nod. Her black velvet outfit with its copper and bronze edging were complemented by oversized amber jewellery. Feen looked at the Captain and gave him a mischievous smile. 'As you wish Captain, I know just the place.' They stood up from their table and slipped out a side door that led them down a seemingly endless corridor. Low level amber lighting reflected off the copper walls with doors leading off to the sides.

She stopped suddenly at one of the doors. 'This is it.'

The Captain could see no difference between it and any of the other doors, so how would she know, he thought. Who cares, he thought, just look at her, she's fantastic! As they stepped into the room, he took her hand, turned her around to face him, put his right hand on the small of her back and pulled her towards him. She did not resist and he gave her an open mouthed passionate kiss. She responded willingly, but finally stepped back and gently pushed him away. Breathing fast, her hard nipples and well formed breasts were clearly visible through the latex dress.

'Aah Captain,' she looked at his crotch. 'You are such a man, and you smell so good. Please make yourself comfortable while I freshen up.' She turned and left the room through a side door. The Captain began to take notice of the room and was surprised to find that there was no bed, only an oversized chair and nothing else. Above the chair was a circular, bronze and amber light fitting. Everything else, even the walls, ceiling and floor were black velvet with no reflected light anywhere.

He walked over to the chair and took his jacket off before he sat down. He put his jacket across his lap, crossed his legs and sat back. He had only waited a moment when Feen's soft voice emanated from out of the gloom. 'Captain, would you indulge me by removing your clothes?' He was taken aback by the request, but decided to play along. He stood up and started to remove his shirt. A black basket on a velvet rope descended from the ceiling and came into view. He put all his clothes into it, but kept his shorts on. His whole body was covered in a fine mat of curly red hair.

He felt a bit embarrassed by his corpulence and thought he must look a pathetic sight, but Feen's words gave him the confidence he needed. 'I like a man to have such an abundant and wealthy belly. You have such powerful arms and thighs. Please....John...remove your shorts, I really want to see your penis,' she continued breathlessly. By the tone of her voice he could hear that she was genuinely turned on by the thought of it, so, he turned his back towards her voice and removed his shorts. He put them in the basket which ascended out of sight.

He was not embarrassed by the size or girth of his male member as he had never had any complaints before. His anticipation showed in its semi-erectness. He turned and faced where her voice was coming from and heard a sharp intake of breath. He saw her appear out of the black gloom and walk towards him. She was wearing nothing except her boots, gloves and a black skull cap type mask that covered her forehead and framed her eyes. Her red hair was like a mane gushing out behind her. Her breasts were even more succulent with their large dark pink nipples. Her trimmed red bush above her pudenda seemed to have a life of its own as she walked.

By the time she reached him his phallus was fully erect pumped hard and swollen beyond anything he had experienced in his adult life. She indicated for him to sit and when he had done so she straddled his waist, took hold of his priapus and slowly lowered herself onto it. With her knees on the chair she began to undulate her hips, riding him faster and faster. Her lips were white with sexual tension and a hunger he had not expected. The heat inside her had become almost unbearable when suddenly she pulled him out of her. As she climaxed her abdomen rippled and she let go spurts of urine that suffused his genitals with an unexpected heat that caught him by complete surprise and triggered his spasmodic release across his belly.

He was still in a dazed state of unexpected sensual delight when he felt her lift his arms and cuff his wrists with leather bound bonds hooked to a chain that reached up into the ceiling. 'What...' Before he could say any more Feen kissed him hard on the mouth.

'Just a bit more John, please,' she said breathlessly and got off his lap. 'Now, stand up.'

He stood up meekly and felt the chain pull his arms up. Feen got on her haunches and attached his ankles to chains on the floor that pulled his legs apart.

'What's this?' he asked feeling more alarmed this time.

Feen stood up and produced a black velvet cloth with which she hurriedly wiped him down. She hugged him for a moment and then kissed him. 'I'm sorry John, you have been a real gentleman and to me you are such a man.' With that she turned around and disappeared into the gloom.

The Captain stood there for a few moments trying to work out what had just happened. One minute he was having the time of his life, the next, he was chained, naked in a pitch black room. 'Feen!' He called almost feebly into the dark. 'Where are you?' There was no answer, so he called out in a stronger voice. 'What kind of game is this now?' From behind him there was a feminine chuckle that put a chill up his spine.

'So Captain, did you truly think that you could have the pleasure of Feen without sharing it?'

He knew that voice! 'Uli...this has nothing to do with you.'

'Oh, on the contrary. As head wife I always have a share in the spoils. It's the privilege of my station.' She walked up behind him and touched his back with her velvet gloved hands. He recoiled, but couldn't go far. Uli chuckled again. 'Oh Captain, it's not so bad. You might just like what I have to offer.' She chuckled again. She gently fondled his buttocks and hummed her approval.

'Get away from me woman!' he said with a veiled threat.

'Or what?' she challenged. 'I assure you Captain, there is no need to feel so threatened.' The next moment she tied a velvet blindfold across his eyes. The captain shook his head trying to dislodge the blindfold, but to no avail. 'Try to relax Captain. Now...' she broke open a popper under his nose. 'Breathe deeply.' He breathed in reflexively and felt the rush of blood in his veins and the explosion of pleasure in his brain. Unlike the ones he was accustomed to, this one was much more powerful. He could feel all his nerves un-knot and his thoughts start to flow with their own rhythm.

He could feel velvet hands gently caress his body. Suddenly there were four hands, then six. After that he lost count. He didn't care anymore. Every crevice of his body was being explored at the same time. He felt himself getting hard again as velvet hands caressed his testicles. He felt a flexible dildo slip into his anus and slowly massage his prostate as another hand stroked his erection. Someone broke another popper under his nose and he breathed the gas in. It felt as if every nerve was being sensuously touched and stroked. As the blood rushed in his ears the sensual gush in his brain brought about the most intense orgasm he had ever experienced.

He felt the dildo release him and many velvet hands pushed him onto the seat. He felt his ankles being released. He felt his hands uncuffed and his arms laid at his sides. He felt drained and totally satisfied, yet completely paralysed by the effects of the drug and sexual excess. He lay there on the oversized chair for a long time after...

●

'Where am I?'
Monica heard the voice in her dream.
'Upi.' She answered.
'Where is Upi?' She frowned and wondered why anyone would ask that. Everybody knew where Upi was.
'Well...I don't.' She heard the voice answer.
'In the Onusa quadrant,' she answered a bit irritated.
'What is the Onusa quadrant?'
Monica awoke with a start, her hands numb and shaking slightly with the shock of waking up suddenly. She had fallen asleep at the makeshift lab table while researching alien DNA and making comparisons with Coda's. She knew she had been dreaming, but the voice had seemed so clear, like it was talking from inside her. She picked up her glass of water and was about to take a sip when the voice repeated in her head.
'What is the Onusa quadrant?'
The shock of it felt as if someone had shoved her hard up against the back of her chair. The glass fell from her hands and bounced off the carpet, spilling the contents on the aquatic design. She looked up at Coda and found him staring intently at her from inside the tank. She sat very still, looked at Coda and thought, no...no this can't be, I must still be dreaming.
'You...are not dreaming and yes, I am talking to you.'
Monica felt her body go cold for a moment. Never in all her experience had she ever heard of any being who could truly communicate telepathically as well as read minds with such clarity. It suddenly struck her that Coda was conscious and communicating, that the feeding was working. She felt encouraged and emboldened by that knowledge. She stood up, walked over to the tank and stood in front of him.
'How are you feeling?' she thought while scanning him with a

portable scanner.

'I feel like I have been asleep for a very long time. My head hurts...I'm hungry and it feels like I can't move my limbs.'

'Do you have pain anywhere else?'

'In my joints when I try to move...what place is this?'

Monica looked at him for a moment and realised there was more to worry about.

'Can you tell me your name?'

'Yes of course, it's...I...don't recall...'

'Can you remember anything at all?'

'I remember...the light.'

'What light?'

'The light of life...where everything exists at the same time.'

'Do you remember anything else?'

His mind was quiet for a short time before he answered. 'I remember when you touched me...it trapped me in this body. I know this body is mine, but it somehow does not fit correctly.'

'You are very emaciated. Maybe that's why. Do you recall where you come from?'

'Yes, I...no, I don't. Why can I not remember anything and how did I come to be in this place?'

Monica told him everything she knew so far and ended with. '...and we think your name is Coda.'

He turned away from Monica and seemed to retreat within himself. As he closed his eyes Monica felt his mind shut her out while his tentacles tentatively explored his body.

He remained quiet for a long time after...

●

'Where is it?' The Chief asked.

'Behind the ridge there...across the crater. Should be out any second now...there!' Shay pointed at the shuttle.

'Well now, it's about time. He's two hours late!'

'Man, he's coming in fast!'

'Yeah, I suppose he's trying to make up some time,' the Chief said. He stood up from the burgundy coloured silk couch and walked over to the glass wall of the departure lounge that overlooked the crater. The giant orb of Onusa was the perfect backdrop and completed the magnificent view. Ah well, the chief thought, two extra hours of this view was not to be scoffed at. Shay and he had had a lot of fun out there, ripping up the dirt with the all-terrain vehicles. He smiled when he thought of the bet he had lost to Shay who had won the race to the top of the crater.

As the gravity was low on Upi, the race had turned out to be a bit of a slow motion dance. The steam bath and massage after had left them relaxed and in good humour. The comedy show at dinner had capped off a good break from the stresses of space flight.

Shay stood up and walked over to his friend. 'David, that flier is either very good or very reckless. If he doesn't check his speed soon he won't make his landing.'

'Yeah, you're right.' The Chief responded thoughtfully.

They watched anxiously as the shuttle came in and pulled back at the last second. The pilot flared out its emergency brake and hit the reverse thrusters to full capacity. The shuttle landed hard, testing the hydraulics of its landing gear to their limit. The landing pad descended to the docking bay and the roof sealed shut above it.

Shay and the Chief breathed a sigh of relief, looked at each other, picked up their bags and headed for the docking bay doors. Three passengers entered through the doors ahead of them, looking pale and drawn from shock and anxiety. Both Shay and the Chief felt a sense of foreboding, however, they were due back so there was nothing they could do, but go on the flight. As they neared the shuttle they saw the pilot doing his exterior checks. He looked drawn and fatigued with dark rings under the eyes. He was dishevelled and his behaviour was anxious and hurried. He had obviously not had a rest for some time.

'Are you my passengers?' He looked up at them.

'Yes, that would be us.' the Chief answered.

'Come aboard then, make yourselves comfortable.' He turned and continued with his hurried inspection.

With silent comprehension that they had a fatigued pilot, Shay and the Chief went on board. This shuttle was nothing like the one they had come with. This one was a staff transporter. In comparison it was much smaller and its passenger compartment was tatty and utilitarian. It had not been cleaned in weeks and it smelled of stale sweat. The compartment was separate from the pilots' cockpit with only a hatch for communication. The Chief sat with his back towards the cockpit and Shay sat opposite him facing forward. They felt the craft tilt with the weight of the pilot as he came on board and seated himself at the controls. Shay noticed him pop two pills into his mouth and drink it down with whatever liquid was in his flask.

The pilot turned and called through the hatch. 'I'd suggest you fasten your seatbelts as this will be a bumpy ride. The auto pilot is not working properly, so I have to compensate most of the time. This old bucket had to stand in for the shuttle today. An electrical fault grounded it, so it's out of commission until further notice. So, sit back, relax and enjoy the flight!' With a yellow toothed smile, he turned back towards the controls, put his headset on and began the start up and take-off procedure.

Shay and the Chief fastened their seatbelts and sat back. Through the small porthole windows they saw the landing bay platform ascend to the now open roof. They felt the engines vibrate to life and heard their whine accelerate into a high pitched scream as the shuttle lifted off and pinned them to their seats. It did a hundred and eighty degree turn and headed off across the crater. It steadily picked up speed and height until it finally levelled off and the engine's pitch dropped down to a more comfortable hum. The pilot shut the hatch and left Shay and the Chief to their own thoughts. The Chief broke the silence. 'I wonder how Monica is getting along.'

'I think she'll be just fine…really. Coda is far too weak to get up to any mischief just yet, besides, I think there's some sort of bond happening there, some connection that started when she first touched the ice. I don't sense that he would be a danger towards her, towards us maybe, but not towards her I don't think.'

'Well, I hope you're right. We don't really know anything about him or how his mind works. Judging by his weaponry and the scarring on his body, this being has been in many conflicts and survived. It says something about him. He must obviously have exceptional skill at arms and survival. Who knows what other talents he might have?'

'Let's look at this logically,' Shay responded. 'Here's a being that has come from some remote corner of the multiverse, has probably lived a very long time, has obviously been in numerous physical battles, probably emotional too, with his final battle ending in a long freeze. A bi-aquatic surface being who has been frozen for eight hundred years, who has only just woken up and has to be fed like a baby, so…how much damage can he inflict?'

'You weren't in the water with him. If you were, you'd be

singing a different tune.'

'I suppose...did you see that?' Shay asked with an alarmed expression on his face.

'What?' The Chief asked and looked out the window.

'We just passed a rock formation that we should have been flying over. We're flying too low!'

'You're right!' The Chief unhooked his safety belt, stood up and prised the hatch open. 'Pilot!' he shouted. 'Why are we...?' He saw the pilot slumped over on his right side with white spittle on his lips. It looked like he was having some sort of seizure. The Chief put his arm through the small hatch and shook the pilot by the shoulder, but he was too far gone to be revived. He then tried to reach the control wheel but it was too far away. He looked up and saw the edge of the mountainside approaching fast. He knew they were done for. He turned and sat down fastening his seatbelt.

'The pilot's out with a seizure and we're heading for the side of a mountain. Brace for impact!'

A few seconds later the shuttle struck the side of the mountain at a tangent that spun the craft violently down towards the surface. The impact ripped Shay's seat off its bolts and catapulted him directly into the wall in front of him. As the shuttle spun, Shay was bounced around the passenger compartment like a child's toy. The shuttle hit the surface with a sickening crash and bounced over the side of a deep ravine. It tumbled down the side picking up more momentum until it finally hammered onto the rocks below.

As the dust settled, the silence was disturbed only by the hiss of released oxygen from ruptured pipes...

Coda's eyes opened suddenly, his mind fresh with visions of chaos. He looked at Monica whose back was turned towards him. Suddenly she spun around with shock and horror in her eyes. She walked up to the tank and thought, 'Are you saying that there has been an accident? Has something happened to Shay?' Like a gagging suffocating gas, her anxiety ballooned out and engulfed her.

'Your loved ones are in mortal danger,' Coda thought with tangible empathy.

It was at that moment that she realized how much Shay meant to her. She had kept him at arms length all this time and for what? She felt her panic start to strangle her mind when Coda interrupted her.

'The Captain is the one to find them…you must be strong now.'

His thoughts steadied her nerves just enough to keep the panic at bay. She turned towards one of the guards and got him to contact the Captain. 'How do you know this? Are you an all seeing, all knowing sort of being? How does this work?'

'I see only the energies I tune into. I know only that I can.'

'What do you see now?'

'Darkness and pain. They are in the bottom of a deep ravine. They must be found soon or they will not survive.'

●

The Chief groaned as he lifted into consciousness. He had a massive headache, his neck hurt and when he tried to move his left leg the pain was raw and excruciating. It must be broken, he thought. He vaguely remembered Shay's seat hitting his leg as he was tossed about the cabin. His eyes flew open as he thought of Shay. The darkness was like a thick blanket you could touch. Its texture seemed to change as his eyes became more adjusted to the barely perceptible light through the port window. It revealed a scene of destruction and chaos that was upside down and tilted to the right.

He was hanging from his seatbelt with his legs dangling down towards the ceiling. He fumbled with the safety belt clip, but could not get it loose as his weight was pulling it too tight. Remembering the small pocket knife he always carried, he dug it out of his right trouser pocket and slowly sawed through the belt. As he fell on the ceiling, he tried to break his fall with his right leg, but still fell heavily on his left. He reflexively grabbed his left leg and let out a wail of pain that broke a sweat on his forehead. Gritting his teeth he waited for the wave of agony to wash over him. When he got his breath back he gingerly explored his leg to see if there was any protruding bone and where it was broken. The fibula had a clean break about four inches above the ankle, so in a sense he was quite pleased that the damage was no worse.

'Shay!' he called. 'Are you okay?'

He was answered by a soft mumble from the far right corner. At least he's alive, he thought. 'I can't hear you! What's that you say?'

'Pain...everywhere...' The Chief could almost feel the effort it had taken Shay to say that. His breathing was laboured and in the dim light he could see that Shay was not moving.

'Can you move?' There was no answer, only the laboured breathing. 'Shay, are you with me?' There was no response. He must be unconscious the chief thought, not a good sign. He reached up to the seat above him and found the first aid box that was usually under the seat. He pulled it out, opened it up and found the glow sticks. He cracked one and the neon green glow revealed the surreal scene. In the far right corner he saw Shay's broken body still strapped in his seat. He was lying at an awkward angle and his legs were un-naturally bent.

From the pain in his head, the Chief knew that the oxygen was running low in the cabin. It was also getting cold, the kind of cold neither would survive for long. He took one of the emergency packs off the wall, strapped it to his back and put the oxygen helmet on. He then clipped it to the seal of his flight suit collar that automatically opened the oxygen valve. He found the small water tube at the side of his mouth and took a drink. The packs water rations had not been changed for some time and had taken on the metallic taste of its container, but he didn't care.

He found a support pack and wrapped it around his broken leg above the ankle. He then pulled the activation strip that caused a chemical reaction that stiffened the pack to form a splint that would support the leg. He took another emergency pack off the wall, took hold of the first aid box and crawled over to where Shay was. He was horrified to see the state of his long time friend. He was lying with his face on the ceiling, his right arm was pinned under him and his left was twisted behind him. Strapped into the seat, his waist was at an unnatural angle to his torso. His left leg looked okay, but the right leg had a piece of shin bone sticking out where it had broken. The foot was almost completely the wrong way around and there was a pool of blood under the break.

His back was most likely broken, the chief thought, probably head injuries as well. He wasn't too sure where to begin helping him, but decided the best place to start was probably to give him oxygen. Before he could do that, he realised, he'd better give him something for the pain, just in case he came to. He rummaged in the first aid box and found the vial he was looking for. He then opened a hypodermic needle pack, broke the top off the vial and filled the syringe. He wasn't too sure how much to inject, but thought it would have to be fairly substantial as any movement would most likely cause extreme pain. He found the spot at the base of the skull and injected the pain killer directly into the nerve meridian. It was a bit of a blunt instrument, but for the field it was the best as it cut off all sensations of pain.

He found the first aid oxygen mask, strapped it over Shay's mouth and nose and connected it to the emergency pack's oxygen supply. He then applied a tourniquet just below the right knee to stop the bleeding from the wound created by the broken shin bone. He placed a field dressing over the wound and then wrapped a support pack around the lower leg and activated it to form a splint. The ankle was also broken, so he did his best to straighten it out as gently as he could and wrapped another support pack around and activated it. Straightening out the left leg he noticed an intense swelling in the knee. He wrapped an elasticised bandage around it.

The Chief sat back for a moment, cracked another glow stick and surveyed his friend. What he needed to do was get him comfortable and warm, maybe do something for the shock. He decided to leave him strapped into his seat which was in a partially upright position. He groaned at the pain in his left leg as he got on his knees to lay the seat on its side. He thought the best thing would be to get Shay to lie on his back, that way he could make him more comfortable.

He cut a seatbelt off one of the seats above him, tied the cut ends together and looped it around the back of his seat. He slowly lifted Shay's shoulders until they touched the back rest. He slipped the buckled ends of the belt under Shay's armpits and clipped them together across his chest. The seat was now on its side with him strapped in it. The Chief looked around him and found one of their bags. He dragged it closer and gingerly lifted Shay's legs as he tilted the seat onto its back. He then shifted the bag under his legs and gently lowered them onto the bag. He looked at Shay's face and found his eyes open and staring at him.

'I can't feel my body.' Shay said breathlessly.

'That's good. I gave you a pain killer, so at least it's working. Can you move?'

Shay moved his head, fingers and arms and then said, 'I can't move my legs!'

'Yeah...I think you have a back injury.'

As the shock of it slowly registered on Shay's face, he asked, 'What else...?'

'From what I can see, your right shin and ankle are broken and your left knee has some bad swelling on it. Beyond that I'm not sure. Now, I want you to lie still and try to stay calm.' He looked about and found his own bag and opened it up. He took out whatever articles of clothing he thought would help to keep Shay warm and lay them over his body. From the emergency pack he took the electrified space blanket and tucked Shay into it. He turned on the power pack and checked to see that it was working. 'This will keep you warm. We have lost a lot of oxygen and the cold is intensifying. Now, I have to get your helmet on you. Can you lift your head?'

Shay lifted his head slightly and the Chief slipped the first aid mask off. He then took the emergency helmet, put it over Shay's head and connected it to his collar. He reconnected the oxygen pack and sat back. 'How are you feeling?'

'High, like I'm floating on air. That painkiller is fantastic. I can breathe a little better with the helmet on...What do you think our chances are?'

'I don't know. I'll go check on the pilot and see if we can get a signal out. We're in a dark place here and I know we fell down a long way. Maybe...' Shay was unconscious again. The chief turned to get on with what had to be done...they were running out of time...

●

Captain John Masters could not keep his mind from wandering. Visions of Feen kept interrupting his thoughts as he piloted his shuttle at the head of the search party. Her musk lingered on him and he could still feel her soft hairless skin as he gently fondled the flight controls. They were all consuming flashbacks that overwhelmed him and distracted him from the task at hand. All his senses seemed sharper and he felt lighter, as if he had taken some sort of drug that brightened colours and focused his vision. His half smile betrayed his sense of well being. An electronic sounding voice crackled over the coms system and snapped him back to reality.

'Captain, shall we spread out a bit further? We may have a better chance of picking up the debris trail.' Ehzhu's lieutenant asked. He was flying in one of four shuttles seconded from Ehzhu's ship.

'Yes,' he cleared his throat. 'Rescue fleet one, this is your Captain speaking. Spread out to your maximum monitor range.

Remember, we are looking for any organic heat source, flair, debris trail or flash; anything that would indicate survivors. They may be at the bottom of a ravine or gully, so don't overlook any possibilities. Time is the enemy...good hunting!'

He kept his eyes on the monitors and watched the motley group of nineteen shuttles as they flew over some of the roughest territory on Upi. There were mountains formed by deep impact craters. Gullies and ravines shaped by Upi's violent geological past frozen in time by the permafrost in its soil. The light from Onusa's star cast jagged shadows off odd shaped rocks that had burst from Upi's belly and left shattered monuments in fields of megalithic ruin. The idea of his chief engineer and navigator going down in that wasteland sent shivers down his spine. They were not only key members of his crew, but were also among the few he could trust.

He'd had some difficulty with what he considered to be that telepathic mumbo jumbo until Coda had spoken to him directly. It had seemed as if Coda's voice was talking to him from inside his head and not through his ears. What he could not ignore however, was the fact that there was no contact with the shuttle and that it had disappeared off the radar screen. Maybe the alien did know something. He had mustered every available shuttle at the research station and had launched the largest rescue mission this base had ever seen. At least he had an idea of where to look; any deep ravines or gullies along the crashed shuttles flight path. He hoped they would be in time and that they were alive.

Without some form of electronic or visual signal, they were doomed, he thought. Such inhospitable terrain could swallow you up without a hope of discovery. He looked at his scanners...nothing. Where are they, he thought. How long has it been exactly? How badly injured are they? Are they even alive? He had to believe they were, after all, Coda had been correct about the shuttle going down and if they were alive, the cold would get them in the end. Time was of the essence!

●

The Chief crawled through the hatch into the pilot's cockpit. He cracked another glow stick and looked around. He found the pilot's lifeless body hanging upside down; held in place by his harness. The impact had crushed part of the flight console into his chest. There was nothing he could do for him, so he looked at the console to see if there was any power; perhaps he could fire up the coms system and get an emergency signal off. He turned on the main and auxiliary power systems, but there was no response. He looked up at the floor where the power cells were stored and found it steeply crushed into the cockpit. It had taken a heavy blow and would have destroyed the power cells. The windows had all shattered out and the cold was becoming intense. He hurriedly scratched around in the debris lying on the ceiling and to his surprise and relief he found a box of flares. He backed out through the hatch into the passenger compartment and closed the hatch.

He checked on Shay and found him in a dead sleep. The painkiller was doing its work, but he was worried about the heat loss. He found several heat packs in the first aid box; put one under Shays neck and one on his chest. He pressed the button on the packs that activated the chemical reaction and they rapidly heated up. Resting his back on the wall, he sat next to Shay. Digging in the first aid box he found a box of pain tablets. He touched the button on his helmet that unsealed its visor with a hiss of released pressure and lifted it up. The first thing he noticed was the lack of oxygen in the cold air. He quickly put three pills in his mouth and swallowed them down with some water from the tube at his mouth. He touched the visor button and the visor came down and resealed again.

Looking around him he took stock of their situation. Their chances of rescue were very slim. Equally precarious were their chances of survival. He had to find a way of getting some kind of homing signal out. The strength of that signal would depend on how far down the ravine they had fallen. Cracking another glow stick, he looked to see if there was anything he could use.

Deciding to take another look in the cockpit he crawled over to the hatch and opened it. He crawled through and, ignoring the cold, started on the pilot. Rifling through his pockets he found the small pilot's bag that held the multipurpose tools of his trade. He took out the laser and cut away part of the mangled console. Cutting through the silicon fibres he found the tiny circuit board he was looking for. He unplugged it with cold numb fingers and as it came loose he banged his hand painfully on a structural bar. Ignoring the pain and the cold, he cut away a handful of cables to take with him. He found the pilot's head set, picked it up and crawled back through the hatch, closing it behind him.

He checked on Shay and found his eyes open. 'How are you feeling Shay?'

'Cold, thirsty...' Shay took a drink from the tube at his mouth. 'What's our situation like?'

'We're in bad shape, but with a bit of luck, we might get a signal out with this.' The Chief indicated with the small circuit board he held in his right hand. 'Do you feel any pain, are you comfortable?'

'Numb...nauseous...look...if I don't make it...'

'Ah Shay, you are going to be fine,' the Chief tried to sound reassuring. 'With the medical technology available now, you've got every opportunity of a full recovery.'

'Yeah, I know, but just in case, tell Monica I love her. I still haven't told her yet. I just haven't had the courage.'

'I'm sure she knows.'

'There's also something else...I have some property no one knows about. You will find the deed amongst my things. I want you to make sure it goes to Monica.'

'Now, don't talk like that. You're still going to live to be an old man.' The Chief could see his friend slipping back into unconsciousness, so in an effort to keep him conscious he continued. 'So, where is this property anyway? How come you've never told anyone about it?'

Shay's eyes seemed to come into focus. 'I discovered it by accident... while flying over the Wikopi desert.' Shay took another sip of water and continued. 'A sandstorm...forced me to land in what looked like a volcanic pipe. It turned out to be a small enclosed valley.' While Shay spoke, the Chief redressed the wound on Shay's broken right leg and checked his vital signs.

'After the storm cleared...I saw mature trees...growing under a large rock overhang. Beyond them...I was...astonished to find a small lake.' The Chief watched as Shay's energy seemed to drain out of him.

'That's amazing. I wonder what kind of trees they are. How any trees can survive our climate in the wild is astounding...' There was no response from Shay as he had slipped back into unconsciousness again.

The Chief sighed and continued with his makeshift signalling device. With the small laser he attached the power pack of a space blanket to the circuit board. He then attached the circuit board to the space blanket, turning it into a large antenna. He then attached one headphone cable to the antenna cable. With the other headphone cable he touched the outlet from the circuit board and heard the signal as a long high pitched whine. When he broke the contact the whine stopped. He spread the blanket out on the ceiling and began the long tedious task of tapping out the standard space academy emergency signal. He checked his time and decided to fire off a smoke flare every fifteen minuets, if no one heard the signal; they might see the smoke…

●

'So, this is the infamous Coda.' Ehzhu said as he walked around the tank. Looking through the glass plasma he felt safe; protected from this giant being that so much had been written about. He was incredulous that he, Ehzhu, would be the one who would claim the bounty that had remained active for almost two thousand years.

'Are you sure this is the famous warrior you spoke of?' Dr. Dennis Craven interrupted Ehzhu's thoughts.

'Oh yes, those tattoos are well documented, I'm sure…' Ehzhu froze in mid-sentence as Coda opened his eyes and looked directly at him. What had seemed at first to appear like a specimen in a bottle preserved for science, was suddenly very much alive. As he stood impaled by Coda's gaze, he felt the worm of fear twist in his ample belly.

'He's quite harmless you know.' Dr. Craven said. 'He does that every now and then. It seems to have a novel effect on people; besides, there are four sentries here who are armed to the teeth, so how much damage can he do?'

This man has no idea what he is dealing with, Ehzhu thought. He is so full of his power that he really believes nothing can touch him. He knew differently of course. Coda's reputation alone was enough to shatter the strongest resolve. He would take no chances with this being who had been particularly hard on the Sabalians. His family had suffered great losses in the past thanks to the deeds of this warrior. No, he would take no chances whatsoever.

'So, how soon can you take him away from here?' The Dr. was anxious indeed to get his hands on this ship, Ehzhu thought.

'I think it best to leave him here in your care until he is well enough to travel. Once in my hands your funds will be transferred in

Interversal Gion as agreed.'

'Oh, very well then.' Dr. Craven could barely contain his irritation.

Monica entered the room and stood protectively next to the tank. She folded her arms across her chest. 'Is there something I can do for you Doctor?'

'Yes there is actually,' he vented. 'I want a full report on my desk first thing tomorrow morning on the alien's condition and an estimated date of when he will be well enough to travel. Now, Ehzhu, shall we continue with our little tour?'

As they left the bridge, Monica looked at Coda and thought, 'What did they want?'

'The fat one seems to know of a bounty on my head and the Doctor wants my ship. There is an exchange agreed.' Coda thought.

'What do you suggest we do?'

'With your help, I need to get out of the water to speed up my recovery.'

Monica called one of the guards over to help with the hoist and ascended the stairs to the makeshift gangway at the opening of the tank. The guard pulled on the hoist chain and as Coda's head rose above the surface she detached and sealed the catheter from the feeding tube. She indicated to the guard to lift him out and as Coda's gills cleared he expunged a stream of water from his mouth and took a deep breath. As he exhaled he coughed out more liquid until his breathing settled down to normal.

Monica swung his body over the side and indicated to the guard to lower him. She then descended the gangway steps and pushed the examination trolley she had used to rest on under him. She pushed the trolley closer to the monitor table and moved the scanner from in front of the tank and positioned it above Coda. She called Professor Astor over the com-link.

'Monica?'

'Are you free to come onto the bridge?'

'Yes I am. What's going on?'

'I've had to take Coda out of the tank. I'll explain the rest of it once you are here.'

Distracted by thoughts of Feen, Captain John Masters almost missed the faint regular tap on the analogue scanner. He listened intently, but it faded away before he could get a fix on it. For a moment he thought he was just imagining it, when he heard it again. It was faint, but regular. With a shock it suddenly struck him that what he was listening to was the Academy distress signal! It was unmistakable. Over the coms system he called Ehzhu's lieutenant.

'Lieutenant, can you hear a tapping sound on your analogue scanner?'

'Yes Captain.'

'That's our Academy distress signal. Can you get a directional fix?'

'It's very weak and spread over a wide area. The general grid reference is way off their flight plan and seems to be wavering between several different points.'

'Yes, it's what I thought. The signal must be echoing off rock formations, but seems to be coming from a north easterly direction.'

'I concur Captain.'

'Right then, rescue fleet 1, change course to north east and tune into channel 4 on your analogue scanner for the Academy emergency signal. Keep visual alertness for any flares or smoke.'

The Captain felt a sense of relief as he changed direction. At least one of them was alive! He could only hope that they would get there before the cold took them…

'How is he?' Professor Astor asked as he wheeled onto the bridge.

Monica looked up from the task of sponging Coda's body down. 'He's weak, but he is breathing on his own. I tried to give him an oxygen tube, but he refused it. It's remarkable that after eight hundred years his lungs can still function normally.'

'Fascinating.'

'His skin is completely hairless you know,' Monica continued. 'I've never come across anything like it before. There was a thin layer of slick mucus that completely covered his body. According to the scanner it's mostly glycerine and fatty acid naturally produced by the body when in the water. It would most likely have contributed to his survival as glycerine effectively prevents ice crystals forming in the cells. That's why there is so little cell damage.'

'That almost defies logic,' the Professor said, 'as most of his DNA is human. There is however a strong mix of aquatic and dare I say…canine strands which would make our Coda one of the most unique beings in all this multiverse.' The Professor handed her a black rough silk shirt and drawstring trousers. 'I took the liberty of asking our seamstress to make these for him. She took the measurements from the clothes you found. I hope they fit him.'

As Monica turned Coda onto his side to wipe his back down, Coda's ankle length hair twisted into a long rope which moved like a thick tentacle and lay across his neck to give Monica access. For the first time she could see his tattoos up close and noticed that the skin under the tattoos had been severely burnt from his shoulders all the way down to his ankles. The tattoos looked like they had been done essentially to cover the terrible scarring that had resulted, however, the designs were so strikingly integrated with the scar contours, one could almost think that the scarring had been deliberately created as part of the design itself.

'Do you remember how you got these scars?' Monica thought.

'I remember nothing.' Coda answered telepathically. 'Even the brief you gave me of my recent past has no meaning for me.'

'Have you had any dreams, anything that seems familiar?' She started to dress him.

'Only the deep black of the ocean.'

Monica felt a chill go up her spine at the thought of such deep water. 'How do you know it is deep water?'

'Because the jailer is with me.'

'Who…?'

'Aah, the food is here!' the Professor said as the kitchen attendant wheeled a trolley laden with a pot of steaming fish broth into the room. 'I ordered dinner on the way here; I thought our guest might be hungry.'

Monica had finished dressing Coda, so she lifted his backrest to put him in a semi seated position. 'I hope he eats fish soup.'

'Well, judging by the fact that we found nothing else edible on the ship, I assumed this would be it.' He ladled the soup into the bowls.

'Does he not speak Monica?'

'He's a telepath, Erick'

'Yes, but is he collectively telepathic? Can he communicate with both of us at the same time? Does he know our language?'

Before Monica could respond, they both heard Coda's answer in their heads. 'Yes…I can…and…it is the reason why I can speak any language.'

In a stunned silence the Professor passed a bowl of soup to Monica. He regained his composure. 'Well…I hope you like the soup.'

Coda sipped at the spoonful Monica offered him. 'The taste is…pleasant,' he thought and took the bowl and spoon to feed himself. As they sat silently enjoying their meal the Professor was uncertain whether to think anything at all as his thoughts were not private in the presence of Coda. After a few moments deliberation he decided to keep his mind on the task at hand. He looked at the slow, deliberate and painful way that Coda was feeding himself. With every helping his hand shook a little with the effort of bending his arm at the elbow and lifting the spoon to his mouth. To get his body functioning normally was the first priority, he thought, everything else would flow from that. After eight hundred years of lying dormant, it was amazing he could even get soup into his body.

'Do you feel any pain?' he asked speaking normally so that Monica could participate.

'Yes.' Coda had finished his broth and Monica took the bowl from him.

'Where?' Monica asked.

Coda leaned back, resting his head on the pillow. 'My joints are the worst.'

Monica took the small hypodermic pump loaded with painkiller, held it to the side of his neck and pressed the release button that painlessly injected a controlled amount of the powerful drug. 'There…that should give you some relief. Now…this dream you had…could you tell us more of the jailer in your dream?'

'In the black deep…I see only the jailer. There are no others. I feel…fear. I…become the jailer…I feel no more fear.' Coda's energy seemed to be draining out of him with the effort to digest his food.

Monica readjusted the backrest to a prone position. Coda was already asleep by the time she pulled the sheet up over his chest…

It was time to set off the next flare, so the Chief crawled through the hatch into the pilot's cockpit. Everything had a thin layer of red dust on it from his earlier smoke flares. He set off the next one and as the red smoke started to billow from it he tossed it out of the broken front visor. As the smoke started to rise he went back through the hatch and closed it. Shay was still unconscious, so, with cold shaking hands, he continued to send the signal out with his makeshift signalling device.

It had been almost ten hours since the accident and the cold was starting to penetrate into his bones. He found another heat pack, activated it and tucked it into the front of his flight suit and continued sending the signal. He thought of Shay and the many missions they had been on together and the horrific injuries he now had. How would Monica take it? Such a tragedy, he thought, they were only just starting to find each other.

His thoughts were interrupted by the high pitched whine of a craft's engine as it descended into the gully towards them. Through the small port window he could see the lights of the rescue craft, tinged red from the smoke of the flare. He breathed a sigh of relief. At last they were found!

Shortly after, he heard the Captain's voice over his helmets coms system. 'Hello! Is anyone alive down there?'

'It's David here…I'm glad you found us Captain!'

'Ah, Chief, it's good to hear you're okay. What's your status?'

'We're in bad shape Captain. The pilot is dead, I have a broken leg, but Shay is the worst off. He has a broken right leg and ankle, his left knee is badly swollen and I think his back is broken.'

There was a brief silence before the Captain responded. 'I'm sorry to hear that…I have the medical rescue team here with me, so we'll have you out of there in a few minutes.'

The Chief could hear the Captain's craft land and several men come up to the shuttle's fuselage.

'Stand back from the door; we're going to cut it open!'

The laser cutter was a powerful precision instrument that could cut at different depths. Its hot beam had been set to cut two or three inches beyond the fuselage door and no further. The Chief watched as it melted the metal until a rough square shaped chunk was ripped out of the side. The first in, amid the back lit smoke and fumes from burnt metal, was the Captain himself…

●

'Thank you.' Monica took the glass of water offered by the Captain. The waiting room seemed cold and unfriendly with its pale blue walls and hard green chairs. Both were silent; lost in their own thoughts. Monica was surprised at how deeply affected she was. The thought of losing Shay had forced her to acknowledge how she felt about him, but upon learning the extent of his injuries, her emotions had heaved and twisted inside her like a tempest in a fragile glass bubble that threatened to burst and overwhelm her. At least he's alive, she thought, and as long as he's alive there is hope.

The Chief was wheeled in on a wheelchair with a brace on his broken left leg. 'Has there been any word yet?'

'Nothing yet,' the Captain answered. 'How's the leg?'

'Almost as good as new Captain.' He wheeled himself closer to Monica and took her hand. 'How are you holding up my dear?'

'Well enough.' Her face was pale and drawn, but with a determined set of the jaw. I am not going to give in, she thought.

'Good woman.' There was a profound gentleness in his voice. 'He's a strong lad, Shay is. He'll pull through this, you know that hey?'

'Yes.' She nodded, holding it together and wishing he would stop. She took her hand away.

'So tell me,' the Captain interrupted. 'What went on out there?'

The Chief turned and faced the Captain. 'Well…'

As the Chief and the Captain fell into conversation, Monica tuned out and lost herself in her inner space where she felt safe and protected. What seemed like an eternity later, the surgeon came into the room. He pulled up a chair and sat down.

'What news Doctor?' The Captain asked.

'His leg and ankle are in bad shape, but will heal well enough with time. The left knee had torn ligaments which we have done surgery on and again will heal with time. The injuries to his back are much more serious and will need specialised treatment not available here. I would recommend nanobot surgery on Moeba. The technique has proven to have a high success rate for spinal injuries, but you would have to get him there as soon as possible.'

'We could have the Nullax Rover ready for teleportation in 48 hours,' the Captain responded.

'Very well then,' the surgeon stood up. 'I'll make the arrangements for surgery on Moeba.' He left the room.

●

'What can you tell me about these?' The Professor asked as he opened up the leather roll that contained the eight throwing and two eighteen inch fighting knives. 'Do they bring back any memories?'

Coda was seated in his oversized, wing backed red leather chair that seemed to perfectly fit his proportions. It was remarkable how quickly he was recovering, almost as if every meal and exercise session had an immediate effect. Only twenty four hours had passed and his joints were already more supple. Although still stiff, there was much less pain. His organs had started to function normally and Monica had trimmed his nails which had grown long and bent in the ice cocoon. He leaned forward and touched the knives laid out on the table in front of him. He picked up the fighting knife and with effortless grace and speed, bourn from years of familiarity, he went through the complex motions of changing the position of the blade to affect the cut, thrust and parry of close quarters combat.

'I know how to use them…' Coda answered telepathically. 'But there are no memories. Only…a heavy, dark energy.'

The professor went through all of the weaponry from the bag at his feet, but nothing seemed to jar Coda's memory, until he lifted the flute out of the bag. With a quick intake of breath, Coda sat forward with a start. He took up the flute and played a few of the most haunting notes the Professor had ever heard. Coda was quiet and composed before he started playing the melody again. It was a meditative melody with long drawn out notes that flowed seamlessly. It took hold of the Professor's emotions and led them on a journey of beautiful peaks and valleys. It showed him a place of ecstatic joy and a love he had only experienced once as a teenager. It felt as if someone had dropped him back in his seat as the melody abruptly ended.

Coda had a far away look on his face. He lowered the flute onto his lap and sat back with a sigh. 'I…remember…my father…' he said with an emotionally laden deep voice. They were the first words he had spoken aloud…

3500 years earlier
XN5, Northern Deep mine, Sabalian Realm

A discordant note sounded as the flute arced through the air and viciously struck the bald man on the back of his head. With a sickening pop, Thaif could feel the skull give way beneath the force of the blow. As the bald one crumpled dead to the floor his tall snake eyed partner released Ola and with the knife in his right hand rushed at Thaif. Side-stepping the knife thrust, Thaif punched Snake Eyes a hard sharp blow to the face and broke his nose. Snake Eyes grunted with pain and came at Thaif again with a blur of slash and thrust. Thaif was shocked at how painful it was as the blade sunk into his left side. With reflexive force he brought the flute down onto Snake Eyes wrist and felt the satisfying crush of bones. Snake Eyes howled with pain as his nerveless hand left the knife buried in Thaif's side. Thaif lifted the flute to hit him again, but Snake Eyes turned, ran up the alley and disappeared into the dark night.

Ola, who had stood frozen at the wall, rushed to his side. 'Thaif!' she exclaimed while trying to cover herself with her torn clothing. 'You are hurt.'

'Ola,' Thaif reached for her. 'Did they hurt you?'

'No,' she lied. 'Let me help you. Sit here.'

He sat on the metal crate. 'Did they hurt the baby?'

'No, you got here before they could do any damage. Now, let me look at that wound.'

The knife had a straight double edged twelve inch blade and was still stuck in his side. It was a flesh wound that had exited through the other side, but had missed his vital organs. 'Pull it out as fast as you can,' Thaif said and took a deep breath.

Ola took hold of the hilt. 'Ready?' He nodded and she pulled hard. Thaif gave an involuntary roar as the blade came out with a sucking sound. As the wound started to bleed, Ola tore a piece of cloth off the hem of her robe.

'Press this hard against it.' She tore another strip off her hem and tied it tightly around his waist.

'I'm sorry I was late, Bala kept me on the mine and I couldn't get away.'

'I thought it had something to do with him. Now, let's get you to Dr. Elwyn.'

Thaif picked up the knife and put it in an inside pocket of his coat. She helped him up and he put his left arm across her shoulders. Ola supported him as he limped down the alley towards Dr. Elwyn Rosmadden's home.

Thaif and Ola were two of a population of humanoid clones produced in the genetics labs of XN5 to serve the Sabalians as slaves. They were designer clones, resistant to the effects of radiation and bred with a mixture of DNA for specific purposes. The technique of combining human DNA with nonhuman DNA had taken almost a thousand years to perfect. There were limitations that had not been overcome yet, namely a forty five year life expectancy. It was first thought that all clones were sterile, but occasionally there would be occurrences of fertility. All clones were made and owned by the realm; therefore, any naturally born children were claimed by the realm. They would be institutionalised, programmed for suitable tasks and later sold.

There were many labs on several planets and moons, but XN5 was one of the biggest with rich deposits of mesorite, a radio active metal used mainly for the production of weapons to expand the Sabalian realm. Its seas were permanently frozen over with hundreds of feet of ice. All of the mining colonies were built on large or small volcanic islands that rose up from the seabed through the ice fields.

Thaif was designed as an aqua-miner, bred for the dangerous task of deep water mining below the ice fields. This was done by guiding massive vacuum pipes that sucked up the mesorite rich silt from the sea bed which was later processed in the refinery. He was a bi-aquatic surface humanoid who had both gills and lungs. His hairless body was designed to withstand the extreme cold and pressure of the water under the ice. His aquatic origins were lost in the mists of time.

Ola was a domestic servant, designed with the submissive and loyal canine DNA. She had a short soft layer of fine golden fur on most of her body with only her hands, face, neck and feet hairless. Her skin was a creamy brown with a soft inner glow. She had a mane of long dark brown hair which grew from a fine ridge of brown fur that ran from the cleft of her buttocks, along her spine and up the back of her neck. She usually tied her hair back to be more practical. Her face was human with finely balanced features and soft brown eyes. She had worked for Dr. Elwyn Rosmadden and his wife Honora for the past five years and had learnt to trust the Doctor and to avoid his wife.

Honora always treated Ola with disdain. She made Ola use a separate tin cup and plate for her meals with a designated set of old cutlery. Ola had to address her as Madame and the Doctor as Master. She lived in the small back room and was to be permanently available. She was allowed one day and night off every two weeks at the discretion of the Madame. Ola was not to have any visitors, a rule broken twice a week when Thaif visited for a few nightly hours of companionship.

Tonight was her night off and they had intended to enjoy a meal together in a local eatery that had a warm atmosphere and good music. They were to meet there as it was never certain what time Thaif would be free. Ola usually took a rickshaw to get there, drawn by those hardy runners, bred for speed and stamina; their bodies completely covered with lush fur to withstand the rigours of extreme weather. It was a particularly mild evening, so she had decided to take a walk instead.

She had gone a little more than half way when she was attacked. She had fought her attackers off with a ferocity born from fear and desperation until the bald one landed a powerful blow on the side of her head. She was stunned and disoriented long enough for them to restrain her. That was when Snake Eyes had put the knife to her neck. He had breathed his repulsive breath on her and started to lick her face with his wet corrosive tongue when Thaif arrived. She had never thought Thaif capable of such violence. He was a mild mannered, spiritual man who would never hurt even the smallest creature. Now he had left one man dead and another maimed for life.

They arrived at the back service gate to Dr. Elwyn's house. Ola unlocked the gate and they entered the courtyard. There were two entrances to the house. One was to the kitchen and the other was to the small surgery the Doctor used to treat the workers. Ola unlocked the door of her room at the back corner of the courtyard and stepped in. It was tight and claustrophobic with its grey walls, a single fold down bunk, a metal table and a stool. Thaif had set up a pipe across a corner of the room for her to hang her meagre collection of clothing. A small damp bathroom closet with a cold water shower, toilet and basin was situated at the foot end of the bunk.

'Sit here,' she said, indicating the metal stool. 'I'll go and see if the Master is in his study.'

Ola left the room and crossed the courtyard to the kitchen door. She opened it and made her way through to the study. Dr. Elwyn Rosmadden was seated in his armchair facing the small gas fire place. He was snoring softly with a book on his chest. She padded quietly across the room and sat at his feet. Touching his knee she shook it slightly hoping that would wake him, but the snoring continued. She tried again, a little more forceful this time and the snoring stopped. He opened his soft brown eyes and looked at her with a mixture of sleep and surprise.

'Ola, you're supposed to be off tonight.'

'Yes Master, but something has happened and I ask for the Master's help.'

Dr. Elwyn sat forward and lifted the book off his chest. 'What has happened Ola?'

'Please Master, come quick.' She stood up and went to his side to help him out of the chair. Dr. Elwyn was a big Sabalian man with patchy dark and light-blue skin. He was in his fifties and was from an influential family, but he had been exiled to XN5 for standing up for the rights of clones, a fact Honora would never forgive him for. XN5 had eroded him and he was dying a slow death from radiation poisoning. No amount of anti radiation pills or other more extreme treatments had been of any benefit to him. His body had almost no resistance to the radiation of XN5.

On his feet he said, 'Lead the way then,' and shuffled hurriedly behind her as Ola led the way through the surgery to collect his bag.

'Who is this man?' Dr. Elwyn asked on entering her room.

'His name is Thaif...he...is my man.'

'Ola, I never knew. You've never mentioned him before.'

'No,' she said simply. 'Can you help him? He saved my life tonight.'

'I say. So, what's the problem then?'

Thaif pulled back his coat to reveal the bloody dressing.

'Can you take your coat off and sit on the table please, Thaif.'

Thaif was unaccustomed to being asked to do anything in such a polite manner and was unsure of how to respond. He looked at Ola and she nodded. Thaif stood up and in the small room he seemed like a giant with his nine foot five inch height. If it were not for the open pitch of the roof he would have remained stooped. He removed his coat and sat on the table.

Dr. Elwyn opened his bag and went to work. 'So, Thaif, you work on the mines?' Thaif nodded. 'Who is your supervisor?'

'Bala.' Thaif grunted at the burn of the antiseptic that Dr. Elwyn applied.

'You poor man. Bala is particularly…unsavoury. How did you get this?'

'I was attacked,' Ola interrupted. 'Thaif fought them off.'

Dr. Elwyn glanced at her. 'You have chosen well then. Too many are defenceless against these abominations of nature. Protection is only for the wealthy; everyone else has to fend for themselves.'

'Yes master.'

●

Thaif watched the pale sun rise over the ice flats; its perishing light was a distant star, too far to offer any heat. It was his morning ritual, his quiet hour of meditation to contemplate the beauty of this stark and unforgiving icescape. He took up his flute and started to interpret his emotional responses into long harmonious notes that seemed to pick out the subtle shades of yellow, grey and light blue as the crisp morning light caressed the ice.

From his high vantage point atop a mountainous grey slag heap, he could just make out the distant mountains of ice. He had always felt drawn to them as if somehow he was meant to go there; perhaps there would come a time... A tiny dark speck in the sky above the mountains caught his eye and distracted his thoughts. He stopped playing the tune and watched as the speck got bigger and took the shape of an off world freight shuttle. As it got closer he noticed it was not the usual lumbering Sabalian freight shuttle, but the smaller one he had seen several times before. It came in low and fast and landed amongst the slag heaps behind him.

He determined to take a closer look this time and ran across the flat top of the slag heap, taking care to stay on the solid ridges to avoid falling into a sink hole. As he got close to the edge he went on his hands and knees and crawled forward, careful not to silhouette himself against the skyline. He looked over the edge and saw the space craft standing in a clearing between two other slag heaps. Its rear freight doors were open with miners carrying what looked like mesorite crates up the ramp.

Suddenly, he saw Bala get out of the enclosed transporter from which the crates were being carried and walk up the ramp into the space craft. Until that point, Thaif had only a mild interest in the proceedings, but upon seeing him he knew something was amiss. Anything to do with Bala had to be treated with suspicion. He had always reeked of corruption, but there had never been any evidence. Even if he could prove it, he was a clone and nobody would take a clone seriously. Most authority here was completely corrupt anyway. Even the mine owners back on the home planet Sabal were only interested in their profits. No one truly knew what was going on here nor did they care if their supervisors skimmed a little off the top, as long as their production targets were met. Bala was in control of three of the seventy eight mesorite mines on XN5 and a fourth mine that was not on the books. He was amassing a fortune in Interversal Gion as well as precious stones and metals and there was almost nothing to stop him.

Bala was a product of XN5, conceived with the violent rape by his Sabalian father of his cloned domestic servant. He was born into a world of hate, bigotry and violence. As a half breed bastard child he was unloved by either his father or his mother who was abused and maltreated for the remainder of her short life. When she died, his beatings became more frequent. His father actively encouraged Bala's own tendencies towards violence and bullying. He was put to work on the mines as a young boy, but when, at the age of fifteen, he had killed his first man in a brawl, deep in the ice tunnels, he was finally posted as assistant supervisor under his father.

He learnt to hate his father even more. He had always craved his father's approval, but was routinely met with cruelty and suppression. There came a day when his father had beaten him senseless that Bala resolved to kill him. He plotted and schemed for months, but the opportunity came quite by chance. They were inspecting one of the old tunnels when part of it collapsed and trapped them.

His father was lying on his belly with his legs trapped under a heavy pile of ice and silt. Both were unconscious with Bala having taken a blow to the head and lying under loose debris. He came to and worked his way free from beneath the chunks of loose ice and found his father conscious and moaning feebly.

'Bala, help me.' His father pleaded. 'Help me my son!'

Bala snorted derisively. 'Oh, so now I'm suddenly your son, am I?' His laugh had a penetrating chill to it. 'Its funny you know, all my life I've wanted you to call me your son. Now that I don't care, you acknowledge me and that only because you know you will die if I don't help you.'

'Please son, be a good boy and get me out from under here.' His father came up on his elbows and tried to crawl forward, but screamed with the pain. His chest heaving for breath, he reached out to Bala. 'Please my son, I'll never hurt you again…I'll share all my wealth with you…please, just get me out of here…I promise I'll be a good father.'

Bala laughed triumphantly. 'At last, it is me you need. Grovel old man,' he said with venom. Then, with all the hatred and pain his father had inflicted upon him, he slapped him hard against the side of his head. 'Beg all you like you old bastard, its music to my ears.'

As his father begged and pleaded, Bala laughed and danced on his father's back, eliciting more screams of agony. He finally tired of the game he was playing and viciously kicked his father in the ribs. 'You know old man, you don't have to share you wealth with me as I'm going to take it from you today.' Bala was rummaging through the debris lifting chunks of ice and discarding them until he found the one he wanted. It was silt laden ice which made it heavy. He took it with both hands and kneeled in front of his father. 'I have waited a long time for this day.' Breathless from emotional excess he continued, 'You remember that day in the pump house? Do you know what it feels like to be beaten with a wrench? Well, it feels something like this!' he lifted the ice chunk high above his head and brought it down with brutal force, smashing the left shoulder blade.

His father screamed with agony and whimpered. 'Please…stop.' He started to babble with panic as the realisation of what was to come struck him. Bala laughed, put his face down to his father's ear. 'Do you remember when you cut my face in front of everyone just for a laugh? Well, it felt like this!' and he lifted the ice again and pulverized the right shoulder blade. His father continued to scream and babble.

'Look at you now, you pathetic old bastard!' Bala shouted and lifted the ice again. 'I hate you!' he screamed and swung the ice down on the back of his fathers head. The babbling abruptly stopped, but he was not satisfied. He repeatedly lifted the ice and struck the back of the skull, screaming, 'I hate you, I hate you, I hate you, I hate you…'

The skull caved in like a ripe Sabalian melon. Blood, brain and chips of bone splattered across Bala's face and chest until the ice slipped from his blood soaked hands. Like a lanced boil, he let out a long moan, expelling all the pent up stench of pain and hate he felt towards his father. As he gained control of his breath, he started to laugh, first as a derisive chuckle that escalated into an almost hysterical cachinnation that reverberated his relief and satisfaction off the tunnel walls…

●

'Give it to me,' Honora snapped and snatched the jacket from Ola's hands. 'You ectype's are all the same. Could they not have made you with a little more intelligence?' she tutted and inspected the small tear in the fine cream coloured fabric with its intricate white silk embroidery. 'You've ruined it. You obviously have no idea how much this cost, do you? You realise of course that the whole outfit has to be thrown out now.' Honora backhandedly threw the jacket back into Ola's hands. She grabbed the ankle length skirt of the same fabric and threw it also at Ola. Out of fear Ola could not move as it struck her in the face and landed at her feet.

Ola found her voice. 'I'm sorry Madame, but I received it like that from the cleaners.'

'Oh, that's rich. Now you expect me to believe that the cleaners, who have never messed up anything of mine before, now suddenly, ripped my clothes? I don't think so. Now pick it up, throw it out and…I think you should polish the floors today. I want to see my face in them by the end of the day and while you're at it you can dust everything off as well. I don't want to see even one speck of dust. Do you understand me?'

'Yes Madame.'

Honora turned her back on Ola and sat down at the dressing table. She picked up the bottle of moisturising cream and started to apply it to her blue skinned face. She looked at Ola in the mirror, still standing behind her with an astonished look on her face. 'Well? Don't just stand there, get on with it.'

Ola picked up the outfit and left the room. She walked through the kitchen and crossed the courtyard somewhat dazed and numb. Her morning sickness had been particularly bad this morning and her worsening headache was accompanied by a persistent ringing in the ears. She felt weak and exhausted and wondered how she was going to get through the day. As she reached the refuse bins at the back gate, she decided that the outfit was far too good to throw away. She darted a quick look over her shoulder to make sure no one was watching and opened the door to her room which was right next to the bins. Once inside, she folded the outfit neatly and tucked it under her mattress. She left the room, pulled the door closed behind her and went back into the kitchen. From the metal utility closet, she took the polish and rags and went to work on the living room floor.

On her hands and knees she applied the polish, careful not to miss any spots. When the whole floor was covered she started to rub it from one end of the room until the stone tiles began to shine. The dizzy spells and nausea she felt increased and her vision began to narrow. It felt as if her body became lighter as she floated to the floor in a dead faint.

Ola regained consciousness from the sting of a hard slap on her cheek. 'Wake up you lazy bitch.' Honora's venom poisoned the air as she continued. 'You ectype's are all useless. You can't even polish a floor without going to sleep. You are all hopelessly incompetent. How the institute expects us to put up with such dregs is beyond me. How they could possibly think that this type of domestic clone design would be adequate help is beyond me.'

'Hold on now, Honora,' Dr. Elwyn walked through the doorway. 'Let me take a look and see what's wrong with her.'

'Elwyn, I wish you would stop referring to these ectypes as if they were people. They're clones…nothing more.'

'We all know your feelings on the matter Honora.' He walked up to Ola and helped her onto her feet. 'Come with me to the surgery and let's take a look at you hey.'

Honora put her hands on her waist. 'That bitch better finish the floors today.'

'Ola does not look well and she won't be working at least for the rest of the day, so call the institute and have them send out a temp until she is well enough, okay?'

'Aaargh!' Honora exclaimed with indignant exasperation. 'You are such an "ectype lover". It's your fault we are stuck here in this ghastly place. I'll never forgive you for it, never.' And she stormed out the room.

'Never mind her.' He supported Ola to his surgery.

After examining her bruises, torn fingernails and taking into account that she had taken a blow to the head the night before, Dr.

Elwyn suspected a concussion. However on further examination he discovered her pregnancy. His immediate reaction was surprise and then elation as this was the rarest occurrence amongst clones. As he sat down behind his desk, the gravity of the situation dawned on him and he realised just how tenuous Ola's chances were of holding on to that small life within her. When Ola had got dressed she went and stood in front of the desk.

'Please sit down Ola.' He indicated the chair. She sat down and Dr. Elwyn continued with a humorous twinkle in his eye. 'Congratulations my dear, I assume Thaif is the father?'

Ola's shock was complete. She had hoped to keep it a secret somehow. She looked at Dr. Elwyn with fear and anxiety etched into her face.

'Now now, don't fret. I'm sure we can work something out. For the time being we must be cautious. I want you to take a few days rest...'

'But the Madame...'

'Don't mind her. I'll send her off to Sabal for an extended holiday with the family. It's the institute and their agents we must be wary of. Now...go and rest and call me when Thaif comes again, we have things to discuss.' He gave her a bottle of pills for the headache and she left the surgery.

Thaif crumpled to the ice as Bala hit him on the knife wound with the metal baton he always carried. 'Now what am I going to do with you fish boy!' Bala shouted. His face was dark with anger. 'You're no good to me if you can't swim you ectype scum.' He lifted Thaif's chin with his baton, bent down and spoke into his face. 'Now you listen fish boy, you are the property of this mine and your only purpose here is to work. So, until you are well enough to swim you will work the silt face in tunnel thirty six, is that clear?' Bala straightened up. 'What is your name fish boy?'

'Thaif.'

Bala hit Thaif hard across the back with his batten. 'Thaif what?'

'Thaif...master.'

'Get up you lazy ectype bastard and get your fishy ass over to shaft number two. Move it fish boy! I'll be watching you.'

As Bala moved on to his next victim, Thaif got to his feet, feeling grateful to have got off so lightly. Many had been severely beaten by Bala and many more maimed by his baton. Others were taken away after their beatings and never seen again, so he felt almost lucky as he made his way to shaft number two. He reported to the mine foreman who sent him off to the shift supervisor who kitted him out with his miner's helmet with its inbuilt lamps and power pack. Thaif joined the rest of the mine crew as they made their way into the shaft elevator. The cage tender waited until everyone was on board and then closed the gate. He pulled the lever and the cage descended with him and the crew into the bowels of the ice.

A silence came over the crew as they descended past each tunnel, deep in their own thoughts. Mining the mesorite rich flows in the ice was a hazardous undertaking done by clones that had been specifically designed for underground mining and those hapless beings that had become expendable. Thaif's thoughts turned to Ola and the warm night they had spent together. She was his ocean of peace and harmony. Her embrace was the salve of his existence. Her intelligence engaged him and ignited his imagination. Her kindness and compassion juxtaposed the constant cruelty of XN5. How he loved to look upon her beautiful face and savour her subtle perfume. The sound of her laughter and the sparkle of her amber eyes were fresh in his mind when the cage came to a stop.

The tender opened the gate and they stepped out of the cage and into the damp and cold tunnel thirty six. Were it not for the dim lights hanging from the roof it would have been dark. With their helmet lights on the crew got on board the open crew train. The tender walked to the front and got in to the driver's seat, released the brake and stepped on the accelerator. The electric motors hummed and the train trundled forward, taking its passengers deeper into the mine. It soon joined a larger tunnel with four rows of tracks. Shuttle cars loaded with ore bearing silt and broken rock were hauled in the opposite direction by motorised cable to the central loading point. The ore would then be tipped into the huge container that would be taken to the surface by the ore lift.

As the train took them deeper, Thaif looked at the roof held up by a network of arched pit props. It testified to the violent nature of

XN5. It was an ice moon, trapped in an elliptical orbit around planet Orro, a giant dark gas ball that wreaked havoc on XN5 and was responsible for its season of storms. Millennia ago, the volcanoes of XN5 had spewed their mesorite rich ash and lava into the seas that eventually froze due to the darkened atmosphere. Every time XN5 came within Orro's gravitational influence its ice crust twisted and bulged creating catastrophic ice quakes. Its three active volcanoes blasted out massive columns of ash and bled its lava deep into the ice. Violent winds created radioactive ash laden sleet storms that buffeted the populace, imprisoning them for months indoors. It was at this time that mining was at its most dangerous, but even during the mine season ice quakes were frequent. Subterranean ice falls were a common occurrence in the tunnels. Despite the machinery and safety precautions, the death toll of mine clones was always high.

The tense atmosphere was made worse by the constant crack and rumble of the ice flexing and twisting under its own weight. Its crushing intent felt malevolent, as if at any moment it would overpower the feeble pit props and squash the constant intrusion into its subterranean belly. They reached the face where the mine crew were winding down their work in readiness for the relief crew. To Thaif's surprise there were no Sabalian supervisors, only the short stocky mine clones. The supervisor was slightly taller than most and had an air of authority about him. As they disembarked the crew train, he came over to Thaif and asked pointing his chin at him, 'You the aqua miner Bala sent?' Thaif nodded.

'What's your name?'

'Thaif…master.'

The supervisor laughed cynically, turned and walked along the train as the old crew embarked. Thaif walked alongside him. 'I'm no master, only those half breed Sabalian scum think they are. My name is Chi'Dorolam; call me Chi if you like. Now…down here, we all work hard and try to look out for each other. This place is a death trap that likes to kill. Sometimes she gives, sometimes she takes and when she takes she takes us all. These men all want to live, but they know their fate. For us it is noble to die in the mines.'

As the relief crew went about their tasks, Thaif was put to work carrying rail tracks to the end of the line that was to be extended further into the tunnel. At the face the "constant mine machine" was started up. Ditholium picks attached to the rotating drum in the front of the machine bit into the frozen mesorite flow, breaking away chunks of radioactive ore that would be shifted by small excavators and loaded into dumpers that ferried the ore to the shuttle cars.

Even though Thaif was accustomed to hard physical labour, he found it hard going in the confines of the tunnel. The air was bad and the floor surface was uneven and slippery. Being much taller than everyone else, the roof of the tunnel was almost too low for him and he found himself stooping to avoid the hanging lights and brackets that held up the myriad of pipes and cables that supplied electricity, oxygen and compressed air among others. It would be some hours before he could take a break…

●

The squeal of the "constant mine machine's" rotating drum came to an abrupt stop as it hit a solid wall of rock. Chi'Dorolam walked up to the rock face and deliberated with his crew. It was not uncommon to find large rock deposits in the ore flows and the scanner showed what looked like a large pocket of ore behind it. With the Blaster they marked the best positions to place the explosives and called the two drill operators. They connected the compressed air pipes to their massive compression drills, cleared a path to the rock face and wheeled them in to place. They lined the bits up to the marks and pulled the levers on the handles. With deafening percussion the drills sprang into life and hammered their bits into the rock. Once the holes were deep enough the Blaster placed his explosives and set the electronic detonators. He led the detonator wires to the firing station and connected them up to the ignition box. They cleared the area of all men and machinery and hung a heavy flyrock absorption mat in front of the blast site. They were ready. The Blaster flipped the blast siren switch that sounded its warning for two minutes. Everyone put their hands over their ears and waited.

The silence was deadly as the siren stopped. As time lay suspended in its grip, Thaif felt a terrible foreboding that paralysed his limbs and gagged his vocal chords. The Blaster hit the button on the ignition box and a moment later the explosives detonated. The explosion was short and muffled by the flyrock mat, but the air compressed and flung itself at the crew as they huddled behind the firing station. In its aftermath the crew waited with bated breath for the crackling in the ice around them to settle as it absorbed the shock. As they breathed a sigh of relief a loud crack sounded like a whiplash from behind the flyrock mat. As more cracks appeared black silt and water squirted through. What they thought was a large pocket of mesorite ore, turned out to be a large lake of silt and water.

As the waters burst through, the rumble drowned out the terrified wails of the crew. Thaif leapt up to the roof of the tunnel and grabbed hold of the pipes. Chi'Dorolam had done the same; his shouts for his men to do the same were drowned out by the cacophony of destruction all around them. There was no escape as heavy machinery, flying rock, water and silt slammed into them, engulfing and dragging them along the length of the tunnel. The lights went out and the only light available was that of their helmets. As the water filled the tunnel to the roof Chi'Dorolam and Thaif held fast as the current threatened to drag them away. Thaif let out the air in his lungs and opened the side flaps of his coverall to let the water flow through his gills. He saw Chi struggling with the compressed air pipe as he tried to pry one of its extension couplings loose, but couldn't. Thaif inched closer until he was beside him and helped him with the coupling. As it came loose a blast of compressed air bubbled out. Chi pinched the pipe shut, let the stale air out of his lungs and breathed a controlled breath from the pipe. He passed the pipe to Thaif who declined. Chi smiled as comprehension dawned on him that Thaif could breathe underwater.

Thaif could feel the current abate and realised that the water had begun to run its course. He let go of the pipes and let the diminished current take him along. He looked around for something he could use for Chi and found a tool drum wedged between some machinery. He tipped it over and threw the tools out. The current had almost completely stopped, so it was not difficult to swim with it up to where Chi still clung desperately to the pipes on the tunnel roof. Thaif indicated to him to take a deep breath from the pipe and when he had done so, Thaif took the pipe from him. He then held the drum with the open end at the bottom and filled it with air. As it floated to the roof he indicated to Chi to put his head and shoulders in. When he was in Thaif pumped more air in until it was three quarters full.

'Thaif, what of my men?' Chi called from inside the drum.

Thaif ignored him, took hold of the handle on the side of the drum and started swimming towards the elevator shaft. There were drowned and crushed men all along the tunnel. Thaif weaved his way through a maze of tangled wreckage. When he reached the shaft gate he found a drowned man who in his panicked death throes had latched a death grip onto the handles. Thaif had to break his fingers to loosen his hands. Thaif could see why the man could not get the handles open. There was a lock pin that had to be pulled before the handles would unlatch.

Their ascent was much quicker with the buoyant drum, so Thaif had to slow it down. As soon as he saw light from above, he stopped their ascent by holding on to a cable bracket on the wall. He had to allow a minute for Chi's body to start the decompression sequence. They had been deep in the ice and the water pressure would have been high. Every ten feet or so Thaif stopped again to allow the inert nitrogen gasses in Chi's body to dissipate. When they reached the surface of the water, Thaif pulled Chi out from under the drum. As they broke the surface Chi gasped for air and Thaif closed his gills and breathed in deeply.

'My men...they must all be dead.' Chi'Dorolam had a pained, almost lost expression on his face.

'We can do nothing for them now.' Thaif confirmed with compassion. He pointed up the shaft and said, 'We still have a long climb ahead of us. Perhaps by saving ourselves we can remember the dead.'

'Your thoughts are true Aqua man. Lead the way then.'

Thaif swam to the side and took hold of the cable that ran alongside the shaft, lifted himself out the water and started the torturous climb to the top of the shaft. With Chi'Dorolam behind him, they sweated and cursed their way up the shaft until with numb and quivering muscles they reached the elevator. They had to climb up the side of it and onto its roof. As they clambered onto the roof a cheer sounded from the small group of men waiting anxiously at the elevator entrance. They were met by eager hands that helped them down the ladder that was put up for them.

The foreman elbowed his way through and barked. 'Are there any other survivors?'

When Chi slowly shook his head a disappointed silence fell over the small group of men.

The foreman broke the silence. 'What happened?'

'Flood.' Chi'Dorolam answered simply. Everyone knew the causes and they knew that no-one survives the floods. As if he knew their thoughts he pointed to Thaif. 'I would not be here if the Aqua man Thaif had not saved me.' They all looked at Thaif, some with respect, others with awe, but all with gratitude in their hearts...

●

'What will they do with you now?' Thaif asked.
'I'm not sure,' Chi'Dorolam responded. 'But I think they will use me on one of the new mines down south. Now that my men have died I will be a common labourer. The men will look upon me with suspicion. You're not supposed to survive the floods.'

He stared across the ice flats, his powerful shoulders were sagged and his head hung heavily on his thick neck. 'I am nothing without my men. Either I work my way up the ranks again or I work myself to death.' With a deep sigh, he lifted his head, straightened his shoulders and looked at Thaif with bloodshot eyes. 'It is the way for us miners. What better way to die than in the mines.'

'There is an alternative.'

'Oh...?'

'We can defy the Sabalians and their oppressive ways.'

'And how do we do that?'

'We join the Nation'

'The Nation.' Chi had an incredulous look on his face. 'If they exist at all, what makes you think I would want to be hunted for sport? I have heard the rumours, besides; they are supposed to be mostly free born. Without children it is said, you won't be accepted.'

'They exist all right and they are the only resistance to the Sabalians.' Thaif hesitated. 'I need your help.'

'You need only ask.'

'You see, if you help me with this, there will be no turning back.'

'It sounds almost like an adventure, go on.'

'My woman is pregnant and the only way we can save the child is to join the Nation in those mountains.' Thaif pointed his chin at the distant mountains across the ice flats.

'Blow me over!' Chi exclaimed with wonder. 'You are a rarity among men. How can I Chi'Dorolam, who knows nothing of children, be of assistance to the likes of you?'

'I need to stage my death: that way Bala will be off the scent. This is where you come in…' They stood there on the edge of the ice flats and worked out the details until it was dark.

'Here he comes.' Dr. Elwyn said as the dark silhouette of the shuttle truck weaved its way through the slag heaps. 'It's a black night, so the chances are good that you won't be seen heading across the flats.'

As Chi brought the truck to a halt opposite them, Dr. Elwyn opened the passenger door and helped Ola up onto the seat. 'Don't worry now Ola, everything has been arranged. Take good care of her, Chi.'

'Oh, you can be sure of that now.' He put the truck in gear. 'Tell the Aqua man, we will wait for him at the southern end of the crevasse and that he must be careful. That Bala is not to be taken lightly.'

Dr. Elwyn handed up Ola's two bags and the box of supplies they would need. 'Drive carefully now Chi and just remember,' he said, the concern etched into his face, 'you have two to take care of.' He looked at Ola and squeezed her hand. 'Watch yourself my dear and good luck.'

'Thank you Master Elwyn.'

Dr. Elwyn closed the door and with a smile Chi hit the gas and the truck headed off into the dark. Ola was apprehensive of the new, yet excited at the same time. She had no idea what lay ahead of her or how she would cope, but the one thing she did know was that her baby would live free…

Thaif met Dr. Elwyn at the fence behind the compound building. His scheduled night shift was about to begin and he was anxious.

'They are away,' Dr. Elwyn said.

'Chi came through then.' Thaif was visibly relieved.

'Oh yes, like clockwork. He said for you to be careful of Bala and that he would meet you at the southern end of the crevasse.'

Thaif nodded. 'Doctor, you have been very kind to us…'

'Think nothing of it Thaif. Take care of your family when you get there. I'll be thinking of you.' Dr. Elwyn turned and walked off into the night.

Thaif stood there for a moment, then turned and walked towards the shaft headgear; the giant lift machinery with its massive wheels that hoisted men and machinery up and down the shaft.

As Thaif joined the other aqua miners at the cage, Bala and the shift boss was there taking roll call. As Thaif's name was called out Bala looked at him. 'Ah so, our hero of the day! Tell me ectype; did it feel good to save that worthless miner? Did it make you feel special? Perhaps a little better than the others hey?'

Thaif felt more defiant this night and chose to ignore him. Bala's derisive smile turned to a sneer. 'I'm talking to you fish boy.' He walked up to Thaif and took his baton out. 'Don't…push…me…fish boy.' He punctuated the words by hitting Thaif with sharp blows to the abdomen. 'If it weren't for the fact that I need you to fill your quota tonight, I'd tear you to pieces and have the chef cook up a nice stew for those tunnel boys you love so much.'

Bala stepped back and said loudly for the others to hear. 'You fish boys can thank your hero here for just increasing your quota by half a ton each, so ectypes, get in that cage and go fetch me my mud!'

The aqua miners entered the cage. The tender closed the door and pulled the lever that started their descent. As the cage went down the men prepared themselves for the water. They all put on their miners helmets with their powerful aquatic lights. The cage hit the water and continued downwards. The submerged men breathed out and opened their gills to let the water flow through. They continued downwards until suddenly the shaft opened up as the cage came out into the open sea below the ice. A second shaft beside the crew was filled with large vacuum pipes and cables that extended into the dark depths like giant live worms. The cage continued for another hundred feet before it came to a halt. The tender opened the gate and the crew swam out towards the pipes. Each man located their particular pipe by its number and followed it down to the seabed. They then took over from the operator in the steel framed single seated vacuum extraction pod at the end, who in turn swam up to the cage that would then take them up to the surface.

Thaif took over the controls from the miner he was relieving and started working the thrusters to position the pod just high enough to keep it above the disturbed silt cloud, but low enough to keep the vacuum pipe in position. He looked around to see where the others were. The pupils of his eyes were totally dilated with a thin membrane covering the eyes. This membrane served a double purpose; it was an infrared underwater lens that also protected the eye. He had excellent underwater vision and could see heat signatures over long distances. The other aqua miners were all hovering above the silt clouds in their pods intent on their tasks. They were working a wide plateau bordered by a cliff face on one side and a deep abyss on the other.

Thaif slowly manoeuvred his pod closer to the abyss. As he got closer, he pulled the wrench he got from Chi, from inside his trouser leg and started working the anchor bolts loose from the pipe above his head. He had to make the accident look lethal and spectacular. He took off his helmet, put it on the floor, moved the pod until it was half way over the edge and worked the bolts. As they came loose the pod started to sag dangerously to one side. With the unbalanced position the thrusters started to vibrate violently shaking the pod. The vibration became so intense it broke the bolts off. As the pod broke loose and fell spinning onto the silt laden edge, Thaif lost his grip on the wrench and jumped free.

Under cover of the silt cloud he swam over the edge of the cliff into the abyss. As the pod churned up the silt squealing with broken metal against rock, Thaif swam as fast as he could, straight down into the black depths. Suddenly the squealing above stopped and he looked up. Through the silt cloud he could see the pod falling towards him; it's twisted and broken metal reaching for him. It had broken loose from its power cable and was tumbling silently with deceptive speed into the abyss. Thaif had just enough time to avoid the pod's lethal embrace. He swam into the slipstream behind the pod as it fell past him dragging a trail of silt with it.

Thaif had to go as deep as possible or his heat signature would be seen by the miners and they would know he was alive. If he was alive they would try to rescue him, so he needed distance and fast. With a burst of speed he caught up to the pod and took hold of it to let it carry him down. When he judged it deep enough he let go and swam out into the open sea. He had tremendous speed and now he pushed himself to the limits of his power. The ice above him stretched on for miles and cut out most of the light. Fluorescence in the ice was the only source of light for him to keep his bearings. When he was far enough away he slowed down and began to pace himself for the long swim to the crevasse…

●

Thaif knew he was not far from the crevasse when eight hours later, in the distance he saw a dim shaft of light. It was the beacon he had arranged with Chi. As he got closer he decided to be a little more cautious and surface further up the northern end. In a dark corner of the crevasse he slowly raised his head above the water. He was relieved to see Chi and Ola standing on the edge. He looked around to see if there was anything unusual on the skyline. When he was satisfied he drifted closer to the light.

'He said he would take possibly ten hours or so, so I guess we should just…wait a minute, what's that?' Chi pointed the light at the ripples and found Thaif slowly making his way towards them. 'There he is!' he said and tossed the rope over the side. A hundred and fifty feet below, Thaif reached up and took hold of it. Chi had tied the other end of it to the shuttle truck which he started and put in reverse. Slowly he reversed the truck and lifted Thaif out of the water and up the wall of the crevasse. Thaif used his feet to guide his way up the face and when he reached the top he stepped effortlessly over the rim onto the ice flats. As he let go of the rope Ola rushed into his arms. They remained in their silent embrace until Chi arrived back with the truck.

'I'm glad to see you made it, we were starting to worry.'

'It was a long swim, but making the accident look good was the hard part.' He took his coat and boots that Ola handed him and put them on. 'We must be on our way; we have no time to lose.'

'I was just thinking about that.' Chi said and they got in the truck.

Within the hour Thaif could feel the monotonous motion of the drive sap the remainder of the energy from his exhausted body. His bones became too heavy to lift and he could not remember when his eyelids fell shut. Hours later he awoke when the motion of the truck stopped. He looked around and found they had halted between two jagged blocks of ice. They jutted up from below the flats like two ancient weather worn megaliths. The morning light had a directionless eerie silence to it; saturated with a foreboding energy that pulsed with erratic gusts of wind, like a rabid animal panting for breath.

'A storm is approaching,' Chi said. 'Looks like sleet. Let's hope these blocks will give us enough protection.' He opened the door and got out. 'I'll fire in the anchor bolts while you set things up in the back.' Chi went around to the side of the truck and opened the tool box. He took out the bolt gun and four bolts. At each corner of the truck there was an internal winch with a long cable. Chi pulled the cable out as far as he thought necessary and attached the bolt to the end. He charged the bolt gun and fired the bolt deep into the ice. He then walked back to the winch and touched the button that started its motor in reverse to take up the slack in the cable. As the bolt started to lift, the reverse action released two barbs in the bolt that dug into the ice and formed a solid anchor. He did the same with the other three corners of the truck, thereby anchoring the vehicle firmly to the ice. The winds that drove the sleet storms were very powerful and would regularly destroy anything that was not tied down.

Chi got in the back of the truck where Ola had the small electric stove going. She had opened up a ration pack from the box of supplies and was cooking up a soup with melted ice in the field pot.

'Ah, there's nothing like a good hot soup while waiting out a storm.' He sat on a pile of mining gear and took an energy bar from the ration pack and began chewing on it. He looked at Thaif. 'So, how did you two meet?'

Thaif was surprised by the question and perplexed at how to answer. He looked at Ola for a moment and decided to just say it.

'We met in our dream.'

Chi looked up from his bar. 'You're having me on right?'

'No…we met in a mutual dream that happened at the same time.'

'How so?'

In the silence that ensued, Thaif took his time to compose his thoughts. 'We had been having the same dream for several weeks. We had never met before and this was the first we knew of each other's existence. We could not see the others physical characteristics, but rather each others energy imprint. More like…a presence. After a while the dream changed. We could see each other in a place. Finally the place became clear. It was under the three arches bridge at the market. We met there in our physical form and we have never looked back.'

Chi was motionless in his astonishment. He speechlessly stared at Thaif and Ola who smiled shyly and continued with the task of stirring the soup. Chi finally found his voice. 'Now that has got to be the most...you mean to say...you actually...' he pointed the energy bar at them. 'You mean to say that you met via some sort of energy transference?'

'Spiritual.' Thaif replied.

'Ah now, only the Sabalians have spirit, we are only flesh.'

'They lie.' Thaif handed Chi a mug of soup. 'The Sabalians would have us believe that they are superior beings by virtue of the fact that they are supposed to be naturally born and therefore only they have spirit. We on the other hand were made by Sabalian science and therefore do not possess spirit. We are considered to be mere electrically charged organisms designed to fulfil the whims and labour quotas of the Sabalian realm. In times of need we are food for them. When we have children they are claimed by the institute as their property. On the question of spirit; what of our children? Are they not naturally born? Do they then not also possess spirit? It is our opinion that we all have this thing they call spirit.'

'What then is spirit?' Chi sipped his soup.

'Perhaps the one they call "Raman of the Nation" can answer that question.'

Before Chi could answer the storm hit with the scream of ten thousand voices. It shook the truck with vindictive mischief. It drowned out their words and left them to contemplate their thoughts.

●

By nightfall the storm had abated but the wind remained. It whipped up the loose sleet into lethal sheets and rivulets above the ice that could cut through steel. They had not had any sleep during the night due to the noise of the storm and now they had to remain where they were, sheltered by the great blocks of ice until the wind stopped. Thaif took out his flute from the inside of his coat pocket and started his morning meditation tune. Its long nostalgic notes infused the small group with inward thoughts and feelings of peace and harmony. To Thaif and Ola this experience was normal, but to Chi it was a first.

Thoughts of the men he had worked with and who had died in the flood began to drift through his mind. He remembered friends he had toiled and got drunk with. His always steady and controlled emotions were thrown into turmoil and took hold of his throat. They squeezed until the tears burst from their ducts and rolled down his cheeks in great rivers of sorrow that could not be held back any longer. His body shuddered and heaved against the tide, but the silent flow was too strong. He saw their faces as they sang and laughed. He heard their screams and moans as they drowned. He hugged himself and rolled into a foetal position as sorrow turned to unbearable pain.

Ola came to his side and held him, gently rocking. Chi had never experienced this kind of tenderness and lost himself in her embrace. The tune Thaif was playing changed to subtle notes that soothed and cushioned. Its calming melody engulfed Chi until his spent body lay calmed in sleep. Ola lay him down and moved over to Thaif who ended the tune. They lay in each others arms until sleep took their exhausted bodies and carried their dreams on the mournful wind…

●

It was the silence that awoke them. Chi was the first to get out of the truck and busied himself with the cables, embarrassed by his display of emotion the day before. He hit the release button and a small electric charge ran down the cable and detonated the tiny explosive embedded in the bolt ring. Its metal crumbled and released the cable. He held the reverse button down; the electric motor sprang to life and pulled the cable back out, leaving the disposable bolt deep in the ice. When the cable had rolled up neatly on the winch drum, he stomped to the next winch and repeated the process. How was it possible for music to move him in such a way, he thought? He was always fully in control of himself.

Thaif got out the back of the truck and stood next to him. 'It seems a good night to travel.'

'Indeed it does. Listen…Thaif…about earlier…'

'You lost many good men. Men you had worked with for years. It is good to honour their memory with your grief. We are grateful you shared that honour with us.'

They were silent for a short time, before Chi answered. 'They were good men. It is good to die in the mines. That's our way. It is a great honour to die in the mines.' He punched the final release button and winched the cable up.

'Ola has a stew on for us. Let's eat and be on our way.'

Chi's mood seemed to visibly lift. 'Now you're talking.'

After the meal they set off into unknown territory in the general direction of the mountains. For the first five hours they had good going across the ice flats until they reached the Drift, a current of broken and drifting ice that crossed their path and barred their way, making it impossible for the truck to continue.

'So what now?' Chi asked.

'We set off a flare and we wait.'

'For what?'

'Dr. Elwyn said we would be met here by a guide who would take us across the Drift.'

Thaif took one of the flares out of the supply box and got out of the truck. He walked to the edge of the Drift and set off the flare. Its phosphor yellow rocket shot high into the air. When it reached its zenith the slow burning fuse ignited the chemicals that burned brightly and released its small parachute which opened and slowed its descent. As it slowly fell to the ice, Chi lifted his hand to shade his eyes and squinted into the dark, trying to see beyond it.

'I don't see anyone.'

'Neither do I, but no matter, we'll set off a flare every three hours so that he knows where we are.'

'Well, let's hope he takes us across that in the day,' he pointed at the Drift. 'Can you imagine going across there in the dark?'

'We have to wait and see.'

Massive blocks of ice, broken and jagged, that reached twenty feet above the water, were slowly drifting along a warm volcanically heated sea current of roughly five miles wide. They collided with each other with crushing force and pulverised anything caught between them. Jets of water would erupt from among them creating a perpetual intermittent rain. The constant sound of snapping, breaking and cracking ice assaulted their nerves and kept them on edge. Thaif continued with setting off the flares and every now and then he would cover his eyes with their outer membrane to look for heat signatures, but found none. They waited for two days and two nights, but still...nothing.

Chi had set up camp in a more suitable place, sheltered by big ice boulders on three sides. He had become accustomed to the meditative music Thaif played in the morning. At night they played some of the miner's board games they had learnt in the mine compound. Thaif played some of the popular tavern tunes on his flute and they enjoyed the creative variations of ration fare that Ola cooked up for them. They changed the watch every three hours.

It was early dawn of the third day when Chi set off the flare. As it lit up, he was shocked to see a tall man, who had appeared as if by a bolt of lightning, standing at the entrance of their small enclosure. Chi noticed that his entire body was covered in a thick shaggy coat of grey and white fur with a white mane that grew from his head and spread across his neck, shoulders and thorax. He was obviously one of the rickshaw men, but unlike any he had ever seen before. His stance was confident and proud and he radiated an aloof power. The canvas cross-bands, connected by a release buckle where they crossed his chest, held his large back pack. He wore a long pale grey canvas loin cloth and knee length fur lined snow boots, nothing else. In his right hand he held a long metal staff. Above his long nose and pointed jaw, his pale blue canine eyes stared intently at Chi.

He walked up to Chi, lifted the staff and rested the bottom end on the ice. 'I am Merrix, your guide.' Chi was taken aback at the gentleness in his voice. He looked up at Merrix. 'I am Chi'Dorolam, the miner. Come…you must be hungry.'

Merrix nodded and followed him to the truck. When they got there, Chi reached into the back and shook Thaif awake. 'Our guide is here.' Thaif and Ola got out of the truck a moment later and introduced themselves. They invited him into the truck, but he preferred to remain outside, so Thaif and Chi remained with him while Ola went back into the truck to prepare their meal.

'How many days have you travelled?' Chi asked.

'It has been seven days and seven nights.'

'How did you know we were coming?'

'I was told.'

'Yes, but by whom and how did he get the message over such a distance, there are no communications cables this far out.'

'Raman of the Nation. He calls us when we are needed.'

'Yes, but how?'

'He is…a telepath. We are all connected.'

'How so?'

Merrix was contemplating the answer when Ola brought out the food. They all filled their bowls with the hot broth and sipped it down while chewing on energy bars. Thaif finally broke the contemplative silence. 'How long do you think it would take us to get to the Nation?'

'The terrain is difficult and we must consider Ola's condition. If the weather is good then we could do it in fifteen to twenty days.'

'But, you had just said that you have travelled for seven days.' Chi interjected.

'Yes, I was only seven days and seven nights away from you when I got the message. The storm slowed me down, that is why you had to wait here for as long as you did.'

'How soon do you want to begin?' Thaif asked.

'Tomorrow morning. We have to hide the truck and you must pack what food and supplies you can carry. We will be travelling on foot for the rest of the way. Do you have anything we can use to build a litter or sleigh for when Ola needs to rest? Take extra blankets for her too. I will join you again at first light tomorrow. Thank you for the meal. I need to rest now.'

Merrix finished his meal, scrubbed out his bowl with some crushed ice and walked in amongst the ice debris until they lost sight of him…

●

First light and they met at the Drift. Each wore a fully loaded back pack. Ola, Thaif and Chi each had a long pole they had scavenged off the truck that they would use as a staff, and tied together, as a litter. They watched Merrix as he judged the huge floating chunks of ice. A rounded one with a level top floated close to the edge. He pointed his staff at it and squeezed the recessed release lever. A spring loaded grappling hook with a thin cable attached to it, shot out and landed on the pinnacle. He touched the retrieve lever and a small, but powerful internal motor wound the cable back into the staff. The grappling hook dug into the ice and Merrix started walking backwards to pull the ice tower closer to the edge. Once it gathered momentum he stopped walking and let the motor do the work.

As it crunched into the edge they all scrambled onto it. Merrix released the grappling hook and folded it back into the staff. They all then used their staffs to push away from the edge. As the current took hold of their tall tower, it started to sway and bob precariously.

'Move to the three corners and use your staff to keep the other blocks from crashing into us!' Merrix called to be heard above the din of falling and cracking ice. Thaif and Chi moved to the edges and pushed the other blocks away while Ola stayed in the centre. 'We have to try and manoeuvre diagonally across. As the current takes us, push off the other blocks to get us going in that direction!' Merrix pointed at an oblique angle that would take them across the Drift.

They worked hard at maintaining the general direction Merrix had pointed out and keeping their ice raft intact. They had drifted several miles down stream and had lost sight of the edge when the wind picked up and pushed them from behind. Their speed increased, but so did the danger of breaking up with a collision. A spout of water burst upwards as they struck a glancing blow off an adjacent ice block and inundated them. Their footing became treacherous and made it even more difficult to hold their balance.

'Look out!' Merrix shouted and pointed at a large block they were bearing down on. Thaif was the closest who waited until it came within reach of his staff and then with a mighty shove, pushed it out of harms way. As their speed picked up so did the frequency of obstacles rain upon them. As the day wore on they became more exhausted and drenched by the constant spray of water. They had all been designed to handle extreme cold, but Ola had to rest in the small shelter Thaif had set up for her in the centre of their raft. She could also stay somewhat dry, while the others did the work of keeping them afloat. The only time to take a break was in the short lull between fending off the ice blocks. During these breaks Ola handed out energy bars and drinks in their disposable bags. By nightfall they were only a third of the way across and the real danger was about to begin. As darkness fell, Chi strapped on a power pack and tied his miner's lamp on his head. He could not see in the dark as well as Thaif and Merrix. The wind had died which slowed them down and eased off the pressure they had been under for most of the day.

In the darkness the constant cacophony around them was amplified and began to sound like tortuous moans of agony and spasmodic squeals of hysterical anguish as the great blocks rubbed and ground into each other. Out of the darkness loomed ghostly forests of ice that endeavoured to hold and pulverise them. With Thaif and Chi on either side, they continued to work throughout the night, with Merrix on point, guiding them inexorably through the Drift.

By daybreak the wind had picked up and they found themselves trapped amongst a series of blocks that locked them into a deadly dance of swirling ice.

'What now?' Chi asked.

'We go with it. The wind will eventually break it up. It's a good time to eat and get some rest.' Merrix answered. 'I'll take first watch.'

They all went to the small shelter in the centre where Ola had cooked up a hot meal on the small pile of combustible bricks under the field pot. 'Ah, something hot at last!' Chi exclaimed with appreciation.

They ate their fill of the carbohydrate and protein gruel. They munched on energy bars and drank the hot Sabalian tea Dr. Elwyn had put in their supply box at the last minute. When the meal was over Thaif and Chi lay down under their blankets in the small shelter and almost instantly went to sleep. As Merrix walked around the perimeter Ola joined him with more tea.

'How long have you been with the Nation?' she asked.

'I was free born, but have not always lived among them.'

'How so?'

'When I became a young man, I began to feel uncomfortable among them and preferred my own company. I began to stay away for longer and longer periods, exploring the mountains. Eventually I became a guide in the service of Raman of the Nation. I am suited to a solitary life.'

'Don't you ever feel the need for company?'

'Company is often…overrated.'

He handed the empty cup back to Ola and walked to the forward edge. There he busied himself with pushing and shoving at the ice blocks that trapped them. Ola went back to the shelter and lay down next to Thaif.

●

The wind had done its work. By mid afternoon they had broken free and the left bank was in sight. Storm clouds were building up behind them and the wind was lashing them with blustering gales. They collided into bigger blocks of ice and giant waves gushed up between the fractured ice that engulfed them and threatened to wash them off their now battered ice raft. Ola's shelter had been packed up and each wore his own back pack. There was no time to talk or eat. Their exhausted bodies burned with fatigue as they worked their staffs against the tempest all around them.

'We are almost there!' Merrix called. The others looked up from their tasks and saw the left bank was only a hundred feet away. With renewed vigour they worked their way through the gaps between the broken ice blocks and angled their way towards the bank. As they got closer Merrix kept some smaller blocks between them and the bank and allowed their raft to bump directly onto the blocks ahead of it to slow them down. When they were close enough, Merrix shot the grappling hook out towards a large block wedged into the bank. As the hook took hold and they drifted past, the cable pulled taut and swung them like a pendulum the last few feet towards the bank. As they gathered momentum he released the brake on the motor to give the cable some slack and slow their approach to the bank. As they touched the bank, he put the motor in reverse and tensioned the cable to hold them in place.

'Quick, jump off! The current is too strong to hold it for long!'

Chi and Thaif took hold of Ola and the three of them took a running leap onto the bank. As soon as they were off, Merrix released the brake again and ran to the edge of the raft furthest from the bank. He then engaged the brake and as the cable tensioned up again he ran towards the bank. The raft had begun to drift away from the bank, but as he leaped off, his momentum coupled with the taut cable, catapulted him across the gap. He let go of his staff and broke his fall by rolling over on the ice. He stood up and retrieved his staff. He started the motor and as it wound up the cable he walked towards the grappling hook. He released the hook and folded it back into the staff. He then walked up to the others who were on their feet busy re-adjusting their back packs.

'Is everyone okay?' He looked pointedly at Ola.

'Yes, we're okay.' she answered.

'Good. We must find shelter. The storm is almost upon us.'

They leaned into the wind as they walked away from the drift towards what looked like an outcrop of large ice boulders. The ice particles carried on the wind scoured them as the first sleet began to slap into them. They found a sheltered place among the boulders away from the wind. After rigging the canvass over the top of their small enclave it was tied down and anchored with smaller ice blocks. With ice debris they blocked the small gaps between the boulders, to keep the wind out.

In the cramped space, they all lay exhausted as the storm raged across the ice flats. Thaif took out a few combustible bricks and boiled some clean ice in the field pot. He left Ola to sleep while he cooked up a broth from their rations. Chi stared into the flames and said, 'I don't think I have ever been this hungry before.' Thaif and Merrix chuckled spontaneously. 'It's amazing how food always tastes better when you are really hungry.' Another chuckle erupted from his companions. With the heat of the small fire and the pleasant smell of cooking, they fell into thoughtful silence and re-lived their journey across the Drift…

●

They had travelled for ten days and White Mountain was in sight. The undulating icescape was punctuated by massive ice blocks and mesorite rocks which were strewn everywhere. The ice was dirty; grey with mesorite dust and ash from the volcano deep inside the mountain. It had erupted a long time ago and had been deemed dormant, not rich enough in mesorite for mining by the Sabalian mine survey teams. White Mountain was not just one mountain, but a range of mountains and outcrops of ice and mesorite rock.

'So…that's white mountain,' Chi said. 'It doesn't look like much.'

'That's because you can't see it yet.' Merrix answered.

'What do you mean?'

'The clouds are too low. Wait until they lift.'

'I thought the sky was just grey. How far do we still have to go?'

'Three days.'

They were all exhausted. They had travelled hard over some of the worst terrain imaginable. They had been battered by severe storms, but still they prevailed. Two at a time, they pulled Ola along in her makeshift litter. Each took their turn at the ropes. Thaif and Chi were labouring at it when they saw what they thought was White Mountain. They stopped and Merrix changed places with Chi. With their destination in sight, they set off with renewed vigour. By late afternoon the clouds lifted to reveal White Mountain in all its majestic splendour. It was white, but with an ugly black gash down the right side, as if a big bite had been taken out of it.

'That must be where it had erupted,' Chi said. 'I have never seen anything like it before. I never knew places like this existed. When you live in one place all your life it becomes your entire existence. This is magnificent!'

They found a good place to shelter for the night. They set up camp and marvelled at the pale twilight as it reflected off the white side of the mountain. It seemed to shimmer and glow with an inner light that infused them with awe and wonder. As they took it all in, they were filled with new hope and anticipation for the future…

●

By the third day they were standing at the base of White Mountain, where they took to the steep path that led up the northern slope towards Raman's cave. The path was narrow with a sheer drop on the left. Loose ice and rock made keeping their footing treacherous. The steep angle of the path sapped their strength as they hauled at the litter. After three hours of toil they took a break with still two thousand feet to go. In the thick mist that surrounded them Ola made tea and they chewed on energy bars.

Chi looked at Merrix. 'I have heard it said that the Sabalians hunt the Nation for sport. Is this true?'

'Yes.' Merrix answered bluntly. 'It is during the calm season that they are most active. During the season of storms we are left in peace. Most of the time they kill the older men and take the young men, women and children.'

'But, can you not fight back?'

'Yes we do. Only about a third of their raids have been successful. We have beaten them back and killed many, but they have the technology and far superior weapons. It is a fact of our life here.' Merrix took a sip of his tea and continued. 'In a sense, it is a rite of passage for us, to kill a Sabalian and survive your first battle. Our young men become fighting men at age fourteen and sometimes younger. It's ironic, but this has become their passage to manhood now.'

'Bastards,' Chi choked the word out. 'Who do they think they are? Just because their scientists made us, does not mean they can do with us as they wish. We live, we think, we have feelings…just who do they think they are?' He was shaking with rage as his worst fears were confirmed. What he had heard was true. Right there he resolved to fight them with every ounce of his energy. He would fight and he would kill as many as he could get his hands on. All the injustice that had befallen him in the mines seemed to be breaking out in painful boils that chafed against his peace of mind and would only heal with the killing of Sabalians.

Merrix finished his tea. 'Come, it is time to go.'

Ola got on the litter and Chi took up both ropes. His anger was such that his fatigue had vanished. He applied all his great strength against the ropes and pulled furiously up the slope. Thaif and Merrix had to stretch their stride to keep up and Ola held on tight. Thaif knew not to interfere as the fire in Chi needed to burn out first. With Merrix they stayed close to Ola to guide the litter in case it threatened to topple off the edge. It took almost two hours before Chi finally collapsed, heaving for breath. Nobody said anything; they just sat where they were and rested…

●

By nightfall they had reached the mouth of the cave high above the clouds. The distant sun shone its last light bleakly into their faces as it sank into its soft blanket of cloud. They turned and entered the cave. Ola was on her feet and the litter had been dismantled. What at first seemed like a small shallow cave, narrowed towards the rear into a dark descending passage. Chi put his miner's lamp on his head and turned it on. The passage was a natural volcanic tube carved from molten rock. Its surfaces were treacherous, lined with rock blisters that if stepped or leaned on would break and cause a grievous injury. There were partially formed blisters where the lava had cooled into sharp spikes and lethal knife sharp edges.

'Put your feet on the same places I do, if you fall through one of those blisters there's no telling if you'll fall to your death or just break your bones.' Merrix twisted the top of his staff which extended by an inch and turned on the powerful light in the inner glass tube. He extended the staff ahead of him and led the way.

The passage followed a tortuous twisted route that at times widened out and then became so narrow, they had to remove their back packs and squeeze through sideways. At some places the roof was too low and they had to crawl through on hands and knees. The air became oppressive and close with the weight of the mountain above them. It felt claustrophobic and humid with the intensifying heat. Time became nonexistent until the passage opened up into a small chamber with several passages leading from it. The air smelt of sulphur and there was a metallic taste on the tongue. They all took a rest. Thaif attended to Ola who sat at an entrance where the air was a bit fresher, while the others drank water from their water bottles.

'How far do we still have to go?' Chi asked. He was used to conditions underground and was bred for the task of underground mining; however, he had never got this close to a volcano before. They had not encountered molten lava yet, but even the rocks around them were hot and the heat was unbearable.

'Raman's cave is not far now and the air will be better soon. This is the back way in and the shortest route. If we were to go in the front, our journey would have taken another five days to go around the mountain.' Merrix drank more water. 'These tubes are a frightening maze. Many of them are dead ends and are so tight that once you are in you can't turn around and walk out. There are rivers of boiling lava beneath some of the thin blistered floors; one miss step might be your last.'

He pointed his water bottle towards a narrow entrance across their small chamber. 'If you go down that one, it ends abruptly about five hundred feet above the main lava flow. You see, the lava here does not just come up in a great big spout; it flows like a river along the entire mountain range. It's the internal heating system that makes it possible for us to live here. I have been through these tubes many times and know my way, but for a stranger there awaits almost certain death.'

'Which way do we go from here?' Chi asked.

'This way.' Merrix led the way into an unlikely narrow passage that Chi would not have considered. It had several turns and cutbacks that made them lose all sense of direction. The rocks were hot and the going was slow. As they worked their way around a particularly tight bend, the air suddenly began to cool and smell fresh.

'Its not far to go now,' Merrix said and led them along a curved passage that seemed to lead into a dead end. It turned out to be another tight cutback. Once they were through, they abruptly stepped into a cave with a high ceiling. Long stalactites disappeared into darkness high above. Some joined their corresponding stalagmites and formed pillars like great arms that pushed the mountain away from the floor. There were several shafts of light that came through tiny holes in the ceiling that gave the different stalactite formations an inner glow that lit up the cave like magnificent chandeliers in a great hall.

'Aah!' Chi exclaimed spontaneously. 'I have seen many caves, but nothing as spectacular as this. The light is a marvel.'

'It changes with the direction of the sun. It fades to black by night. Come…this way.'

Merrix led the way past clear pools of water that reflected light onto the walls and made the atmosphere alive with movement. They stopped at one of these pools and washed the grime of the passages off their hands and faces. They tidied themselves up as best they could and refilled their water bottles from a small trickle running down from the roof. They moved on towards a dark entrance that led to another smaller chamber. At the entrance they waited. After a few minutes they heard a susurration from the dark beyond.

'I see you Merrix.' The voice that came from the dark was strong and confident.

'I hear you Great One.' Merrix answered.

'Come.'

As their eyes adjusted to the dark within they became aware of a soft glow from the lavender quartzite crystal canopy above them. On the floor was a carpet woven from black and white Sabalian cloth. Its pattern was that of a white bursting star in the centre on a black background. The black edges of the carpet seemed to cover the entire interior of the small chamber. On a raised shelf of rock also covered with black carpet and black cushions sat the most extraordinary looking man.

Raman of the Nation was tall. Despite the heat, he wore a long black robe with a thick soft red collar that was pinned with a white metal diamond-shaped brooch at the centre of his chest. The robe was finished with an intricately patterned red border. What at first seemed like a turban on his head, was on closer inspection, his brain, which was covered not by bone, but by red skin. Around his oversized brain he wore a white metal web-like frame that supported its great weight and maintained its shape, thus allowing normal movement of his head. Where his eyes should have been were cheekbones. In the centre of his forehead was an eye that was overgrown by red skin that ended at the bridge of his nose and spread over the cheekbones. His mouth and lower jaw were human with a normal white skin tone. By normal standards he was physically blind, but with his enormous brain and his middle eye he could discern more than mere sight. He could see everything from the appearance of a being to its aura as well as read and communicate with the mind. He was in every respect all seeing and did not need eyes.

As he spoke the strong determined set of his mouth and jaw line softened. 'You have done well Merrix.' The strength of his gratitude was in the tone of his distinctly powerful voice, not the words. Merrix bowed his head in silent acceptance. 'Welcome to the Nation,' Raman continued. 'Please, take off your packs and rest.' He indicated to his left. 'Zizi here has kindly joined me today with food and drink for us.' A shadow seemed to detach itself from the dark and walked towards them. Over her black fur covered, plump body she wore a comfortable black dress that seemed to float with the shadows. She had a friendly smile that revealed an even row of white teeth.

She walked up to Ola and in a sweet bubbling voice said. 'You must be Ola.' Ola took an instant liking to her as Zizi took her hands. 'Come with me. I'll make you more comfortable and get some good food into you then you can tell me all about your journey and how you're feeling…' Ola looked back at Thaif with a shy smile on her lips as Zizi led her to one side of the chamber where there were more cushions for her to rest on.

After they had dined on food only Merrix was familiar with, they all sat at the base of the raised shelf of rock upon which Raman sat. He looked at Thaif. 'When they made you they created a being far beyond their mandate. You are nothing like the other aqua miners. Your intellect and spirit are too high for you to be a slave to the Sabalians, but it is your seed that is unique. Your offspring will be the one with the key. His power will span the multiverse and his name will live forever. Your teachings will be the window to his soul and,' he looked at Ola, 'yours will unlock the multiverse for him.' He looked towards Chi. 'Chi-Dorolam, you will have your chance to repay your perceived dept in full. Now, go with Zizi, she will help you settle in. Merrix, stay with me a while.' They got to their feet and Ola, Thaif and Chi thanked Merrix warmly for he had not only been a good guide, but their friendly companion throughout their journey. As they turned to follow Zizi out, Raman said, 'Come and see me often, I like company.'

White Mountain was a labyrinth of caves, tunnels, passages and secluded valleys. It had a deep narrow lake that although sometimes frozen at the surface was heated at the bottom by volcanic pipes that created an environment that had spawned a multitude of underwater life unique on all of XN5. The Nation fed on its fish that were fished by beings like Thaif. His role as aqua miner was quickly adapted to that of fisherman and he became a productive member of the Nation. Although heavily pregnant, Ola became a teacher in their local school. She had a natural ability for mathematics and was a valuable addition to their community.

On one of his fishing dives, Thaif and two of his companions had a run in with a twenty foot killer siux eel. It was a particularly nasty predator from the deep. It struck from the darkness below with such speed that no-one could have seen it coming unless they were looking directly at it. Its massive jaws with their serrated teeth snapped shut on the man next to Thaif and severed the lower half of his body. The siux eel turned and came back and swallowed the rest of the dead fisherman down in one gulp. Thaif knew that the eel would not rest until it had all of them. He took the long knife he had taken from Snake Eyes, what seemed so long ago, from its sheath on his thigh and waited for the eel to make its turn and come back.

It headed straight for him. Thaif waited until the last minute before he dodged the eel's lethal strike. The mighty jaws snapped shut beside him and as the eel swam past, Thaif struck upwards with a powerful thrust into the eel's soft under belly. Thaif took hold of its leathery scales and was carried along with the now maddened eel that was twisting and thrashing wildly, trying to bite Thaif and pluck the source of its pain from its belly. Thaif held on with all his strength and worked the knife deeper and deeper, slashing and hacking at the eel's insides until he hit the heart. As he pulled the knife out for another thrust a powerful gush of dark blood engulfed him and the eel convulsed into a death spasm and shuddered into limp stillness. As the eel started to sink into the depths, the other fisherman came alongside and helped bring it up to the surface. The siux eel was a rare food and many would feed on its huge body. When they finally got it to the surface there were many helping hands to lift it onto the stone pier.

'I have never seen anything like it.' Thaif's companion told the men on the pier.

'He took that monster single handed. The siux went mad and trashed wildly, but Thaif held on like his life depended on it.'

'His life did depend on it!' One of the men responded. A chuckle rippled through the small group standing around the eel carcass.

'If he didn't he would have met the same fate as your friend!'

They cut the stomach open and stared in fascinated silent horror as the two halves of the man who was swallowed whole slid out onto the pier. They took the body, cleaned it up and wrapped it in rough canvas to take to his family for burial. Thaif was given the skin of the siux as a trophy which he shared with the fisherman who had helped him. They were also given the choicest cuts of meat before it was taken away for processing.

Zizi had taken the skin and with Ola's help had cured it and sewed it onto the back and shoulders of Thaif's coat. It offered warm weather protection and would last a long time. During the day Chi worked with Merrix and the other men who were in the local militia. He improved their explosives and taught them how to make them more stable and how to transport them safely. Used to leadership, he soon became a cell commander specialising in explosives. At night he remained close to Zizi. Her warmth and bubbling personality had become indispensable to his well being.

On the day of Ola's confinement neither Thaif nor Chi had any idea of what to expect. Zizi had taken Ola to Raman's cave were she gave birth in one of the warm volcanic pools. She was not a swimmer, but the pool was shallow enough. Thaif stayed with her in the pool, supporting her as she leaned against him. Zizi was also in the pool attending to her while Chi ran errands and prepared things for the new baby. Ola was exhausted after twelve hours of labour and each contraction was driving her into an almost delirious state.

'I can see the head!' Zizi said. 'Okay, now, one more big push…that's it…push!'

Ola took one more deep breath and pushed with the last of her strength. 'Yes…yes!' Zizi said as the baby emerged into the water. 'It's a boy!' She took him into her hands and cleaned him of amniotic fluid and blood before lifting him out of the water. As she lifted him out, the shock of the cold made him take his first breath and bellow an indignant cry. Zizi handed him to Ola who was overcome with emotion and exhaustion. Zizi handed Thaif a sharp knife and showed him where to cut the umbilical chord and tie it with a length of twine.

She continued to work below with the afterbirth and wrapped it into a cloth that Chi handed her. She then took the baby from Ola and wrapped him in a soft blanket. She walked out of the pool and placed the baby into the small hammock Thaif had made for him. They helped Ola out of the pool and placed her on a stretcher. Thaif and Chi lifted the stretcher and took her to the bed prepared earlier on the warm rock slab close by. They moved the hammock on its stand closer to the bed. Thaif lifted the baby out and sat on the bed next to Ola who was fading in and out of sleep.

She looked at Thaif and the baby. 'What shall we call him?'

Thaif lifted him up and looked at him for some time before he answered. 'He is the most beautiful boy, like the musical phrase at the end of a tune; his name…shall be Coda.'

●

Coda had started playing the flute at a very early age and now at age seven he could deliver a virtuoso performance. Today he played a special tune as today was a special day. Thaif and Ola had decided to make their partnership more binding to each other by making their love vows. While he played he watched his father who stood tall in his full length black coat with the siux eel skin. He wore a white shirt with black trousers and boots. His mother stood next to him. She looked lovely in her cream outfit with its intricate patterns of white silk embroidery. It had an elegant high collared jacket with long sleeves and an ankle length skirt.

Coda could feel the love and affection that radiated from their shining faces as they watched him play. They were standing in the main chamber of Raman's cave. Ola had asked Raman to witness their vows and he had taken it upon himself to invite everyone. The cave was filled to bursting point with the beings of the Nation who were so many; they spilled out the entrance and down the mountainside. There was nowhere left to stand. The whole chamber was aglow from the midday light caught in the stalactites hanging from the high ceiling like great chandeliers. Pools of water on the floor reflected dancing lights in all directions as everyone listened in silent reflection.

There was a few moments' silence after Coda sounded the last note that ended the pensive tune. Raman's voice was strong and carried physically and telepathically to everyone present. He was seated on the high base of a stalagmite that reached high up towards the ceiling. 'We are here to witness the love vows of Ola and Thaif. This will bind them in body and spirit, now and in the afterlife. A vow made in love is the most powerful and binding vow that can ever be made. Its power resonates across the Universe and attracts the forces of manifestation.' He looked down at Ola. 'May we hear your vows?'

Ola and Thaif turned to face each other and took each other's hands. 'I am Ola...mother and teacher. When we met in our dream...you became my reason for life. You protected and sustained me and our son has made me complete. Thank you for Coda and bringing us here...to live free. You and Coda will always be my reason for life. I love you Thaif. I will always love you...no matter what.' Tears began to well up in her eyes as the strength of her emotions choked her.

'I am Thaif...father and fisherman. Since we met it has felt like I'm still living the dream.' A spontaneous murmur of humour rippled through the crowd. 'Before we met, I did not know love. I did not know such emotions were possible. You and Coda are my entire existence. Nothing else matters. Every breath I take and everything I do will always be in gratitude of your love. I love you Ola. I will always love you...no matter what.'

Raman indicated to Coda to go forward with the hand-fastening cord and black ditholium bracelets Chi'Dorolam had made for them. Thaif took Ola's bracelet and put it on her left wrist. 'This bracelet is the symbol of my love for you.' Ola took Thaif's bracelet and as she placed it on his left wrist she repeated the same words.

As Coda bound Thaif's right hand to Ola's left with the silk cord, Raman concluded. 'This cord is the symbol of the bond you have pledged this day. May your bond resonate for eternity.'

Thaif and Ola sealed their bonds with a tender kiss to loud cheers from the Nation. They bowed to Raman and turned to face the crowd. Coda stepped in front of them and began playing an upbeat tune. The Nation opened a path for them to walk out of the chamber and down the mountain. With Coda in the lead they all followed to a clearing by the lake where a banquet of food and drink awaited. Thaif and Ola felt very special as all their community and friends congratulated them and partied late into the night.

Bala stared uncomprehendingly at the wrench. 'This is what broke the vacuum turbine,' his mine manager said. 'It's the only thing that could get past the sonic resonance field that usually breaks up the rocks or debris that comes up the pipes.'

'Yes, but how did it get there. Aqua miners don't use wrenches.'

'I sent one of my men down there and he found this.' He put a crushed helmet on the table next to the wrench. With a sharp intake of breath, Bala sat up with keen interest. He looked at the number on the helmet and knew whose it was.

'That miner we lost seven years ago…it's his helmet.'

'I'm surprised it was still there with the currents the way they are,' the manager said. 'But, how would the wrench get down there, unless that miner had something to do with it.'

'That would mean that the miner…Thaif was his name, is still alive…and had effectively staged the accident to escape.'

'It's a long way to the mountains.'

'Not for an aqua miner. With enough food they could roam these oceans for ever.'

'What food? These oceans are barren.'

'Hmm…I understand the hunting hasn't been very good these past few years. Maybe our luck will be a little better.' Bala's intent was evil and murderous. Because of Thaif's escape he had not reached his target that day and now that the main turbine was down he would lose another two days production until they could transfer the suction pipes to the backup turbine. How dare that fish boy do this to him, he thought. He would make that slime encrusted ectype pay for this…in blood!

Thaif looked at his son as he played the morning meditation tune. His heart filled with pride and love for him. This young boy had become the centre of his and Ola's existence. Already he knew all the tunes and had proved to be a good student. He knew his letters and could read well. His love of mathematics was owed to Ola who was expert in the field and worked as a teacher in their local school.

They were seated on a rock beside a small stream that ran down the hill into the long lake. They had a clear view of the sunrise as it ascended between two peaks at the opposite end of the lake and gently moved the shadows off the water. When Coda finished playing the tune, he put the flute on his lap and with his legs crossed he put his hands on his knees. He focused his mind on the sound of the water as it chuckled and bubbled over the rocks.

For the past few weeks he had been working on the techniques he had learnt from Raman and his father on how to slow the heart rate down to the point where his whole body was turned off. As he watched the sun rise, he felt the light touch his skin. His vision narrowed as the light washed all thoughts from his mind. He felt his heart rate decrease and the void within start to open. A flash of light from one of the near hills distracted him and he felt the void contract. He tried to ignore the irritating glimmer, but he could not regain the moment.

He looked at his father and noticed that he was equally distracted. 'Perhaps we would be better off if we went for a swim, what do you say?' Thaif asked.

'That's a very good idea.' Coda loved to swim. He revelled in the freedom to breathe underwater, to race with the fish and help his father with the daily catch.

Thaif and Coda looked alike in many ways. Both had hairless bodies. Between their ribs were gills that were covered with muscular skin flaps that opened and closed in conjunction with their diaphragms. Their skin was almost totally without pigmentation except for the ability to change the colour of the back of their bodies to black. On Thaif's large bald head where hair would normally grow on a human, the skin was a gradated speckled black that continued down the back of his neck and onto his shoulders. His face was human with a strong jaw line and red-brown eyes. Instead of a sharp pointed nose he had more of a bump with flaps of muscular skin that opened and closed his nostrils.

Coda had his father's body and skin colour, but he had ropy hair on his head which was black with fine thin muscles that ran inside the length of the hair. He had his father's eyes and strong jaw line, but the finely shaped nose of his mother with the muscular skin flaps that opened and closed his nostrils. His smile was full and reached his eyes which sparkled with joy and innocence. He had not yet known cruelty and was filled with the wonder of life.

They stood up and took the path to the lake. 'Race you there!'

Thaif said and slowly jogged behind Coda who ran ahead giggling and laughing. Thaif marvelled at the way he could run. He would let him win of course…

●

Merrix watched the snake eyed man who lay on his belly and peered though the lens of a visocom. Raman had contacted Merrix four days ago and told him that there were strangers in their midst, that they brought death to the mountain. He had known that a new hunt was imminent. Their defences were in place and had been put on alert. Merrix had found the small aircraft and followed the tracks into the mountains. Snake Eyes had proven to be sloppy and easy to track. Merrix looked in the direction Snake Eyes was pointing the visocom and saw the two figures on the rock. Snake Eyes had been concentrating on Thaif and his movements for the past two days. Could it be that Thaif was a target of some sort? What was Snake Eyes' interest in Thaif? Who was he spying for? He watched as Snake Eyes awkwardly worked the buttons of the visocom with his right hand that was partially disabled from a badly healed broken wrist. He was transmitting pictures and text to a receiver somewhere.

Merrix knew what he had to do. He quietly stepped out from behind the rock he was crouched behind and cautiously moved towards Snake Eyes with his staff at the ready. As he was about to engage, Snake Eyes rolled over onto his back and was on his feet in an instant. He had a small laser gun in his left hand, but before he could bring it to bear Merrix knocked it from his hand with the staff and with the same motion, brought the staff down with a sickening crack onto the side of Snake Eyes neck. Snake Eyes crumpled dead to the ground. Merrix had not intended to kill him, but had not realized how fragile this spy was.

He switched the visocom off and searched Snake Eyes' clothes and back pack for any clues. The visocom had a playback function so they would know what footage and text had been sent. In one of Snake Eyes pockets, he found an Interversal Gion credit note from Bala. Raman would know what to do, he thought. This Bala probably is the one who hired the spy. He had to move fast. He picked up the bag and visocom and left the body where it was. He would be back for that later. As he ran down the path that led to Raman's cave he knew that the hunt had begun. Would they have enough time…?

'What just happened?' Bala barked.

'We lost the signal.' The pilot answered.

'I can see that! Why have we lost the signal? Is it the equipment or is it our man in the field?'

'The readings on our equipment show that they are not faulty. It must be the man in the field.'

'Then we have been discovered. The element of surprise is lost; we have no time to lose!' He leaned forward. 'Start the engines.'

As the engines of the amphibious flier whirred into life, Bala gave the order for the other five craft to proceed slowly to the surface. They had been waiting in the dark depths of the lake for the past two days. Snake Eyes had killed the sentry on the peak, thus making it possible for them to get into the valley and into the lake unseen. Bala was anxious. The others could do what they wanted, but he had a fix on Thaif now and he wanted him so bad he could taste it.

He was looking through the observation window when a dark shadow moved across them. At first Bala did not comprehend and then it happened again. 'Did you see that?' he asked his pilot who was concentrating on his instruments.

'Did I see what?'

'Ah...it was probably nothing.'

Suddenly a chorus of terrified screams broke radio silence and was cut off. Bala grabbed the coms mike. 'What's going on there?'

'Some kind of monster just bit number two craft in half!' The voice was screaming in panic. 'Here it comes again. Get us out of here! Full ahead, full ahead!'

Bala stood transfixed as he watched in horror. He had never seen a siux eel before. He could not believe how big it was. He was awestruck at the size of its vicious jaws as they ripped number three craft apart. In what seemed like less than a minute they had been reduced to four craft. He would be held accountable for those Sabalians he lost today. He would make Thaif pay for this!

'To the surface, full ahead!' He spat the command out like hot venom.

'I'm going to catch you!' Thaif called as he chased after Coda. Fresh squeals of laughter and giggles erupted from Coda as he looked over his shoulder. He ran full tilt at the high embankment and took a leaping dive into the lake. Thaif dived in right behind him and continued the chase. He sure is fast, Thaif thought, as Coda dodged him and sped off to the right. Coda weaved and dodged Thaif's playful attempts to catch him when Thaif felt the ripple from below. He looked down and saw the heat signatures of the five craft below and the scattered remains of the sixth as the siux bit it in half.

He caught Coda effortlessly as he raced after him in earnest and headed for the small beach. He held Coda to his chest as he sprinted up the beach and onto the path that led to their small village. He had to get Coda and Ola to safety. Coda had always thought his father was indestructible and was confused to see him so distressed. His father had never run from anything. As he clung to Thaif he asked. 'Why are we running Da?'

'Because there are some bad men in the lake. I must get you to your mother.'

'Are they going to hurt us?'

Before Thaif could answer, he heard the four amphibious fliers roar through the surface of the water and level out. He could feel the heat from the laser bolts as they whipped past him. He started to run in a weaving pattern and managed to dodge them. Rocks and boulders of ice disintegrated as they were hit.

Suddenly the air was filled with loud percussive explosions as White Mountain's defences came to life. Chi'Dorolam had built explosive weaponry and trained many anti aircraft units over the past seven years. Ditholium bullets ripped into one of the invaders aircraft and punched great big holes in it. As its engines were struck they set alight and the craft lost control. It struck the ground with a dull thump and exploded.

Coda was astonished at how fast his father could run as debris was scattered all around them. He always thought he was faster than him. They were running up the mountain path towards the village when the second aircraft was brought down. It hit the side of the mountain near them. A large piece of shrapnel took Thaif's right leg off below the knee as he ran. Coda was thrown clear as Thaif hit the ground hard.

'Da!' Coda called.

Thaif lifted his bloody face off the ground and looked at Coda. 'Run Coda, run to your mother!'

'Da!' Coda called again; shocked with tears running through the mud on his face.

'Run!' Thaif called. 'Run as fast as you can.' He watched as his son turned and ran. 'I love you!' he shouted. As he felt the laser cut through him, he watched Coda run. That boy sure can run, he thought. As his vision dimmed to a fine point of light he knew that his son was the one good thing he had done, and died…

●

'No!' Bala screamed as he saw his prize cut down in front of him. His revenge was denied by the panicked men in the other flier who were shooting at anything that moved.

He picked up the coms mike and shouted into it. 'Cease fire! Cease fire you incompetent fools!' But the firing did not stop as the men in the other craft were in full battle and were not listening anymore. Bala fixed on Coda. If he couldn't make Thaif pay, he thought, then his offspring will. 'Follow him,' he said to his pilot.

Bala followed Coda from the air as the other flier wreaked havoc on the village and kept its defences occupied. It too was finally brought down in a spectacular explosion, but as it hit the ground it killed many of the Nation. Bala watched as the boy was met by a domestic woman and the two of them ran off towards the high peak. 'Quick we must cut them off, I want them.' The pilot brought the flier above them and opened the door to the hold. They hovered above Ola and Coda, dusting them with the thrusters which trapped them in one place. Bala rushed to the hold and manned the net. He expertly threw it and caught the two of them. He hit the button on the motor that tightened the net around them and indicated to the pilot to go up. He then turned on the winch that pulled them up into the hold. Once the door was closed he said. 'Get us out of here. Full speed ahead.' He would have his revenge, he thought, no matter what…

Present
Upi, Onusa Quadrant

Professor Erick Astor leaned forward with keen interest. 'Aah…so your memory is starting to come back.' He leaned back in his wheelchair. 'So, what of your father, what can you tell me about him?' He watched the play of emotion on Coda's enigmatic face. There were tears in his eyes and the effort it took to hold them back made his hands shake a little. Seated in his wing-backed red leather chair, he looked at the flute on his lap. His father must have something to do with that flute, the professor thought.

'Yes he did,' Coda answered. 'This…was my father's flute.' Coda's voice was hoarse and dry, laden with heavy emotion. He stroked the flute's metal and followed its contours. 'He played it beautifully you know.' He swallowed several times to hold back the overpowering grief he felt. 'He was…a man of love and vision. He was…a kind spiritual man. A warrior who was cut down in his prime.'

'How did he die? Do you remember?' the professor asked, mindful of Coda's mind reading ability.

'He died…protecting me.'

'How old were you then?'

'I was…very young, a small boy.'

'Do you remember what happened after that?'

'It is all…unclear. It's as if the memories are on the edge of my mind, but I can't bring them into focus.'

'Well, I think we have made good progress so far. You might take a look at your library, maybe something will come back to you. Would you like to try and walk across to it?' the Professor ventured. He knew that Coda was in some sort of danger, although he did not know the nature of it. All the more reason to accelerate his recovery, he thought. 'Perhaps you could lean on the wheelchair handles while I slowly make my way there.'

Coda nodded and the professor called two of the guards over to help Coda up. As Coda came shakily to his feet the Professor turned his wheelchair and reversed closer for Coda to take hold of the handles. Coda could barely put one foot in front of the other as the Professor slowly moved forward. The guards on either side of him had to give further support as, even though he was seriously emaciated, he was a tall man and his body had not carried any weight in eight hundred years. His body shook with the effort and pain of resting his full weight on his bare feet. The stress on his joints was made more extreme as the crystals and bone growths in them were crushed and ground down. By the time they reached the library console, Coda was drenched in perspiration. But for the support of the two guards he would have fallen into the console chair.

'Would you like a painkiller?' the Professor asked.

'No…it will pass.'

'Perhaps I should leave you to browse through this on your own. If you need anything the guards will assist you. I need to see how Shay is doing since his return. I will be back soon.' Coda nodded his assent and the professor left the room.

●

Captain John Masters really felt Shay's absence. He was his best officer and now that he was seriously injured he had to do all the preparations for departure from Upi himself. Even Chief Wall, hobbling around on crutches to take the weight off his broken leg, could not perform his duties properly. Amidst all the activity his mind was constantly distracted by thoughts of Feen. It was as if she had taken over his mind and had become the central focus of his every thought and physical function. At night, when he awoke from dreams of her, he would find himself with an aching erection. Never in his life had he ever been so profoundly affected by anyone.

He had seen her for the first time at the dinner party he had held for Ehzhu and Etha Dax in his apartment what seemed like years ago. Even then his loins had stirred at the very sight of her. He still remembered it like it was yesterday. The intensity of that first shock of knowledge that she was the one he had never dared to dream of still burned bright. The experience with her on board Ehzhu's ship, no matter how contrived, had confirmed for him that she felt the same way. He had since learned that Ehzhu had purchased her as a captured slave. She had been given the status of junior wife, but was in fact only their sex slave.

He walked across the launch platform and up the steps that led into the Nullax Rover. He had to find a way of freeing her bonds to Ehzhu, he thought. He could try and negotiate, but what could he use as collateral. Ehzhu was a man of expensive taste and had everything Gion could buy, so that was a closed door. He had shown an interest in the alien. Perhaps that might be worth a thought.

As he entered his quarters he was surprised to find Ehzhu's assistant Elmee seated on the couch in his small living room.

'Elmee! To what do I owe the pleasure of your visit?'

'Hello Captain. Please excuse me taking the liberty of meeting you here, but the matter is of a delicate nature and I thought this would be more appropriate.'

'Oh…?'

'Yes.' Elmee stood up from the couch and walked across the room. She handed him a letter. 'I have been asked in confidence to pass this letter on to you and await your reply.'

Captain Masters took the letter and opened it. His hand shook slightly when he saw who it was from. The colour in his face changed to a bright red and the skin glowed with heat. When he had finished reading, he looked up at her. 'I will find a way to meet with her. Perhaps we could organise a pre-departure briefing on Ehzhu's ship or something.' His expression was hopeful.

'You realise of course that if Ehzhu finds out, he will slaughter her like an animal and feed her flesh to the crew like it was a delicacy. His possessions are not to be trifled with, you see.'

'I see. I had no idea he was that sort of man.'

'There is a lot about Ehzhu you don't know.'

'What is your interest in this scenario then? You are Ehzhu's assistant, so how do I trust you in this matter?'

'Uli and Ehzhu have inflicted great cruelties on Feen and have forced her to do the most demeaning things. I too am one of Ehzhu's possessions and have endured his…treatments. Feen is like a daughter to me and has cried on my shoulder many times. I am totally committed to her well being.'

'Then why put her in such danger by encouraging this meeting?'

'From the first day she met you she has loved you. I have tried to dissuade her, but her heart is set on you. This puts her in even more peril as it has become so much harder for her to endure Ehzhu's treatment. A chance at life with you or maybe a quick death is preferable to a long slow wasting insanity. She believes that you have the courage to negotiate her freedom. Do you think you can do it?'

'I was thinking those very thoughts when I walked in here. The idea of her being a slave sickens me. Now that I know that her conditions are life threatening I will do everything I can to secure her freedom.'

'I am pleased to hear that. What else shall I tell her?'

'Tell her that…I am filled with joy and am impatient for our next meeting. She must be strong. I will be with her soon.'

Elmee's black face split into a white toothed smile. Her features became soft and feminine as she turned her hard muscled body and left the room. Captain Masters poured a drink at his small desk and swallowed it down in one gulp. He poured another and sipped it while he paced across the room repeatedly. All thoughts of the imminent departure to Moeba were banished from his mind as he thought of a plan to free Feen…

Shay Duncan felt as if he was falling. His body felt weightless and numb. He heard subdued voices, but couldn't make out what they were saying or who they were. He opened his eyes to what at first seemed like dimmed lights, but upon looking around he found himself suspended in an anti gravity tank. There was a gravity assisted IV drip in his left arm with the tube exiting the tank above him. The only sound inside the tank was the slight hiss of oxygen as it flowed through. It was not a big tank, nothing like the one on the bridge of Coda's ship. It was more like an elongated egg with about three feet of space all around him.

He lay on a body contoured brace that was strapped to his waist and legs to prevent movement except for his arms and head. The brace was connected to the tank with thin metal cables to prevent him from floating around. He looked down his body and noticed the excretion catheters that ran down to the external evacuation pump which deposited the contents into a holding tank. The indignity of it, he thought. Fortunately he was covered with a light wrap around-sheet. In his left peripheral vision he saw someone approach him.

'Shay…?' The internal speaker crackled to life.

'Huh?' he croaked.

'Ah…it's Erick here. How are you feeling?'

'Numb…thirsty.'

'If you turn your head to the right you'll find the water tube.' As Shay put the tube in his mouth and sucked in a mouthful of water, Professor Astor continued. 'We've put you in the antigravity tank as it will be the least stressful on your back while we do the teleport jump back to Moeba. On Moeba you will get the treatment you need, but for now you have been stabilised. With the medication we have given you, you will feel no pain, that's why you feel so numb.'

'What's the diagnosis, Professor?'

'Your right ankle was crushed and twisted and both knees have torn ligaments with the left kneecap also split in two. The worst damage however is the spinal cord which is severed between the first and second lumber vertebrae. Now…with nanobot surgery all of your injuries can be repaired, but the body still has to go through its own healing process which will take some time.'

'How much time…?'

'Well, the recovery period is a lot quicker than it used to be and with good physiotherapy you should be on your feet within about six months, but it will be maybe another six months of hard work before you will be able to walk reasonably well. That's all I can tell you for now. Your surgeon on Moeba will monitor the situation as you go along. However, we have had a high success rate with nanobot surgery for conditions like yours.'

Shay turned his head towards the Professor and stared at him for the longest minute, letting the shock of it sink in. He wasn't keen on tiny robots crawling around inside him, but that seemed to be the most effective treatment. After that it would be maybe a full year before he could function and then maybe another year or two before he could fly again. All this, just when things were going so well with him and Monica. Monica…how would she take this? In his heart he knew that she cared for him, but how much? They had not made any long term commitment to each other. Was it even reasonable to expect her to have any future plans with him now that he would be an invalid, even if it was only for two or three years. If she stayed on Moeba to be near him that would be long enough to disrupt her career. Aah…he had to stop thinking like this, he thought. You have to take the positive route, get a handle on it and shorten the time it would take to full recovery, he thought, that's the only way.

'Piece of cake Professor. I'll be on my feet in no time then.' He smiled.

'That's my man. You keep thinking like that and you'll be flying sooner than you think!'

●

Feen screamed and sobbed in agony and fear as Ehzhu violently pummelled her anus from behind with his giant priapus. Her hands were tied to a post and her bent knees were strapped to two chairs spaced apart to expose her. The full weight of Ehzhu's stinking sweating body was behind each painful thrust. Uli had a handful of her beautiful red hair. Pulling her head back and twisting her neck she spoke hoarsely into her ear. 'Scream honey, he loves it that way.' She straightened up and hit her as hard as she could with the strap across her back. A fresh scream erupted from Feen as the tip of the strap curled around and bit into the side of her breast. 'Louder!' Uli shouted and brought the strap down again. As Feen screamed and sobbed she could see that Ehzhu was getting more excited. Uli's sense of power over Ehzhu expanded and she laid into Feen with renewed sadistic vigour. The more she beat Feen the more frantic and powerful Ehzhu thrust into her. Uli did not let go of Feen's hair as she hysterically screamed at Feen and drew blood from the brutal cuts of the strap. As Feen lost consciousness, Ehzhu's phallus began to convulse and he grabbed Uli by the neck. He withdrew his penis and forced her head down to it. She knew what to do, she let go of the strap and cupped his testicles with her hand. As she opened her mouth to fill it with the angry head she felt his balls retract and the powerful muscle convulse. She moaned with pleasure and guzzled hungrily on his acidic semen as it spasmodically spat onto her face and in her mouth.

As Ehzhu's breathing slowed and he regained his composure, he disdainfully shoved Uli aside who chuckled knowingly. She looked up at him with a triumphant gaze, knowing that she had satisfied him for the moment at least. Ehzhu picked up his dressing gown and put it on, his mind already on other things. It always amazed him how clearly he could think after sex.

He left the room without giving Uli or Feen a second glance and went to his study. It had a wonderful view of Upi and its holding planet Onusa through the large observation port next to his desk. He sat down with a sigh and poured himself a drink. As he drank from the silver goblet his eye fell on the book "A Treatise of Manna" which he had purchased from Captain Masters. He reached across the desk and opened it at a random page. Try as he might, he had not been able to decipher the language or the symbols used in it. He would have to find someone who could translate it. Someone he could trust did not exist, so other arrangements would have to be found.

A movement in his peripheral vision made him look out through the observation port and saw the private shuttle of Captain Masters heading towards his ship. Perhaps…just perhaps that's where the answer lay, he thought and smiled an ugly smile.

●

Captain Masters had been kept waiting for over an hour and was irritably pacing back and forth in front of the small reception room's observation port. The magnificent view was completely ignored as he mulled over the problem he faced. He had to find a way to negotiate Feen's freedom and somehow contrive a meeting with her without Ehzhu finding out. The long wait however had left him with a sense of foreboding that something was amiss.

Elmee came through the doorway and nervously looking over her shoulder she strode across the room towards him. 'Captain, you must beware…'

'Elmee!' he exclaimed in surprise and moved towards her. 'What's the matter?'

'Ehzhu has become aware that Feen has a romantic interest in you and is now treating her worse than ever. I think there is a listening device in my quarters. Please, be very careful.'

'Is there still a chance of meeting with her?'

'I'm afraid she is very badly beaten and does not wish for you to see her in this state.'

Captain Master's face went pale and his lips were white with anger. He felt a fury build up in him that he did not know he was capable of. He resolved to make Ehzhu pay for this. One way or another, I will make him pay! he thought. I will find a way to hurt you, Ehzhu, and you will know why.

'Captain,' Elmee interrupted his train of thought. 'You must compose yourself, for Feen's sake. Come, I was sent to bring you to

Ehzhu. I am taking care of her and she will recover, but these episodes will become more frequent, so time is of the essence.' She turned and started for the door. As the Captain followed her out she whispered over her shoulder. 'Keep your wits about you and never forget that Ehzhu is a master at subterfuge.'

When they got to the great doors of Ehzhu's private quarters, Elmee said, 'Good luck Captain,' and knocked on the door. The door opened and they were met by Uli. Her blue skin was aglow and she was smiling having just shared a joke with Ehzhu. She wore a long tight fitting cobalt blue evening gown. Why was the cleavage always low cut and revealing, the Captain thought? And there's that peculiar smell off her again. He was never sure if it was her musk or her perfume, but it always managed to turn his stomach.

'Aah Captain…please come in,' she looked past him and her face hardened. 'You may go Elmee.'

As the Captain entered, the door automatically closed behind them and Uli asked with a knowing smile. 'So Captain, how may we pleasure you this time?' and she chucked derisively.

He ignored the question. 'I have come to speak with Ehzhu.'

'Ah yes of course, business first. He's in his study, this way please.'

She led the way through a cavernous hallway that looked like the inside of a molten copper ball. The walls shimmered with a soft reflected amber glow from lights that seemed to float on either side of the base of the magnificently flared glass staircase. It led up to the next floor with the edges curving inwards and then flaring outwards again at the top. The treads seemed to be suspended in mid air, as if held in place by some energy field. He followed Uli up onto the landing. She turned to the left and walked a short distance. They then took the right hand passage of three that led off of the landing. Even down the passage the walls seemed to shimmer from the soft amber light that floated above them.

The passage took a sharp turn to the left, but Uli walked straight on into what seemed like the wall. When she disappeared through the wall Captain Masters realised it was a holographic barrier and gingerly followed her through. He found himself in a small antechamber. Across from him Uli stood in front of a doorway. She waved her ring across a small panel on the side which turned the force field off that blocked the door. They stepped through and into Ehzhu's study.

Ehzhu had not bothered to change and was still in his deep purple dressing gown. He was deeply engrossed in his book and was chewing noisily on a sweet. He looked up as they entered.

'Captain…' Ehzhu nodded with a quizzical tone. After a moments pause he said. 'Leave us Uli, the Captain and I have things to discuss.' Uli left, still with that smile on her face. Ehzhu picked up another sweet and popped it into his mouth. He sucked noisily on it and looked out of the observation port. 'So Captain, what news from Upi?'

'Well…as you know my Lieutenant has broken his back and we have to get him back to Moeba for treatment. I have come to find out if you wish to teleport with us.'

Ehzhu looked back at him and paused for a moment. 'What of the alien? Is he on his feet yet?'

'Yes. As far as I know he is still in bad shape though.'

'Will Dr.Craven also be returning to Moeba?'

'Yes. He has engagements he has to attend.'

'Heh heh,' Ehzhu chuckled. 'I'm sure he has. How will you teleport the alien and his ship? Towing a ship through space is one thing, but teleportation requires a very different approach.'

'Well, I was wondering if one of your cargo bays had enough room and if you'd be willing to carry his ship back to Moeba?'

Ehzhu's smile was a little too friendly, the Captain thought.

'Bay four is free. Will he be on board his ship?'

'Yes I'm afraid so. Unfortunately he is still in quarantine and has to remain on his ship until we reach Moeba. He will have four sentries with him at all times on a rota basis.'

'Will they be your sentries or mine?'

The Captain knew of Ehzhu's interest in the alien, just maybe… 'Well, that depends.'

'On what?'

'Whether you would consider an exchange.'

'Oh?' Ehzhu's eyes held a knowing incredulousness tainted with humour.

'I understand Feen was purchased as a slave.'

'Aah…so you want Feen do you?' His smile was ugly again. 'I have purchased many wives. Feen happens to be very special to me. What makes you think I will let her go?'

'Because I know of the bounty you will receive for the alien. That should more than compensate for your financial investment.' He hesitated for a moment and then decided to risk all. 'I also want Elmee with her.'

Ehzhu frowned and sat forward with a hard look in his eye. It was at that moment the Captain realised just how dangerous Ehzhu was. 'I am not in the habit of trading my possessions. However, in this instance your proposal is not…unappealing.'

'Does that mean Elmee is released to me as well?'

Ehzhu sat back and considered for a moment. 'Very well. How soon can you deliver?'

'I need 24 hours.' He paused and decided to press on. 'I must see Feen before I return to Moeba.'

'She is…indisposed.'

'I insist!' The Captain was irritable and concerned for Feen. Elmee had said she was in a bad way, but he needed to tell her there was hope.

Ehzhu leaned forward and hissed. 'Seeing her before delivery is not part of the deal!' He stood up and was around the desk in an instant. He grabbed the Captain by the neck with his huge left hand and lifted him out of his chair. He held his face close to the Captain's and said with a foul breath. 'Do not test my generosity, Captain.' His voice was calm and reasonable, but his grip crushing. 'You will have your bitches.' He set the Captain down on his feet and released him. 'Elmee will see you out.' He turned and sat back in his chair. 'You may leave, Captain.'

●

After the Captain left Uli entered the room. 'How did that meddling little man know about the bounty?'

'He is not without his own resources it seems. First I must pay that leech Craven and now lose two of my women as well. This is proving to be a little more costly than what I bargained for.'

Uli was secretly pleased that she would finally be rid of Ehzhu's two favourites. She knew he would let them go of course as the capture of the alien was too important to him. The prestige of avenging his family's misfortunes at the hand of this alien was too good to miss. She thought she might sweeten the deal for him. 'Their condition was not part of the deal, was it?'

'No...it wasn't.' Ehzhu answered thoughtfully while staring at the view through the observation port.

'What are your wishes?' Uli asked again with that knowing smile.

'I think we should give Elmee a fond farewell don't you?'

Uli's smile went askance. 'But you have released her from her matrimonial duties!' she blurted. Uli had always been jealous of Elmee's status and her ability to absorb the treatment Ehzhu loved to inflict. Elmee was also a warrior second to none.

'All the more reason to remind her of who she belongs to.'

'But how will you get her to do as you wish?' Uli was afraid of the power this woman had.

'She will do as she is told if she wants Feen to live. Make the arrangements for after the late meal, but Uli, I know your hatred for her, so make sure she survives. Unfortunately I need the Captain...for the moment, so, remember that Coda is the prize.'

Uli smiled triumphantly...

●

As Captain Masters landed his shuttle in the Nullax Rover's landing bay he had a gnawing sense of foreboding. When he had told Elmee how things had gone with the negotiations and that he had demanded she come too, the colour had drained from her face. When he had asked why, she had said never mind, that she knew what to expect and that she would handle it.

He had not expected Ehzhu to be so reactive and threatening over the issue. Love obviously played no part in his relations with his wives. They were his possessions. Perhaps if he did love them, things could have been a lot worse. Which raised the question, did he, Captain Masters, actually love Feen. He had never loved anyone in his entire life. Did he even understand the concept of love or was it just based on desire. Maybe that's where love begins, he thought. And why did he assume Elmee would even agree to come too. Instinctively he knew that if he didn't get her off that ship, she would be in grave danger. But leaving them there now put them both at severe risk. He had to get the alien and his ship to Ehzhu now if he was to minimise that risk. The trick was to get it past Dr. Craven. To lift the alien craft off the surface of Upi he needed the cargo shuttles that only Dr. Craven could authorise. First he had to check on the alien and his progress.

When he arrived at the alien ship, he found the sentries standing on the walkway above the large reservoir looking down into the water. With the power on, the pumps were doing their work aerating the water through the waterfall under the walkway and channelling it through the ultraviolet filters. They couldn't see Coda all the time as he was effortlessly weaving through the myriad of pipes and the dark recesses at the bottom. Every now and then he would stop and inspect something or open a hatch and punch some buttons as if he was preparing for something.

As Captain Masters leaned over the banister Coda's voice reverberated in his head. 'How strong is your love Captain?'

'What?' The Captain was startled and a little confused.

'How strong is your love for the one you call Feen?'

'Where are you? Show yourself!' The sentries were staring blankly at him as the Captain looked around wildly.

Coda surfaced and continued telepathically. 'Send the sentries away so that we can talk.' After the sentries left, the Captain said. 'Well...I still can't get used to you being in my head.' Coda's silent penetrating gaze scrutinised what felt like his inner being. 'Will you stop that and tell me what it is you want to talk about?'

'Your trepidation of the fat one is justified.' Coda spoke normally and his voice was strong. The Captain was again surprised, expecting a feeble old man's voice, but there was nothing feeble in the warning.

'How do you know...?'

'Your thoughts are loud Captain.' Coda swam to the ladder at the walkway and ascended it. As he stood on the walkway, his long hair twisted into two ropes. They twisted around each other and at the waist, wrapped around like a belt with the sharp hooks and hornlike ends evenly dispersed, hanging freely around his hips. 'Your heart is in the right place, but do not put your trust in the fat one.' The Captain could not believe the change in Coda. In such a short time he had changed from emaciated half-dead to a thin walking swimming old man on stiff legs. He must have some sort of accelerated recovery system, the Captain thought.

'Yes Captain, but I still have some way to go before I'm reasonably fit.' In his loincloth he hobbled back to the bridge and stopped at the table beside the tank. He picked up his raw silk trousers and put them on. He took a can of Moeban fish from one of several containers of canned fish stacked on the table, opened it, and emptied its contents on a plate. He sat down and picked up a second can. 'Excuse my manners Captain, but my appetite has returned with a vengeance. Please…' He indicated the seat opposite him and offered a fresh plate whilst opening the can.

The Captain sat down, but declined the fish. 'What do you know of Ehzhu?'

'Only that his nature is very dark. It is that of the slaver who values no life other than his own.'

The Captain was quiet for a minute and regarded Coda as he ate. He found himself perplexed by this new situation. What had at first seemed like a simple exchange of one alien who had no memory and was probably brain damaged, for two women whose freedom meant so much to him, had become much more complex. The alien was obviously not brain damaged and was recovering rapidly. Here he was sitting opposite him while he ate his meal in a civilised manner. He seemed quite harmless. He knew that Ehzhu had a healthy fear of the alien…

'Yes Captain, he does.' In response to the Captain's reaction, Coda continued, 'I'm not quite sure why yet, but the pieces are slowly falling in place. I know how I got here, but my ship's log does not go back far enough to fill in all the blanks. I would have to read my whole library and rely on the pieces of memory that return. In the meantime I'm compelled to eat and exercise.' Coda continued to eat.

'If you can read my mind then you know why I'm here.'

'Yes Captain, which brings me back to my first question; how strong is your love for the one you call Feen?'

'I don't see how my feelings for her have anything to do with you?'

'I ask this question because it has everything to do with her.' Alarm registered on the Captain's face. 'You see Captain: the damage she has sustained will change her. Physically she will eventually recover, but mentally she is very…fragile. The one you call Elmee is made of stronger stuff.'

The Captain's face turned pale. 'I'll kill the bastard for this.'

'He will not kill so easily Captain.'

'You know that you are the trade off.'

'Yes and I'll go willingly under my conditions.'

'Oh? And what makes you think that I'll entertain any of your conditions.'

'My memory may be faulty Captain, but the one thing I am very sure of is my hatred towards slavers. Perhaps we can achieve our goals together.'

The Captain thought about it for several minutes as Coda continued to eat. Perhaps he was right, this alien. He could easily have his men put him in confinement and forcefully transfer him, or he could simply give him what he wanted, thereby acquiring a willing accomplice. If what he says is true about Ehzhu then he would need all the help he could get. Let's see what he wants, he thought.

'What are your conditions?'

'Here is a list of parts I need for repairs to my ship. I also want my weapons back and several months supply of this fish.'

The Captain looked the list over. 'I can get you the fish and your weapons, but I don't know if I can get you all these parts. I'll do what I can.'

'Then we have a deal Captain.'

As the Captain stood up Coda got up. 'You may call me Coda, Captain.'

'Coda.' The Captain said and left.

Monica was restless and irritable. She had not anticipated the impact Shay's injuries would have on her emotions. The last time they had made love she had felt her barriers torn down and then when she got the news of his dreadful condition, it had left her feeling as if she had been imprisoned in a cage of vulnerability and uncertainty. She had been sitting with Shay for the past hour keeping him company and making sure he was comfortable. As the conversation wound down and Shay started to drift off into sleep, Monica stood up.

'I think you should get some rest while I go and check on our other patient.'

'Yes…' and Shay slept.

Monica stood for a moment and looked at him through the glass, surprised at the strength of her feelings for him. Right there, standing next to his antigravity tank, she decided that she would stay with him throughout his recovery. Her career could take second place. Perhaps she could teach or do consultancy work; whatever it took, she would stand by him. She turned and made her way to Coda's ship, the Awa Na Tahu.

When she arrived on the bridge she could not find Coda anywhere. The sentries weren't there either and the place was quiet. On the table was a large cylindrical device with several of its access panels opened. Surrounding it was several burnt-out looms of optic and gold fibre with an array of tools she did not recognise. Patched into a bay inside one of the opened access ports, was a long cable that led to the base of the battle station. Then she noticed the battle station was completely enclosed by its full surround three dimensional screen. As she approached it, the screen separated into sections that retracted into the base of the battle station seat upon which Coda sat. She stopped abruptly and stared in astonishment at him.

The power emanating from Coda washed over her like a warm breeze. She could not believe how much he had filled out in such a short time. He looked infinitely stronger and with the target specs on his face, he had a palpable sense of detached menace. For the first time she felt a sense of trepidation towards him, but intuitively she knew she was safe with him.

Coda took the target specs off and his eyes were kind. 'From our first contact you have had my unconditional loyalty.' He lifted his feet off the footplates and stood up. 'That will not change.' Monica was still speechless as she marvelled at how fluid his movements had become and how strong his voice sounded. As he walked across to the table she saw that he was still slightly stiff-legged and stooped, but nothing like before.

'How have you done it?' she blurted as she found her wits.

'It seems that my recovery system is accelerated.'

'But...your body...It's only been seventy two hours. It defies all precedent. I have never come across or heard of such a fantastically fast recovery. How is your memory coming along?'

Coda picked up a tool and continued working on the replacement cables. 'I know this ship and everything in it. Some of its core systems were damaged by the meteor strike, but the good Captain has provided me with the spare parts I need to get it up and running again.'

'Now I am even more surprised. The Captain is not known for his generosity.'

'We have come to an…arrangement.'

Monica's curiosity burned bright as Coda continued to work in silence. Whatever the arrangement was, Coda seemed content with it and she sensed it would be better not to ask.

'I am sure the Professor will want to know of your recovery.' She touched the tiny mike on her collar and called Professor Astor. When they had finished their brief conversation Coda walked back to the battle station seat. As he sat down, the surround screen deployed and closed around him. Suddenly, with a slight vibration, the cylinder on the table hummed to life. As Coda tested some functions the pitch of the hum changed several times. The hum stopped. The screen opened and retracted back into the base. Coda got up and went back to the table.

He picked up a can of fish. 'Would you care to join me for a bite of your Moeban fish?'

Monica smiled. 'I don't mind if I do.'

Coda cleared the tools from a corner of the table and they sat down. 'This fish has a good texture and taste, what do you call it?'

'Wikopi fish. It's named after the Wikopi desert which once was a sea. Once a year they gather in massive shoals to mate. That's when the fishermen catch their quota for the fish markets and the canning factories.'

Coda handed her a plate of fish. 'According to my log files Moeba is a desert planet.'

'Yes, but we have large underground reservoirs that provide our water supply which is replenished by ice harvesting off world. Of course, the fish in these lakes offer a ready supply of protein.'

'Tell me more about your planet.'

'Well, it's mostly uninhabitable except at two latitudes. One above the equator and one below it. Even then, we have to live in glass-covered valleys because we have nine months of dust storms that choke everything. It gets quite cold during the storms. When the season is over we can venture out, but the sun can get very hot towards the equator. Further north and south we have ice caps where it is too cold for most …' she stopped abruptly as Professor Astor wheeled in on his motorised wheelchair.

'My word!' he exclaimed. 'What an extraordinary transformation.' He was flushed with excitement. 'Would you have any objection to letting us monitor your further recovery with the scanners?'

'I have no objection, but first we should eat.' He opened another can and put some in a plate for the Professor. 'Then I have much to do.'

'Yes, I can see.' The professor said as he and Monica poked politely at the fish. 'So tell me, how are you feeling? How are your joints? And how is it that you can recover so fast?'

'I do not know, other than that it feels normal to me. I cannot stop eating either. Once I have had my fill, it takes only a short time before I must eat again...'

●

Ehzhu slumped back into the couch gasping for breath like a winded animal. His great penis lay flaccid between his fat thighs. 'The bitch won't let me in!' he shouted, frustrated and angry. Elmee had kept her buttocks clenched to keep him out. As much as he had beaten her, he could not get in and had finally gone soft. After that he could not get it up. All the acts that usually turned him on, just didn't work. Uli was equally out of breath. The strap and the rod had done nothing. Elmee, cruelly tied to a bench, was as hard as stone. The only sign that there had been any effect was that she was sweating.

'Let me use the rool.' Uli said in a harsh voice.

Ehzhu was of two minds. He needed satisfaction, but if he gave her the rool Elmee would be ripped to pieces. He didn't often use the rool as it was a particularly cruel whip with sharp metal studs knotted into the five thongs which were of varying lengths. He only ever used it if he wanted to kill someone in the most painful way. Did Elmee deserve such cruelty or did he deserve satisfaction? Uli he knew would be ecstatic and perhaps the sight of blood would make the difference. The mere thought of it made his penis pulse with renewed vigour.

'Twenty lashes, that's all!' he said as Uli started to protest.

Uli dug the rool out from the box behind her. As she lifted it out, its metal studs tapped against each other with a dull solid sound. Elmee began to moan with fear as Uli reached back with the rool.

'One!' Ehzhu called and with all her might Uli laid the lash across Elmee's back. With a sickening sound the thongs struck and its metal studs broke the skin. They sank into her flesh and as Uli pulled the rool away skin and bits of flesh tore away. Elmee screamed in agony and Ehzhu's penis got harder.

'Two.' Ehzhu called and watched the blood start to flow as the rool ripped into her. By the tenth blow she started to babble incoherently. By the fifteenth blow her bladder released and she went quiet. He continued to call out the numbers and watched Uli's face flush with exhilaration as the blood spattered on her face and arms. He watched her aggressive stance and the way her breasts moved with each blow she inflicted. She was naked except for her black flat-soled thigh length boots attached to a belted bodice that strapped around her waist and cupped her breasts. Her short silver hair was offset by her now dark blue flushed skin. Ehzhu's priapus was so hard he feared it might break off; he was so filled with lust for Uli. He had not touched her for a long time, but seeing her this way made him want her like the first time he had seen her beating her maid to death.

He stood up as he finished the count and walked up to her. As she reached back to deliver another blow, he hit her between the shoulder blades, lifting her off her feet. She landed across Elmee's ruined back. Before she could recover he pinned her down and violently entered her. His thrusts were vicious and deep. Uli screamed and laughed with joy as she tasted the blood of her hated Elmee…

Coda went suddenly quiet. Their conversation had been friendly and animated, but had come to an abrupt silence. Coda had an inward expression, his eyes unseeing. Monica and the professor both heard his thoughts. Our time has run out…they heard.

'What do you mean?' the Professor asked.

'Tell the Captain…the strong one will die if we do not make haste. Go quickly…' He stood up. 'I must finish my work.' He took up the hoist chain and attached its hook to the ring on the top of the cylinder on the table. As he detached the cable and closed the access panels, Monica activated the comlink and hailed the Captain.

'He is on his way here.' She said.

'Good,' Coda said. He walked around the table and lifted a floor panel next to the battle station. The cavity below was filled with water. He walked back to the table and hoisted the cylinder up. He wheeled it across to the open floor panel and lowered it into the water. He took hold of the chain and submerged himself into the water. He then guided the cylinder into place under the battle station and twisted its connectors. Trapped air escaped with a bubbling hiss as the internal cables attached with a magnetic click to the rest of the system. Coda detached the chain and pulled himself up out of the water and on to the dry floor. The Captain, flushed and anxious, was standing in front of him.

'What's going on?'

'The strong one will die if we don't assist her immediately.'

'But...how do we get your ship off Upi? I don't have all the shuttles in place yet.'

'If you will permit me Captain, I would try and start my ship's engines. Perhaps we could travel independently.'

'Yes, of course.' The Captain stepped back.

Coda walked past him and went to the console. He typed in the start up data and started the sequence. He turned and walked back to the battle station seat and sat down. The surround screen activated and enclosed him. The Captain, Monica and the Professor stared in silent anticipation at the grey ball that contained Coda, straining their ears for any sound that might indicate life in the engines. Suddenly there was a hum accompanied by a slight vibration. The surround screen opened up, retracted back into the base and Coda stepped out. He walked over to the wooden panels on the starboard side, opened the one that had the slave power cable running to it and detached it. As he did so the ambiance of the room changed subtly. The lights dimmed down to a warmer amber glow. The ball tank in the centre of the room lit up as the touch screen glass came alive with its control panels.

'How do you know that Elmee is in danger?' the Captain asked as he came to his senses.

'I have felt his thoughts...they are...vindictive and I have seen his visions and the one you call Elmee has taken severe punishment. She will die if we do not make haste.'

'And Feen, has she been hurt?'

'She has...changed.'

'What do you mean, "changed"?'

'Physically she will recover, but emotionally she will need time.'

'What has that bastard done?' The Captain's anxiety was etched in his expression. His eyes were bright with alarm and fury as he bellowed his frustration. Frustrated because he knew that there was little he could do. Ehzhu was needed by the Moeban government for his political connections to help improve the trade agreement with the Sabalian realm. If he interfered with that, the consequences for him would be unthinkable.

'Concentrate on your women, Captain. You have made the correct choice. Leave the fat one to me. I have a feeling that we have…unfinished business.' Coda had walked up to the side of the tank where he touched the glass with his thumb. A small bar of light scanned his thumb. A doorway slid open and instead of the water gushing out, it seemed to be held back by an invisible energy field. Coda stepped into the tank and the door slid shut.

'My ship will be ready within the hour Captain,' the Captain heard inside his head. 'Could you have your men remove all of your equipment while I finalise my preparations?'

'Yes…Monica,' the Captain said as he started to leave the bridge. 'Will you head up a medical team on board my shuttle?' She spontaneously agreed, despite all the abuse she had suffered under him. That he was undergoing a profound change was plain to see and she followed him.

After they left, the Professor manoeuvred his motorised chair closer to the tank. 'I have never seen water held back like that before.'

'There are many different technologies on board this ship that stem from numerous different galaxies and universes.' Coda answered telepathically from inside the tank, while checking through the ships systems. 'My ship is a unique creation and its secrets are…enigmatic. It is a robust organism that has evolved over time.'

'Did you build it yourself?'

Coda stopped what he was doing and looked at the Professor for a moment before answering. 'I don't know.' He continued working on the panels. 'I know that I did do some work. Much of it feels too familiar for it not to have been done by myself. Then again…with my memory as faulty as it is, I can't be sure.'

The Professor was trying to jog his memory; bring back pictures or feelings that might trigger some recollection. 'When you move about the ship, do you have any pictures that occur in you mind?'

'I have…fragments. I sometimes see myself working with fire or wood. When I'm in the reservoir I keep looking for the fish.'

'Oh yes, we found thousands of dead and frozen fish. Were they your food source?'

'Yes, they were and one in particular was my friend.'

'Aah…you must be referring to the shoal hound. That's fascinating. I have only come across them in myths and legends. If this is indeed the shoal hound of myth then I'd really like to know everything about it.'

Coda was quiet for a moment before he answered. 'His name was YutZho Phehak. They mate for life you know and when he lost his family he became rogue to his enemies. We became friends after an intense battle with those enemies. He was a marvellously intelligent and loyal being with whom I could have long discussions and debates. I will miss him.'

'Are you saying that he was a conscious being?' The Professor was incredulous.

'We communicated on a telepathic level and yes, he was conscious, more than most.'

'I am astounded. I have never heard of such a thing.' The Professor was perplexed. In all his years of scientific and anthropological research he had never come across anything like this. A fish that could communicate and have a debate on a telepathic level!

'Yes Professor. He was much more than just a friend. He would often monitor these systems when I was busy with other things. He loved to see the places we travelled.' Coda pressed the pad at the door. It slid open and he stepped out of the tank. He walked over to the wooden cabinets and opened one of the compartments.

'He loved the thrill of battle and knew this ship as well as I did.' He took his leather leggings that had been returned to him and returned to the still opened tank door. He dipped them through the energy field into the water, then took them out and placed them on the table. He pressed the holographic pad beside the door and it slid shut. As he took his silk trousers off and put his wet leggings on, he continued. 'You see…eventually I didn't see the fish, only the being he was.'

He attached the top of the leggings to the hip rings on the belt of his loincloth and let the front and rear flaps of the loincloth fall in place. He buttoned up the webbing at the front and back. He then pulled the straps over his shoulders that ran from the small of his back and hooked them onto the ring behind the conch shell at his navel. As the webbing over his hips pulled tight, the leather thongs attached to them fell in place around his waist.

Professor Astor watched in silent awe at Coda's transformation into the warrior he was. The wet leggings would shrink to a more snug fit as they dried. Coda walked back to the cabinets and opening a different compartment, took out the two swords. He tested their weight and then slipped them into their sheaths on his back, which were part of the shoulder straps. He picked up the two fighting knives and continued as he slipped them into their sheaths sown into the outer thighs of his leggings. 'YutZho Phehak had lived many lives and had fought many battles.' He put the armguards with their metal bolts on his forearms. 'He remembered them all you know…his lives I mean.' He lifted the two needle-like blades with their stone handles and put them into place in the outer sheaths of his lower leggings. 'In many ways he had become my battle mentor. He always knew the way to defeat an enemy.'

He put his space boots on and put the throwing knives in place on the inside of the armguards. 'Now that he has died in the Moeban Universe, he becomes part of the fabric of this space. He has escaped Uroha and has joined with the energy of Moeba. Perhaps we will meet again.' Coda took his coat and put it on. His long hair lifted out and twisted into a tight braid that cascaded down his back. The handles of his swords fitted neatly through two slits of the Siux eel skin sown on so long ago. 'This was my father's coat. I have changed it over time, but the siux skin has proven eternal.'

The men sent by the Captain arrived and removed all the Nullax Rover's equipment from the bridge. The Professor was speechless as he looked at Coda whose nine foot six frame stood straight and powerful. He looked in peak physical condition, and for the first time, the Professor felt a little fear. Just how dangerous is this man? The Professor thought.

'You have nothing to fear,' he heard inside his head as Coda smiled at him. 'Tell the Captain I am ready for the fat one.'

Feen was distraught. Elmee had been dumped onto her cabin floor unconscious and bleeding from her wounds. She had no idea what to do apart from what her intuition guided her to do. She knew she had to try and staunch the bleeding. The only thing she could think of was her towels. She folded them into wads and wrapped them tightly over those terrible wounds with strips of her clothing.

Elmee had slipped in and out of consciousness groaning with pain and had asked for water. She was unconscious again, breathing shallow breaths. Tears were streaming down Feen's cheeks as she stared at Elmee's ashen face. The deep lustre of her black skin was gone. It looked dry and dull with a greyness around the corners of her mouth. She felt as if her heart was going to break. The only person who really cared for her had been brutally beaten and could die and she was helpless to do anything about it. Her own bruised and battered body was nothing compared to what they had done to Elmee. She would rather die than live without her. She did not know what would happen if the Captain did not come soon. Would Ehzhu even keep his
word and let them go?

That question would be answered soon she thought as she looked through her tiny port hole and saw the Captain's shuttle towing Coda's ship. Not far behind was The Nullax Rover. Would the Captain still want her now that she was damaged goods? The thought of being with another man sent shivers down her spine. She was in love with the Captain, but since the last session with Ehzhu she was fearful. Fearful of what men could do. They weren't all like Ehzhu were they? The Captain didn't seem cruel. Maybe he could be, but would he be cruel to her? Would he be patient with her? So many questions she thought.

She looked at Elmee and her eyes were open. 'The Captain is on his way. I can see his shuttle through the porthole.'

With great effort Elmee sat up. 'We must prepare to go.'

'Do you really think Ehzhu will let us go?'

'He has no further use for us.' Elmee was weak and lethargic. She reached for the glass of water and Feen hurriedly picked it up and passed it to her.

As Elmee drank the water Feen stood up and went to the small kitchen alcove. She warmed up a bowl of soup she had prepared earlier and brought it to Elmee. 'Please try to eat something, you might feel better.' Elmee accepted. She was too weak to control the spoon as her hands were shaking with the effort, so she drank slowly from the bowl.

Feen smiled with relief and went about sorting through their meagre belongings. She packed a small bag with what she thought they might need and a few things they wanted to keep. She didn't care for the clothing Ehzhu had made her wear and chose only an outfit she wore in her own private time. Elmee had very little, so she decided on the two most comfortable and loose fitting outfits she had. When Elmee had finished her soup she helped her dress and then they waited.

●

The great docking bay door opened like the maw of a giant monster. Captain Masters was anxious. If what Coda had said was true then he must prepare himself for a shock. He had done many things in his life, but falling in love had not been one of them. For the first time he had a real sense of caring for someone else. What had Coda meant when he said that Feen would recover physically, but emotionally she would need more time? How badly has she been hurt? What has that bastard done to her? And Elmee? What of her? Were her injuries really life threatening? She was such a strong and powerful woman. What could have caused her to sustain possible mortal injuries? Ehzhu...that bastard, he thought. Perhaps Coda will give him what he deserves.

The Captain guided the shuttle into the docking bay and towed the Awa Na Tahu in behind it. He hit the release on the tow cables and retracted them into their hubs. He then manoeuvred the shuttle into place beside the Awa Na Tahu. The bay door closed behind them and the massive docking area was re-oxygenated and pressurised. Both craft touched down onto the floor as the gravity drive was activated. The Captain kept the shuttle's engine running as he and Monica disembarked. Four of her medical team were in tow with two wheeled stretchers between them.

As the Captain turned towards the control booth, the loading bay doors opened and a hundred armed military clones rushed through and surrounded the docking bay. They were Ehzhu's cold, deadly personal guard especially bred for the task. The Captain could see Ehzhu behind the control booth window. To his surprise he saw Dr. Craven standing next to him. Craven...the opportunistic leech, he thought. May his fate be tied to Ehzhu then.

'What is the meaning of this?!'

Ehzhu's silken voice snaked through the speakers in the bay. 'So Captain...Where is the alien?'

Before the Captain could answer, the bridge observation shield of Coda's ship opened. They could all see him in the large observation port standing tall and strong. Over the speakers there was an audible intake of breath from Ehzhu who had not seen Coda since he was fragile and half dead in his tank. Even the military clones seemed to waver at the power that pulsed off of Coda. The Captain smiled inwardly, let them try and deal with that, he thought.

'Where are they?!' the Captain demanded.

'Well…I suppose you have honoured your side of the deal…' Ehzhu motioned to some unseen person on his right.

From the dark recess of the loading bay there was the sound of a door opening then a sharp feminine cry of alarm. The door slammed shut and then there was silence. The Captain motioned to Monica and strode ahead of her up the ramp that led onto the loading platform. The two women emerged with Feen supporting Elmee, who would not have been able to walk at all, but for her great strength. Her ashen face showed determined resolve to show no pain, but she held on to Feen's left arm. Feen carried their small bundle of belongings in her right hand and looked worriedly from Elmee towards the ramp. Her eyes lit with hope and love as she saw the Captain…

●

Coda watched the women walk into the light. As he saw Elmee there was a pressure at the edge of his mind. Something, some memory was pushing hard to come through. He focused on her and tried to think what it was. He saw the Captain embrace Feen and then Monica lay them down on the stretchers. He kept wondering what it was about Elmee that kept his focus. He looked up at Ehzhu in the control booth. Did it have something to do with the fat one? He looked at the military clones and wondered if it was a combination of these things.

Then he remembered. It was the colour of her skin. That realisation began a cascade of memories. With it came a flood of emotions: a torrent that seemed to fill him with love, joy, sorrow, pain and then hate. A hatred that turned to fury and then there was a sound. Like a crack coupled with a catharsis. Like a dam that released its water, the fury was suddenly gone. What was left was control. White hot control. A knowing that spanned the multiverse was his. He could feel the power flow through him, expanding his consciousness, and making him at one with everything. He was becoming whole again. He looked at Elmee as she was wheeled into the shuttle and remembered his longest and most trusted friend…Remco…

3493 years earlier
XN5, Northern Deep Institute, Sabalian Realm

As the blows rained down on him, the little brown skinned boy squirmed and crawled as fast as he could. The older boys were lined up between the beds of the large dormitory room, with their feet apart forming a tunnel through which all the new boys had to pass. Each of the older boys took his turn to land as many blows as he could with his belt.

Remco was much quicker than they had expected. Very few blows landed on him until he got to the last boy who caught him between his legs and viciously laid into him laughing almost hysterically. Remco, although small, was stronger than he looked. He pushed and wiggled until he finally shot through. He crawled into a corner of the room and sat with his back to the wall, holding back his tears with stoic determination.

The boy who had beaten him turned and with a slack jawed smile that never reached his eyes said, 'Shame…did you think you would get away?' and ended with an effeminate chuckle that sent a shiver down Remco's spine. He was quite tall and beautifully formed with blond hair and blue eyes, but there was no mistaking the menace of him.

The next boy, whose turn it was, was an aqua boy, but he was not like any aqua boy Remco had seen before. He had hair on his head, unlike the others and his skin was almost without any pigmentation. He was dressed only in a pair of black shorts so everyone could see his gills between his ribs. The interesting thing was that he did not seem afraid. He looked composed and relaxed. With a suddenness that took them all by surprise he ran at them. As he went through the legs of each boy he knocked them off balance or hit them on the back or inside of the knees. They all toppled until he came to the last boy who was ready for him. He trapped the aqua boy with his knees and reached back with the belt in his right hand. As he brought the belt down, the aqua boy bit into his Achilles tendon. The blond boy howled in agony, paralysed by the intensity of it. He released the aqua boy who let go and stood next to Remco. Remco stood up and looked at the boys lying in an untidy heap. He smiled. 'Wow! You sure showed them.' Forgetting the pain from the blows he continued. 'I'm Remco.'

'Coda.'

As the boys stood up, some surrounded the howling blond boy. 'Valdas, what happened?' they asked.

Valdas was sitting on the floor holding his right leg, his face contorted with pain. 'The aqua boy…he bit me. Call Master Cubal. He'll fix him. He'll fix him real good.' One of the boys ran out the door while the others moved towards Coda and Remco. 'So…' one of the boys said. 'What do we have here…fish boy and sewer boy?' A chorus of derisive chuckles sounded from the group. 'Don't they just make a fine pair?'

'Why do you hit us?' Remco asked innocently.

Valdas limped through the group. 'So you know your place sewer boy.'

'I'm not sewer boy, my name is Remco.'

Valdas back-handed him hard across the mouth. 'Shut your mouth you septic little turd. I don't care what your name is…sewer boy.' He looked at Coda but kept his distance. 'You will pay for what you did. I will make sure you do.'

Coda thumbed a bit of blood from the corner of his mouth and deliberately licked the blood off. 'Valdas tastes real good.' And he smiled.

'What's going on here?' Master Cubal asked as he walked into the room. All the boys started talking at once, trying to give their version of accounts. 'Quiet!' They all froze and looked at him expectantly. 'Valdas…you and the fish boy, to my quarters at once. The rest of you, get to bed. You have an early start in the morning.'

●

In the master's quarters, Coda watched as Master Cubal tenderly cleansed and dressed Valdas's wound. His hands caressed as Valdas looked on with a knowing smile. Master Cubal looked up at Coda and the adoring expression in his eyes changed to malice. His blue Sabalian skin was flushed dark with emotion.

'So fish boy. You have only just arrived and you are starting to make trouble already. Bala was right to send you here. That independent streak needs to be straightened out. So…starting tomorrow, for the rest of the year, you will carry poor Valdas's bags to and from the mining college every day. You will make his bed every morning and you will wash his clothes every week. In addition you and that sewer boy will clean the washroom and toilets every night before bed. If you don't, you can expect…more severe punishments. Go back to your bed and sleep well. This may very well be your last good rest.' And he and Valdas chuckled with derisive mirth.

Coda left the room and stood in the empty corridor for a moment. He missed his father. He would have known what to do. And the thought of his mother, forced to live with Bala, brought a tight ball in his throat that suffocated and squeezed. As the pain of it bit he swallowed hard until it went away. His eyes were watery with sorrow and anger. Yes, that was it, he thought, anger. The angrier he got the stronger he felt. Why did Bala kill his father and why did he have to be so cruel to his mother? Why did he have to be sent to this place?

He turned and walked barefoot down the cold dark corridor. He did not feel the cold as he thought of what his father might have done. What had he done in the past? He had escaped. Escape. Could he get away from this place? And if he did, where would he go? He was only seven. How would he live? When he got to the dorm room, he stood in the doorway and looked down the central passage formed by the two rows of beds. On the opposite end of the long room there was a tall window that reached up to the roof. He walked to the window and looked out over the mine fields of Northern Deep. There was a field of grey and black slag heaps. Most were topped with ice and beyond that were the ice flats. Would he ever see Chi'Dorolam and Zizi again? What of Raman and Merrix? For the first time he felt alone. He looked up at the stars and wondered what was out there. There must be better places than this. One day he would go. He will go further than anyone else has been. But, first he must find a way to get away from here. He thought about it for some time, staring out over the mine fields. The whole building was locked, so he went to his bed and resolved to wait until the right opportunity came along. He lay awake for a long time, thinking of his mother and did not remember when he fell asleep.

A whisper, then a repressed snigger. Someone shook his foot and as Coda opened his eyes from a dreamless sleep, a bucket of ice cold water hit him in the face. He sat up gasping and shaking with the shock of it. Gales of laughter rippled from the four boys standing behind Valdas who smirked with the bucket in his hands. 'Nothing like a good dip in the morning hey fish boy?' Coda was drenched, but quickly regained his composure. Valdas's eyes turned hard. 'Get up and make my bed slime ball.' The other boys dispersed, chuckling amongst themselves and re-enacting the look on Coda's face when the water was thrown at him.

Coda got out of bed and wiped the water from his face. He went to Valdas's bed and started to straighten the covers. He noticed that it had not been slept in, but only disturbed to make it look like it had. Valdas was watching him and suddenly burst out with. 'Not like that fish boy, like this!' and he showed him how. Then he pulled the blankets off. 'Now do it again and you better get it right this time.' Coda picked up the blankets and started over. Coda had already learned that to confront Valdas openly at this point would bring down the wrath of his followers and that of Master Cubal. He would bide his time and take the opportunities as they presented themselves.

Valdas seemed satisfied. He went to the locker beside his bed and took out his toiletries. 'When you are finished I want you to tidy up these shelves and put these clothes out on the bed for me. When you have done that you can then get on with whatever it is you do. Just remember that you have to carry my bag to college after morning meal. You'll find it outside the study hall.' He turned and limped off to the showers. Coda smiled inwardly and thought; may that limp be a constant reminder to you, hey…bum boy…

Coda picked up the bag and it was heavy, much heavier than he had imagined. What was in it, he thought? He was taller than most boys of seven, but he had not yet built a lot of strength. He lifted the bag with his right hand and as he walked it knocked against his leg, tripping him up and causing him to stumble. Suddenly Remco was beside him. He did not say anything as he took hold of one of the handles and helped Coda carry the bag.

They struggled along the three mile path that wound through the slag heaps and the back of the reduction plant. The heat from its furnaces had melted the ice and the side of the slag heap. It had created a field of sticky clay and the path led through the centre of it. They stopped and stared. All the other new boys had to tread the same path and most of them were covered in the black clay by the time they reached the other side.

'How do we get over that?' Remco asked.

Coda looked around for a moment. On a hunch he said. 'Let's see what's in the bag. Maybe we can lighten it.' He knew he was looking for trouble, but he was curious. They untied the buckles that held the flap down and opened it.

'Rocks!' Remco exclaimed. 'He put rocks in it.'

'Yes…nice flat rocks.' Coda smiled. As the realisation dawned on Remco they both burst out with gales of laughter. Coda lifted one of the half inch thick slabs out of the bag and dropped it onto the wet clay. It landed with a slap. He took out another slab of rock and dropped it about a steps distance in front of the one he had just dropped. They picked up the bag and with Coda leading the way, they made their way across the clay by stepping on the slabs they took from the bag. All the boys behind them crossed on the same stones, laughing and giggling with glee. By the time they got across the bag was much lighter with only a few books and tools in it.

'That will show him.' Remco said animatedly.

When they got close to the mining college Coda found a pile of rock at the bottom of another slag heap that looked very much like the ones they had removed. He stopped and re-filled the bag with new slabs of rock. 'Maybe this way he won't be any the wiser,' he said. 'I'd better carry the bag alone for the rest of the way. No point in you attracting attention to yourself.'

Valdas and his four cronies were waiting for him when he arrived. The look of malice in his eyes changed to surprise when he noticed Coda was not covered in mud. His whole bullying tactic had been based on his bag being covered in clay. Now that it wasn't he was at a bit of a loss, so to save face he said, 'I see you've made light work of it hey fish boy? Well that won't do, will it now?' He spat on the ground. 'Put the bag here.' He pointed at a spot at his feet.

Coda dropped the bag on the spot and as he stepped back Valdas slapped him across the face. 'I didn't say drop the bag here, I said put the bag here. Now pick it up and do it again.' As he bent forward to pick the bag up, Valdas tried to kick him in the face, but Coda was now expecting something like this and side stepped Valdas's foot. Valdas lost his balance and fell over backwards with the momentum of his kick. The sniggers of the young boys behind Coda made Valdas furious.

'Take him!' he said to his cronies, who grabbed Coda's arms and legs. They held him as Valdas began to savagely beat him. As Valdas landed the third blow to Coda's head, a rock hit Valdas on the forehead, cutting a nasty gash above the eyebrow. He twisted away, howling and covering the wound with his hands. He turned back and as he started his rebuke another stone hit him in the stomach that winded him. His four henchmen turned to see who was throwing stones and were hit with a barrage thrown by a group of six young boys with Remco in the forefront. They dropped Coda and ran at the group, but were beaten back with more rocks. Coda ducked under a wild right-handed cross by Valdas and ran towards the group of boys. As soon as they saw Coda was free they ran off with him into the college grounds.

It was an insect. A black one…with red brown colouring on its abdomen and the edges of its wings. Its huge head moved and looked sideways at Coda with disturbing red and yellow eyes. The interruption did not stop it from chewing on the morsel of faeces it held in its large mandibles. Coda was on his hands and knees scrubbing the toilet floor when he saw it. With a shock he sat back. The movement stopped the insect's chewing and as it turned to face Coda it spread its wings which showed bright red under their black leathery cover. It unfurled its six inch long antennae and pointed them at Coda, sniffing the air. Coda could not believe the size of it. It must be four inches long, he thought.

'Remco!' he called. 'Have you ever seen anything like this before?'

Remco popped his head around the neighbouring cubicle wall and took in the scene. He crawled around and sat next to Coda. 'That's a pit fly! Be careful. If he is disturbed he will fly straight at you and squirt foul smelling black stuff all over youuuu!' They both cringed and fell back as the pit fly suddenly lifted off on its red wings and as it flew over them it did just as Remco had said it would.

They were assaulted by a powerful stream of black liquid expunged from the end of its abdomen which splattered on the floor between them. The pit fly landed on the door post and crawled upwards trailing a black line behind it. They escaped the offensive excretion, but were assaulted by the sharp odour of death and detritus.

'Ugh!' Coda exclaimed, holding his nose. 'I've never smelt anything as bad as that before.'

Remco was watching the fly, and also holding his nose. 'My father told me they came with the Sabalian ships. Makes you wonder what other nasties are on Sabal.'

'Well it's the ugliest thing I've ever seen. I think it was probably made by someone who hated the Sabalians.'

'Yeah, get some of their own back.' And they both laughed spontaneously.

Coda dipped his rag in the bucket of water and began washing the stinking mess off the floor. 'Was your father a clone as well?'

'No. He was a construction slave taken from a far away planet by a slave ship. He worked on the South Crater settlement. Mother was a washer woman for the mine house laundry. She was a clone.' Still watching the fly, he continued. 'They hid me away until my father died when he fell off a building they were working on. My mother went mad that day. She said they had killed him and attacked one of the Sabalian guards. Killed him she did. But then they beat her until she died. That's when they found me and sent me here.'

They were quiet for a time, washing the floor, both lost in their own thoughts.

'What about your father?' Remco asked.

'He was an aqua miner here at Northern Deep. When my mother became pregnant, they decided to leave this place for White Mountain.'

'White Mountain! What's it like? I heard it was beautiful.'

'It is. There is a big lake and everyone lives inside the mountain. I was born there, in Raman's cave.'

'Who is Raman?'

'He is a wise man. He taught us many things.'

'So…you are free born. What's it like to be free born?'

'I don't know. I don't think it is different to anybody else. You are also free born, just in a different place.'

'I am free born…' Remco had a distant look in his eyes. A new confidence seemed to grow in him. 'I am free born.' He repeated with a faint hint of a smile.

'Free born my arse!' A voice boomed at the doorway of the cubicle. Valdas stood there with two of his henchmen. 'You will only ever be a slave sewer boy. Now get out of there I need to use the crapper.' As he stepped forward, the pit fly took off from the door post, squirting its foul black ooze onto his face as it landed on his groomed blond hair.

Valdas's eyes opened wide with horror and he squealed like a girl. He slapped spasmodically at the fly and gagged at the stench. His cronies giggled and fled to get away from the hapless insect while Coda and Remco collapsed in gales of laughter. They stood up and ran past Valdas who shouted after them, 'I'll get you for this you little turds…I'll get you!'

●

Coda lifted the flat rock from the bag and tossed it onto the clay. By now the rocks were forming a wide pathway. Several days had passed without any incident. Remco was helping him to carry the bag, but they were slowed down because of its weight. All the other boys had gone on ahead of them and they were alone.

'So, what happened to your father?' Remco asked.

Coda stopped walking and put the bag down. They sat on their haunches and Coda picked at a thread on the bag. His memories of that day were still clear in his mind. It took him a moment to calm his emotions before he answered. 'He was killed when the Sabalians came to hunt us. Then the one they call Bala captured me and my mother. Now she is forced to do whatever he wants. He sent me here.'

'So it's true what they say, that the free born are hunted for sport.'

'Sport for them…not for us.'

While they were talking, neither had noticed Valdas and four of his lackeys coming up both ends of the path...until it was too late. Valdas grabbed Coda by the hair and lifted him to his feet. He punched him in the stomach and with a murderous look in his eyes said. 'You will pay today,' and punched him again. Remco had got to his feet, but was kicked sprawling into the wet clay beside the path. Before he could get up, two henchmen set upon him, kicking and punching. The other two lackeys came up behind Coda and held him while Valdas rained vicious blows to his face and body until Coda was almost senseless. Valdas stopped and stepped back. 'Now for the tasty bit. Hold him up boys,' and Valdas delivered a straight kick to Coda's abdomen that lifted him off his feet and hurled him backwards into the clay field.

He lay there covered with pain and struggling to breathe. He was disoriented and he could feel his face swelling. Remco was lying curled up on his side unconscious. Valdas and his cronies stood there breathing hard and admiring their work. 'To the pit boys. Each of you grab a foot. Let's go!'

The henchmen bent down, took hold of a foot each and dragged their two victims through the mud and clay to the edge of a natural crevasse that they all referred to as the pit. They suspended them over the edge and let them go. They slowly slid head first down the sloped clay bank and came to rest on the bottom ledge fifty feet below. Valdas looked down at them. 'Let's see if they can find their way out of this one hey boys?' The cronies cheered and turned away, making their way across the clay field.

Valdas stood on the edge for a moment looking at Coda and Remco with a triumphant look on his face. 'Let that be a lesson to those who mess with Valdas.'

●

Coda's left eye was swollen shut, and his face was almost unrecognisably bloated from the beating. The feint light of day had faded to early twilight and it was dark at the bottom of the pit. He turned his head and saw Remco half buried in the freezing clay, still unconscious. He sat up and was overwhelmed by dizziness that made his head feel like it was adrift in rough waters. He crawled over to Remco, and with his hands clawed at the mud and clay to free Remco's body. He splashed some water from a puddle onto his face, but there was no reaction. Coda shook him. 'Remco, wake up,' and splashed more water on his face.

Remco groaned and tried to open his eyes, but they were both too swollen. 'Is that you Coda?'

'Yes.'

'I can't see.'

'That's because your eyes are swollen. They must have kicked you on the nose as well.'

Remco tried to sit up and gasped with the pain in his side where his ribs had been fractured. 'I can't breathe…it hurts too much.'

Coda helped him to sit up. 'I'm going to wash your face,' he said. 'The water is very cold, but might help with the swelling around your eyes.' Remco was quiet while Coda washed his face.

'Where are we?'

'We are at the bottom of the pit.'

'The pit! But…how do we get out? It's too deep and the sides are soft clay.' Coda was silent and continued to swab at Remco's eyes. 'I heard someone died here once,' Remco continued. 'They never found his body you know. It was said that the pit swallowed him up.'

'He must have been buried in the clay. It runs down the sides as the ice melts in it. Can you see yet?'

Remco tried to open his eyes and turned his head from side to side. 'No…can't see anything yet.'

'Look up at the light, maybe it's just too dark.'

Remco looked up. 'Yes…if I look out the side of my right eye I can see the ridge up there.' He shivered. 'It's very cold. Aren't you cold?'

'I don't feel it so much. Maybe if we stand up and try to find a way out you won't feel so cold.'

He helped Remco up and they stood there taking in their situation. They had come to rest on a narrow ledge. Coda, who could see in the dark, looked over the ledge and saw that the crevasse had opened up further into a dark abyss. Feeling a panic building up in him, he remembered the mantra that his father had taught him. He had said that it would centre him and clear his mind so that he could think and feel correctly. Coda used it now, saying it over and over to himself until he could feel the tension drain away and be replaced by a calm clarity. He had to find a way out of the pit. He looked around for a way up the steep slopes, but found none.

'Coda!' Remco called anxiously. 'Where are you? I can't see you.'

'I'm here.' Coda took his hand. 'Come, it is not safe here,' and led him to a wider part of the ledge to what looked like a rock jutting out from the slope. As they stepped on it and moved towards the centre, they felt the rock sink beneath their feet and slowly tilt towards the abyss. The clay under it was water logged and slick. The extra weight shifted the balance that had held the rock in place and it slipped over the edge. Coda and Remco screamed in horror and clung to the rock as it carried them into the abyss. As it gathered momentum, the rock carved a path through the clay. When it hit the bottom three hundred meters below, it bounced off another rock which launched it into the air. Fresh shrieks of horror pealed from Coda and Remco as their missile burst through the opposite wall and continued its mad charge down a lava tube. Sparks flared out from beneath the rock trailing out behind it; lighting up their way.

'We're going to die!' Remco screamed in panic.

'Just hold on!' Coda shouted as the rock picked up more speed and shot down the tube. It carried them up and down the sides as the tube's twists and turns took them deeper into the bowels of XN5. Suddenly their descent began to slow down as the tube levelled off, but the rock's momentum spat them out at the end of the tube into an open cavern. For a moment they seemed to float above a wide subterranean river before the rock plunged them into its icy depths. Coda jumped free, but Remco, blinded by the swelling of his face, could not see what was coming and held on until it was too late. The downward current caused by the sinking rock held Remco in its grip and dragged him deeper and deeper into the water's black depths. Coda dived after him, but his grey coverall hampered his gills, so he kicked his boots off, unzipped the front and wriggled out of it as he swam after Remco. When he reached Remco he swam out of the grip of the rocks downdraft and began a slow ascent to the surface. As they broke through, Remco coughed and gasped, his chest heaved as he desperately sucked air into his burning lungs. 'Coda!' he gasped, 'where are we?'

'I think it's an underground river...there's a current pulling us along.' They floated along for a while and then Coda began to get worried. The current had become stronger. 'Come...we have to work our way across the current and find the bank.'

'Can you see the bank?'

'It's over there, about fifty yards to your left. Take off your boots and your coverall...it will be easier to swim.'

Remco did nothing. 'I'm freezing cold and my hands are going numb.'

Coda realised then that Remco was not suited to cold water the way he was and that he had to get him out fast. He took him by the collar. 'Just relax and try to keep your head above water. I'll get you out.' Coda began to swim backwards towards the bank as he pulled Remco by the collar. He was a swimmer born to the water, but the current had become powerful and made the going hard for Coda. He swam with relentless determination and after what seemed like a very long time, he felt the rocky bank scrape against his back. He turned and let the current take him a little further along to a small stony beach. He dragged Remco onto the beach and took his wet coverall and boots off. He then rubbed his hands and feet to get the circulation back.

It was not long before Remco could stand and rub his own body. Coda wrung as much water from the wet coverall as he could and gave it back to Remco. He gingerly got into it and continued to rub himself all over until the coverall began to warm up from his own body heat. Coda gave him his wet boots. 'Come…you must keep moving until you are dry.' Remco put his boots on and took Coda's hand as they started off downstream in the pitch blackness that only Coda could see in.

Their progress was slow with Remco feeling for every step. 'Coda…what is this place?'

'I don't know. It looks like it was carved out by hand. Maybe it was a mine.'

'Do you think we'll get out? Maybe we'll die here. I don't want to die in the dark like this. I want to die like a warrior. Like the ones my father told me about.'

'What sort of warriors?'

'He said that all of the men of his tribe were warriors. Even the old ones. They had to be. All of the villages raided each other for animals, food and women.'

'Why did they have to fight for these things?'

'If they wanted to marry a woman, their custom was that they first had to blood their spears in battle. Then, with these animals, they had to buy their woman from the father.'

'Sounds a bit mad to me.' Coda led Remco along a narrow bridge of rock that spanned a gully that had been carved out by the passage of water from a now extinct tributary of the river. 'Was that their rite of passage?'

'What do you mean?'

'You know…when you become a man.'

'My father said their initiation was at fourteen years of age. They would be circumcised and sent into the hills for a month. There they had to live in the wild and hunt for themselves. If they survived, they would be men.'

'What is circumcised?'

'When they cut the bit of skin from the front of your widdler.'

'Ouch, that sounds painful.'

'Yeah…my father said it was.' They walked in silence for a short time and then Remco asked, 'Did you have a rite of passage at White Mountain?'

'Yes…when you survived your first battle against the Sabalian hunting parties, usually at about fourteen.' Coda stopped abruptly and Remco bumped into him.

'What is it?'

'Shhh…I can see lights.'

'Where?'

'Down there…ahead of us.'

'Oh yeah,' Remco whispered as he squinted out the side of his good eye. 'I can see them now. Looks like they're moving. Someone must be down there.'

'Yeah…they are quite far off. Let's get closer.'

They cautiously moved forward, following the easiest route down the rock strewn path. Phosphorescence from the river began to cast an eerie glow around them as the rushing water broke over the rapids. Coda took Remco's hand and pulled him down to a crouching position. 'Come, we must stick to the shadows.'

'Why...are we not trying to get out of here?'

'Yes. It's just…we don't know who they are.'

They continued on until they could see the shapes of men lit by their miner's lamps as they worked on a rock face beside the riverbank. All sound of their labour was obscured by the rushing waters. Suddenly Coda sat on his haunches behind a rock and pulled Remco down with him.

'What's the matter?' Remco asked.

'One of them has a blue skin.'

'So…?'

'So, I don't think we should be discovered by them. I don't trust the blue skinned ones.'

'What do you think we should do then?'

'We must wait until they leave…then follow them out.'

'Okay.'

They sat silent for some time before Remco asked. 'What are they doing? I still can't see properly.'

'It looks like they are digging stuff out of the rock. Might be precious stones or something. My father told me that there are stones that are worth a lot to some and are just pretty stones to others. Here the Sabalians seem to value them. I think that's what they are doing.'

'Maybe we should come back here and take some for ourselves.'

As Remco smiled Coda chortled. 'Yeah, that would be a good laugh!'

At that moment a great thunder clap sounded as the tension in the rocks around them released and shuddered. The rock beneath them heaved upwards and tilted, tossing them against the rock they were hiding behind. A large slab of rock broke loose from the roof above them and landed over them. It protected them as more rocks fell around them. Minutes later, when it sounded like the last rock had fallen, Coda asked. 'Remco?'

'Yes.'

'Are you okay?'

'I think so, and you?'

'I think so.' They crawled out from their small shelter and began to laugh. They laughed with the intense joy of having survived a near death experience. Coda laughed with abandon and Remco, haltingly, as he held his left side where his ribs hurt. When they finally stopped laughing, Coda said. 'Come, we must get out of here.'

He stood up and pulled Remco to his feet. He looked around and saw a few beams of light where the miners had been, but saw nothing that moved. 'Can you see anything?'

Remco turned his face to the left and looked out the corner of his right eye. 'Yes…I can see some lights down there.'

'Good…I think we should go and take a look, maybe we can find a light for you.'

They stood up and moved cautiously towards the catastrophic scene of mangled bodies and broken rock. Clambering over the rocks they found a miner's hat with the lamp still on. It had been knocked off its owner's head when the rock face had collapsed onto them. Coda picked it up and put it on Remco's head. 'There…that should help you see better.' He turned away and as he was about to continue on he heard someone cough and moan with agony. Remco turned his head and looked towards where the sound came from. His miner's lamp illuminated the blue skinned Sabalian who was lying on his right side with a huge rock crushing down on him. His breath was spasmodically blowing small puffs of dust as he struggled to breathe. His right arm was outstretched and a few inches from his hand was a bag with the stones they were mining, spilled out into the dust.

'Help me.' He said breathlessly and coughed up some blood, dark against his ashen face. Coda and Remco sidled up to him and stood staring, not sure of what to do. Coda suddenly remembered Remco's idea of coming back for the stones, so he went forward and sat on his haunches by the bag.

'Help me,' the Sabalian puffed out and coughed up more blood. Coda looked into his eyes for a moment and then very deliberately picked up the stones and put them back into the bag. When the last one was in he pulled the cord that closed the bag and looked at the Sabalian again. He had a distant look in his eyes as he puffed out his last bubbling breath and lay silent. His eyes seemed to twitch and then go still and lifeless. Coda stood up and kicked dust into the Sabalian's face and his still open eyes.

'Choke on that, pit fly!'

There must be a way, Coda thought, as he stood on the rocks next to the waterfall. Its waters tumbled down the sheer cliff face and broke over the rocks five hundred feet below where the pool of boiling water frothed and churned against the ice fields that stretched as far as the eye could see. The raging storm had abated, but he knew the calm would be short lived. The season of storms had begun and the tempests were never far apart. Through a rare break in the clouds, Coda could see the dark brooding mass of Orro, the gas planet that forever held XN5 in its gravitational grip.

In the darkness of the cavern, time had ceased to exist as he and Remco had followed the river. They had rested when they were tired and slept fitfully when they were too exhausted to continue. They felt weak from hunger and now they stood on the edge of a cliff with seemingly nowhere to go. Remco leaned against a rock and stared at

Orro across the ice flats. Too fatigued to enjoy the view, he looked with dull eyes. 'So…what do we do now?'

'I don't know.'

'I wonder how those miners got here.'

'I don't know,' Coda repeated. 'Maybe they came from the other direction. Maybe they came from above.'

He looked up the cliff face, but found no way up its sheer face. The water was on his right, so that was a dead end. He looked to his left and saw what looked like a narrow ledge. He walked up it a little way and saw it ascended at a steep angle. He went back to the water and found Remco asleep. He suddenly felt a wave of exhaustion overcome him. All he wanted to do was sleep next to Remco, but he knew, they either had to go back into the cave and find a safe place to rest out of the weather, or go on and risk falling off the cliff from sheer fatigue. He put his hand on Remco's shoulder and shook him gently. Remco awoke with a start.

'What…?'

Coda made up his mind. 'I think we must rest first.'

'Did you find a way?'

'There's a narrow ledge we can go up with, but we must rest first.'

'Okay.'

'Let's go back into the cave and find a good place out of the weather.'

He helped Remco up and they walked back in. They found a sandy spot among the rocks and huddled together. Remco slumped into a deep sleep while Coda watched the storm roll in. Dark snow and sleet, stained by the ashes of a volcano, lashed against the cliff face driven by a sulphurous wind. Like an elemental monster it clawed at them with its foul breath, trying to drag them out and devour them in its cold wet sheets of ice.

Coda was not afraid. He looked into the storm and found some comfort in its violence. The past days in the cave had begun to harden his mind. His anger towards Valdas and his henchmen had turned inwards. It began to feed on itself and gather momentum. Like the storm outside, it turned into a tightly controlled tempest that gave him strength, keeping him awake and restless. Valdas will pay, he thought. I'll make that bum boy feel the pain, one way or another.

It was the silence that woke them. The wind had stopped moaning and the only sound was from the river with the distant thunder of the waterfall. They stood up and began to make their way to the entrance. On an impulse Coda decided to hide the bag of stones before they left the cave. He tucked it away in a small crack in the wall behind a boulder that looked heavy and immovable. One day I might need those, he thought.

Coda and Remco took to the ledge that was slick with ice and made their way up the cliff face. Coda was barefoot wearing only his black shorts. Remco was dressed in his grey coverall with his boots on. The higher they went, the narrower the ledge got. They were eventually forced to walk sideways and find hand holds to keep them from falling to certain death. After two hours of painfully slow progress, their hands were bleeding and Coda's feet were lacerated on the sharp ice.

'My hands have gone numb,' Remco said. 'Can you see the top yet?'

'No…just further up it looks like there's a crack that goes up. Maybe that's the way.'

'I hope so because my hands can't take much more of this.'

'It's not far to go now, just a little longer.'

The wind began to howl and threatened to pluck them off the wall. 'Coda! I'm going to fall!'

'Hold on!'

'I can't'

'Pull yourself into the wall…like this.'

Coda and Remco clung to the rock, too afraid to move. They stayed that way for what seemed like hours. Their young muscles quivered and cramped, but they hung on until, suddenly the wind stopped as abruptly as it had begun. Tentatively they crept up to the crevice. With relief they both finally squeezed into it and rubbed their aching muscles.

'That was close. I really thought I was going to fall off.'

'Yeah…me too. That was a strong wind.'

Remco looked up. 'Look!'

Coda looked up and saw the metal spikes that had been hammered into the sides. 'Looks like someone has been using those spikes as a ladder. Maybe this was the way those miners had come.'

'I think you're right. Let's go.'

They forgot their pained and aching muscles. Their fatigue evaporated and with Remco in the lead they climbed up the ladder. The spikes had been hammered in on both sides of the crevice at about the height of a man's foot and hand hold, which made it more difficult for them to reach, but they were nimble with renewed vigour. Remco clambered up in no time and was over the top with Coda trailing behind. He had slipped a few times on his bloodied feet, but had made good progress when he heard Remco's call of alarm suddenly choke off.

Instantly Coda was wary. He knew something was wrong. He ascended the last few rungs slowly and cautiously raised his head over the edge of the crevice. He looked, but could not find Remco anywhere. Ahead of him was a small clearing at the bottom of a steep hill strewn with rocks and large boulders. Looking on the ground he saw a profusion of jumbled up footprints and the remains of an ice fire. The gas trapped in the permafrost rocks that was common on the volcanic islands of XN5, was set alight. The flames were covered with a layer of volcanic rocks which retained the heat long after the flames had died out.

Coda lifted himself over the edge and onto the ground. He quickly checked the fire and found the rocks still warm. Somebody had been waiting for the miners to come out. He ran to the opposite edge of the clearing and crouched among the boulders. Remco must have been captured, he thought. He crept cautiously among the rocks, not sure of where to look for Remco. Suddenly he heard a sound to his left and he hunkered down in the shadow of a huge boulder. He tried to breathe quietly, but his heartbeat threatened to give him away. Then he heard it again, only this time it was the unmistakable sound of a boot stepping on loose stones. It was close, much too close. As the ugliest Sabalian on XN5 stepped into view, Coda bolted and ran as fast as he could up the hill on what seemed like a natural path between the rocks. He had gone no more than twenty yards when a rock hit him with a slap square between the shoulder blades. The blow lifted him off his feet and he landed heavily, hitting his head on a rock that left him unconscious.

Coda lifted his head, but the pain overwhelmed him with throbbing monotony and forced him to lie back again. He feared that if he opened his eyes, the pain might get worse. He opened them a crack and the ugly Sabalian's face loomed large, staring at him. In the next instance a blinding pain burst in his head as the ugly man slapped him.

'Where are the miners?'

Coda stared in detached fascination at him. One side of his face seemed to be almost caved in. He was breathing heavily through a badly healed broken nose and his open mouth. Mucus caked the side of his top lip where it ran freely from his damaged nose. His foul breath was a cloying stench of rotting food that further assaulted the senses. Another slap brought Coda out of his stupor. 'I said, where are the miner's, ectype worm?'

'They are all dead.'

The ugly man sat back, visibly shaken. 'How?'

'The quake. They were crushed under the rocks.'

Ugly stood up and paced about making absent minded gestures and muttering to himself. That's when Coda noticed Remco tied up and lying on his side behind him.

'Are you okay?' Remco nodded. He suddenly looked past Coda and his eyes widened. Coda turned back and found Ugly coming towards him.

'The stones! Did you find a bag of stones?'

Coda feigned ignorance and said with a blank look, 'What stones?'

'Coloured stones! Some may have looked like glass. The stuff they were mining!' He was agitated. Frustrated by the lack of positive response.

'We didn't know they were mining for stones. When we found them they were all dead. We only wanted to get out of there.'

Ugly looked intently at Coda, trying to work out if he was lying or not. 'You are Institute boys. So what were you doing there?'

'We were left for dead in the clay pit and then we fell in on a rock.'

His laugh was a bark that splattered mucus and foul breath on Coda. 'That's got to be the most ridiculous story I have ever heard...no matter, the Institute pays for gutter snipes like you, so, this will not be a dead loss after all.' He tied a short cord around their necks and untied their feet. 'Up you get…now move.'

Coda and Remco, with their hands tied behind their backs, leaned uncomfortably against each other as the short cord around their necks did the work of keeping them bound together. Remco fell in behind Coda and they walked in step up the hill. There was a dilapidated off-road van hidden among the rocks at the side of the dirt track. When they reached it, Ugly lifted them up and dumped them in the back. He banged the doors shut and got in behind the controls. He hit the starter button and the engine belched into life. With a roar they lurched forward and took to the track.

Coda looked through a small crack between the metal plates that covered the framework of the back. He had to remember where they were and how to get there again. The track wound along a steady incline that finally topped out on the edge of the miners compounds. They were a sprawling expanse of long buildings that accommodated miners and workers of all kinds. Coda had never seen so many buildings or beings in one place. There were clusters of beings standing around fires and women of all kinds carrying food bags and going about their business. But, there were no children.

They drove on, past small food squares where beings sat and ate from small bowls. Long columns of returning miners shuffled down the track they were on. Their shoulders sagged with exhaustion and their faces were black with mesorite dust. The only ones who did not look so dirty were the aqua miners. Some were very tall while others were of average height. Some were bald with pigmentation, like his father had been. Others had long or short, very delicate fins of different colours on their heads. If one didn't know they were fins, they could easily have been mistaken for hair. Only when they were in the water did they show. A pang of sorrow stroked his heart as he recalled his father. Thaif the gentle, magnificent and brave, his sensitive spirit guide who was never far.

The track wound its way through the compounds and into the complex of shaft fifteen. Ugly took a left turn onto the main road and they picked up speed. Buildings and mine shafts sped by for what seemed like an hour. It was dark when the van eventually slowed down and turned off the road. It took a bumpy road that led up a dirty alleyway. The van stopped abruptly.

'Where are we?' Remco asked.

'I don't know. I don't recognise anything. Wait…I see the ugly one talking to someone there in that doorway.' Coda watched them argue and gesticulate in the light that spilled onto the alley. Eventually Ugly backed down and strode towards the truck in a foul mood. The back doors were wrenched open. He leaned in and grabbed Coda's right foot. He yanked them both out violently with the cord still attached to their necks. They were flung out onto the muddy lane where they gagged and choked on the cord that dug into their windpipes. Coda tried to stand up, but Remco was winded and struggled to get on his feet. Ugly grabbed the cord between their necks and impatiently pulled them up.

'Come on…get going.' Ugly shoved them roughly towards the door until they stood, wretched in the light. 'What did I tell you? Look, they are unharmed and in good health. The institute will be happy to have them back. So…how about it…give me another fifty, what do you say?'

'You are lucky to get what I offered. Look at the state of them…covered in mud. One of them has no coveralls and his feet are cut to ribbons. It's going to cost me food, clothing and medicine before I can sell them on. They are damaged goods, so be happy with the price you get.'

'Give it to me then.' Ugly shoved his hand past Remco's head and the man in the doorway placed a small pile of black coins in his hand. He grunted, went back to his van and drove off down the alleyway.

'Well come on then…don't just stand there.'

They stepped past him and stood in what looked like a utility room with half filled refuse bins and assorted clothing hung from hooks on the wall. The rest of the room was filled with sealed crates stacked on top of each other. The man closed the door and turned to them. He was a tall Sabalian with slick black hair and he sucked on a sweet stick. He wore tight black trousers and a white vest that offset his dark blue skin. Most striking was the delicate perfume he used. He pointed to the open door that led into the next room and took the sweet stick out of his mouth. 'Go on…in there.' They walked into a blindingly white kitchen.

'Sit over there by the table.' He untied their hands and took the cord off their necks. He then reached for a small button on the wall and pressed it. 'My man servant will be in to take care of you. Would you like a sweet?' They stared...uncomprehendingly. 'Aah...all boys like sweets don't they?' He walked over to a wall closet, opened it and took out a small glass jar of brightly coloured sweets and placed it on the table in front of them. They stared at it, thinking it was too good to be true. 'Here...I'll open it for you. Hhhm...smells nice doesn't it?' He tipped some out onto the table and picked up a bright red one. He popped it into his mouth.

'Hhhm...tastes delicious.'

The man servant arrived and the man stood back, almost guiltily, as if he had been caught in a private act. 'Clean these two up will you and give them some food. Get them ready for presentation.' He turned and left the room.

●

'Come. The Master calls.'

Coda and Remco followed the man servant down the corridor. He had given them a good meal and they had slept a dreamless sleep on bunk beds in a small room with a tiny window. In the morning the man servant had given them a gruelling scrub in the bath and had treated their wounds with a stinging liquid that sealed over like a second skin. They wore new grey institute coveralls and new boots. Coda wondered where they had got them from and the answer came as soon as they entered the grand sitting room. Master Cubal sat on an opulent couch with an evil grin on his face.

'You two runaways have caused me a lot of grief you know. Not to mention the large sum of Gion I've had to pay to get you back.'

'We did not run away Master,' Coda responded. 'It was Valdas and his pit flies who threw us into the clay pit.'

'Ah...so that's your excuse is it? What pit and why would Valdas do such a thing; he's such a sweet boy. He couldn't harm a hair on anyone's head. No, no...lies won't do and now trying to put the blame on that poor boy is just incredulous."

'I am not lying.'

'Well, we'll see about that won't we? I think I should also do something about that cheeky mouth of yours. Remind you of your place, hey little boy.'

'I'm not afraid of you.'

Master Cubal was off the couch in a flash and slapped Coda

hard on the left ear. 'Watch your tongue boy or I'll cut it out and eat it myself.' His lips were bloodless and his black eyes shone brightly as they bored into Coda. Deaf in one ear, Coda stared back defiantly. Master Cubal straightened up.

'We'll see if you still like this little game when we get back.' He looked at the man with the delicate perfume and pointed at the red box on the side table. 'It's all there.' He looked at the man servant. 'Put them in the back of my transporter.' He turned and left the room.

●

'Choose.'
Coda looked in the box of three foot long plastic welding rods. Some were thick and tapered at one end while others were slim and straight. He realised that there was no escaping the pain that Master Cubal was about to inflict, so it didn't matter which one he chose. He decided to test his theory and chose the lightest one he could see.

'No I don't think so. Much too light for the punishment. I think we'll try this one,' and he lifted out a heavier one with a slightly tapered end. 'What do you think?'

They were standing in Master Cubal's office at the Institute. Remco had already had his beating and was standing beside the closed door. Tears were streaming down his face, but his fists were clenched in stoic defiance. Ten of the best they called it, but Master Cubal never cared much for the count and his aim was sloppy. The pleasure he derived from beating their bare bottoms was evident by the lump in his trousers.

'Drop those shorts and assume the position.'
His breathing quickened as Coda undid the draw string and let his shorts drop around his ankles. He had no sooner bent forward when the first blow struck. He gasped involuntarily at the pain of it. He had never experienced anything like it before. The second blow made it worse; compounding the agony. As each blow landed the heavy rod left deep bruises and stung with the intensity of a hot fire brand. He gritted his teeth and refused to show the pain. The blows began to land on Coda's legs and back as Master Cubal grunted with effort and pleasure while massaging his crotch with his free hand. The twelfth and thirteenth blows were the hardest, but the fourteenth and fifteenth were the feeblest as Master Cubal released his sticky load in his trousers.

Coda slowly and calmly pulled up his shorts. He turned and looked at the dark stain in Master Cubal's trousers and then at the weak smile on his sweaty face. Coda's disgust overcame all pain and caution. On impulse he sniffed into his mouth a large globule of nasal mucus and spat it in Master Cubal's face whose countenance turned dark and twisted with rage. As he lifted the rod to hit Coda, Coda pushed him. Master Cubal fell backwards into the open rod box and hit the back of his head hard against the lid. He slumped sideways, unconscious, into the box. Coda slammed the lid down forcefully onto his legs. He turned to Remco who was holding the door open and they ran down the corridor to the dorm room. There was nowhere else to go as the building was locked.

'That was amazing!' Remco laughed. 'He's going to be so mad when he wakes up. What do you think he's going to do?'

Coda knew that he would not escape the Master's wrath, but at that point he did not care. 'I don't know, but it sure felt good to spit in his face and did you see how he fell into the box?'

'Yeah!' and Remco acted it out, mimicking the look on the Master's face as he collapsed onto the floor. Both Coda and Remco were in gales of laughter when they walked into the dorm room.

'Well now…look who's back boys…fish boy and sewer boy.' Valdas was standing in the middle of the room with his lackeys behind him. 'So, looks like you enjoyed the Master's beating hey? Maybe we should finish it off for him, what do you think boys?'

'Maybe…except, this time, we can see you coming, hey…bum boy. But first, you might want to go and help your master "boy lover" who is out cold in his precious box of rods.'

Valdas stepped back as if he had been slapped with the force of Coda's words. No one had ever dared to call him something like bum boy before. Never in front of everyone. Coda watched as the look of controlled malice in Valdas's eyes changed to uncertainty and fear. And then one of the boys behind him sniggered. Valdas gave Coda a venomous look and walked past him into the corridor and on to Master Cubal's rooms.

Valdas's henchmen faded away to their beds as several of the other boys crowded around Coda and Remco with a thousand questions, hungry for their story.

Coda had slept fitfully during the night. The pain of the beating had woken him every time he turned onto his back. He was also aware that Valdas's boys could harass him at any time while he slept. As the pallid light of morning pushed wanly against the dark, the room became still and peaceful and Coda slept. His sleep was deep and dreamless.

He awoke with a start as the morning bell sounded even louder than usual. Everyone was starting to wake up and get out of bed when Master Cubal walked in with Valdas. Between them they carried the rod box which they dropped loudly on the floor. Here it comes, Coda thought, Master Cubal's wrath.

'Today we will play a little game of conquest.' Master Cubal looked pleased with himself. 'You will divide yourselves into two groups. The first group will be led by Valdas and the other by young Coda over there. You will meet on the clay field behind the reduction plant. Valdas will take the northern end and Coda the southern end. The objective is to take the others territory.' He opened the rod box. 'These will be your weapons. The winning side shall have three days off college and all the food you can eat. The losers will, in addition to doing their lessons at college, clean the building from top to bottom, and have only one dry ration and water per day for three days.'

A shocked silence fell over the room. 'Those with Valdas move to this side of the room,' he indicated with his left hand. 'And those with Coda move to this side.' He indicated with his right. Slowly the boys began to mill about and whisper among themselves. Valdas's four henchmen began to bully and intimidate some of the boys onto their side and others gathered around Coda. A big powerful looking boy that reminded Coda of Merrix the guide from White Mountain, with his fine coat of grey fur and the beginnings of a black mane remained aloof and kept to one side. He had always been a loner and everyone seemed to avoid him, but now he stood there with a quizzical look on his face, not sure of what to do. He looked at Valdas and then at Coda. Suddenly it seemed like he had made up his mind. He walked up to the rod box and chose the heaviest rod he could find. He turned and walked up to Coda, said nothing and stood behind him. There were fifteen with Valdas and twelve with Coda.

'Very well...those with Valdas come and choose your rods.'

They all filed past the box and chose their rods. Coda's group followed. He chose for himself a sturdy, but flexible one. It had to be flexible he thought. There was a plan brewing in his mind already, but first they had to prepare.

'You have one hour to get ready and get yourselves onto the clay field. I will see you there.' Master Cubal gave Valdas a meaningful look and left the room. Everyone began to dress in their grey coveralls, but Coda called his group into the washroom first.

'Keep the door closed.' Coda said. 'Has anyone got any ideas?'

The big powerful boy came forward and took off one of his boots. He put his left hand in it and held his rod with the right. 'I am Sibex. To fight with the rod you need protection,' and he lifted his left hand with the boot. 'And you need deception.' In whistling mock strikes he waved the rod overhand several times and then struck hard to indicate a strike to the ribs. He did it again and then showed a hard strike to the ankle. He turned to Coda. 'Hit me with your rod.' Coda instinctively knew what he wanted and tried to hit him across the ribs. Sibex blocked him with the boot. Coda tried to get through with several other attacks, but Sibex blocked him every time. Coda stepped back and Sibex turned to the rest of them. 'You will not always be successful. You will take many hits, but by the end of this battle you will be a lot better than when you started.' He stepped back amongst the boys and looked at Coda with the same expression of expectation as everyone else in the room.

Coda looked at Sibex and said simply. 'Thank you…Sibex.' He looked at the rest of them. 'Any other things we can use…any ideas?'

Remco stepped forward. 'We can keep the other boot on to kick their butts.' And some of the boys responded with chuckled smiles and exclamations of, 'Yeah…!' punctuated by demonstrations of how they were going to hit and kick the enemy.

When everyone had settled down, Coda said, 'I have a plan that I think might work…'

●

The clay field was flat and empty except for the path Coda and Remco had built. The pit was on the western edge and the reduction plant was on the eastern side. Dark clouds ripped by lightning and deep thunder were blowing in from the north. The breeze was cold and carried a violence they could smell. Coda's group had rolled out large empty metal drums from the reduction plant and laid them out in a straight line across their territory. They crouched behind their drums and looked out over the field. Each one had the tip of his rod primed with a lump of clay laced with gravel and small stones. Piles of prepared clay lay at their feet, ready to reload. Coda, Remco and Sibex were in the centre with the fastest runners in the group placed on the flanks.

Valdas and his group milled about opposite them, a hundred yards away. Master Cubal walked into the middle of the field from the reduction plant and stood on the path. He carried with him a long tapered rod with a thick tip. 'Are you ready?'

'Yes!' shouted Valdas and his group shouted and called abuse at Coda. 'Come out from behind your drums you cowards.' They jeered and taunted. 'Those drums won't protect you from us!'

Coda and his group remained silent.

'Very well.' Master Cubal turned and joined Valdas's group.

'Look…how are we going to fight him?' Remco asked.

'Don't worry about Cubal…I'll sort him out.' Sibex answered.

Remco looked at Sibex. 'But he is a grown man. He's much stronger than us.'

'We have unfinished business and he is not strong. He is weak and uses boys for his pleasure. His day has finally come.'

Master Cubal began egging Valdas's group on, whipping up their battle lust. They roared with bravado and false courage as they tried to intimidate Coda's group. When they were at their peak of excitement Valdas started the charge. Coda watched the charge come full tilt at them. Clay and mud flew up around them as they sprinted towards them.

'Choose your targets well and make them count boys!' He waited. 'Hold!' He waited a little longer until they were about thirty yards away. 'Fire!' he shouted.

With an over handed whipping action of their rods, they let fly with the lumps of clay. The clay whistled through the air and slapped into the bodies of the charging enemy with withering accuracy. Most of the charge broke. Some of the boys were thrown backwards as they lost their footing with the force of the projectiles and others fell headlong into the clay. Coda's boys reloaded and kept up a constant barrage of stone laden clay that left the enemy floundering in the mud. Master Cubal took one in the face and called the retreat. Valdas and his group turned back and ran until they were out of range. Coda's group cheered loudly and congratulated themselves that they had successfully repelled them.

Coda knew that they could not hold them off a second time as they had not had enough time to prepare more clay. He had discussed this with his group before the battle and they knew what had to be done. They waited for their foe to regroup and begin the next charge. The wind had picked up and the clouds were overhead, heavy and cold. They primed their rods again and took off the boot they would use on their free hand. They did not have to wait long before Valdas started the charge.

'Steady!' Coda called and waited until Valdas hit the fifty yard mark.

'Charge!' Coda shouted and they stepped out from behind their drums and took the fight to Valdas. Coda had instructed the centre to run slower than the flanks so that they would form a semicircle, forcing the enemy to be drawn in. They were about twenty yards away when Coda took aim at Valdas and let fly with his clay. It struck him on the outside of his left eye and crushed the bone of his socket. The eye popped out and flopped about on his cheek. He stopped running and brought his hand up to his face to protect the eye. Coda was closing in on him, but before he reached him the boy on his right got to him first. He hit Valdas a wicked blow across the face that made him drop his protective hand. The boy hit him with his booted hand and crushed the eyeball that left Valdas squealing with pain and horror. The boy continued to lay into him with intense retribution and hate for every misdeed he had inflicted on him. Valdas fell on his side and curled up in the mud, screaming in agony.

Coda's flanks were putting up a fierce fight that forced Valdas's group closer together and restricted their movements. They could not swing their rods effectively and were being beaten mercilessly by Coda's boys. Master Cubal was desperately trying to fight Sibex off who blocked his vicious strikes. Sibex was more than his match and expertly broke through his defences. He feinted to the Master's face and struck a hard blow to his ribs. He followed it up with a stinging cut to the right side of the head. He continued to find the spots where it hurt the most and drove him backward towards the lip of the pit.

Remco was much stronger than he looked. He laid one of the henchmen down with a kick to the groin and engaged another with a well placed blow across the ribs. Coda fought off a determined attack by another of the henchmen by kicking him on the kneecap, but not before he had sustained two painful blows to his ribs and gills. Another boy swung at him, but this time Coda blocked effectively and struck him on the side of the neck. The boy lost all colour to his face and crumpled into the mud.

The battle raged on intensely with savage blows and screaming victims as Coda's pincer movement trapped Valdas's group. Blood, mud and steam filled the air around their writhing bodies. Some of the downed boys were trampled on and others were cut and bleeding. In what seemed like no time at all the only one of Valdas's group left standing was Master Cubal who was teetering on the edge of the pit. Sibex hit him hard on the ankle and he fell down the steep slope. As he came to rest fifty feet below he shouted in pain as his weight came down on his now broken ankle. 'I'll kill you for this Sibex!'

Sibex was twelve years old. He knew that to stay at the Institute would mean his death. Well he wouldn't give this detestable boy lover the satisfaction. He had been formulating a plan for some time now. They all knew where Coda had come from, perhaps he could make it there…to White Mountain.

Of Coda's group ten were still standing, rubbing their bruises and welts. Some were bleeding and others were still dazed from blows to the head.

Then Remco said. 'We won…hey, we won!'

Suddenly all the pain was forgotten and they erupted with ecstatic roars of victory and relief. They threw their arms around each other and laughed and cried with abandon. It was then that they noticed a group of miners standing at the reduction plant. They had made bets on who would win and some were shouting their congratulations at them.

Coda wondered if they should get Master Cubal up from the pit or leave him there to die. He realised that the consequences of leaving him there would be death to himself and possibly the other boys as well. He also knew that Master Cubal knew where Bala was and therefore knew where his mother was and that meant that he needed him alive. So he walked up to the miners and asked for help. They all decided to come to the pit and with a long rope, pulled the beaten

Master up. They all laughed and jeered at him then turned and left. Some called their thanks back at Coda for their winnings as they merrily returned to work. Then as a flash of lightning struck one of the metal drums, the storm broke.

●

Sleet and snow battered the large window of the dorm room. It was dark, but frequent lightning lit the scene for Coda, who was standing in his black shorts, in front of the window, looking out over the minefields. The storm had not abated for three days. Master Cubal, Valdas and several of the other boys had not been seen as they were being taken care of at the medical station. Sibex had taken off across the ice flats with a bag of rations stolen from the kitchen, in search of White Mountain. He had no doubt that Sibex would survive the journey as he was not affected by the cold. He would have gone with him, but for his mother. Somehow he had to find her and get her away from Bala. Whatever Master Cubal had in mind for him did not matter as long as he could find his mother. He knew Bala had her, so if he could get to Bala he would find her.

A soft step behind him made him turn suddenly. Two large Sabalians grabbed him and one put his hand over Coda's mouth. Master Cubal was sitting on a wheelchair in the doorway with an evil grin on his lips. Coda's shouts were suppressed, but he kicked viciously, to no avail as they took hold of his legs and carried him out of the dorm room. Silently, they followed Master Cubal down the corridor through the kitchen and out the back door into the service courtyard. They tried to put Coda into the back of the institute van that was standing there, but he put up fierce resistance until one of the Sabalians punched him out cold. They tied his hands behind him and dumped him in the back of the van. They locked the doors and got into the front cab.

Master Cubal came up to the driver. 'You know what to do. Tell me when it is done.' The driver started the engine and drove off. The movement of the van over the bumpy road brought Coda back to consciousness. He struggled to get to his feet and looked out of the small windows in the back doors. They were already on a straight road between the slag heaps. He could see the lights of the Northern Deep mining settlement receding into the distance. So, they must be going towards the ice flats, he thought. Why the ice flats? What did they have in mind for him? He turned and looked around the inside of the van. There was a small bag of rations and nothing else.

The storm had abated somewhat, but the wind that channelled between the slag heaps, violently buffeted the van. The motion of the van changed as they drove onto the ice flats. They drove on for what felt like thirty minutes or more before they came to a stop. He heard the cab doors open and shut. The wind had picked up and masked the sound of the two Sabalians as they walked to the back of the van. The back doors opened with a shock of cold air. They pointed their flash lights at him.

'Come boy!' Coda did not move. 'Come or I'll come in there and kick you out!' Still he did not move. Why should he, he thought, why should he make it easy for them? The Sabalian's face darkened and he stepped up into the back of the van. His big body filled the doorway as he grabbed for Coda, who ducked under his hand and rammed his left shoulder into his groin and pushed him back out onto the ice. The Sabalian was caught completely off guard and fell heavily on his back. His head hit the ice with a solid dull thud that left him dazed and disoriented. Before the second Sabalian moved towards Coda, he jumped out feet first towards him and landed on his chest.

The momentum combined with his small weight was just enough to topple the Sabalian. Coda landed on his back, but with his hands tied behind him he was not quick enough to get up. The other Sabalian had recovered and grabbed his arms. He lifted him off his feet and as he did so Coda brought his head back, butting him hard on the nose. His grip on Coda's arms relaxed and as he wriggled to get free, the second Sabalian hit him with a vicious blow to the side of the head with his flash light. Coda collapsed unconscious onto the ice and lay still.

The first Sabalian stood bleeding from his nose and both were breathing hard. The wind whipped at their clothes. 'Have you ever seen a kid fight like that?' the bleeding one asked. The other put his hands on his knees to get his breath back and shook his head. 'Well…we had better get him in before he wakes up again.' They lifted Coda by the arms and dragged him into a small outcrop of ice boulders. Some of the boulders had been placed carefully to form a loosely shaped room with an overhanging boulder forming a canopy. They went in under it until they reached the back wall. On the floor was a shackle with its chain anchored deeply into the ice. They attached the shackle to Coda's right ankle and untied his hands. One of them went back to the van and brought back the small bag of rations. He dumped the bag next to Coda and slapped his face until he became conscious. He pointed the flashlight beam in Coda's eyes.

'We'll be back in three days. Sweet dreams boy.' And they left.

Coda heard them get back in the van, start up the engine and drive off. As the sound of the engine disappeared into the wind, Coda sat up. He looked around him, but although he could see in the dark, he saw nothing beyond the boulders. They surrounded him like walls and held him in their icy grip. He could not see over them and the gaps between them were too high to see through. His head hurt from the blow he had taken and he still felt disoriented. So, what now? Just sit here and freeze, he thought? Even though he could handle extreme cold, he knew that if he didn't get enough food, he would eventually freeze to death.

The shackle on his ankle was uncomfortable. He tested the chain, but there was no give in it. He wondered how deep it was anchored and if he could dig it out, but there was nothing to dig with. The links in the chain were round and not big enough to get a strong grip to maybe hack away at the ice. He stood up and walked the circle the four yards of chain would allow. He looked in the bag and found only five dry ration bars. Two a day with only one for the third day, he thought. That's assuming they would come on the third day.

The mournful wind was shattered by lightning that made it roar as it drove the sleet and snow ahead of it. Coda shrank from the violence that swirled around him and settled in a small crevice in the back wall. He emptied out the ration bag and sat on it. He wrapped his arms around his knees and tried to marshal his thoughts. His father had always said that to gain control of his body he had to control his thoughts. So, he began to take notice of his thoughts. If he did not like what he thought, he let it pass. If he liked the thought, he dwelled on it until it was replaced by another pleasant thought. And so he continued for three days.

By the fifth day the storm had not stopped and his rations were finished. He realised that no-one would come until the storm passed and that could still be days away. His fatigue had become such that he could no longer focus on any thoughts and his body had begun to freeze. Without any conscious effort he went into deep meditation. His bodily functions slowed down and his heart rate decreased to one beat every two minutes. Soon the ice took hold of him. In his mind he was back at White Mountain deep in Raman's cave. Raman turned towards him and motioned him to sit by the hot volcanic vent.

'It is good to see you again, Coda.'

'How did I get here?'

'Your spirit has travelled here.'

'What is spirit?'

'It is the vital principle; your life energy that holds your body together and keeps it healthy or diseased and contains the soul. It is the conduit between your soul and your mind.'

'What is the soul?'

'It is the essence of your being; it is who you are. It is your spark of life. It is the infinite intelligence part of you; the all knowing conscience that guides you to fulfil your purpose in life.'

'How do I know my purpose in life?'

'When your spirit is clear you will hear and understand the soul's message.'

'If I am here, then I must be dead.'

'Not at all. You are on the astral plane. Look at your solar plexus; there is a silver chord and it is stretched tight. That means that you are still attached to your body. You have only come for a visit. If you wish, with practice, you can visit me this way whenever you want to.'

'I am cold and lonely where my body is.'

'I can see that, but your spirit is still pure and strong. Help is on its way. Stay a little longer and warm yourself by the vent.'

'Did my father have a spirit?'

'Yes.'

'Was it also cut in two when he died?'

'No. His spirit was whole.'

'What happened to his soul?'

'His spirit released him and he has returned to the fabric of creation.'

'Where is his spirit?'

'It has returned to the ether of XN5.'

'Will I ever see him again?'

'He has fulfilled his purpose and will not return, but if you desire it enough he will visit you, but remember, each time you call him you bind him to you. His soul needs to be free of the ether of this place.

Eventually you must let him go. His love for you and his teachings will always be with you, but his soul must continue with its journey.'

Coda's silver cord began to vibrate. 'It is time for you to go. Come and visit me again.'

The words echoed in Coda's mind as he jolted back into his body. It was cold and he began to shiver. The two Sabalians who were carrying him back to the van almost dropped him with shock. 'I thought he was dead.'

'So did I. How does anyone survive like that? The storm would have killed any normal being by now.'

'Well…we'd better get him back to Cubal. It's his problem if the boy still lives, not ours.'

'Yeah. Let's get a move on then.'

They dumped Coda shivering and in pain, in the back of the van. They got into the front cab, started the engine and drove back to the institute…

●

Coda opened his eyes. He found himself in the medical station. He had a throbbing headache and his joints were painful, but inside himself he felt as if he was still sitting next to the heat vent in Raman's cave. He remembered his mother telling him that he had been born there, in a hot pool of water with Zizi's help. Would he ever see her and Chi'Dorolam again? Would he ever see his mother again? Well…he had to find her and somehow get her away from Bala.

He turned his head and found Remco sitting next to the bed with his head resting on the covers fast asleep. Coda touched his arm and Remco sat up with a shock. 'Coda …we thought you were dead.'

'So did I.'

'But…how did you live…I mean…no one could survive the storms like that.'

'I don't know. Except…maybe…because I was not inside my body.'

'I don't understand.'

'I was in Raman's cave. It was warm there.'

'The wise man of White Mountain?'

'Yes. He said I was on the astral plane and could visit him any time.'

'But how?'

'I am not sure, but he said with practice I can do it again.'

'That sounds amazing.'

'It is. Now…tell me what has been going on?'

'Master Cubal is madder than ever and Valdas has been scheduled for an eye replacement. His new eye is being grown in the clone lab. He's only getting it because he is the master's bum boy. The rest of us that were on your side have been on a dry ration per day and have been cleaning the college after class. There's talk that we will be sent into the mines soon.'

'Do you know which ones?'

'I don't know.'

'I wonder what we have to do in the mines and where we will live.'

'I think we will be sent to the miner's compound.'

'I wonder why we didn't see any children there when we drove through.'

'Yeah…maybe they keep them somewhere else.'

'Well…we'll find out soon enough hey.'

They were quiet for a few moments before Remco continued. 'That was an amazing battle we had. You know it's called "The battle of clay pit" now. The miners at the reduction plant give us extra food on our way to college in the morning. Here…I brought you some, it's better than the stuff we get here.'

Coda had not realised how hungry he was. It was a ration bar, but much tastier than what they normally had. He chewed fast and with urgency. When he was finished he drank down the water Remco offered. He lay back panting from the effort.

'Valdas's boys leave us alone now. Valdas is still not back. I think he's…'

Coda drifted back into a deep sleep as he began to digest the food in his stomach. At first it was a black dreamless sleep. After a while the blackness began to lift and he found himself floating above his bed. He could see his body asleep and Remco sitting next to him. He thought of his mother and found himself in a small basement room looking at his mother. He could hear and feel all her thoughts and emotions, but she could not see or hear him. He tried to call out to her, but she still could not hear.

Ola was terrified of Bala. He had beaten her senseless when she refused his advances and then he raped her. Afterwards he had kept her locked up in his basement for three days without food or water. Her right eye was swollen shut and her bottom lip split open where it had burst with the force of his blows. She had found a tiny trickle of dirty water seeping through a crack in the wall that she had collected in an old bowl. She sipped gingerly at it and thought of Coda.

She had no idea how he was. When Bala had said he was going to send Coda to the Institute her heart was crushed. She loved her son more than life itself. Now that she had had some time to think about it, she knew that even though it meant separating them, he would be better off there. At least his basic needs would be taken care of at the Institute. It would be hard for him there, she thought, but better than here. What was going on here would affect him for life. She had to protect him from that. She did not know how, but she had to find a way. Coda was a resilient independent boy, but the not knowing was the hardest part.

She looked around her at the empty room. All that was in it was the old bowl. There was a small window behind her that was about four inches high and two foot wide, high up, just below the ceiling. The room was a narrow space of about eight foot by twelve dominated by the straight staircase that led up to the door. She turned and sat on the stairs facing the window. It was then that she noticed the markings etched out in the grey wall beside her. She saw that they went all the way to the top of the stairs.

She climbed to the top step and saw that the markings were simple downward strokes marking the days. At first they seemed confident and later seemed to become shaky and uneven. After the five hundredth stroke they became drawings that at first were stick drawings depicting beatings and chores of cleaning and cooking. As she descended the stairs, they became more manic. They became a face gouged into the damp brick with deep strokes and later became frantic hackings that drove deep holes into the eyes. Eventually the faces became featureless only recognisable by their oval shape. Whoever carved this had a long slow descent into madness with the eventual total loss of identity expressed by the gouged out faces.

It became clear to Ola that she was not the first and that the bowl must have belonged to the one before her. She knew there was no way out of this for her. There was no law preventing Bala from doing what he wanted to captured clones of the Nation. They were fair game to do with as the Sabalians pleased. Was there any reason to live, she thought? But then she thought of Coda. She would live for him. She would submit to Bala and suffer his abuse for the sake of Coda. She would do everything in her power to protect him, even if it meant dying for him. At least her death would have meaning then…

A key rattling in the door intruded on her thoughts. The door opened and crashed against the wall. Bala's silhouette filled the doorway.

'Come!' he bellowed. 'Make some food, and when you've done that, you can start by cleaning yourself up and then tidy up the place.'

Ola put the bowl down on the last step thinking of the one before her and silently thanked her for the warning she had left behind.

⚫

Coda awoke with a start and sat bolt upright. Then he doubled over with the extreme cramps he felt in his stomach. He had eaten too much too soon.

'Coda! What's wrong?'

'My stomach…I think I ate too much.'

'Here…try a little water. It might help.'

Coda took a sip and lay on his side. When the cramp subsided he said. 'My mother is in trouble.'

'How do you know?'

'I have just seen her…in my dream. She was badly beaten and was in the basement of Bala's house.'

'You mean you've just been there? I don't understand.'

'When I sleep or meditate, my spirit leaves my body and can travel wherever I want to go. I could hear her thoughts and I could feel what she felt.'

Before Remco could respond a Sabalian orderly came in pushing a food trolley.

'Time for you to go,' he said to Remco. 'Master Cubal will be here soon, so make yourself scarce.'

'Okay…see you later Coda.'

'Wait! Let me know as soon as you can which mines we are going to.'

'Okay.' And Remco left.

'Well now…you must be starving. Here, sit up and I'll put this pillow behind your back so that you can be nice and comfortable.' The orderly put a tray of hot watery soup and a ration bar across Coda's lap and continued. 'It must have been terrible out there on the ice. They told me you ran away from the Institute. Why did you go onto the ice flats? Surely you know no one can survive out there especially in a storm like that.'

Coda was too busy eating to answer. So the word is that I ran away, he thought.

'Oh well, never mind. You just eat up and get well. I'm surprised you survived at all to be honest. We've had a few boys over the past few years that died out there. Frozen stiff they were when they brought them in. They were solid blocks of ice. I'm astonished that you had not turned to ice. You must have something special. Something the other boys don't.'

Master Cubal wheeled in on his wheelchair. 'Leave us!' and the orderly left.

'So you survived the cold. I don't know how you did it, but we'll see how well you do in the mines hey.'

'Which mine?'

'Oh, I don't know. Maybe one of Bala's mines.' Coda's heart leaped with excitement. Bala…that means I might find my mother, Coda thought. 'Maybe one of his unregulated ones. The miners have a very low survival rate there. Let's see how long you live there.'

'Long enough to visit you in the night.'

The colour drained from Master Cubal's face as Coda's words sank in. 'The sooner you go the better.'

'That might not be soon enough for you.'

The master regained his composure. 'Well…fortunately you can't do anything about that now can you? Now that you can barely move hey.' And he laughed as he left the room.

Coda watched him leave and continued with his meal. He ate slowly and deliberately. When the orderly returned he asked for more. When that was finished he slept a deep sleep. He awoke late into the night and he felt refreshed. The headache was gone and his joint pain was only a dull ache. He got out of bed, went to the bathroom, and relieved himself. He walked past the orderly who was asleep in his chair in the orderly's office. He left the medical station and walked down the passageway to the kitchen. All was quiet. He walked up to the work top and took a ten inch meat knife from the block. He left the kitchen and walked down the passageway in the opposite direction towards Master Cubal's rooms. With his bare feet he made no sound as he walked past the dorm room door.

He stood outside the Master's door for a moment before slowly turning the doorknob. The door opened easily and he stepped into the Master's office. The room was illuminated by weak strips of light from the mine fields through the blinds on the window behind the desk. He tiptoed past the desk to the opposite side of the room and quietly opened the door to his living room. The heavy drapes on the window were shut, but Coda could see in the dark and found the bedroom door. Like a ghost Coda drifted through the living room and stepped into the bedroom.

Coda stood in the doorway for a moment. On the right side of the room there was a fireplace bordered by two sumptuous black velvet couches. A small gas flame heated the volcanic rocks in it and cast a warm glow onto the large bed opposite it. The bed was flanked by two tall and narrow windows. The light weight dark blue drapes were hung from an elaborate multi leafed bow of the same fabric on the ceiling above the centre of the bed. They covered the entire ceiling and hung down all four walls of the room. Behind the drapes on the walls on either side of the bed, were rows of closets. Above the fireplace the drapes were held up by a large silver framed mirror. The floor was covered by a deep pile black carpet.

Coda padded to the end of the bed and watched Valdas and Master Cubal sleep peacefully between the black sheets under the dark blue covers. Coda stood there thinking about what he wanted to do. These two had been the sole cause of much harm to himself and everyone else. If they were out of the picture all that harm and pain would just go away. It would be easy to end the misery right here and now, he thought. It wouldn't take much to hold Valdas down and slit his throat. Master Cubal might be a little more difficult, he thought, but a few quick stabs in the heart and lungs would finish him off quickly enough.

Then he thought of his mother. He had to find her and get her away from Bala, but the Master was the way to Bala. So…he had to keep him alive. As for Valdas…who cared about a twelve year old bum boy anyway? His day will come. He looked at the knife and decided to put them on notice. He walked up to Valdas's side of the bed. He reached over him with the knife and plunged it silently into the mattress between them. He stood back and watched them for a moment longer. Well…they'll get the message when they wake up in the morning and the Master will know, won't he. Or maybe he won't really know, but he will know that he was inches from death. Coda turned and slipped silently out of the room.

●

Master Cubal stormed into the medical station in his wheelchair. His face was dark with fury and his breathing was laboured. He tossed the knife on Coda's bed.

'It was you wasn't it?'

'What are you talking about?'

'Don't play games with me you little ectype runt. It was you who stuck this knife in my bed last night.'

'I was in bed all night. Ask the orderly.'

'The orderly is not always awake. I know it was you.'

'But…how was I supposed to get there? I can hardly move. You said so yourself.'

'I know what I said. I also know that you are recovering much faster than you are letting on. So…I'll tell you what's going to happen. Tomorrow you and that little brown lackey of yours are off to Bala's mine. It's not a listed mine, so no-one will know where you are. So…when you die…and I know you will because the conditions are very bad there…no-one is going to know or care.'

'We'll see.'

'Oh we'll see all right.' Master Cubal took the knife and left.

Coda was left with mixed feelings. Closer to Bala meant closer to his mother. In a sense he was excited about that, but in another he was afraid of what they had to do in the mine. He knew it was dangerous, but had no idea of how dangerous. And why would he be sending both Remco and himself? What had Remco done? Well…maybe we could look out for each other, he thought.

The next morning, after all the boys had left for school, the two large Sabalians who had taken Coda onto the ice, escorted him and

Remco out through the kitchen and shoved them into the back of their van. Coda and Remco sat quietly, absorbed in their own thoughts. There was nothing to say. They were now Bala's property, for him to do with as he pleased. Coda resigned himself to his fate.

'Who is this man they call Bala?' Remco asked.

'He is one of the mine supervisors. He is also the one who murdered my father and took my mother and me from White Mountain.'

'You must really hate him.'

'Yes…his day will come.'

'I wonder what sort of work we will have to do.'

'I don't know. Something dangerous I suppose.'

They were silent for a while. They sat on the hard floor of the van consumed by their own thoughts. Coda stood up and looked out of the small windows in the back doors. Things started to look vaguely familiar. Then he noticed the shaft numbers increasing. They had travelled past shaft number nine and had just passed shaft number ten.

'Hey Remco…I think we are going towards the compounds.'

'Yeah?' Remco got up and joined him at the back doors.

'Yeah. You see that headgear there? Well…that's the headgear for shaft number ten. Now if we wait a bit we should go past the gate for shaft number eleven.' They waited until they drove past the next gate. As they sped past they could see the number eleven painted on the gate pillars. 'We're definitely heading for the compound.'

They counted each gate as they sped past. Twelve, thirteen, fourteen, but before they got to fifteen, the van slowed down and it drove through gate fifteen. 'We're heading for shaft fifteen. But, that's not an illegal mine. I wonder what's going on.' They drove past several slag heaps and into a large warehouse, filled with mine machinery. The van came to a stop and the Sabalians got out. They stretched their legs and stood around as if waiting for someone. An hour later a black enclosed transporter drove into the warehouse and stopped behind the van. It was a big mine vehicle that often carried mining equipment into the mines. A Sabalian got out and met with the two that were waiting.

'That's Bala.'

'He doesn't look like the other Sabalians.' Remco said. 'There's something different about him.'

'Yes. I heard someone say his mother was not Sabalian. She was a domestic clone. Maybe that's it.'

'Here he comes.' They shrank back from the door and waited.

The door opened and Bala stood looking in. 'So…Coda. You've been a bad little fish boy I hear. Pity your father died so suddenly, I had plans for him you know. Well…you and your little brown sidekick will do just fine.'

'Where is my mother?' Coda blurted out venomously.

'Ho ho…aren't you just full of piss and bile. Won't she just be pleased to know that you are working in the mine for me?'

'Tell me where she is!' Coda barked.

'Ha ha ha…or you'll do what.' Bala taunted with a smile. 'Besides, it's none of your business.'

'What have you done with her you bastard!' and he rushed Bala. He jumped out the back of the van, but Bala was too quick for him and caught him by the neck. Coda kicked and scratched at Bala's hand until it bled, but Bala squeezed harder and harder until Coda was about to lose consciousness. He threw Coda to the ground and put his foot on his throat.

'This is not a game little boy. Ola belongs to me and I'll do with her as I please. You also belong to me and you will work until you are dead.' He looked at the other Sabalians as he lifted his foot off Coda's throat. 'Blindfold them. Then bind their hands and feet so that they can still walk and put them in the transporter.'

Bala drove the transporter onto the machinery lift and got out of the driver's seat. He pushed the down button and the elevator took them to the mid level one mile below the surface. He hit the stop button, got back into the driver's seat, and drove into the tunnel. It was deserted. This one had been mined out years before. About a half mile further he stopped. The rail tracks branched off to the left and went in under a closed double doorway. Bala got out of the transporter and in the beams of the headlights, opened the doors. He got back into the transporter and drove through what looked like an old equipment storage room until he reached the ore truck standing on the tracks. He got out and opened the rear doors of the transporter.

'Get out you two.'

Coda and Remco were still blindfolded with their hands tied in front of them. Their ankles were tied separated by a foot long cord that made it possible to still shuffle along. Bala gave Coda and Remco the ends of a length of rope.

'Hold onto that and follow me.' He took the middle of the rope and stepped off the tracks. With the two boys in tow he walked past the ore truck and stopped behind it at what resembled a wall of metal beams to support the roof. He pushed a rock in the wall and a small door that had been cut into the beams opened inwards. They walked through and Bala stopped. He pushed another rock in the wall and the door closed behind them. They walked on for what felt like several minutes turning in several different directions as the tunnels forked into dead ends. Suddenly Bala stopped again. He pushed another rock in the wall and another door opened. He pushed the boys through. 'Go on then. Carry on walking and you'll find the others. They'll tell you what it's all about.' And he shut the door.

Coda and Remco stood there in the pitch black, listening to Bala's footsteps receding. They took their blindfolds off. Coda's eyes adjusted quickly, but Remco could see nothing. They untied each other's hands and then their ankles.

'What do we do now?' Remco asked.

'Here… tie this piece of rope around your waist. I'll tie the other end around mine and you can follow me.'

'Yes, but…where will we go. We don't know where these tunnels lead. We could get lost and die somewhere.'

'Don't worry. You know I can see in the dark right?'

'Yeah?'

'Well…the tunnel we are in has foot prints in the dust. We could follow where they lead. I think we have to be more worried about who we find than where we go.'

'Okay…let's go.'

Coda led the way. They followed the footprints cautiously. At one point the tunnel widened out into a large space where rock pillars had deliberately been left in place to keep the roof up. The footprints were all over the floor and it was confusing to determine the right way to go. Coda stopped.

'What now?'

'The footprints…they're all over the place.'

'What do you mean?'

'We are in a big space with pillars that keep the roof up and there are footprints everywhere.'

'The footprints we were following…can you describe them to me.'

'Well…they are boot prints…about my size.'

'Are there any distinct markings on the soles?'

'The heels are worn and the inside big toe on the right foot seems to be more worn than the left. Oh…there seems to be a part of the outside right heel broken off. Like a piece of sole was torn off.'

'Okay…see if you can find the same prints and follow those.'

'That's a good idea.' Coda said and moved forward. 'How did you know about reading footprints like that?'

'My father taught me. He was a hunter in his tribe. Everyone was, he said. Reading sign was central to the hunt. He showed me many ways to tell if someone had been this way or that and even to tell when they were there or which direction they were going.'

'That's amazing. Well…these prints are clear and over the others, so I guess they were made after. They also go in both directions. It seems like he walked to the door we came in and then walked back the same way he had come from.'

The tracks led into a tunnel on the far side that seemed a little larger than the others that fed from the chamber. After a while Coda noticed a glow ahead of them. It seemed to be coming from the right side of the tunnel. When they got there, Coda looked cautiously into the space beyond. It was a large room with four central pillars left in place as it was carved out. In the centre of the floor was a large fire. Around it sat a dozen children and what looked like an old man sitting on a metal box, telling them a story. Some were staring into the fire mesmerised by the flames and lost in the story and others looked like they were asleep. It was then that Coda noticed that many of the children had misshapen arms and legs with thick joints. Some had bad burn scars and all were dressed in rags. When he and Remco stepped into the room, they all looked up and a silence befell them.

'Bala sent us,' Coda said simply.

'Come and sit with us,' the old man said. 'I am Jarlath. What are your names?'

'Coda.'

'Remco.'

'You are welcome here. The others are working the east face. These cannot do the heavy work anymore.'

'Why?' Remco asked.

'Their bones have gone soft. Some have breaks that don't heal. What has Bala told you?'

'Nothing.'

'Where did you come from?'

'The Institute at Northern deep.' There was a stir amongst the children. Darkness flashed behind Jarlath's eyes.

'Tell me…is the detestable Cubal still there?'

'He is the reason we are here.' Coda said.

'That puss infested pimp is the reason many of us are here.'

'Well…we gave him a broken ankle, so he'll remember us for a while.'

Jarlath took real pleasure in that. His mirth was deep and his chuckle was infectious. 'Then you are true heroes. We who know him have dreamed many dreams of inflicting such hurt upon him. However, he will not recognise us as we have all changed. I have become old in a very short time. My hair went from blond to white and my skin became dry and wrinkled. Most of my teeth have fallen out and my bones have become brittle. They take very long to heal when they break.'

'What do you do here?'

'We have to mine the stones Bala wants in return for food. We would starve to death otherwise. What we have now is a longer, slower death from disease, accidents, and dietary deficiencies. We are consoled by the knowledge that everyone must eventually die. We will just die sooner than most. So, we try to make life as comfortable as we can. But, enough of us for now. You will find out everything when you go out with the others. Tell us your stories.'

Instinctively Coda knew that they were starved for fresh news and mental stimulation. He began. 'I am the son of Thaif the fisherman, and Ola the teacher. I was born in White Mountain and am one of the Nation…

●

Coda passed the bucket on to Remco. They were in a cramped space close to the face. They could see what they were doing from the small miner's lamps placed ten yards apart along the narrow tunnel floor. A line of young boys and girls were passing the buckets of blue coloured ore down the line. Remco took the bucket and carried it off to the sorting room. Jarlath was there overseeing things.

'Where does this go?' Remco asked, almost blinded by the clusters of miner's lamps hanging off the ceiling.

'Over there. The stone bearing ore must be separated from the flammable permafrost rocks we use for our fire place. Then the ore is crushed with hammers over there. When that's done they scoop it up and put it into that large drum that's got the angled bottom plate.'

'Then what?'

'We fill it up with water from our well at the back of the room over there.'

'Where does the water come from?'

'There's an underground river. It also pushes air up and helps ventilate the whole place. There are some old ventilation shafts in the tunnels that help circulate the air.'

'So, what happens when the drum is full of water?'

'See those two boys there? They stir the mix up with those two paddles. The heavy stones sink to the bottom and the lighter muddy stuff floats to the top and goes into the overflow pipe which ends in that container there.'

'So, how do you get the stones out then?'

'See the narrow gap cut into the bottom edge? Well…the gravel and the stones flow out and over the greased steps of the chute there. Now, the gravel, which is wet, flows away and is collected in that drum at the bottom of the chute. The stones we are after stay dry for some reason and stick to the grease.'

'It seems like a lot of work to pick the stones out of the grease.'

'No, no, there's an easier way. You see that boy there? He's the scraper. When the water stops flowing, he scrapes the grease off and puts it in that pot which he gives to that boy there. The scraper then puts recycled grease back on the steps for the next flow.'

'So, how do they get the stones out of the grease then?'

'Well, that boy there,' he pointed to the one who took the pot from the scraper. 'He heats it up over that small fire. When the grease has melted he then pours it into another pot through a sieve that catches the stones. The grease pot goes back to the scraper and the stones go to the cleaner who washes the remaining grease off and puts the cleaned stones into that metal box over there.'

'What happens to the stones?'

'Well, they go to Bala don't they. It takes about two hundred to two hundred and fifty work hours to fill that box. Then we take it to the

207

drop off point where one of his men exchanges it for food, battery packs, grease, and a few other supplies we bribe him for.'

'What sort of supplies can you get?'

'Well, it depends on his mood really. He's a surly bastard and keeps asking for more stones for the smallest things. We try to get better food, clothing, and medicines, especially pain killers. The pain killers cost more than everything else.'

'How much?'

'It could take about seventy work hours worth. The boys with the soft bones help by sifting through the gravel drum. They are experts at finding the small stones that get through.'

'What happens to the gravel and the slag? You must end up with lots of it.'

'It all gets used. I don't know if you have noticed the tunnel walls and the roof. The slag, the gravel and the ash from our fire gets mixed together with the used water. We then use metal shuttering to form a mould up the walls and roof. We then fill the mould with the mixture which, when dry, sets hard like stone and keeps the tunnel from caving in on us.'

'That's amazing. How many are you down here?'

'Thirty five, with you and Coda.'

'Well…I'd better get back. They are probably wondering where I am by now.'

'We all take a rest as we need to. Some more than others, but the work gets done.'

Remco picked up the empty bucket and joined Coda who was at the back of the line. Coda took the empty bucket and passed it up the line. 'There are four full buckets here for you. Better hurry as we are slowing things down.' Remco took two full buckets and hurried back to the sorting room. Minutes later he was back to take the other two. When he returned there was another waiting for him, but he waited for the second one.

'What took you so long?'

'Jarlath was explaining how the sorting process worked. It's very interesting…'

It was Coda's turn to be at the head of the bucket line. There were only three in the line this time as the previous shift had widened out the tunnel. It was less cramped so they could walk past each other to get to the face and collect the full buckets. It was Coda's job to fill them and pass them on. Here he could see, first hand the work being
done.

Working the face was a strong looking stocky boy of about five foot six who reminded him of Chi'Dorolam. His name was Valax and he swung his pick carefully and with determination. Every few strokes he stopped and tested the roof by knocking it with a hammer to see if it was safe to continue. If he was not sure, he put a metal post in under it. Then he continued.

It was hot at the face, brutally hot. Everyone was stripped down to their shorts and Valax who worked the hardest of all wore nothing. His body was covered in rivers of blue dust and sweat. An older girl came around with the water bucket. She reminded Coda of Zizi except that her fur was brown and slick with perspiration. Her smile was infectious and her personality bubbled with an upbeat energy. They all stopped for a break and gratefully drank the cool refreshing water.

'So, you're the White Mountain boy.' She smiled at him.

'Yes.'

'What's it like there?' and she passed a cup of water to Valax.

'The mountains are high and the air is fresh and cold.'

'Ooh…I could use some of that right now. I understand you ate fish. What is fish?'

'They are small animals that live in the lake. They are very tasty.'

'Ugh…sounds horrible to me, eating animals.'

'Well…we ate other things as well.'

'I'm sure you did.' She filled Valax's cup again and gave him a ration bar. 'You can tell me more about that later, okay?' She took back the cups and said as she left, 'Lots of thirsty workers here, so I'd better get some water to them.'

Coda looked at Valax who was still chewing on the ration bar. 'Where does she come from?'

'From a girl's Institute in the south.'

'I didn't know there were girl's Institutes.'

'Yeah…there's one here at Northern deep as well. There are two girls who come from there and one from the west. They all stood up for themselves. That's why they're here.'

'Where did you come from?'

'I was picked up off the streets.'

'What about your mother, did she not hide you?'

'I didn't know her or my father or if I even had a mother or father. I could quite easily be a clone for all I know. My earliest memory is of stealing food and bringing it to an old man. He died and I just carried on with what I knew.'

'Where did you live?'

'Enough questions for now,' Valax picked up his pick and tapped the roof. 'We have work to do.'

As the pick hit the rock a small spark ignited a layer of gas along the roof. 'Fire!' he called and fell on Coda bringing him down to the floor. The fire seemed to suck itself back into the face and a second later an explosion blew the top half of the face into the tunnel followed by a flash fire that quickly consumed the gas in the tunnel. Slabs of shale fell off the roof and landed on and around them.

Valax was the first to get out from under the ore rock and dust. He lifted Coda up and together they started digging with their bare hands for the other three. Within minutes, a swarm of boys and the girls were there. Fortunately the blast was a small one and had not proven deadly. All three were finally dug out. One had concussion, one had a broken arm, and all had cuts and bruises.

They were all taken to the sorting room where the dust was washed from their eyes and their bodies. Jarlath attended first to the one with the broken forearm. Amid screams of agony and tears, he set the boy's arm. He then wrapped it in strips of freshly boiled and dried rags and put a thin layer of the mortar mixture over the rags and left it to set. The girl from the south was attending the one who was concussed. He had come to and was vomiting in a bucket.

To Coda it looked like the aftermath of a battle. Valax was staunching the blood from a cut at the back of his head. Coda's left hand was swelling up where a rock had fallen on it and his body felt like it had been brutally beaten. They were leaning against the grease chute.

'Where does the gas come from?'

'Sometimes, the ice in the permafrost rock we use for our fireplace melts in the heat and releases the gas. There is usually some gas in the tunnel, but if there is a pocket of gas in the rock like that, we end up with an explosion. All it takes is a little spark to set it off. This time we were lucky it wasn't a big explosion.'

'Well, if that's a small explosion, I'd hate to see a big one.'

'Only a few of us have survived a big explosion.'

'What do you do with the ones who don't survive?'

'They are buried in the tunnel walls. We mark where they are by placing a flat rock in the mortar with their name etched on it.'

'Oh yeah, I've seen those. I wondered what they were. There are so many of them.'

'Yeah…'

The girl from the south came to Valax and looked at him with concern. 'How did it happen?'

'Now Lilia, don't get mad. I didn't know there was a point of flint.'

'You are our most experienced cutter. How many times have I told you to always look twice before you tap?'

'I know, I know. I was distracted and wasn't concentrating.'

'Oh, you silly man.' She hugged him to her. 'I thought you had died this time.' After a few moments, she stepped back. 'Now, let's take a look at that cut.'

Valax turned and sat on a metal tool box that he had pulled out from under the chute. Lilia washed the wound out with warm water that had just come off the boil. She was very careful to clean out any bits of stone, hair, and dust. It was a nasty L shaped cut that went down to the bone. She lifted the pointed flap of skin and washed under it. He flinched, but sat still. She carefully put it back in place and parted the hair away from the cut. Lilia opened a sealed tin of sterilised grease and put a layer of it over the cut. She then put a clean strip of rag over it. Then she bandaged it in place with more clean rags.

'There…that should hold you together and stop the bleeding. Before the next shift I'll put a clean dressing on again.' She cleaned out all his other cuts and scrapes and applied the grease to them.

'Now, Coda, let's take a look at that hand of yours. You're lucky it's not broken you know.' She put a bandage on and then filled a bag with small chunks of permafrost. 'Hold this against it. Keep it cool. That will bring the swelling down. Also,' she lifted his hand up across his chest. 'Try to keep your hand up. That will also help.' She then fashioned a sling to keep his hand in place. She washed his cuts and scrapes and put a layer of grease on them, then went off to attend to the other boys.

'Lilia is very good at this.'

'She's had lots of practice.'

'So, how do we work now?'

'We'll be off for the next few shifts.'

'But what about filling the box for Bala?'

'We have a stockpile for these occurrences.' Valax smiled at him. 'The work won't stop. The next shift will clear out the tunnel and process it. Then they will make it as safe as they can before they mortar up the walls and roof. As soon as we are healthy enough we'll go back again. That's kind of how things go.'

●

Coda tossed a few fresh permafrost rocks on the dying embers of the fire. Small blue flames appeared as the gas in them ignited and slowly grew into a bright ball of hot light. Everyone was asleep in their alcoves cut into the walls. It was quiet here as the sound of the work was another mile further down the main tunnel. He sat on the metal box and stared into the flames. The pain in his hand had kept him awake. In an effort to ignore the pain he began to relax his body and go into the no mind state of meditation. He thought of Raman and found himself in his cave.

'It's good of you to come for a visit again. Come and sit by the vent.'

As the heat of the vent touched him, he felt calm inside. 'Why has Bala done this to us?'

'The one you speak of has caused you much misery. He is motivated by power and greed.'

'But why does he use the children?'

'Because he believes he can.'

'I don't understand.'

'He thinks because you are children, you have no power and cannot oppose him.'

'So, what do we do? We are deep in a mine and have to give him the stones for food. We cannot escape and many of the children cannot walk as their bones have gone soft.'

'Is there another way to access the mine?'

'We get our water from a well that has an underground river.'

'That is very good. Can you hang a light into it?'

'Yes…why?'

'I will send someone who will find it and bring you the right foods and medicine.'

'How long must we wait?'

'First you must tell me everything you have seen.' After Coda told him everything he knew, Raman said. 'Then it will take several days. Do not despair. Soon your water bucket will not only bring you water, but many other things as well.'

Coda's silver cord began to vibrate. 'I must leave you.'

'Come again soon and bring a list of what you need.'

Coda snapped back into his body to find Remco's hand on his shoulder, shaking him gently. He had been working the opposite shift, which had just ended.

'Coda? Are you okay?'

'Yes. I was in Raman's cave.'

'I wish I could do that.'

'He said he would help us.'

'How? We are locked in here for the rest of our time.'

'Don't worry. You will see.'

'Come on now…tell me.'

'Come with me then. I have to speak to Jarlath.' Coda led the way out into the tunnel. 'We need a miner's lamp with a good battery.'

'Is that all? How's that going to do it?'

'Wait, you'll see. It's brilliant.'

They found Jarlath in the sorting room. After Coda discussed things with him, Jarlath was sceptical and reluctant to use up such a scarce and costly piece of equipment.

'I don't understand how this is going to happen. And what is this as…tral travel you speak of. I've never heard of such a thing.' After much discussion Jarlath finally agreed to give it a try. 'I just don't want to give the boys a false hope and it all becomes a great disappointment for them.'

'This will not fail.'

'I hope you are right.' Jarlath opened the supply box and took out a good miner's lamp and battery. He found a rope that was about twenty foot long. 'I think this will be long enough.' They tied the lamp to the one end and turned it on. They anchored the other end to a metal rod hammered into the wall and lowered the lamp into the well.

'So, now we wait.' Coda said.

'Now we wait.' said Jarlath with a smile.

News of the pending supplies travelled fast in their small community. It had been a very long time since they had looked forward to anything. An air of hope and anticipation filled them. Coda had contacted Raman again and given him the list of their wants and needs. Raman promised to do the best he could. And now they waited. Nine shifts came and went and the battery was changed three times. Coda contacted Raman again.

'Come…sit by the vent,' was Raman's customary greeting. 'You must be wondering what is taking so long.'

'Yes.'

'I had to send three aqua miners up the tributaries of this most powerful river. It is in fact the one that you and Remco had fallen into, but it has many branches that feed into it. One of them finally found your light and the supplies are now on their way. Perhaps another five or six hours I would say.'

'That is such good news. They will be so happy.'

Raman nodded…after a moment's silence he said. 'I have contacted your mother.'

'How is she?'

'Now that she knows you are well, she will endure. Bala is cruel, but her mind is strong.'

'I hate that Sabalian worm.'

'And you have every right to, but you must learn to channel your hate for the right opportunity.'

'When will be the right time?'

'You will know when the time is right and I will help you prepare for it.'

'How?'

'You must work the mine and develop your body as you will need all the strength you can muster against the likes of Bala. You have the heart of a warrior and were born with the instinct for battle, but your skills must be learned. Come to me when you are not too tired and Merrix will begin your instruction.'

'It will be good to see Merrix again.'

'You must go now. Your supplies will arrive soon.'

Coda was back in his body. He opened his eyes to find Jarlath staring intently at him. It had taken him some time to accept the theory that Coda could astral travel at will.

'So…what did he say?'

'Five or six hours.' Coda smiled. 'He said it took three aqua miners some time to find our light as there are many rivers that flow into one.'

'Three aqua miners. How is that possible? What did he say about the medicine?'

'I did not ask, but he did not say there was anything he could not get for us.'

'Then we must hope for the best. It will be fantastic if we get everything we asked for hey.' Jarlath's eyes were bright with hope and expectation.

'Oh yeah…it will be fantastic. That's for sure.'

●

The fifth hour came and went and all the well bucket contained was water for the drum. There was an expectant silence among the boys working in the sorting room. Every time the bucket came up everyone looked to see if this was the one with some supplies. Coda looked down the well for the hundredth time to make sure the miner's lamp was still working and of course it was. The bucket went down again, but this time there was a hesitation when Coda tried to reel it back up. When it came up brim full of ration packs it was with silent disbelief that everyone looked. The magical moment was broken by a sudden whoop of joy from the scraper.

Everyone was infected by it and it was as if the room suddenly became brighter as they all cheered and danced with joy. It was not only the idea that the supplies were finally here, but that they were not alone. They were connected with the outside world. Their fate was known.

Coda emptied the bucket onto the floor and sent it down again. Bucket after bucket came up with fresh supplies of batteries, medicine, clothing, footwear, and more food than they had ever seen at any one time before. Three story books came up in the last bucket with a note that read. 'Be strong. We will be back in ten days.'

Never had they ever had such a bonanza before. All work stopped for the occasion. Everyone came in to marvel at the large pile of goods. There were cans of off-world fish that some remembered from the Institutes they were in and rations that were only supplied to the miners.

'Let's eat,' someone said.

'Yes! Let's eat!' Everyone chorused.

'Hold on! Hold on now!' Jarlath called above the din. 'Okay…we'll take a few hours off and have a feast to remember this moment and give special thanks to Coda who made it happen for us.'

'Coda!' They all cheered. Coda smiled graciously and was taken aback by all the sudden attention and the shining smiles on everyone's faces. Suddenly as if by common consent they all began picking up the supplies and carried them off to their common room. There they built up the fire and put buckets of water on it for cooking. They put in ration bars that melted and became a thick tasty broth. They opened up a box of canned fish and distributed a tin of fish to each and everyone. They opened them, drank the oils, and scooped the fish out with their fingers. Some stuffed their mouths and chewed hungrily while others took their time and savoured the taste of the delicate flesh.

The chatter was animated and exciting as they sorted out the clothing and footwear amongst themselves. Jarlath and Lilia were sorting out the medical supplies when Valax came up to Coda and asked. 'So how does it work…this astral travel of yours?'

'To be honest, I can't really explain it. When I meditate or sleep I can choose to go anywhere and before I know it I'm there.'

'Can you teach others to do this?'

'I don't know. I've never tried.'

'Do you think you could try to teach me? I would like to see daylight again. Breathe in the fresh air and feel the cold on my face.'

'I can try. Maybe it will work.'

'Yeah…maybe.' Valax smiled. 'Looks like the soup is ready.'

After they had all satisfied themselves on bowls of broth they sat quietly staring into the flames. Their bellies full, some began to doze when Jarlath picked up one of the books and began to read aloud.

'***Mystery in the Forest of Greed***, by Magnus…A drop of water slipped softly from a purple leaf. Mystery watched it grow large as it fell towards her…'

●

'The end is very near.' Raman was holding a long crystal with its end submerged into a bowl of water. 'A dark force is approaching us and there is nothing we can do about it.'

Coda had just turned fifteen. He was seven foot tall and his body was beginning to fill out with hard muscle borne of gruelling hours at the face. His hair had grown into long ropey locks that reached halfway down his back. His locks grew around long slender muscles that enabled them to move as if they had a life of their own. The tips of the locks ended in hardened spikes. 'What do you mean by "a dark force"?'

'A consciousness, so dark, I fear most of us will not survive.' Coda could feel Raman's urgency. 'Your training is almost complete. I think you are now ready for the next phase. This will empower you and increase your chances of survival.'

'What's going to happen?'

Raman turned towards him. His eye in the centre of his forehead moved behind the skin. Coda knew him well enough to know that he was agitated. 'Total destruction. Those who survive will be taken and sold into slavery.'

'But we are already slaves and I have been sold once already.'

'The cruelty you have experienced here holds no comparison to what will come.'

'What more can they do to us that has not already been done?'

'Do not dwell on it. We have little time and much left to do. In the next delivery of supplies you will receive a small bag of herbs. Go to your meditation chamber and light your fire. Then empty out the contents into a bowl of water and bring it to the boil. Let it steep for a few minutes and then drink it all. Go into your state of meditation, but do not travel here. This is a journey you must take alone.'

'What must I expect?'

'You must be strong for you will experience many things. Above all, do not fear for you will be reborn. If you survive it, the secrets of this universe will be yours. Everything you need to know will come to you as you need it.'

Coda's silver cord began to vibrate. 'When must I come to you again?'

217

'After you have taken the infusion. Go now and enjoy the last hours as Coda the miner, for you will not be the same after.'

'I will do as instructed Raman of White Mountain.' Coda bowed his head with what had become their customary departure.

'Your company has been my pleasure Coda of White Mountain.'

In an instant Coda was back in his body. It was Remco standing at the entrance to the meditation chamber. He had lost almost all of his skin pigmentation from all the years living underground. 'Sorry to disturb you, but it is time for your class.'

Coda was seated on a woven cloth mattress. It was in the wall alcove of his meditation chamber. It was a small room he had carved into the wall of one of the unused tunnels that had some ventilation. He used it for meditation and sometimes to sleep. Usually he would sleep in the common room with the others, but their community had grown to forty two by now and was sometimes too noisy.

Their survival rate had increased with better food and medical supplies. They had kept the supply of stones at the same rate, which meant more time off to do other things. A school had been created that was attended by everyone on a regular basis. Coda taught mathematics and music. Jarlath taught letters and reading. Lilia taught her nursing and hygiene skills and Valax his strong engineering skills. It had all been Jarlath's idea.

'Very well…it's so hard to keep track of time. If it wasn't for the time piece, we'd be lost.' Coda stood up and followed Remco out.

'That's for sure.' Remco was short, but of stocky build. He had become physically very powerful. He was able to lift things no one else could, and in their wrestling matches he was only second to Coda who had learned his skills from Merrix while on the astral plane. He had taught Coda all of the fighting arts who in turn had passed those skills on to the others. Theirs had become a literate, fighting community that Coda was proud of.

When they reached the recreation room, which served as a kitchen and classroom with a central fire, it was filled with the raucous uncoordinated noise of everyone playing or warming up on their various instruments. There were clusters of two or three boys playing their own thing and individuals practising their orchestral movements. The instruments were all hand made, invented with what was available. Drums were various sized metal buckets. Remco had made timpani drums from two large metal containers he had found down one of the old tunnels.

Different sized flutes were made of pipes. A variety of other windblown instruments like trumpets, bugles, horns, and didgeridoos were made by Valax. He had also made a xylophone and tubular bells. There was all manner of other percussion instruments designed by anyone who wanted to join in. It was a wind orchestra that had grown organically.

As soon as they saw Coda they settled down. He looked at them. Their faces shone with eagerness and a hunger for knowledge. He smiled and picked up his father's flute. His father's belongings had been sent with Merrix across the ice flats. He played a note and everyone with a wind instrument played the same note. The note ended and an expectant silence fell over the room.

The bass didgeridoos began with a low moody hum…

Coda looked at the battered time piece and called. 'Time!' Their shift had finished at the face. He had become a cutter like Valax, but instead of working naked, he had taken to wearing a loin cloth. He put his tools down for the next shift and walked down the tunnel. Halfway down, one of the two boys that worked at the face with Coda said to the other indicating the slop bucket. 'It's your turn.'

'Ugh…I suppose it is.' He bent and took the handle. As he lifted it the contents sloshed about releasing a fresh whiff. 'Ugh…' he repeated. 'It smells worse than ever.'

'Ha-ha! It smells like that all the time. It was no better with our last shift. Careful you don't trip and spill it all over yourself.' He smiled.

It had become a long corridor with several side branches that led to the volcanic pipe they were mining out. They had rigged up a simple trolley system with a cable on each end to exchange the four full buckets of ore from the face with empty ones. When the trolley got to each end, they swapped the buckets out and pulled on the bell cable that signalled the boy on the other end to pull it back.

Valax met them at the end of the tunnel with the new crew. 'How are the gasses at the face?'

'Mild this time, but there's a lot of flint about, so watch

yourself.'

'Right then,' he responded with his usual cheer. 'Let's go get some stones boys.'

When Coda got to the sorting room he and the four boys headed for the shower room that had been carved out on the left side of the room. Several gravity feed bucket showers had been set up. They had holes in the bottom with a sliding plate above the holes that was moved with a twist lever to release or close the flow of water. The used water would then drain off back to the well and into the river. A shower boy would refill the buckets and clean up.

While Coda stood under the shower and felt the cold water wash the grime off his overheated body, he thought of a conversation he had had with Raman years ago.

'But why can't we leave? We know there is a way out now.'

'Now is not the time. We cannot hide you all and it will only mean that you will be re-captured and put back in the mine. We do not have a way of bringing you all across the ice flats either.'

'When will be the time?'

'When you are ready.'

'When will that be?'

'I cannot yet see that far ahead. For now you must learn from Merrix. Learn the war arts from Chi'Dorolam and continue with your meditations. It will be sooner than you think.'

That had been eight years ago. During that time he had learnt his lessons well and passed everything on to their small subterranean community. He knew they were as ready as they were ever going to be. Was this the time? Was this the end time Raman had referred to in relation to the dark force? Was taking the herbs the final piece of the puzzle?

His thoughts were interrupted by one of the young boys who had cramps and had to rush off to the toilet. He ran through the sorting room, wet and naked, generating jeers and laughter, as he headed for the room on the opposite end. Their toilet had been a much bigger problem to solve. In this room they had placed slabs of rock on squared off blocks. Holes had been cut in the slabs to create five seated toilets. They did their business into a bucket beneath. The waste was then covered with a handful of dry slag. A small bowl of water from a water bucket at each toilet was used to wash. One of the great luxuries they now had was soap.

The slop buckets would be changed with each new shift and emptied out onto one of the new compost beds being prepared in three of the old tunnels. Two low stone walls had been laid out in the centre of these tunnels so as to form a path down the middle with the compost beds on either side. When it was dry, another layer would be put on top. They had found that these beds of waste were excellent for growing mushrooms. It was another of Raman's instructions.

When Coda finished with his shower, he took his clothes from one of the many pegs on the opposite wall. He dried himself off with a large rag and got dressed. In the recreation room he helped himself to a light meal from the pot and listened to Jarlath discuss the plot of a new book the class was studying. When he was finished he washed his bowl and went to his meditation chamber and slept for a few hours.

He awoke refreshed and relaxed. He added some permafrost rocks to the embers of his fire and a small flame appeared. Soon they were burning well. He poured some water from a bucket of water he had prepared earlier, into a small metal bowl. He placed it onto the fire and added the herbs from the bag. He stirred it in and let it come to the boil. Then he moved the pot to the side and let it steep for a few minutes. He poured the infusion into a cup and let it cool off just enough to drink it. When it was ready he took the full cup to his mattress and sat in his customary position. He lifted the cup to his lips. He thought of Raman's words. "Do not fear for you will be reborn" and drank the contents down.

He stared into the flames wondering what might happen. What did Raman mean by "reborn"? Was he going to die? Would he need help? Should he have asked Remco to sit with him? All these thoughts began to go through his mind. He tried to relax. He closed his eyes and tried to meditate, but he felt too keyed up. He was restless and anxious of what might happen. He began to feel nauseous and wondered if he was going to get sick. He decided not to get sick. Waves of nausea and exhaustion seemed to follow.

Then he began to see sparks of light flashing against his eyelids. He opened his eyes and stared once more into the flames. They were blue and pulsing. The shadows on the walls began to move as if they were somehow alive. When he looked, they were not there. When he looked away, they moved again. Must be a trick of the light, he thought. The air in the chamber became thick. He lifted his hand and drew it across his vision and the air rippled like water between his fingers. He could see the air enter his mouth as he breathed it in, distorting and contracting the room as if he was breathing the room in. When he breathed out the room seemed to expand outwards.

He closed his eyes and he felt himself sucked into a tunnel. He tried to resist it but found the pull was too strong and no matter what he did it would not let him go. It felt like this was his death. He was totally consumed with fear. Fear of dying. Then Raman's words came to him. "Do not fear for you will be reborn". The light at the end of the tunnel rushed at him. His fear increased as he came into the light and found himself in the chamber, but it was different. It felt more sinister. The shadows had detached from the walls and were looking at him with glowing eyes. They were ragged boys all trying to speak at once, reaching out to him, their faces dark with sorrow.

He could feel tears streaming down his face, burning deep furrows into his cheeks. As the drops landed on his thighs, they seemed to sizzle with heat. It felt like he had entered another dimension where he was connected to everything and everyone. Soon the shadows entered him and he understood their needs. His fear dissipated and was replaced by a feeling of intense euphoria, as if he had just survived the battle of his life, only more intense than that. The euphoria continued for what felt like an hour. He felt at one with everything. He was the energy of life itself, the binding force that held everything together and turned it into matter.

The room seemed very bright and the walls had become iridescent with many colours that seemed to flow and swirl between the stones. The stones seemed to come alive and crawl around in random patterns. He began to feel a pressure in his head, like a knife pushing against a membrane. Suddenly there was a loud crack and what felt like a rip.

Then he heard voices, only what they were saying was more like thoughts. They crowded into him. Overwhelmed him. He put his hands over his ears and tried to shut out the noise. It felt as if he was standing in a crowd and could hear everyone's thoughts. He opened his mouth and tried to scream, but no sound came out. He was in a dream, but not a dream. This was all happening to him and he knew it was happening, as if he was watching and feeling it all. He felt like he was and was not in control all at the same time. It was a conscious experience.

The voices in his head felt real and almost natural, like it was normal to hear other people's thoughts. He tried to focus on the thoughts, but they were passing too fast. They were too mixed up to find any order. Some were loud and others were soft and then they went silent. Everything in him became still. Suddenly he found himself on top of one of the slag heaps. There was fire and explosions all around him. He saw the head gears above the mine shafts falling. Some were bent and destroyed. The compounds were on fire and the village of Northern Deep was destroyed.

A strange looking space craft appeared in front of him. He felt an intense terror, but could not run. It hovered there for what felt like hours while everything else burned. The craft inched forward and his terror became something he could taste. His tongue turned to hot metal that scorched the inside of his mouth and fused with his pallet. As the craft began to hover above him he felt a pull on his body that lifted him. Paralysed by its power, he was elevated into an open doorway. Then everything went black.

He looked behind him and saw himself sitting with a terrified expression on his face. His distended pupils made his eyes look surreal in their blackness. Gently he got back into his body. He looked at his hands and arms and black shadows were expelling themselves through his pores and returning to the walls. The light from the fire began to dim to normal and he felt himself returning.

He had been dead and reborn. Not dead as in deceased, but re-made from his living cells. As if he had been taken apart and re-assembled. Woken up to a different reality. That everyday life was the lie, and reality existed in that other dimension he had briefly been immersed in. What did the vision mean? Was it something that would come to pass? He knew that his mind had not absorbed everything that he had experienced. As time went on it would come to him. Five hours had passed. He was exhausted. He curled up on his mattress and slept for another twelve hours.

●

'Can you make it stop?' Coda asked Raman.
'You have been given the greatest gift of all. When I gave you the infusion, I had no idea what would happen; only that your latent talents would become manifest. In all of creation there has never been and I don't think ever will be one with your abilities.'

'What's the point of an ability when it's driving me mad? I can't hear my own thoughts with all this noise in my head.'

'You must learn to tune into the thoughts you want to hear and the others will subside.'

'How do you know? What makes you the expert at reading minds?'

'I am a telepath. I am attuned to the community of White Mountain. It is as if everyone is connected to me. I communicate through energy that generates specific emotions. To do this I have to tune in to that individual's energy. But what you have is unique in that you can hear their thoughts and feel their emotions. It's as though you are inside that being's head. You can also communicate directly in a conversational way with language.'

'So all I have to do is tune in or out?'

'Yes, but it will take practice. Lots of practice.'

'How much time do I have?'

'You have the rest of your life, but for now you must learn to tune out, so that you can find order and control.'

'No...I mean, how much time before the dark force?'

'Very little. You must prepare to leave the mine.'

'How much time?'

'Forty eight hours. There will be three rafts waiting for you on the river. The three aqua miners who have been your suppliers all these years will also be there to guide the rafts out and to hide you before the...harvest begins.'

'What do you mean by "harvest"?'

'Many of you will be captured and taken from here.'

Instinctively Coda understood that many would also not survive, including Raman. 'But what of you? How can you be so calm about it?'

'Death is only another state of being. I will continue to exist. I will become part of the fabric of creation. I will become part of all of those I have been connected to. Yours will be a very long life and I will be a part of your journey.'

'Who will do this to us?'

'Pirates...slavers who answer to no-one. They destroy planets and trade the spoils at the whim of their leader.'

'How can we stop them?'

'Only you will find the way, but it will take a very long time. You must hurry now. Come and see me again when you are safe.'

'I will do as instructed Raman of White Mountain.'

'Your company has been my pleasure Coda of White Mountain.'

●

They were all ready. Everyone had gathered in the common room and was looking at Jarlath. Coda had stilled his mind and had built up a barrier to tune out. The noise was finally quiet, but when he looked at someone he could hear their thoughts, whether he wanted to or not. Many were afraid. To most, the mine had been their only home and they were reluctant to leave. Only the threat of imminent death had convinced them. Jarlath was especially reluctant to go, but had busied himself with the preparations. There had not been much to do. They had gathered up their meagre belongings, tying them up in small bundles. Lilia had fussed over what medical supplies to take and Valax had fretted over leaving his hand made tools. Remco had made sure they were all warmly dressed as they had forgotten the cold. Coda had his father's boots, his coat and flute and also the knife he had taken from Snake Eyes all those years ago.

They had all eaten a large meal and as was their habit cleaned everything up. There was a mixed sense of panic and joy among them that came to a head when Jarlath divided up the stones. Jarlath divided up the stockpile they had accumulated, equally among them. He kept three portions aside, for the aqua miners who had supplied them all these years. Somehow it had made things real for them. Some of the young boys and girls had cried. The older ones had been more stoic. Now that everyone was ready, Coda could feel Jarlath's pain.

'We have lived and worked here for so long, it feels like there is nothing else.' Jarlath took a deep breath to bring his emotions under control. 'But there is. What you will find is fear and cold. Our little community has been spared all that, until now. Those of us who survive what is to come will remember this home as a place of love and compassion. Many of our friends are buried in these walls, but they will travel with us in our hearts. They will not be left behind.' Jarlath looked around the room. There was a sober realisation on everyone's face. 'What is to come is beyond our experience, but if we stick together we might live. You must be strong and above all, do not fear. Fear is the killer.'

A deep silence fell over them. Coda took his father's flute and played the haunting meditation melody his father had taught him. Everyone listened introspectively to the soothing notes. When Coda reached the end of the tune he lifted the mood of it and turned it into something hopeful and joyous that brought brightness to the room and lifted their spirits. Lilia and Valax began a dance that infected everyone and made some join them in a celebration of love and togetherness. Even Jarlath had a smile. Coda played his heart out and when the tune finally ended, they were all flushed and in an elevated mood. The air was electric.

'It's time.' Jarlath said.

They all picked up their bundles and went to the well. Each took a miner's lamp and checked the battery. They did not have to wait long for the aqua miners were on time. Coda, Remco and Valax took turns at the winch. Lilia was the first to go down, and then the young boys and girls followed. The older ones went down after them. When it came to Jarlath's turn he hung back.

Coda looked at him and knew his thoughts. He said nothing out loud, but communicated telepathically. 'Do not stay Jarlath.' Jarlath swung around and looked at Coda. He was uncertain if he had heard correctly. 'Do not stay.' Coda shook his head. 'This will be certain death.'

'What life is there for me but this?'

'You are the force of cohesion to us. You are and will be needed in the time to come. This place is not your life. We are your life.'

'I don't know if I have the strength.'

'Do not fear. Our strength will be yours to share.'

Jarlath looked at the well for the longest time. His mind and emotions were numb with shock. The shock of having to enter into the unknown. Coda could feel his panic. He looked into his mind and transferred a calm clarity that seemed to quiet Jarlath's emotions and clear his thoughts. He looked at Coda and with a resigned shrug sat on the edge of the well. He swung his legs over the side, took hold of the cable, and put his foot into the bucket. He looked up at Coda for a long time as he was lowered down.

Valax was next and then Remco. Coda let the cable out a little further and anchored it to the winding mechanism post. He took a last look around and felt a pang of nostalgia for the home he had known for the last eight years. He bade it a silent farewell, took hold of the cable, and climbed down to the subterranean river. When his foot touched the raft he could feel it being pulled to the bank where everyone was waiting. Once Coda was ashore they divided themselves up into three groups and boarded the three rafts which the aqua miners anchored with ropes around their waists. They were barrel rafts held together with cables onto an upper metal frame. The floor was made from the metal sheeting of barrels cut open and flattened out. When they were all aboard they set off down river.

Jarlath and one of the older boys had taken the poles at the front of the lead raft with the largest of the aqua miners on the oar at the rear. Valax and Lilia were on the second raft and Coda was on the third with Remco. They floated gently into the stream picking up speed as the current took them. The light from their lamps pierced the dark and illuminated the cavern carved out by the river over thousands of years. Great chandeliers of stalactites hung from the roof and the water was crystal clear.

Soon they joined one of the tributaries and the current strengthened. They had to negotiate a series of rapids that threatened to topple them off. When they reached the third tributary, their speed increased considerably. Some of the boys were terrified and others were exhilarated by it. The ones at the oars and poles were too busy to think about it. In what felt like four or five hours they began to see light. The oarsmen manoeuvred the rafts closer to shore and out of the central current. They beached the rafts on a sandy bend three hundred yards from the waterfall's edge. They huddled together on shore, cold and fearful of what was to come. The aqua miners lit a fire and told Jarlath that they had to wait for nightfall to go on. Remco and Coda walked to the entrance.

'Remember this place?' Remco asked.

'Yes.'

'I wonder if the stones are still there.'

'Let's go take a look.'

Close to the entrance they found the heavy rock. Coda looked behind it and found the small crack in the wall where he remembered he had put the bag and it was still there. He took it out and opened it. He emptied some the stones into his hand and looked more closely at them.

'These are smaller than I remember, but bigger than the ones we have been mining.'

'What do you think we should do with them?'

'I'm not sure. What do you think we should do with them?'

'I don't know.' Remco scratched his head. 'Maybe we should hold onto them. Maybe your mother will need them.'

Coda looked at Remco. He felt a great gratitude towards him. 'Perhaps you are right. I have seen her many times in my meditations and she is not doing well. I must get her away from Bala.'

'Do you think she even knows that you're there?'

'Sometimes I think she does. Sometimes she looks straight at me. I know she can't see me, but I'm sure she knows I'm there. I have not been there since I can read minds.'

'Maybe that will make the difference.'

'Maybe.' Coda put the stones back in the bag and put it in his pocket.

They went to the entrance and looked out over the ice flats. The late afternoon sun was on their right and cast long shadows off the massive ice blocks that jutted out of the flats. They seemed to have broken through the floor like giant spear tips violently thrust up from the depths beneath. Some were jagged and pure white. Others were grey and black. There was some that were blue and transparent as the bleak light filtered through. A billowing cloud of water vapour picked up a few yellow rays where the waterfall met the ice at the bottom of the cliff. Its thunder drowned out all sound.

Valax, Lilia and several of the younger kids joined them. 'I've waited a long time for this!' Valax called with a smile on his face. 'I never thought I'd ever say the ice flats were beautiful!' Lilia hugged him; glowing with joy.

They all stood there until the light faded and the night sky lit up with millions of stars like sparkling dust on a black pond...

After they had eaten it was time to go. The tall aqua miner led the way up the cliff face. Every one was tied to each other with a long rope. When the aqua miner reached the top he anchored the rope to a large rock and kept it taut. Some of the younger children slipped and if it were not for the rope they would have fallen to certain death below, but the aqua miner was strong and held firm. Like subterranean beings they boiled over the edge and silently filtered into the rocks. The last to come over the edge was the third aqua miner.

They gathered in a small clearing among the rocks. When they were all accounted for, they followed the tall aqua miner up a narrow path that wound between the boulders and up the hill. It ended at the side of a muddy service road. It was quiet so they crossed quickly and disappeared into the dark on the other side. One of the aqua miners wiped their tracks with a wet sack they had kept hidden among the stones. They had just started moving when they heard the truck. Everyone froze and lay down in the shadows. Headlights lanced the night and waved about as the driver tried to keep the truck on the road. Its engine roared and gears crashed as it skidded through the mud. There were whoops of laughter coming from the two drunken Sabalians in the cab as they returned from the tavern in the village. The truck finally passed. Like shadows detaching from the rocks, they all stood up and continued up the hill.

When they reached the top, there was another road and beyond that, the compound. This time it was not so easy to cross the road. There was too much traffic. They hid behind the boulders and waited. A cold wind picked up and lashed them into huddled shivering groups; pinning them to the shadows for two hours before the traffic slacked off. Only when solitary vehicles finally passed did they begin to cross in small groups.

The compound was dark with no street lamps. The only light was that which spilled out of the open windows and doors. Everyone followed close behind the tall aqua miner as he made his way through the alleyways until he stopped at a dark building that looked like a low store house with no windows. The tall one took out a key and unlocked the door. The ragged boys filed past him and he shut the door behind them. He turned on the light switch and three light strips came on in the roof. The light was blindingly bright in comparison to the dark. There were sky light windows in the roof which were blacked out with sacks that could be removed in the day to let the light in. It was indeed a store house, but a disused one. There were piles of sacks on the floor, a stove in the centre of the room and a heap of permafrost rocks for the fire against one wall. There was a stack of supplies against the opposite wall and three taps for water that had been recently plumbed in. On one end of the room there were two old toilets that still worked and two showers also recently plumbed in.

The tall one gave the key to Jarlath. 'It is very basic, but it will have to do until the harvest. We have three…maybe five days. Be careful when you go out and keep the young ones in until it is time. Then…you must go to the top of the slag heaps. That way you will be found.'

'Thank you. Thank you for everything you have done for us all these years.'

'We did as Raman wished.'

'What is your name?'

'It is not important. This will be the last time you will see us.'

'Where will you go?'

'To White Mountain. It is our choice to be with Raman on the final day.'

'Give him our thanks and gratitude.'

'It will be so.' He turned to Coda. 'Live long Coda of White Mountain.'

'Give my father my greetings Tall one of White Mountain.'

'It will be so.' And he left the room with the other two aqua miners.

●

E veryone was asleep. The room was dark and Coda sat by the stove. He went into deep meditation and thought of his mother. He found himself in the small basement room she was forced to use. She was lying asleep on a small cot under the stairs. She was breathing with difficulty and he could see she had a fever. He stood by her bed and looked at her face. She slept with a frown and she was perspiring.

'Mother…can you hear me?' he thought.

Ola seemed to flinch. She opened her eyes, closed them again, and turned to face the wall. She pulled the thin blanket over her shoulder and instantly fell back to sleep.

'Mother…can you hear me?' he thought again.

'What?' Ola sat upright, wide awake. 'Who's there?'

'It is me mother, Coda, your son.'

She pulled the blanket to her chest. 'My son is in Bala's mine. Who is this...Show yourself!'

'It really is me, Mother. I'm in spirit form and I'm standing in your room beside your bed.'

Tears burst from Ola's eyes and streamed down her face. She

looked haggard and aged. 'If you are here in the spirit then you must be dead.'

'Please…dry your eyes. I am not dead. I am alive and well. I have learnt to astral travel and I can now communicate telepathically. That is why you can hear me.'

'This must be a dream. You are in Bala's mine.'

'I am not in Bala's mine anymore. None of us are. I have come to you to see if you can leave Bala's house.'

'If it is truly you then answer me this. Who was my midwife at your birth?'

'Zizi of White Mountain.'

'Then it must be you. Your voice sounds like your father's.' Ola strained to see him. She looked all over the room with fresh hope in her eyes. 'How is it that you can do these things?'

'I began to travel soon after I went to the Institute. I followed Da's teachings of meditation and I thought of Raman and the next instant I was in his chamber.'

Her face lit up. 'Raman has been a source of constant strength for me. I have thought of him often when things got bad and I have felt him near me many times. I have had similar experiences when I thought of you. Have you been here before?'

'Yes mother…many times. It is only now that I can communicate directly.'

'But, how is that possible?'

'Raman has guided me. I can now not only communicate in this way, but read minds as well. I am still learning to control it.'

'Where are you now then?'

'We are in the compound. Can you get away from Bala's house? I must get you away from him.'

'Oh…I can't leave. He will find me and kill you.'

'Please, Mother. You must trust me.'

'He lets me out to go to the market for some Sabalian fruits and other things. I can try to get away.'

'Can I meet you there tomorrow?'

'I will try to get away for midday. It will be so good to see you again.'

'Where should I wait for you?'

'You will find me at the fruit stall under the three arches bridge.'

'Is it the one where you met Da?'

'Yes.'

'I will see you there then, but now I must go back to my body. I can only stay for so long.'

Ola reached out in front of her. 'Thank you for coming.'

'I will see you tomorrow, Mother…'

●

Coda and Remco had waited all morning in the alley across from the fruit stall before Ola arrived. She wore a black hooded cape that hid her face. She looked around expectantly and then when she didn't see Coda, hesitantly began to pick up and inspect the Sabalian fruits.

'There she is.' Coda's thoughts were directed towards Remco. He looked at Coda, then at Ola and nodded. They had no need to communicate vocally.

'Continue with what you are doing, Mother.' Coda thought to Ola. She looked up and side to side looking for him. 'We are in the alley behind you. Pay for the fruit and then come to us as casually as you can.' Ola took four bags of the smaller fruits, paid and turned around. She walked across the street and into the dark alley. Coda stepped away from the doorway he was waiting in, but kept to the shadows.

'Coda?' Ola asked, not recognising the seven foot tall teenager standing in front of her. He stepped forward into the light. 'Oh Coda, it is you!' She rushed forward and hugged him with all the pent up longing of all the years they had been apart.

'Mother.' His emotions were intense and overwhelming. He

'Mother.' His emotions were intense and overwhelming. He could not believe how fragile she felt.

'Let me look at you.' Ola broke the hug and held him at arms length. 'You have grown so much. You look more like your father than ever. And so strong. I thought the mine would kill you, but instead you look so healthy.'

'We had a lot of help from Raman.'

'Raman? But how?'

'It's a long story, but first we must get away from here. I want you to meet my friend Remco.' Ola nodded and smiled. 'We arrived at the Institute on the same day.' They turned and went up the alley.

'Where will we go? Bala will be home at nightfall and if he finds me gone…'

'What will he do? What can he do? We are all out of his mine and he has no idea where any of us are. He can do nothing. And in three days it won't matter.'

'What do you mean? Why won't it matter in three days?'

'I will explain later, but for now, we must get away.'

'Very well.'

They clung to the shadows of the early afternoon as they made their way to the compound store house that was their temporary home. Coda knocked on the door with the pre-arranged code and it was opened by Valax. All eyes were turned towards them as they stepped into the room. Ola had not seen so many children in one room since her classes at White Mountain.

'This is Ola. She is my mother.'

Jarlath stepped forward. 'I am Jarlath. I'm so pleased to meet you. Coda has taught us all your mathematical theories.'

Ola seemed lost for words. One of the youngest boys tugged at her cape and pointed at the fruit. 'Can I have one of those?'

'Oh…yes…of course.' She opened a bag and offered. The boy took a handful and turned. Ola was promptly swamped by all the young ones. Lilia stepped in. 'I am Lilia. I'll share those out for you,' and took the bags from her. She walked over to makeshift table and emptied the fruit into several small bowls and passed them around.

Everyone introduced themselves to Ola and after some time, left her to be with Coda. They talked for hours. After the evening meal they listened to Jarlath read a story from one of the books he had brought with him. They had switched off the main lights and used a few of the miner's lamps that created a warmer and more intimate atmosphere around the stove. After everyone went to their beds, Coda and Ola sat close to the stove and communicated telepathically until late into the night. Ola finally slept on Coda's bed.

Coda went into meditation and travelled to Raman.

'I see you Coda of White Mountain.'

'I see you Raman of White Mountain.'

'Come…sit by the vent.'

'We are safe for now.'

'I am pleased to hear that. The aqua miners who helped you will be here soon.'

'I have my mother here with me.'

'You must take her to the Doctor.'

'Who is "the Doctor"?'

'Dr. Elwyn Rosmadden. Your mother used to work for him.'

Coda was taken aback. 'Why would I take her to someone who used her as his slave?'

'He loves her and was very kind to her. His ex wife was the cruel one. He and I have worked together for many years to run people and supplies out of Northern Deep. He has now come on hard times, but will be able to nurse your mother back to good health. But, you must take her there tonight and persuade him to leave XN5 with her on the morning shuttle. It is their only chance to survive the harvest that will arrive some time tomorrow.'

'Tomorrow! I must warn the others.'

'They must go atop the slag heaps if they want to live. What life they will have I can't say, but your mother has a chance with Dr. Elwyn. Beware of Bala. He will try to stop her from leaving and then he will come for you.'

'I have no fear of him.'

'Be cautious. Bala is tough and dirty. He has much experience and has killed many times. Do not underestimate him.'

'I will do as you say, Raman of White Mountain.'

'I bid you farewell and a long life. You have been a good student and you are now ready. I will see you in the afterlife Coda of White Mountain.'

Coda found himself back in the store house next to the stove. He went to his bed and sat down next to his mother. He looked at her face. It was peaceful but with deep wrinkles of worry around her eyes and mouth. How much she has suffered, he thought. What kind of abuse had Bala dished out? Such an intelligent woman forced to live in that damp basement room for eight years.

This man deserves no mercy or compassion for what he has done, he thought. Not only what he has done to us, but to countless others. Coda felt his pulse quicken as his rage began to boil inside him. Who does he think he is? Who do these Sabalians think they are? I will make them all pay, he vowed. I will make Bala pay in blood. I will make him pay for murdering my father. He will pay for hurting my mother. He wanted to shout it out at the top of his voice. His head was bursting and his chest constricted. He had difficulty breathing and his hands were shaking. He clenched his fists and forced himself to breathe. Slowly his training took over and he regained his control.

Silently he stood up and went to Jarlath. He shook him gently and Jarlath opened his eyes. 'Coda? What is it?'

'I am sorry to wake you.'

Jarlath sat up. 'You won't wake me for no reason. What is it?'

'Tomorrow is the day.'

'Tomorrow? How will we know when to move?'

'I don't know. Perhaps at the first sound of trouble you must take everyone onto the slag heaps.'

'Very well.' Jarlath looked at all the quietly sleeping boys in their beds. 'They look so peaceful. We have several hours before dawn. I'll let them sleep a little longer. What do you think?'

'I think dawn would be a good time for an attack.'

'Then I will have them ready by dawn. What will you do?'

'I have to get my mother to safety. If I survive then I will be harvested.'

'Go with caution then brother.'

'And you brother.' Coda went to his mother and woke her.

Coda and Ola hesitated at the back gate. The alley was dark and quiet in the hours just before dawn. It had been a long walk for her and she was much weaker than Coda had thought. They had to stop several times to let her rest. She had a racking cough that took hold every time she exerted herself. After the spasms ended and she got her breath back they had moved on. They had made much slower progress than he had hoped for.

'Is this his house?' Coda looked up and down the alley, but nothing moved. Ola nodded, afraid she might cough. Coda tried the latch and the gate opened under his hand. To their surprise the light was on in the surgery. They crossed the courtyard and knocked softly on the door. There was a cough and a moment later a shuffling step approached the door.

It opened and Coda looked upon a bent old man in his night gown and slippers. He was very thin and he had lost most of his hair. His blue skin was almost colourless, but his eyes were still lively and alert. 'Ola…It is so good to see you again.'

'Master…' Ola bowed and went on her knees.

'Ola, please, stand up and come here.' She stood up and came to him. He put his hands on her shoulders and looked into her eyes. 'Never call me master again and never go on you knees again. I will always be Elwyn.' And he hugged her. He stood back. 'Come in,' they walked into his little surgery. The small waiting room was dusty and untidy. 'Please forgive the state of the place. I haven't had anyone looking after it in years. Let's go through to the study, its warmer there.'

The study was in an equal state of disarray with piles of books on the floor and on the table and chairs. When they had seated themselves around the fireplace, Dr. Elwyn looked at Coda.

'I can see whose child you are. I see your father in you and you have your mother's eyes. What a fine man you are becoming.'

'Thank you doctor. I would have preferred to meet you under different circumstances, but we have little time.'

'Yes. I am aware of the situation. Raman has been in touch with me. You see…I am left with no means. When my wife left me she cleaned me out. All my assets as well as my entire income are hers now. She now lives in my house on Sabal and enjoys all the fruits of my family's labour. I have been living on the generosity of those I have been administering to. So…to purchase a seat on the shuttle will be impossible.'

'I was told of your situation. I also know that Sabal will not be a suitable place for you or my mother.' He took out the bag of stones he had recovered at the waterfalls edge. 'Will this be enough to start over on a different planet?'

Dr. Elwyn took the bag and opened it. He gasped and looked up at Coda. 'But…how…do you mean all of it?'

'Is it not enough?'

'It is too much. What of yourself? Will you not need this?'

'I have many stones.'

'The smallest of these will secure our seats.'

'Where will you go?'

'Well…the shuttle will take us to the Universal teleport. I have been thinking of Atna lately. I went there with my parents when I was young. It's on the edge of the Ekuno galaxy of the Sabalian realm and has a warm climate. Not too many Sabalians there. I think that's where we'll go.'

'Where on Atna can I find you?'

'There is a small town called Elasu; named after the Elasu crater. It's an enormous lake now. It is a good place, or was when I was young. I hope not too much has changed.' They were quiet for a few moments, taking in the heat from the fire and the ambiance of the room. As if bidding it a silent farewell. 'Come with us Coda.'

'I have unfinished business here, besides, I will not be allowed onto the shuttle. My mother can pass as your domestic. I will come to visit when I can.'

'Well…it's true.' Elwyn looked at Ola. 'I still have your documentation. They will think you are my domestic. Even Bala can do nothing about it.'

'That settles it then. Are you packed and ready to go?'

'I need only my medical bag, my pills and these two books.' He picked them up and put them in his bag one at a time. 'This one is a book of poetry and this one is a book of guidance written by a Sage many years ago.'

They stood up. Coda looked at the clock above the mantle piece. 'When does the shuttle leave?'

'In an hour.' Dr. Elwyn put on his coat and his boots.

They went out the way they came in. As they stepped into the courtyard, Dr. Elwyn switched off the surgery lights and locked the door. He turned and saw the look on Coda's face. 'Old habit I'm afraid.' He pocketed the key. They crossed the courtyard and went through the back gate into the alley. To their surprise there was a rickshaw waiting for them.

The rickshaw runner was tall and covered in black fur. 'I was told to be here at dawn.'

'Who told you?' Dr. Elwyn asked.

'The one who speaks to us all.'

'That's good enough for me.' Dr. Elwyn helped Ola into the large rickshaw seat. It was big enough for the three of them. 'Take us to the Universal shuttle as fast as you can.'

The runner stepped between the long handles. He bent down and lifted them. His back and shoulder muscles bulged as he leaned forward and his powerful legs pushed against the rickshaw's weight. As they moved forward and they gained momentum, the runner straightened up and began to run with a mile eating gait. The alleyways were narrow, but he ran with confidence, never slowing down for an instant.

'Never thought I'd ever get away from this place.' Dr. Elwyn looked at Ola. 'Now I find you by my side once again and we're off to a place where we can enjoy each other's company in peace.'

Coda noticed how she took Dr. Elwyn's hand and snuggled up to him. She looks so tired, he thought. The Doctor also looks ill. I hope they can help each other. The runner lengthened his stride as they came onto the main road to the shuttle launch pad. Coda had never been on a rickshaw before and was amazed at the speed of this runner. Traffic was light and the rickshaw lane was clear. It felt like they were floating on a cushion of air. In what felt like no time at all they turned into the road leading up to the terminal. They stopped outside the front door and got off the rickshaw. Dr. Elwyn and Ola went in and Coda thanked the runner.

'Where will you go?'

'I will join Him in the afterlife.' The runner smiled and left.

Coda turned and walked into the building. He was wearing his father's full length black coat with the siux eel skin that Ola had sown over the shoulders and onto the back. His miner's boots were scuffed and open at the top. He was seven foot tall with long black ropes of hair that reached halfway down his back. He immediately caught the attention of the terminal security staff.

'Stop right there ectype!' A square block of a Sabalian man stepped in his path. 'What's your business here?'

'I have come to see off some friends of mine.'

The security man stepped back disappointedly. 'Make it quick then. Gates close in ten minutes. Blast off in twenty.'

Coda walked to the ticket counter where Ola and Dr. Elwyn were waiting close to the front of the queue. As he approached he noticed a man in line leaning heavily on his walking stick. To his surprise he recognised him. It was Master Cubal. He looked old with deep wrinkles that only long term pain could cause. His eyes were dull and empty with drug enlarged pupils. He looked at Coda with a mindless stare. There was no recognition in his eyes. Coda could not help but feel a pang of pity for him. His ankle had obviously never healed properly and it looked as if his mind was going as well.

Ola and Dr. Elwyn had moved forward and were already at the ticket counter by the time Coda reached the front of the queue, so he waited at the barrier. He watched anxiously as Dr. Elwyn handed over their documents. The ticket clerk fussed over them and looked up on the computer to verify Dr Elwyn's ownership of Ola. There seemed to be some reluctance on the clerk's face, but then Dr. Elwyn handed him a small, but very bright stone. The clerk's demeanour suddenly changed and he printed out their tickets with a glowing smile.

They joined Coda at the barrier and followed it until they reached the turnstile gates. 'Now young man…I'll take good care of your mother. I don't know exactly what is going to happen here, but you must survive. Remember, Ekuno galaxy, Atna, Elasu crater. Come and visit us if you can. Until then…good luck Coda of White Mountain.' He hugged Coda warmly. Coda was taken aback at the formal greeting.

'Live long…Elwyn of Northern Deep.'

Ola was weeping as she hugged him. 'I have been without you for so long and have missed you so much. Will I ever see you again?'

'I will do what I can to come to you, but you will know when I am with you. We will still have many conversations.'

Ola broke the hug and stepped back. Her eyes were full of hope and joy. 'Yes. Come many times and we will talk.'

Coda looked at her wrist and saw the wedding bracelet she still wore. 'I have something for you.' From his pocket he took his father's matching bracelet. 'This was amongst Da's things that Raman sent. I thought I'd give it to you before you left.'

Ola looked at Dr. Elwyn and then at him. 'Your father will always have the most special place in my heart, but it is time for a new beginning. I have mine which will always remind me of him. This one is now yours. Keep it and remember him for the man he was and the love he gave.'

'Thank you mother.' Coda put it on his left wrist.

'I love you my son. You must be strong. I will see you soon.'

'And I love you mother. You will always be in my heart and fresh in my mind.'

'Stop them!' The call came from behind Coda. He swung around and saw Bala rushing through the front doors.

'Go quickly.'

Dr. Elwyn took Ola and scanned their tickets into the turnstile. It opened and let them through. As they hurried along the gangway to the waiting shuttle Coda caught his mother's eye as she looked back and he said telepathically. 'Farewell mother.' And she answered. 'I love you my son.'

Coda turned and Bala hit him hard on the jaw, lifting him off his feet. A black bomb exploded in his head. Almost unconscious he crashed through the barriers behind him and landed heavily on his back. The back of his head hit the floor and another bomb shocked his brain. In the next instant, Bala kicked him in the right side. He felt the pain ripple through him, but it was enough to snap him back to full consciousness. He waited for the next kick and as it struck, he grabbed Bala's foot and then his training took over.

He kicked Bala's other foot out from under him and as he fell, Coda got to his feet and slammed the heels of both his palms under the ribcage of the oncoming guard. Coda was at an angle lower than him and as he pushed and straightened his arms, he lifted the guard off his feet. The guard fell back into two other guards; the momentum was such that they crumpled into a heap. Bala was still trying to get up and there were two more guards bearing down on Coda with truncheons. He rushed at the one closest to him. He feinted with the left and as the guard dipped his head Coda elbowed him with a vicious uppercut to the chin that knocked the guard out cold.

The other guard was upon him with his truncheon high in his right hand ready to bring it down on Coda's head. Coda hit him with a hard body blow to the short ribs on his right side and winded the guard who crumpled over, bringing his right arm down to protect himself and Coda hit him with his knee under the chin. The guard's head snapped back and was unconscious before he hit the floor face first.

From the corner of his eye, he saw Bala was now on his feet and so were the three guards he had pushed over. He realised the odds were against him, so he turned and ran for the front doors. Bala's transporter was standing there. He jumped in and hit the starter button. The engine came to life and suddenly he was at a loss. He didn't know how to drive. He put his foot on the pedal and the engine roared, but nothing happened. He was standing still. Bala and the guards were almost at the door. Then he remembered the gear leaver. He tried it in the first level and again, nothing happened. Bala was at the door and running down the steps. Coda pulled the gear lever into the next position and as Bala reached for the door the transporter leaped forward. Coda put his foot down and sped away.

It took him a moment to bring the transporter under control and then in his rear view mirror he saw Bala push a guard away from the security transporter and get in. Coda turned onto the main road and sped in the direction of the slag heaps at the edge of the ice flats. He looked behind him and saw Bala's frantic turn into the main road, pushing a mine vehicle off the road.

He smiled and knew that Bala had taken the bait. He had lured him away from his mother and now he could finish his business with him. As he sped along he saw the shuttle take off in the early morning light and his thoughts became solemn. He knew that he would most likely never see her in the flesh again. As he watched the shuttle blast through XN5's atmosphere an explosion lifted a mine vehicle off the road ahead of him. It broke up into great chunks of twisted metal that flew in all directions. He swerved to the side of the road to avoid the blast crater and flying debris. A piece of smoking metal crashed through the wind screen of his transporter and he had to kick the rest of the shattered glass out in order to see. He almost lost control of the transporter, but he managed to get back on the road. The harvest has begun then, he thought. At least my mother and Dr. Elwyn have got away.

In his rear view mirror he saw Bala was gaining on him. His transporter engine was revving at a very high pitch and he could not increase his speed. Then he noticed the gear lever had two more levels, so he pulled it into the next level and as it kicked into gear the transporter seemed to get a second breath and blasted forward, pushing him into his seat as it increased speed. He passed several mine vehicles, narrowly avoiding the oncoming traffic. Explosions were raining down all around them, but he barrelled on, avoiding flying debris and craters that opened up ahead of him.

As he reached the slag heaps and turned in amongst them, he headed for the largest of them and drove up the service road that went around the sides of it and ended at the top. He stopped the transporter when he reached the flat plane. He opened the door, stepped out and looked at the scenes of devastation unfolding across Northern Deep.

Tall plumes of black smoke rose high into the air as the village burned. Large and small alien craft were raining fire down on the compound where the miners lived. He watched as thousands ran in panic, not knowing where to go. Hundreds were being cut down by the alien craft in an orgy of slaughter. Buildings and equipment were blown to bits. Debris was flying in all directions. Then he noticed Jarlath and the others from Bala's mine scrambling up to the top of one of the lower slag heaps. At that moment Bala roared onto the plane and sped directly towards him. His transporter was behind him, so he waited until the last moment. He could see the triumphant smirk on Bala's face and then he jumped straight up into the air. Bala's transporter slammed into the side of Coda's. He landed on his feet in a cloud of dust. Bala kicked his door open and got out.

There was a gash on his forehead with blood running down his face, but he was steady and menacing on his feet. Coda could feel his intent, but for some reason he could not read his mind. Bala rushed at him, but he was still off balance and could not get out of the way quickly enough. He stepped to his right, but Bala hit him a glancing blow on the left shoulder with his short metal club. Coda's left arm went numb and lame. Bala lifted the club and brought it down towards Coda's head, but he fell backwards, still off balance and landed heavily on his back. Bala leaped onto him. Coda instinctively lifted his knees and hooked his feet in Bala's inner thighs. Bala tried to bring the baton down on Coda's head again, but his left arm had recovered and he took hold of Bala's right elbow, preventing the blow from landing with any power. He was not quick enough to stop Bala's left fist from crashing into his face.

Coda, while still holding onto Bala's right elbow, instinctively hooked his right hand behind Bala's left shoulder and pulled him down towards him. As Bala's head came towards him Coda reached upwards and bit into his left cheek. He felt his teeth sink into Bala's flesh. Bala roared with pain and tried to stand up and pull away from him, but Coda held on and began to grind his teeth together. His hair wrapped around Bala's head like tentacles and trapped him. The ropey muscles in his hair contracted and held him in their lethal embrace. Bala struggled to get free and as panic began to set in he somehow got his right arm free and butted Coda repeatedly and viciously in the ribs. Pain burst through him as he felt his ribs crack and he slackened his grip for a moment. As Bala broke free and stepped back, Coda bit down hard on his cheek. The flesh ripped away and Bala screamed in pain as he covered his face.

Coda stood up and spat the piece of meat into the dust. 'That's for my mother!' he put his right hand into his coat and pulled out his father's flute.

'What…you going to play me to death boy? Ha ha ha ha ha…' And Bala rushed him again. This time he was ready for him. Bala feinted with the left and brought the baton in low for a butt strike to the abdomen. Coda parried with the flute and struck him a hard blow on the left side of his jaw. The three foot long flute was made of ditholium pipe. It was the hardest metal used on the mines and it was heavy. As it struck, the bone shattered.

Bala was tougher than most. He just grunted and kept coming. Coda side stepped and as Bala rushed past, he brought the flute down on the back of his head. He felt the bone give way under the heavy metal of the flute and Bala crumpled into the dust.

Coda stepped back, but Bala was still conscious. He lifted himself up onto his elbows and was trying to bring his knees up under him. Coda put his flute back into its inside pocket and took out the knife his father had taken from Snake Eyes. Bala had his knees under him and he sat up still groggy and disoriented. Coda came up behind him and held his head back with his left hand on his bloodied forehead. He put the edge of his blade on the left side of Bala's neck.

'And this…is for my father.'

He sank the blade deep into the side of Bala's neck and as the blood began to spurt out he pulled it across to the other side with such force he felt the blade scrape along the vertebrae of his neck. He heard the blood bubble up in Bala's air pipe as he expelled his last breath and his body went limp. Coda shoved his body to the side and as the blood soaked into the dust he lifted his blood-stained blade to the sky.

His voice was strong as he declared himself.

'I am Coda of White Mountain! Son of Thaif the fisherman and Ola the teacher. Today I am a man! I have slain my enemy and avenged my father. I have defended my mother's dignity and survived in mortal combat. To all who hear me this day…I am Coda…a man…of White Mountain!'

An explosion rocked the mangled transporters and a piece of shrapnel flew at high velocity and hit Coda's left shin just below the knee. It snapped and Coda crumpled to the ground. Moments later he saw the alien craft exactly as he had seen it in his vision. He watched it as it hovered above him. The explosion had deafened him. Dazed and confused he saw the underbelly of the craft open and a beam of light fall on him. He began to feel weightless as the beam lifted him up. It drew him into the craft and as the hatch closed behind him the light went out. He fell heavily onto the floor and he called out in pain as the fall jarred the broken bone in his left leg. Someone grabbed him by the coat collar and dragged him. He was lifted up and shoved into a seat. As his captor attached the safety harness, he said. 'This one's damaged.'

'Who cares? We'll lose a percentage anyway.' The other one said. 'Let's go. We have our quota.'

Coda saw that all the seats opposite him and along his side were filled. On the seat in the far corner he noticed a blond man who looked familiar. There was something wrong with his left eye. The right eye was blue, but the left was brown and the socket looked slightly deformed. As if it was a bit smaller than the other one with a scar that followed its contour. The man turned and looked at Coda. Recognition struck him like a hammer blow…Valdas. The look in Valdas's eyes changed from bewilderment to recognition to pure hatred. Coda looked at him impassively. The beautiful young boy has become…less so, Coda thought. Our fight is not yet over, he sighed and looked away.

The two captors took their seats and strapped themselves in. Coda felt the craft lift and tilt as it flew towards its carrier ship. Through the opposite porthole he could see the harvest. A craft was taking up the last of the boys from Bala's mine. Small groups of stragglers were being picked up everywhere. The bombing had stopped and the air was dark with smoke. The craft they were in suddenly slowed and with several loud clanks and whirrs they connected with their carrier ship.

When all the small craft had connected the carrier ship began to move across the ice flats towards White Mountain. They flew higher and higher and when they were above the mountain range they circled it for two full cycles. Coda could see that the battle still raged on. The Nation was fighting back! Small craft were being shot out of the sky. Their carrier ship was hovering just above the height of the flak detonations; out of harm's way. In a co-ordinated fashion the small craft suddenly all returned to the carrier ship and as it lifted up a large black ball dropped from it. It seemed to fall slowly and then about a hundred yards above the lake it exploded into a fantastically bright light that spread outwards. Coda shut his eyes and turned his face away. When he opened them again, a giant mushroom cloud had formed over White Mountain and rose high into the air.

He felt his heart shrivel and sink within him. He knew that

Chi'Dorolam, Merrix and all the fighters of White Mountain were dead. Those inside the mountain may still live, he thought with a little hope. Their carrier ship lifted higher until they were above the stratosphere. He could see the other carrier ships above the stratosphere going in the same direction towards the mother ship. As
they got closer he could read the name on it; AXA GAFF.

After they had landed in the huge loading bay they were all herded out onto the loading platform. Coda was helped to walk by one of the miners. They were then all shoved and pushed into cages made of metal bars. The floors were on wheels and they were all hooked up like the ore trucks in the mines. When the cages were full, the engine at the front pulled the train down a long corridor that after several minutes, opened out into a wider room. The train stopped opposite a wall with large port windows. The wheels under them turned towards the windows and all the cages moved towards them. When the bars touched the wall they were automatically clamped in place. The frame attached to the wheels under the floor detached and moved back out from under them. The wheels turned back to their original position and the engine at the head pulled them away. The cages and their prisoners were left suspended two feet above the floor, attached to the wall with one large window per cage, looking out at XN5.

Everyone was silent as they watched XN5 move further and further away.

Suddenly someone said. 'Look!' A red crack had appeared on the surface of XN5. It began to spread like arteries and veins and then suddenly, the entire planet blew apart. The shock was total and painful as they watched their planet and whatever life and friends they had, blown into space.

Coda felt the tears streaming down his face as he thought of never seeing his friends again. Chi'Dorolam, Zizi, Merrix and his mentor and spiritual guide Raman...

Present
Upi, Onusa Quadrant

It felt like someone had twisted his insides and pulled them taut as the trauma of his early childhood rushed through him. His emotions were left uprooted and scattered like debris after a flash flood. The memories only took a moment, but their effect was devastation as they smashed through the fog. He knew the rest of his memory would return in time. How much of it did he want to know? How would it taint his present? The unfolding of his life was going to be a journey he had to brace himself for.

Coda stood like a monolith, now, three and a half thousand years later, on the bridge of his space ship; the Awa Na Tahu. It was on the landing bay, on board a spacecraft owned by one of the most influential and dangerous Sabalian men in all the Multiverse. Their power was influence and persuasion brutally imposed by their ruthless clone militaries.

He watched the clones that surrounded the landing bay of the detestable Ehzhu Moriwe's ship, knowing that they would obey his every command.

He felt his power grow as control pulsed through him like hot blood. Only the Adovacians had ever defeated them. But, Coda was not Adovacian...he was freeborn...a citizen of the Nation of White Mountain...from a planet destroyed three and a half thousand years ago.

The one thing he was dead sure of was that there was unfinished business here...

To be continued in book two...

Glossary of Terms

A

Ado crater: Impact crater on Upi; one of three moons of planet Onusa in the Moeban realm.

Ado observatory: Stellar observatory with hotel and spa facilities. Used as a recreational centre and observatory for staff and visitors to Upi's research station.

Adovac: Principle planet of the Adovacian realm. The Adovacians are a warlike culture.

Ajari Province: A province of planet Moeba. Its capital is Mt. Ross.

Astor, Erick Professor: Professor of anthropology and alien studies stationed on Upi.

Atna: Small recreational planet in the Sabalian realm.

Auto-tram: Automatic tram service.

Awa Na Tahu: Coda's woman in book two and the name of his ship. It means river of light.

Azul: Moeban underworld

AXA GAFF: Multiversal slave ship.

B

Bala: Half breed Sabalian with domestic clone mother. Mine supervisor on XN5.

Bidan realm: Realm which spans five Universes on the outer rim of the Multiverse.

Black cloud: A frigid black cloud of gas and dust that floats through interstellar space with temperatures of below -250 degrees Celsius.

C

Chi'Dorolam: Clone designed for underground mining. Explosives expert and friend to Thaif, Ola and Coda. Partner to Zizi.

Comlink: Internal communications system on board The Nullax Rover.

Coms button: Communications button on the shirt collar or surfaces of desks or doorframes.

Coms network: Interstellar communications network.

Constant mine machine: Machine designed to work the mesorite face. It has large rotating blades that break up and scoop the ore onto a conveyor belt.

Craven, Dennis Doctor: The minister of science, culture and technology on Moeba and a member of the Moeban Progressive Party (MPP).

Cubal, Master: Homosexual pedophile and Sabalian headmaster of the boys' institute affiliated to the mine college.

D

Dara: An alcoholic spirits drink

Dax, Etha Mentor: Head of the Pathfinders' guild on Moeba.

Ditholium: A hard black metal used in aqua mining.

Duncan, Shay Lieutenant: Navigator on board The Nullax Rover. Lover of Dr. Monica Lynn.

Drift, The: A fifty mile wide river of ice blocks that flows across the ice flats.

E

Ectype: Copy. Derogatory term used to describe clones.

Ekuno galaxy: Sabalian realm. Galaxy of the Atnan solar system.

Eko: Extinct planet of the giant oselha.

Elasu crater: Sabalian realm. Ekuno galaxy, planet Atna. Water filled crater.

EV: electric vehicle

F

Feen: Seventh wife of Ehzhu Moriwe.

Flyrock: Flying debris from mine blasting.

Flyrock absorption mat: Mat used to absorb flyrock.

G

Giant Oselha: A giant arctic beast with tusks and white fur from the extinct planet Eko.

Gion: Known as Interversal Gion and is used as the Multiversal currency.

Green, Walter Admiral: Admiral of the Moeban space fleet.

H

I

Ice fire: The gas trapped in the permafrost rock that is common on the volcanic islands of XN5 is set alight.

Interversal Gion: Multiversal currency.

J

Jarlath: Moral leader of the boys in Bala's mine.

Jexxar star constellation: Star constellation in the Nev galaxy of the fifth Universe of the Bidan realm.

K

L

Lilia: Free born female to rickshaw clones with brown fur in Bala's mine and Valax's partner.

Lynn, Monica. Doctor: Doctor of anthropology and alien studies. Partner of Shay Duncan.

M

Manna: White powder manufactured by the Pathfinders. Elixir of long life and vitality produced for the pathfinders who map the Multiverse.

Mannas: A corrupt version of Manna which was an addictive drug that strongly enhanced the physical sensations with a euphoric hallucinogenic effect.

Masters, John Captain: Captain of the Nullax Rover.

Megaverse: Outer space. Unexplored; believed to be empty.

Merrix: Free born from rickshaw clones. Silver fur. Raman's assistant and Coda's martial arts mentor.

Mesorite: A radio active metal ore found in abundance on XN5 and used mainly for the production of weapons.

Moeba: Realm consisting of a single Universe. Acknowledged to be the origin of humanity.

Moeban Progressive Party (MPP): Coalition partner of the Moeban government.

Moriwe, Ehzhu: Influential and well connected Sabalian businessman.

Mt. Ross: Capital of Ajari province on Moeba.

Mt. Toyin: Another city in the south of Moeba.

Multiverse: Held by the Megaverse and contains Ninety nine Universes.

N

Nation, The: Free born and escaped clones that have a homeland on White Mountain.

Nekob: Principle planet of the Nekobian realm.

Nekobian priest: Priest of their state religion of mind science.

Nev galaxy: Part of the Bidan realm on the outer rim of the Multiverse.

Nullax Rover: Moeban research space ship, captained by Captain John Masters.

O

Ola: Domestic clone and Coda's mother.

Onusa: Planet in the Onusa quadrant in the Moeban Realm.

Othaxal cloud: Black cloud in the Onusa quadrant.

Orro: Gas planet of XN5. Cause of annual earth quakes, volcanoes and storms.

P

Pathfinder: Highly developed spiritual traveler who maps the Multiverse.

Pathfinders' guild: Organization that represents, trains, and monitors all pathfinders.

Pit fly: A four inch roach like insect with six inch feelers. It is black with red brown colouring on the abdomen and the edges of its wings. It has disturbing yellow eyes and large mandibles.

Popper: A small glass vial containing a highly intoxicating recreational drug.

Q
R

Raman of the Nation: Spiritual leader of The Nation and mentor to Coda.

Remco: Brown skinned lifelong friend of Coda.

Rool: Whip with sharp metal studs knotted into five thongs which are of varying lengths.

Rosmadden, Elwyn Doctor: Sabalian doctor exiled to XN5 for his sympathetic views on clone rights.

Rosmadden, Honora: Dr. Elwyn Rosmadden's wife.

S

Sabal: Principle planet of the Sabalian Realm. The biggest and most influential realm in the Multiverse.

Sabalian: Blue skinned citizen of Sabal.

Shoal hound: Conscious fish from Uroha, Coda's friend.

Sibex: Orphaned free born from rickshaw clones with grey fur.

Siux eel: A gigantic eel that lives in the mountainous lakes of White Mountain.

Slag heaps: Heaps made of mine tailings; the residue after the mesorite ore has been processed.

Snake eyes: A snake eyed clone abomination.

T

Taras: A Moeban planet with large ice caps harvested to replenish water levels on Moeba.

Thaif: An aqua miner clone and Coda's father.

Teleport: A man made portal at the entrance to a stable vortex used for Interversal travel.

Treaties of Manna: A text on the preparation of Manna.

U

Uli: Ehzhu Moriwe's first wife.

Upi: One of three moons of Onusa. It's the only one suitable for its research base.

Uroha: Principle planet of the Urohan realm. A mysterious planet under constant cloud cover consisting mainly of water with violent storms.

V

Valax: Orphaned from mine clones. Cutter in Bala's mine and partner to Lilia.

Valdas: Homosexual antagonist and mate to Master Cubal at the institute.

Var: Moon of Moeba with a research station. Docking station of Moeba's teleport.

Vidal flats: Launch complex of Moeban space program.

Vortex: Wormhole passage to different Universes.

W

Wall, David. Chief engineer: Chief engineer on The Nullax Rover.

White Mountain: Mountain range home of the Nation.

Wikopi Desert: Was a sea on Moeba before the seas evaporated.

Wikopi fish: Fish of the underground reservoirs on Moeba; named after the Wikopi Sea.

X

XN5: Small planet of rock and ice with frozen seas. Used as a mining and cloning colony by wealthy Sabalians. Elliptical orbit around Orro causes annual earth quakes, volcanoes and storms.

Y

YutZho Phehak: Coda's shoal hound friend and companion.

Z

Zizi: Free born from rickshaw clones. Black fur. Raman's assistant and Chi'Dorolam's partner.

About the Author

G.M.Ellerbeck was born in South Africa and now lives in Dublin, Ireland. After his military service, his more memorable pursuits were lighting technician in theatre, national chauffeur and tour guide, as well as audio visual technician on cruise ships before finally settling down to write.